MACGYVER: MELTDOWN

MACGYVER: MELTDOWN

ERIC KELLEY
LEE ZLOTOFF

Prince
of
Cats

Literary
Productions

MacGyver: Meltdown

Copyright © 2020 MacGyver Solutions LLCIn Association with Prince of Cats
Literary Productions

Trade Paperback ISBN: 978-1-952825-14-9
Ebook ISBN: 978-1-952825-15-6
Cover design by Kind Composition

Cover Art copyright © 2020 Elizabeth Leggett, Portico Arts
Interior layout and design by Kind Composition
Prince of Cats Trade Paperback Edition 2020

Published by MacGyver Solutions LLC
In Association with Prince of Cats Literary Productions
New Jersey, USA 2020

DEDICATION

To Melinda ...
For all she is and does.

As with all MacGyver projects, a portion of the proceeds from this
book go to support the MacGyver Foundation

To learn more about the Foundation, or other MacGyver projects,
please visit www.MacGyverGlobal.com

CHAPTER 1

EVER HAVE *one of those days where nothing goes right? Because, in my line of work, this happens way too often.*

Say your name happens to be MacGyver, and you've been tapped by the Department of Homeland Security to look into some separatist militia to find out if they're planning to steal a nasty bioweapon.

Then say you find out they haven't just planned it, but they did it.

And say it's all part of some wacko scheme to prevent a particular vote in the United States Senate.

And that the bioweapon is only Plan B.

Plan A is kidnapping a Senator's daughter.

So, you gotta make a choice.

A big one.

Yeah, no two ways about it. It's going to be one of those days.

◖◗

"This would be a lot faster if I could use the siren," the cop complained.

MacGyver shook his head. "Do that and these militia guys won't have just one hostage, but a whole school full."

The other cop finished her call. "Okay, got several units rolling to the school, no sirens. But it's gonna be fifteen minutes at least if they can't clear traffic on the way."

"It'll have to do," Mac said. "Let's just hope we get there before the militia does."

"I still don't know why DHS sent just you on this," the first cop whined. "If it weren't for direct orders, I wouldn't have bought it."

What could Mac say to that? He was a contractor for various United States intelligence services. He didn't operate domestically very often, but DHS had called him in special for this one.

"How the hell did a bunch of militia loonies get their hands on something like that, anyway?" the female cop in the back muttered.

"Don't know," Mac said. "All I know is that they're targeting a Senator, and they're kidnapping his daughter for insurance."

"And that helps them how?"

Mac could only shrug. "Not sure. But we can't just stop them. We need to question them, because I also don't have a location on the Senator right now. And it's happening today."

They swung around the corner to see the upscale New York private school up ahead. "Okay, they'll be in the garage somewhere if they're here." Then to the driver, "You, park the car down the street and cover the entrance." Then to the one in the back, "You're with me. We'll intercept them heading inside if we can; if not, we'll have to keep them in the garage."

"We should tell school security that we're here," she said.

"No," Mac said. "They've got an inside man. I don't know what he looks like, but his job is to take the whole place hostage if they're detected. We can't move until our backup gets here."

Neither cop looked happy, but they followed instructions.

MacGyver's eyes got used to the dim parking garage quickly, as the city sounds abated and the smell of exhaust fumes increased. He gave the lady cop his weatherworn leather jacket to wear over her uniform.

"Not much of a disguise," she said.

"Just has to pass a casual glance," he said, stalking down the rows looking for the visitor spots. It didn't take long.

The cop tapped his arm. "Over there."

The militia truck stood out by the underground elevators, being old, beaten, and sporting an amazing number of offensive political stickers.

"He's still in the cab," said the cop. "Facing away from us."

She started forward, but Mac grabbed her arm. "There were two. The other's already inside."

She cursed. "What can we do? Ambush? That'd risk them hurting the kid."

"We need to stall them. Car trouble would do it."

"He's not gonna let us get under the hood, pal."

Mac's mind went into overdrive, holding a quick conference with itself.

Potato in the tail pipe?

Do you have one? Does she?

No.

Let the air out of the tires.

He'll see us in either mirror.

Can we even approach the thing?

It's pretty dark in here.

From behind maybe, crouched real low?

But if we move out to one side he'll see us.

So, we just have the undercarriage to work with.

What can be done there?

Brakes.

That'll just make them crash. Might hurt the kid.

Electronics!

Short it out.

Need a power source.

And a way to trigger it.

He whipped out his phone and pocketknife. "I need something with wires in it. Your radio. Just gimme the handset."

The cop reached under the jacket, took the mike from her shoulder, and unplugged it from the main unit while Mac popped open his phone with his knife. He knew right where the battery was and the leads he needed.

"What are you doing?" she asked.

"Making a switch," he said, working quickly. His knife made short work of the radio cord, opening it to see the transmission wires inside. He cut two lengths from them and stripped both ends. Tiny bits of duct tape would hold the leads to the phone circuit, and the other ends would get taped into the car's electrical system.

"Give me your phone," he said, and input his number. "When I'm done, you short their power system by calling my phone, which will be under their truck, but only after they start the engine. Got it? If you ring it early, it won't work. Back in a minute."

He crawled beneath the car they'd been hidden behind, down its length, then across the lane, always directly behind the militia truck and out of sight, belly down on the grimy garage floor. It wasn't far, but his elbows started grumbling after just a moment. *Getting too old for this, Mac,* he thought as he crawled under the truck. His forty-sixth birthday was coming up soon, and right now he felt every damn bit of it. Down by the engine, he found a place to wire his phone into its electrical system, taped the whole thing quietly to the undercarriage, then wriggled back out.

He had just straightened up beside the cop after crawling the whole length back again when the school door banged open. A broad-chested man wearing a grizzled beard and building security outfit hauled a dark-haired girl in a school uniform along by her arm. He was limping, so she'd put up a fight, but a patch of duct tape slapped across her mouth had prevented much in the way of noise. The man had a gun in the other hand.

The cop's thumb moved towards dial, but Mac stopped her. "Engine has to be running," he reminded her.

"And this'll work?" she hissed back.

"Yeah. Sure. Usually."

She tore her irritated glance back to see the militiaman yanking open the door.

"Get in!" he snapped, shoving the girl ahead of him, then, to the driver, "Go—GO!"

The truck fired up, coughing smelly exhaust, then just as quickly died as the cop called Mac's phone. MacGyver could hear them curse as they tried the engine again and again. He grinned slightly at the cop as she nodded, impressed. The driver popped their hood as his uniformed partner jumped out to check the engine.

"Okay," Mac murmured. "They're distracted. Cover the driver from here, and I'll take out the guy under the hood. Try not to shoot him," he said as she drew her gun.

"Not my first rodeo," the cop leveled at him.

Mac didn't like the gun, but he knew from long experience that getting police to forego their weapons in this kind of situation was nearly impossible.

He didn't crawl under the cars this time, but crouched low and scooted around the passenger side, while the cop took up a position to cover the driver's door. The driver had his head out the window and was yelling advice to the other one, who shot back that he could come do it himself if he was so damn smart.

By the passenger door, Mac leaped up and slammed the hood down on the guy beneath. A single punch to the stunned man's temple dropped him like a sack of flour.

The other gave a startled yell and kicked the door open. "They're here!" he yelled into a walkie-talkie. "They're here! Send the rest!"

"Freeze! NYPD!" shouted the cop, weapon and flashlight trained on him from less than six yards away.

The militiaman's weapon came up.

"No!" Mac shouted.

A gunshot boomed through the garage like thunder, and the militiaman's head jerked backwards. He fell against the open door and collapsed. Mac spun up to see the life leave his eyes, blood oozing down his face from the hole in his skull.

"Dammit!" Mac said as the cop ran in. "A kill shot was your only choice?"

"He *pulled* on me," the cop said, voice shaky.

Mac hated it, but what was done was done. "But now we don't know where the Senator is."

"Bathhouse," said the girl from inside. She was thirteen or so, Mac knew, dry-eyed and angry as she stared at the dead man. "It's in Chinatown. His aide hates it, but Daddy likes to dictate letters when he's relaxing."

"Can you give me the address?" Mac asked.

She nodded.

"I have to go," he told the cop.

"You can't! They've got backup coming, and you've got a *lot* of questions to answer."

"Bioweapon," he said. "Remember? I'll need your cruiser."

"Bioweapon?" the girl squealed.

Nice one, Mac, his brain said. "It'll be okay," he said, trying not to make it sound like a lie. "This is my job."

"Help him, please," the girl said, looking small.

The cop handed over her keys. "*Via con dios,* pal."

Try as Mac might, the ancient woman at the Asian bathhouse absolutely would not allow Mac into the facility. "You not police!"

"No, I'm with Homeland Security," he said, waving the ID at her for the fourth time. "I have to get in there!"

"You no have warrant. And this look fake! Not police!"

Mac could only groan. Shots had been fired at the school, forcing the whole thing into lockdown and drawing virtually every police officer in the city. He'd heard it on the cruiser radio as he'd sped downtown, siren blaring. That meant that whoever had the bioweapon would be upping their timetable.

"Okay then, how much for a bath?" he asked at last.

In five minutes, clad only in a towel, he searched room after room for the Senator. Most of them were empty. He got yelled at a couple of times, but he found what he was after—just a minute too late.

He cracked the heavy door to a room and found a gun in his face.

"Get in here!" a big man wearing a pro-gun T-shirt and a dirty bandana around his head barked.

Mac's hands went up, and he followed directions, briefly wondering how the hell *this* guy had gotten past the dragon lady at the front desk.

The militiaman wasn't alone. Two other men were in the room, both wearing towels, one older, portly, but with a full head of hair, the Senator himself. The other was younger, the senator's aide. He had a notepad covered with writing.

"Who the hell are you?" the militiaman demanded.

"MacGyver. I'm a ... fundraiser for the Senator," Mac said, moving to stand between the pair and the militiaman. Mac's eyes widened at the small cylinder clutched in the man's offhand. The bioweapon canister.

"So you're just another one of them global warming assholes who can't see this country is falling apart—and that it's pinkos like him that's doing it to us!"

MacGyver shrugged as well as he could with hands high. "Well, I'm a tech guy more than anything else. But why don't we just talk about this, huh? You don't need to shoot anyone, and you really don't need to set off whatever that thing in your hand is." Regular Ebola couldn't last but a few seconds in the atmosphere. This stuff was far worse. Homeland Security had been right to be scared.

The militiaman spat through his teeth. "Goddamn sheeple! Ya can die with them!" He hit a button on the canister's release and tossed it at MacGyver.

Mac caught it as the man bolted through the door, slammed it shut, and three quick shots cracked into the lock from outside.

Mac leaped to the door and shoved. Nothing. "It's barred. And the handle's shot off."

"What do we do?" demanded the Senator—sounding close to panic.

Mac didn't even have his pocketknife.

His mind went into slow motion as the timer counted down.

Bio-canister, gas release, four minutes.

And dropping.

Disable the timer?

No way without my knife.

Canister's not big. Not a lot in there.

Doesn't need a lot. It's weaponized Ebola.

"Oh, my God, we're gonna die!" shouted the aide.

"Keep calm! I'm thinking."

"There's no time!" he screamed.

"There's always time," said MacGyver automatically.

Steamy atmosphere, perfect conveyor, especially as particulates.

If we could freeze it—

In a bathhouse? Nope.

So, go the other way.

He went to the hot stones that people ladled water on for steam. A little searching got the cabinet underneath open. The plate was heated by gas fed through a thin pipe coming up through the floor. The burner was attached with screws. Without his pocketknife, he'd never get it loose. The pipe was solid, but thin, and rattled a little when he tested it.

MacGyver pointed to the Senator. "Grab that pail over there and fill it with hot water from the bath." He pointed at the aide. "You grab that extra towel and help me out here." He soaked the towel in the bath, then folded it twice lengthwise.

The aide watched, confused. "What are you doing?"

MacGyver coiled it once around the pipe. He handed the other end to the aide. "On three, we yank backwards, hard as you can. Ready? One, two, *three!*" The pipe held, but MacGyver felt some give in the fitting. "Again! One, two, THREE!"

The pipe bent badly at its base, but broke free of the burner. He could hear it hissing and smelled the thiol-based odorant added to natural gas.

"Are you trying to blow us up?" the Senator bellowed, standing there with the full pail.

Mac didn't respond. To the aide, "Drag that little table over here." He himself retrieved two of the stones and looked them over. Smooth, solid granite. He struck them together over the hissing pipe once ... again ... and the spark caught. They started back from the jet of flame that erupted from the pipe, strong but controlled. "Put the table right there—and put the pail directly in the flame."

While they set it up, he grabbed the canister. Two minutes and change.

That had better be enough heat, he thought, eyeing the flame.

What's the thermal output on something like that?

We'd need to know the flow rate. It looks like ... well, a lot.

We hope.

MacGyver dropped the canister in the rapidly heating water and watched it count down.

At one minute, bubbles were forming, but nowhere near fast enough. "Stand back," he told them.

He used the soaked towel again as a hot pad against the searing metal pail and dumped out half the water. The canister was still completely submerged.

The water began to boil.

The timer approached zero as the boil grew vigorous.

"If it's neutralized, the gas it emits will be green," he told them.

"And what if it's not?" demanded the Senator as he and the aide stared, wide-eyed.

The timer hit zero, the canister valve hissed open, and—after a seemingly endless beat—*green gas* jetted into the boiling water to be carried away in the bubbles.

Mac finally exhaled as the others just gaped, still too afraid to do *anything.*

"Well," said Mac, trying to ease the tension, "glad that worked."

The aide was incredulous. "You weren't *sure* it would?"

Mac shrugged. "I hadn't really done the math. But trust me, the infection's dead. So there's that ..."

The door yanked open, and two policemen leaped in with guns drawn. "Freeze!"

All hands went up.

Mac's towel fell down.

CHAPTER 2

THE STRIKING REDHEAD examined her bogus ID carefully for any flaws as her cab swung through the Barcelona airport entrance. *Ellie Shaw, Interpol Washington, ECD,* it said. She'd used the alias often enough to be second nature, though taking on any new name only required a little work.

She paid particular attention to the picture. It was close enough. Not her, but if she smiled just so, it would fool anything but the sharpest visual inspection. If they imaged it and tried to pull it up later, it wouldn't match anything attached to her real name in the computers. Key was the hair, scarlet red. More than once she'd wished for a nice brown or straight black rather than her natural color that betrayed her Scottish roots as surely as her native accent. She'd have happily kept her head shaved, but bald women attracted even more attention than redheads, no matter how startling the red may be—and the wigs always itched.

It'll have tae do, she told herself. *Besides, it's Barcelona-El Prat, nae Paris de Gaulle nor Ben Gurion where security is practically a religion.*

The cab bumped the curb, and the driver turned around to find a fistful of bills waiting for him. "Dinnae mind the bag, laddie. I'll handle it meself." She wasn't sure the driver understood, but better to be a baffling Scot than say anything clearly in Spanish.

As airports went, Barcelona El-Prat wasn't huge, and finding a good place to stake out the ticketing and baggage drop-off stations was simple enough. Smartphones had developed into a godsend for operatives. One could spend hours seemingly scrolling through social media and news feeds while still observing the room at large. No one seemed to bother anyone using a phone. She'd used books and magazines in her earliest days in this business, but people always wanted to know what she was reading, especially men, as if a woman alone with a book was advertising for company. The phone kept such distractions to a minimum.

A half-hour's worth of lurking produced no target.

Must have got past security already.

She glanced at an arrivals display, selected a recent American flight to note the number, then went in search of a security officer. "Hey, excuse me," she said, accent perfectly American. "Could I have a word with your supervisor?" She showed him her badge.

His eyes widened a little, and he said, "You, ah ... *uno momento, señora?*"

She nodded, smiling.

Indeed, he wasn't long. "I am Senior Officer Saldivar," said a youngish man in shirt-sleeves and tie. He was accompanied by the original officer and a third. "You requested some assistance, *señora ...?*"

"Shaw," she said, handing over her ID. "Ellie Shaw. Just Ellie, if you like. This isn't exactly a formal visit."

He fingered the ID, checked it carefully, including the holographic watermark. She wasn't sure he knew precisely what he was looking for, but this was an old procedure. He wasn't checking the card for authenticity so much as her for nervousness. She gave him a similar smile to the one in the photo. He handed it back. "'ECD,' Ms. Shaw?"

"Economic Crimes Division," she said. "Nothing terribly exciting. *Umm*, this might be a sensitive matter. Could we go somewhere less public?"

He showed her the way with a polite smile, punching a six-digit code to get through the door into the airport's depths. He didn't hide his keypresses, indicating to her he was at ease.

He stopped at an interrogation room, plain and simple. He closed the door and turned, eyebrows expectant.

"Well, it's a little embarrassing," she began, "but I wondered if you could have your computers look through your security footage for someone." She gave him her phone with the target's image on it. "I ... well, I thought I spotted him going through security a while ago as I was coming out. In fact, I've just spent the last thirty minutes or so at the restaurant out there convincing myself it wasn't him. But ... well, I can't let it go."

He chuckled. "Yet surely, you can contact your own people for this. Interpol is not without reach. We could do this quite officially."

She accepted the phone back and chewed her lip a moment. "Yeah, that's the thing. Like I say, it's embarrassing, but I'm supposed to be here on vacation. Doctor's orders, in fact. I ... work too much. You know how it is, I'm sure." She smiled at that, and he returned it, still amused. "It looked like him, but I didn't get the best view, and we've been after this guy a while. Sure, I could ring the local office and we can get someone out here fast and ground a bunch of flights, or whatever, but ..."

"You do not wish to do this on a 'hunch'?" He seemed pleased with the slang.

She laughed lightly. "Yes, exactly. But, mostly, I don't want my boss getting wind of it."

"Ah. Your vacation. Yes, I can understand. However, you must know I cannot show you anything—"

"No, no!" she interrupted. "Not at all. I'll just send you the image, and you can run it through. It would've been in the last hour or so, that's all. If there's nothing, then good. If there's something, though, then yeah, things will get official real quick." She laughed again.

"At which point, I hope you might be forgiven."

"Oh, yes," she said with a big nod. "If it's him, this is a big fish to catch, even if he's just a vice-president of a major bank. Not really dangerous. Well, except for your wallet, maybe." The joke was lame enough, in all truth, but Officer Saldivar gave her a number, and she texted the image there. He bade her wait, and had an officer send around some water. It didn't take long.

Saldivar brushed in, keeping the door open. "*Señora—er* ... Ellie? If you'd follow me?" He wasn't smiling.

On instinct, she ran through everything that might've gone wrong. He hadn't asked for her previous flight or boarding pass, and thus hadn't confirmed her side of the story, so that wasn't it. He'd given her back her ID, so he probably hadn't run it. Nor had he brought armed guards with him, which was the surest sign that nothing was amiss. Not on her end anyway.

He led the way to an office with his name on the door. "It would seem we have possible matches," he said. Three men in their mid-fifties to -sixties graced the monitors, full heads of silver hair, clean-shaven, in good shape for their ages: the very image of "distinguished men of business." The one on the right was him.

There yae be, yae bloody bastard.

Flight information was listed beneath each image, though no names.

JFK? What're yae up tae, old man?

The flight was boarding in twenty minutes. It would be close, but she could get to him if she hurried.

She went through the motions of examining each one next to the photo on her phone, then sighed and shook her head. "Sorry. It's not him."

Officer Saldivar frowned and pointed to the third. "Are you certain? This certainly looks like him."

"It does," she agreed. "But look at his suit. It's an American make and cost a couple hundred dollars at best. And that bow tie? Hideous! No, our man wears only the best from Italy and France, and they cost more than I make in a year. It's not him." She slumped a little, shaking her head again. "I appreciate you looking. I suppose I do need this vacation after all." She laughed again.

Saldivar smiled. "Well, if you say so, Ellie. It was certainly no trouble. Anything for our friends at Interpol. I do not suppose you have a companion on your journey? I would be happy to show you our fair city."

She smiled at the inevitability of the line. "I might like that. You have my number." Being a stunner always gave her an edge, and she used it often.

He escorted her back to the terminal and left her with a broad smile. She smiled back as she turned away—and her smile vanished. She opened her phone, changed the number, and went to the restroom to swap clothes, put on a wig, and brace herself for the itching. It was time for her own trip through security.

If all me trainin' is tae mean somethin', it has tae be now.

CHAPTER 3

By the next morning, MacGyver had grown sick of the disinfectant smell steeped into the orange jumpsuit the cops had given him. He'd been through interrogation six times, given the same story twenty times each, and the cops still couldn't bring themselves to believe him. Being fair, most people reacted that way when he described his methods.

"Yeah, I boiled it. It killed the virus easy. It was all green smoke coming out of the canister. If the virus was still active, it would've been red, and symptoms would've started cropping up last night. Then we'd be in real trouble."

The detective ran his hand across his bald head. "Mister MacGyver, if that's your real name, I don't think you're getting that you're neck-deep in a world of shit."

Mac sat back and sighed. Naturally, he'd been there under the direction of Homeland Security and the CDC, but his one phone call to his DHS contact had gone to voicemail. Understandable, if he was still rounding up the last of the militia group's goons. There had been a firefight at the school, short but fierce, and no one was telling Mac what the outcome was.

The door opened, and a stern-faced man with a deeply receding hairline stepped in. Arms crossed disapprovingly, he said, "Mac-

Gyver. Next time I won't bother with your phone. I'll just call the local police stations when I need you."

The detective got to his feet. "Hey! I'm in the middle of an interrogation here! Who the hell are you?"

The irritating man held up his ID. "Demerest Boone, CIA. And this one works for us."

The detective snatched the ID from his hand to study it a moment. "He's been saying Homeland Security."

Boone smiled indulgently, like he was talking to a slow child. "That was yesterday. Now, he works for me." He pulled some papers from his jacket pocket. "An order for MacGyver's immediate release, and one to transfer all your prisoners into CIA custody."

The detective's temper was cracking. "CIA has no charter to operate domestically! You can't just seize all my prisoners."

"CIA on behalf of DHS then," said Boone, taking back his ID. "There's a paper in there for it. Your ass is covered."

"They killed a cop!"

Mac sat up. "What? You didn't tell me that!"

"You didn't need to know," the detective said.

"Who?"

"Not that it matters to you, but Sergeant Jeremy Barnes was shot and killed, *after* you commandeered his vehicle and departed the scene."

Mac slumped.

Boone bore in. "Hey, Detective, pay attention; *my* prisoners are going in some deep, dark hole until we find out how a bunch of homegrown loonies got their hands on a top-secret bioweapon. If you want to argue, DHS will be along shortly. In the meantime, get this man's clothes ... Now."

The detective glowered at the papers, Boone, and Mac, in that order, then slammed the door on his way out.

"You've got a real way with people, Boone," said Mac.

"The locals should remember who's fighting the real battles." He glanced at Mac and took in the jumpsuit. "Prison orange. That's a good look on you."

Mac sighed. "You're still pissed about last time, huh?"

"You think? Everything was going fine until you got dropped into the middle of my op and managed to sail off with all the credit. Now I'm no longer next in line for the deputy directorship. I'm just the asshole they send to pick you up."

Mac stood. "Because you've got another situation?"

The door opened, and the detective wordlessly dropped in a plastic bag stuffed with Mac's clothes before slamming it on his own glare, again.

Boone handed the bag over. "JFK. We've got a problem with a plane."

Mac started digging. "In the air?"

"On the ground. We can't hold the passengers more than a couple more hours. That's why they're calling you in."

Mac, still digging, "Passengers? People aren't exactly my forte."

"No. One's missing."

"Missing?"

"Two hundred twenty-five people boarded. Two hundred twenty-four landed, including the seven flight crew. One is missing. Just poof. Gone."

Mac paused. "Huh. That's quite a magic trick."

"One with a disappearing scientist, an expert on nuclear fusion."

Mac blew out a breath. "Oh, okay, yeah, but I can't go anywhere yet."

"Jesus, MacGyver, what now?"

Searching through the bag, Mac said, "My knife isn't in here."

Boone glowered, grumbled, then yanked open the door. "Would someone *please find this man's goddamned pocketknife?*"

CHAPTER 4

SOMEHOW, I managed to get this reputation for hyper-competence. I'm not really sure where that came from. I'm good in a bind, okay, but then so are most agents. I just tend to go about things a little differently than the manual suggests.

For one, science is a lot more useful than people give it credit for these days. Knowing how things work and are put together lets you take them apart, find useful components, and put them back together to suit your immediate needs. To be honest, that might be harder than it sounds, but it's not brain surgery, either.

Still, I've managed to ruffle more than a few feathers among my so-called colleagues, and that doesn't always help get the job done.

In fact, it can be a real pain in the butt.

👓

MacGyver was checking his pocketknife over while Boone complained at the driver. "Never mind the traffic. Use the siren. Get it done!" It was New York City, just past noon, with all the delays the vast city could muster. "We should've taken the damn chopper if you're so important."

MacGyver ignored the jab and slipped the knife into his pocket. "Big date tonight or something?"

"Hopefully with a kidnapper," Boone said, getting out his phone. "Okay, here's the rundown." He popped open an image of a smiling man. Mid-sixties, full head of silver hair, bushy eyebrows, wearing a lab coat and an ostentatious bow tie. "Meet Doctor Arnold Verone, one of the world's leading experts on nuclear fusion. He works for Lockheed Martin—"

"On the T-X fusion reactor," said MacGyver, nodding, voice wondering. "Have you heard of this thing? It's amazing. It's not finished yet, but they're close. Small, too, the size of a semitrailer— well, a *big* semitrailer—"

"How the hell do you know about that?" Boone groaned.

Mac shrugged. "Tidbits here and there on the internet. And I try to keep up on the physics' white papers."

"*Anyway*, he's missing from flight 1142 from Barcelona-El Prat. Disappeared right out from under his handler's nose."

"Handler? Like a watchdog?"

"Standard procedure for a high-value asset abroad."

Mac glanced at him over the word "asset" but said nothing. "He's pretty important, yeah."

"Strategic level. This conference happens every three years. It's one of the only things we let him off the leash for."

Mac didn't let it go by this time. "He's not a dog, Boone; he's a person, you know."

"Yeah, a missing person who also happens to know more about fusion power and technology than anyone else on the planet. Can I finish?"

MacGyver glanced over the driver's shoulder. Traffic was finally moving towards the freeways, but the airport was at least half an hour away. "Be my guest."

"Security at the conference was top-notch. He had a four-man team of handlers on him from the moment he got off his plane five days ago, to the moment he went back through security at BCN. After that, he was with one agent who flew with him. Sat right next to him on the flight, direct from Spain to JFK. A little under ten hours, nonstop."

Mac's brow was furrowed as he stared at the scientist's image. "And then he just vanished?"

"According to his handler, twenty minutes before landing, right before the seat belt lights went on, he went to the restroom and never came back."

Mac frowned.

Boone continued, "Ten minutes before landing, his handler checked the restroom. It was empty. He got the flight crew involved officially, and he checked every single person and potential hiding place on the plane, from the cockpit to the tail galley. Nothing. They delayed landing by half an hour to take a manual head count. As I said, two hundred twenty-five people got on, but two hundred twenty-four were on the plane just before it landed. He was simply gone."

Mac thought about it a moment, eyes wandering as his mind ran through the possibilities. Usually the running flow of thought was subconscious and freeform, resulting in a solution. This time, Mac's brain churned hard, but came up with nothing.

Traffic was finally moving when he ultimately whistled. "Wow. That is a good one."

Boone soured. "Glad you're impressed. Best thing we've got is maybe some kind of plane got him off, or maybe he had a chute and jumped—"

Mac was shaking his head. "Crack the pressure vessel? Even as low as a couple thousand feet, someone's going to notice. You wouldn't believe how noisy it is. Or cold."

"I didn't say it was a *good* theory. All we know is that he was *on the flight*. Slept most of the way, right next to an experienced agent who knows his way around kidnappings. Even if he were completely incompetent, you can't just yank someone out from under your nose and not notice."

"Only someone did."

Boone grumbled, "Yeah. That's why the Deputy Director sent me to fetch you."

"Well, this is a little out of my expertise, but I'll see what I can do."

"Good. Faster the better. Something screwy went on, and we can't hold those people for much longer."

Mac was puzzled for a moment. "Hold them—They're not still on the *plane*, are they?"

"No, MacGyver, I'm an asshole, not a monster. When the handler radioed in the emergency, they landed at a secured runway, and the plane was surrounded by DHS and airport security when it stopped. They did some preliminaries on the runway, then towed the thing into a cleared hangar. Everyone was disembarked with eyes and cameras everywhere. IDs checked and rechecked. They're encamped further down the hangar in pup tents, completely surrounded by security. Plenty of food and water amid all the interviews and interrogations. They're just getting a little rowdy now. To say nothing of the press."

"Not surprised."

"We can legally hold all the Americans for twenty-four hours without charge. We're doing that. As for the foreign nationals ... well, we'll see."

MacGyver always hated that kind of talk. "Just like you're holding those militia guys I stopped yesterday?"

"They're friggin' whack jobs."

"Yeah, but whack jobs with rights. Or didn't I hear you ordering that they be tossed in a hole?"

Boone snorted. "Domestic terrorists can have their rights when I *say* they can. Besides, DHS will handle it. *After* we've had a word."

Mac's mouth was set in a line. "The Constitution is just a set of suggestions to you, huh?"

Boone didn't answer as the car raced down the off-ramp towards JFK.

Boone parted security like the Red Sea at the hangar, a vast space containing the aircraft in question surrounded by armed airport security and patrolling K9 units. Boone waved to the plane. "Okay. There it is. Do your 'thing,' MacGyver."

Mac had had some time to contemplate the matter while getting to the hangar. Now, he nodded at the massive 787 Dreamliner and said, "He's either here, or he's not."

Boone stared at him a moment, then started a slow clap. "Oh, amazing, Mac, just stellar. How could we have not seen *that*?"

Mac gave him a wry expression. "What I mean is, he's either still on this plane, or he was never really on it."

"His handler was next to him the whole time. How?—"

Mac held up a hand. "Let's talk to the handler first, preferably right where they were sitting."

On their way, an older man in his early sixties or so intercepted Boone. "Excuse me," he said, accent British, "but you would be Agent Boone, would you not, sir?"

"Food and water are that way in the tents. Please excuse—"

"Yes, yes, I'm terribly sorry to be a bother, but it has been twenty-four hours, has it not? We may leave at will now, and I wish to be on my way."

"The *Americans* can leave in about ninety minutes," Boone said. "Foreign nationals *may* take a bit *longer,* especially if they're pushy, annoying, or otherwise get in my way. Sir."

The older man didn't back down. "You will appreciate then that I'm a naturalized American citizen, and that I'm on something of a timetable. This communications blackout you've imposed has been intolerable, and now I'm hearing rumors of a bioweapon attack downtown."

Boone got icy. "Where in the hell did you hear that? Never mind. I don't want to know. It's a false report. Now, sir, I think you can appreciate that your government is following every procedure to keep you safe. We're sorry about the inconvenience, and that's all the apology you'll ever get out of me. Good day."

Boone brushed past the man with MacGyver in tow. Mac shared a look with the old man and shrugged by way of apology.

"You're a real loss for the Diplomatic Corps, Boone," Mac said, catching up.

"Save it. You haven't been dealing with two hundred civilians whining about their 'rights' for the last twenty-four hours. The handler is on the plane. Come on."

In fact, they found the agent sitting in seat 4A, portside window near the nose. "MacGyver, this is Agent Holcomb. He was with Doctor Verone the entire time, and somehow still managed to lose him." Holcomb, a deep black African-American, rose wearily from the seat. He seemed early to mid-thirties, broader across the shoulders than Mac, though not quite as tall. His rumpled suit spoke of perhaps a few hours' sleep snatched on a cot, and the bags under his eyes belied the stress eating him up.

They shook hands. "So, you're the genius the Deputy Director has up her sleeve?"

Mac flashed a brief smile. "Don't believe everything you hear. But we'll do our best. This was his seat?" Mac pointed at 4D in the center row. This was business class, pristine under brilliant white cabin lights. The seats were well-padded, comfortable, and could fold backwards into a cot that wouldn't disturb any other passenger. Quite a change from the military transports or economy seats MacGyver was used to.

"That's it," said Holcomb as Mac sat down, looking things over. "And this was mine, facing backwards, to see anyone coming up the aisle from the main cabin."

Mac checked over everything, including the flight safety and menu pamphlets. Nothing sprang to his eye, though he hadn't expected much. "Okay, walk me through it from the time you left the hotel."

Holcomb took a deep breath and began. "It was our four-man team picking him up at his room. He was almost chipper. Happy to be heading home. Talked to me about his notes and some ideas he'd had all the way to the airport."

Boone snorted. "You understand any of that?"

"A little, but mostly it's just fun to see someone so excited about their work, you know? And the doctor loves his work. Anyway, at the airport we stopped for a drink at the bar. He always liked one to calm his nerves. He's not the best flyer."

"Before or after security?" Mac asked.

"Before, with my full team there. I'm good, but I don't have eight eyeballs to keep an eye on his beverage plus the room around us. We were over an hour early, went through the priority checkpoint, and got to the gate. At this point, it was just me watching him."

"Why's that?"

Holcomb shrugged. "Team was needed for another assignment, and I don't need that many eyeballs through security, unless he's gonna eat. Anyway, we were in line to board and he complained a little about his stomach. Wasn't feeling well." He leaned forward. "Now, that's not unusual for the doc, given his flying issues—which is another reason I had the window seat, so I didn't think anything of it. When the two of us and the rest of first class got settled, he went to the restroom up there." He jabbed a thumb over his shoulder towards the nose lavatory by the cockpit. "He was gone about ten minutes and came back reporting his guts were giving him trouble. I gave him some antacids and he took a sleeping pill. The flight's ten hours, so, again, pretty normal. He dozed off as soon as they let us put the seats down."

Mac could see it play out in his head. "Sounds reasonable. Did he sleep the whole way?"

Holcomb gestured. "Right where you're sitting, straight through. Didn't even get up for lunch. Woke up about thirty minutes before landing. That's when the trouble started."

"Go ahead."

Holcomb took another breath. "Okay. He complained a little bit more about his stomach. Took some water and another antacid, but went to the restroom just as the seat belt lights went on."

"No one said anything about that? Flight crew didn't object?"

Holcomb shrugged. "You know how it is. Last minute trip to the head with the plane flying smooth ... nah, the attendants didn't mind. But then he was gone ten whole minutes."

"Show me the lavatory," Mac said.

Holcomb took them forward to the nose restroom. "Right here. Only one up here. He was gone ten minutes before I got that feeling on the back of my neck. I came and checked, and it was standing open. Empty."

MacGyver, thoughtful, stepped into the tiny restroom. Larger than the main cabin restrooms, it was nonetheless cramped. "Okay," he said, turning towards them. "I'll be a minute."

"Didn't you go at the police station?" Boone scoffed. "Anyway, our people have been all over it, Boeing contractors, too."

Mac shrugged. "You wanted me here for this. Let me work. Clock is ticking on your detention camp, right?"

Boone scowled, but returned to the front cabin to confer with Holcomb.

It was like any other aircraft lavatory, though it had a window right over the toilet.

If something happened in here, it happened with the door shut.

He shut the door, locked it, and stood for a moment, just looking around. The harsh interior light put everything in stark relief. A faint whiff of something rank in the trash meant that they hadn't even emptied the waste bins since the plane landed the day before. He gave it a cursory look, found a bit of discarded food, pulled the liner out to examine the bin itself, found nothing, and dismissed the trash as irrelevant.

He looked over the window, examining the seal lightly with his fingers, then tentatively with his knife.

Waste of time. Window's too small for anyone bigger than a six-year-old to get out.

Plus the pressure differential would set off a hundred alarms, like you already told Boone.

And would that door even hold?

He pushed on the flexible door. It might hold, but it had give.

There'd be a racket from the buffeting.

Someone would've noticed. There are seats not six feet away.

He abandoned the window and checked the cabinet. It was compact, like everything else, having only a first-aid kit, which he popped open.

Anything missing?

Bandages, strips, pads, gauze, wire splint, eye wash, antiseptic cream, moist towelettes, inhalants, gloves ... even forceps and tiny scissors.

It's all there.

He put it away and examined the sink. The front panel came off like a hatch. He set it aside and unscrewed the service panel underneath.

Hot and cold pipes.

Drain and trap.

Yep. It's a sink all right, he thought wryly.

He ran the water for a moment to look for unusual behavior. Nothing.

Toilet next. It was a standard aircraft toilet, designed for minimal water usage. He flushed it to watch the action for anything strange. Completely normal.

How well is it bolted down?

He tried to move it. It didn't budge. He looked for a way to remove it. The entire outer panel up to the ceiling would need to come off. There'd be almost no room in there to move around.

No good.

Flooring. Is it loose at all? Some kind of hatch down into the hold?

He tested the rubber flooring for any give, shaking his head the whole time.

No give at all.

No secret springs.

Nada.

What next?

The hold? Could he survive in there?

It's pressurized, after all.

If he did manage to get in there, he'd be okay.

Cold though.

Yeah, but still okay, especially for only twenty minutes on descent.

He opened the door, gave one last look around, then went to Boone and Holcomb who stood up at his approach.

"Well?" asked Boone.

"Whatever happened, didn't happen in there."

Boone snorted. "Great. So much for your genius. And we've got less than an hour now, you read me?"

👓

Mac drafted an airline technician and spent the next hour going through every conceivable space big enough to hold a human on the plane: bathrooms, galleys, luggage bins and cargo holds—crawling in and around any gap or passageway in the one hundred and ninety feet of the air frame. Which left him knuckling the small of his back and stretching when he finally emerged.

Need more yoga, Mac, he thought, as Boone approached like a thundercloud.

"Tell me you have something," Boone demanded.

"Other than a sore back, nada," Mac said. "I'm sorry, Boone. He's not here."

At that moment a timer went off on Boone's phone. Boone swore like a sailor and looked like he might hurl the thing the length of the hangar.

A nearby aide, looking meek, said, "Sir?"

Boone swore again, red-faced. "Fine. Let them go. Only the Americans, though. Keep everyone else until their lawyers find some judge dumb enough to authorize it."

"That won't take long, sir—" the aide began.

"GO!"

Mac's face darkened at Boone as the aide scurried off, but

arguing for the foreign nationals would do no good. He kept considering the plane while Boone paced, fumed, and cursed.

Finally, he stopped in front of Mac. "I thought you were infallible."

"I don't know what gave you *that* idea. I screw up all the time," Mac said.

"Not according to the rumor mills. You're supposed to be Captain friggin' Marvel."

Mac could only shrug. "I wasn't *trying* to make you look bad on that last op, Boone."

"But you did! And who's left to shovel up your shit now? Me! Good old Boone, more than happy to—"

Mac snapped his fingers. "Wait, has anyone checked the sewage tank?"

It was Boone's turn to snort. "He's not in there. Pretty sure."

"Not for him, but for anything else."

"Have you seen how small the toilets are? What could possibly fit down one of those—"

"I don't know," Mac said, finally tired of Boone's questions. "I'm assuming it hasn't been drained. Or if it has, then they'd be holding it somewhere?"

Boone sighed and pulled out his phone. "Yeah. Nothing on or off without my say-so. You want to be present for the grand opening or something?"

Mac nodded. "It's literally the last place to look."

Boone cracked a vicious smile. "Okay, let's do it. Nothing would give me more pleasure than seeing you up to your ass in crap right now."

👓

The sewage from two hundred twenty-five (or -four) people for ten hours took up the better part of a large inflatable pool.

Mac was *really* glad to be inside a self-contained hazmat suit as he and two techs literally raked through the muck. Boone, Holcomb, and a few others stood by behind a plexiglass barrier watching them comb through the filth, debris, and other things people had flushed.

It didn't take long.

With a sinking feeling, MacGyver reached down into the brown slush and pulled up a latex mask, torn and decaying. It had silvery hair and eyebrows like Doctor Verone's.

Mac turned towards the barrier and held up the dripping mask as everyone stared, dumbfounded. "Doctor Verone was never on the flight," he said over the suit speaker. "Agent Holcomb was babysitting an impostor."

All was silent for a moment until Boone's next expletive shook the barrier.

CHAPTER 5

In a dingy hotel room that stank of the last occupant's French cigarettes, the red-haired woman sat down in front of her computer. Her target's phone had been encrypted, but she'd gotten close enough to yank nearly everything off it while he waited to board in Barcelona. The algorithm was finally complete.

"Now, what were yae up tae, yae bastard?" she murmured.

She ran through texts, contacts, emails, and anything else the phone had. Three hours she spent before standing to stretch and rub her eyes. Dark had long since fallen. She cursed the screen and poured herself a drink to contemplate and brood.

The data showed a purely ordinary life. Texts with a wife and grown son talking about grandkids and an upcoming holiday. Emails in the same vein. Daily phone calls to the wife spanning the last two weeks. She perked up momentarily about an incoming call from a contact that traced to a realtor, but it turned out to be a place in New Mexico specializing in summer houses. Ridiculous. Her target would never retire. All of it was a front. Indeed, the lack of anything at all on a professional level spoke of a smoke screen.

"Who are yae huntin' now?" she growled at the screen. "An' why JFK? What business have yae got with the bloody Colonials?"

Her phone beeped an alert at her:

Flash traffic. Medium importance. CIA flags.

INCIDENT AT BCN. MISSING PERSONS. INTERPOL CONTACT: SPECIAL AGENT SOLANA CASTILLO.

She contemplated delving into the attached case number, but ultimately decided against it. Whatever had happened was done now. She'd wait for developments before taking the time to examine the file.

A thought occurred to her. Barcelona-El Prat would now come under closer scrutiny. It was possible they might trip to her having been there. But if that occurred she'd handle it in the usual way—and the consequences be damned.

She turned back to her target's worthless data. There wasn't much left but the spam folders, rejected calls, and files with no extension. But she'd be thorough, for conscience's sake if nothing else, as she murmured to herself "Back into the pits with yae, lads."

◉◉

Mac spent a fair bit of time in the shower, ostensibly scrubbing off the stink, but mostly thinking the situation over. Normally by zoning into such a simple task as a hot shower, he could detach his mind to drift and wait for it to return with solutions, sometimes bizarre, but usually plausible. This time: nothing.

Dressed back in his battered leather jacket and jeans, an agent directed him to Boone's co-opted office in the middle of security territory at JFK. The outer office reminded him of any ordinary business with cubicles: computers decorated with a few personal effects, and windowed offices with shades drawn. He didn't really need to see Boone to find him, though. The man's voice carried.

Mac opened the door on Boone upbraiding Holcomb. "I'm recommending a formal review. You sat next to a man who wasn't your asset for *ten hours* and didn't notice anything at all."

Holcomb's weariness conveyed itself through his eyes and tired shoulders. "Sir, I've been over it in my head a thousand times. He slept for almost all of it. We barely spoke. Hell, an upset stomach would make *me* want to sleep for a long flight. I had no reason to suspect a damn thing was wrong until we were landing."

Boone's phone rang. He glanced at it, then said, "Yeah. Good luck with that in front of the committee." He thumbed the phone and turned away. "Deputy Director, what can I do for you?"

While Boone talked in the corner, Mac turned to Holcomb. "You okay?"

Holcomb sighed and shook his head. "Nothing that sixteen hours of sleep and a nuclear physicist wouldn't cure."

Mac nodded. "If it helps at all, I doubt anyone would've noticed the switch. Way outside the playbook."

"Thanks." He shook his head again, thinking, but just sighed. "I'm just fried. And starting to wonder what I'm doing here, sometimes."

MacGyver thought of the policeman, dead before his time, and the militiamen who should be on trial for their crimes. "Copy that. Seems like no matter how many slimebags I round up, more just keep coming. Or vanish, to concoct another nasty scheme. Like pushing a rock up a hill."

"Yeah," said Holcomb. "I want to get the guys that did this, but mostly I just want the doc back. He's a lab coat, you know? Just wants to make the world better by building something that will help a lot of people."

Mac smiled. "Amen to that."

"I'm no brain, maybe." Holcomb sagged. "But I'm good at protecting people, and today I blew it." He shook his head again. "Boone's right about the review committee. There won't be much mercy there, especially if Boone pulls out the thumbscrews."

"Well, if it helps, Boone isn't the committee. And if you need a statement or anything from me, just say the word."

Holcomb managed a dejected smile. "Thanks, man. But I asked around about you. No one seemed to know what division you're with."

Mac had heard this one many times. "I'm kinda an odd duck. More a freelancer of sorts."

Holcomb grunted. "Must be nice not having a boss."

Mac glanced at Boone. "Oh, I have plenty of suits to answer to."

Holcomb almost chuckled, grin lingering. "Glad he's not my direct superior. But his word carries weight. We'll see how it goes."

Mac was about to reply when Boone turned back their way.

"Yes, ma'am, he's here, but—"

Mac raised an eyebrow as Boone continued.

"No, ma'am, I'm sure—Yes, ma'am, but I've already got Interpol on—Ma'am, I can easily—Yes, ma'am." He handed MacGyver the phone, mouth sour, eyes narrow. "The Deputy Director wants a word."

"Deputy Director, how are you today ...? Me, too, me, too. How can I help ...? It's a strange one, that's for sure ... No, no indication at all. Hell, anyone could've missed it ... Yes, ma'am, whatever went down happened at Barcelona-El Prat ... No, no plans for now ... Okay, sure. Good to hear from you. I hope to have some good news soon ... Yes, ma'am." He handed the phone back to Boone without a word.

"Yes, ma'am ...? Deputy Director, with all due res—" He cut off, just listening.

Holcomb and Mac traded a glance as Boone's face got redder.

"Yes, ma'am. I'll handle it. Yes, ma'am. Thank you—" He looked at the ended call a moment, then glared at MacGyver. "You're going to Barcelona. First direct flight. I'm supposed to ask if you need anything."

Mac looked himself over, then shrugged. "Traveling light, I guess."

Boone's gaze shifted. "Holcomb. Arrange a flight for MacGyver back to BCN. *Cheap.* Then go home. We'll be in touch."

Holcomb straightened up, held Boone's gaze a long moment, then shook Mac's hand. "Good luck."

"You, too."

When the door closed, Boone said, "I'll be straight with you, MacGyver, I'm not happy about this. Today was not perfect, and I don't think it should be rewarded. But the DD wants you to be the

CIA liaison with Interpol on this, representing our interests in Barcelona."

"Okay."

Boone hissed. "'Okay,' he says, like it's something he does every week. Don't think this is some vacation without a handler, Mac. *I still pull your strings.* You'll report at least daily or more often, if possible. Don't be without your phone. I'm on you, got it?"

At most times Mac would've been called easygoing, or even laid-back. He didn't think getting his temper up solved much of anything. It usually just interfered with rapid decision making, and it definitely interfered with objective analysis. At that moment, though, he could feel the pushback rising—or maybe it was an age thing?

"Let me be clear, Boone. I don't work directly for you. I'll report to you in this case, sure, but I'm not out there to follow your implicit instructions. I'm there to help Interpol, not manhandle them. We want Doctor Verone back safe and sound. Everything else is secondary. And, frankly, if the Deputy Director thought you were the right man for the job, she'd have you on that plane instead of me. So, spare me the chest-thumping, will ya?"

Boone was bright red again, jaw clenched, trying to sort through all the things he was aching to say until he found some measure of composure. "I'll be certain to remember your comments when it comes time to renew your deal. That's coming up soon, isn't it?"

"Burn it for all I care." Mac leveled a look of peeve and pity at Boone and let the slamming door's thud on his exit end the conversation.

Mac settled into the first-class seat, stretching into legroom he rarely enjoyed.

Gracias, Holcomb, he thought. *His smile faded as he wondered if this would cost Holcomb in the committee for going against Boone's instructions for a "cheap" flight. Who could tell?*

Boone, MacGyver continued the thought, shaking his head.

No question the man was highly effective as an intelligence officer: quick, perceptive, decisive, and completely ruthless to anyone he perceived as in his way, friend or foe alike. As the aircraft taxied into the fading light, Mac stared out the window wondering what drove someone like Boone.

Ego? Power? Patriotism?

He must've been moved to serve the country enough at one point to join the agency, no? That's what got you here, after all.

But now? With all the infighting and politics oozing from guys like Boone, was that still enough to keep putting my ass on the line?

No particular answers came as the plane accelerated and slid into the twilight sky.

Mac attached his phone to the aircraft wi-fi, waited for the algorithms to secure his connection to the CIA, then received the case file. Up front and center was Doctor Verone's smiling photo. Mac flipped through a few more, each of them the doctor with a colleague, a friend, or with family members. Always a big, genuine smile.

I doubt he's smiling now, wherever he is—wondering if he'll ever take another picture like this. Or if anyone's coming for him. Like me.

'Cause if it weren't for the secrets in his head, he'd be like those poor folks Boone was abusing at the airport. Would the CIA be mobilizing like this for one of them?

The cynical thought squatted in his head like an ugly toad. Mac didn't like it there, no matter how true it was. And he knew it wasn't just Boone. He'd done more than a few missions lately where the outcome, while successful, had been far from satisfactory. People shuffled off to God-knows-where to face charges, or not, based upon some bizarre code of justice the covert community had devised. Mac wasn't naive enough to believe everything should be out in the public eye, but at the end of the day, it was still people they were whisking off to secret sites—or worse.

Because it seemed there were the deaths now. Preventable, unnecessary deaths. Sure, the militiamen had shot the cop and the other cop had shot the other one. But Mac should've seen it coming.

And, in the end, was the world really changing at all? He'd been doing this since his mid-twenties. Two decades of globe-trotting and black ops and what had it gotten anyone? Then, catching himself, *What is this, Mac? Self-indulgent brooding? That's not like you.*

No, it wasn't. He took a deep breath, feeling his ears pop a little as the plane ascended. He went back to his phone.

He reviewed the case details so far. Scant clues, little information, and only one real fact: Doctor Verone had vanished.

Correction: He appeared *to vanish. Exactly,* he told himself. *It was like a stage magician's trick.*

Misdirection was a classic tool in the covert ops toolkit. Mac relied on it himself quite often. Some chemicals from a janitor's closet for a quick flash grenade. Some shorted wiring for a fire in a disused outbuilding. A little olive oil and lighter fluid for blinding smoke. He grinned at the memories, the quick sleights of hand. *Fun.*

This kidnapping had similar markers, writ somewhat larger. He'd taken that plane apart, and nothing. The more he thought about it, the more it had to be. Verone had never left Barcelona. It had been ten hours before anyone thought anything was amiss, and it had happened at an airport. Even before the investigation began, Verone could've ended up almost anywhere on Earth. By distracting them so late into the operation, the perpetrator had bought themselves all the time in the world.

Well, look on the bright side, Mac. Earth's a small place to search —relative to the rest of the universe at least.

But hardly amusing to the lead Interpol agent, who would probably find a nerd crack like that inane at best. Who is heading this for Interpol, anyway?

Her name was in the file, and when he saw it, his silent rambling stopped dead.

SOLANA CASTILLO, INTERPOL MADRID.

The same one? Had to be. How many people in Interpol could there be with that name?

The picture confirmed it, and he realized he'd just forgotten to breathe. A Spanish knockout with classic Castilian features, especially her jet-black hair and dark eyes, that promised she could surrender herself—or take your head off—with an equal passion. Mac knew her. Intimately.

They'd worked together a few times over the last six years. Each time had been ... intense, and most especially the last time in San Sebastián on Spain's north coast. They'd posed as newlyweds for more than a week. In the end they nabbed their arms dealer, but they'd also resolved never to work together like that again. It had been an amazing time and hadn't involved much acting on his part in the role of a besotted groom. Good thing, since his skill set didn't extend far into maintaining a deep cover for long. Not that either of them had planned what happened. It just felt ... right.

And that was why they'd agreed never again. In the field those kind of feelings only got in the way. Reckless joy was just as dangerous as rage or grief.

Even then he'd been questioning his place in field work, regardless of which agency he'd been working for. That once, he was glad to have assisted in what amounted to a straight-up sting and arrest. The arms dealer had gotten their day in court and wouldn't be in a position to hurt anyone else, not for a long time. *That* felt like justice. If someone was going to be condemned, it'd better damn well be by an actual court, not by Boone's brand of summary judgment, no matter how horrible the perpetrators were.

The plane had leveled off while he scanned through the file. Mac wasn't surprised to find himself nodding off in his seat. He'd read the last two paragraphs without retaining a single word. Even though this flight would be just over seven hours (*thank you, jet stream*), he'd still be arriving at dawn local time. He could do with some shut-eye.

He lowered the seat into its cot configuration and lay back. His mind wandered, finally free of the case that he could do literally nothing about while thrusting over the Atlantic at 30,000 feet. But there was no containing the images of San Sebastián now: her alluring smile and those smoky eyes pouring into his as they danced.

It wasn't just that she was beautiful. Solana had somehow seen him fully as a man—no, as a *human*. She got his nerdy jokes (well, most of them). She shared his view of their work. And he'd understood her just as well. The way she gave herself art almost regardless of form: movies, books, paintings, sculptures. Who in this business did that? She was fearless to let herself be moved by it. And he got her highbrow jokes (well, most of them).

They'd felt pretty strongly for each other, and that doesn't work in the field, no matter how neatly that might work in the movies. So, they'd resolved to meet again after a time to see if things still clicked or it was just one of those momentary things. But neither of them had reached out for that yet. And it'd been two years.

Two years, Mac. Lots of things can change in two years.

Like you?

You're talking to yourself, but you've always done that.

I'm just not as sure of my place in the world as I should be. Midlife crisis? Or finally waking up to a bigger truth?

But forget me. Will she feel the same?

But something told him he'd know the answer to that the moment he saw her. And, allowing that reunion to carousel around in his mind, he drifted off to sleep, waking only to the flight attendant gently tapping his shoulder to rouse him for their final descent into Spain.

👓

The dawn's warm light crept in through the dingy blinds, finally diverting the red-haired woman's attention from the computer screen. Almost at once, the weariness she'd been ignoring manifested in an epic yawn. She took a moment to rub her eyes and breathe deeply. The sickening scent of that damned French tobacco was in everything. She'd tuned it out while she worked, but now it came roaring back. Had the former occupant bathed in the stuff?

She needed sleep, that much was certain. She'd already been at it for almost forty-eight hours, between the airport and decrypting this data dump. She should lay down, close her eyes, and wake with a completely clear head.

"Should" bein' the operative word, she thought.

Instead she rose to boil water for coffee on the tiny kitchen burner.

She'd finally resorted to sifting the data files with no extensions, tags, or other markers to indicate which application had created them. Encrypted data often took on this form. But, her software was top notch, the best the intelligence community had devised for field work. She fed it another file to crunch and got up to stretch and enjoy her coffee, black, and strong enough to make an elephant forget—everything. She liked that about Spain: coffee with impact. She felt energy seeping back into her limbs and mind. It was purely artificial, but it would do.

Another hour, another cup, and another file. Slow going, this slog. If only she'd had more warning of his presence at the airport. But she'd been following one of his associates and had never expected the bastard himself. There was much to be said for a surprise attack, but not if she expected to escape. She couldn't afford that kind of exposure.

The file summary appeared. A calendar of events!

Well now, what're yae about?

She leaned forward, scanning the lines.

Ordinary stuff for the most part. Birthdays. Meetings. Meals, long since digested. One item from the previous month caught her eye. She read it aloud in a murmur. "Shipment departure. Freighter *Kutup Ayisi* from Mersin, Turkey ... 'Kutup Ayisi' ...? Turkish for polar bear. Good a name for a freighter as any, I suppose." There was nothing else, but with the name, dates, and ports of call she could find more information from the internet. It didn't take long.

Kutup Ayisi was a medium-sized, long-haul freighter, owned by its shipping company for eleven years. It often ran from Turkey to various points in the Atlantic, down the American coasts, then returning to Turkey. Nothing unusual, nothing odd, except that its current manifest listed only heavy industrial equipment. Previous manifests had been much more detailed and much more varied.

An' nae tae mention, what're yae doing in this bastard's calendar?

Again, it didn't take long to discover. The *Kutup Ayisi* had been reported missing, not six days ago. Searches along its projected course to Brazil had found nothing. Currently, the ship was presumed lost, barring some other clue as to her fate.

She sat back, contemplating. *"Now what would yae be wantin' with a freighter, old man? What indeed?"*

Nothing came to mind, despite the coffee.

She took a deep breath, sat up, and loaded another file.

CHAPTER 6

SPECIAL AGENT CASTILLO was waiting for Mac at the customs checkpoint with that sly Mona Lisa smile on her face. "Well, look what the *gato* dragged in."

She's here, thought Mac. *She could've sent someone or texted me with where to meet but ... she's* here.

And he could feel that click in his gut, like the final tumbler falling into place before the safe door swings free—and he realized he was blushing.

"Solana, good to see you," he said. "Or should I say 'Special Agent' now?" He felt the urge to touch her somehow but she solved the problem by pulling him into a brief hug.

"You should avoid too much formality when it's just us," she said. "Or do you have some title now that you're working for the CIA?"

"Still just ... MacGyver," he replied, breathing in the scent of her hair before she released him, still wearing that impish grin.

"MacGyver is as MacGyver does, no?" God, he'd missed that accent. She continued, "And I know we'd agreed to not work together again, but this is a very different case. Not exactly La Concha beach."

Mac hesitated, then said, "True enough. But maybe we should talk about that ... at some point."

Her eyes danced right through him. "Maybe so." Then she shut it all down and got serious, flashing her badge to lead him through customs towards the airport's security offices. "We'll see what time the case affords us. We haven't had much headway since we got word, but this may be connected to a string of unusual cases that I've been investigating."

That was interesting. "Interpol has had similar disappearances?"

"No kidnappings, until this case. There's a service crew missing here, too."

Whoa. "Hadn't heard that."

"Food services, resupplying the plane. They never reported in after their shift, despite all the aircraft being supplied. Three men, varying ages. No connection between them other than their work here."

"So, we're looking for four people now, all just vanished."

"Correct," she said. "As I say, there have been a few significant thefts that match this modus operandi."

"This is a strange one, all right," Mac said, turning to her as they walked.

"Like a magic trick, no?"

"Exactly."

She nodded. "I'll tell you all about them. And we do have a person of interest."

"Even better. At least we're not completely in the dark. The investigative side isn't exactly my thing."

"No, but you've got good instincts. This I noted more than once."

He grinned briefly. "You don't say." She returned the grin, and, just like that, the dance was back on.

She swiped the door to the security offices with her card and held it open. "I was glad they got you to look at the plane in New York. If you didn't find anything, then I believe there was nothing to find, despite what your man Boone says."

Mac stifled a groan. "Yeah, Boone was not a happy camper."

"The man's—how you say?—a pompous boor. This way."

She led him through corridors of busy security officers, some in uniform, some not. Again, Mac remarked how offices throughout the world looked similar based on function. No matter the country, people were people. She knocked on a windowed door, then opened it to a good-looking man in his thirties. He'd obviously been awake for some time.

"MacGyver, this is Senior Officer Saldivar. Officer Saldivar, MacGyver with the CIA."

They shook hands. "*Señor* MacGyver," said Saldivar. "It is not often we deal directly with CIA agents."

Mac rolled his head a bit. "Well, I'm not really an agent. More of a … contractor, you might say."

"Yes, Mister MacGyver has a rather unique skill set," Castillo said in Spanish.

Saldivar replied in that language, "Spanish is acceptable?"

Mac nodded. "*Sí, español está bien, si Ud prefiere.*"

Saldivar nodded his appreciation. "*Sí, gracias.*"

Castillo continued in that language, "Let's start with your encounter with my POI."

Consternation crossed Saldivar's face as he hit some buttons on his computer. The woman's image appeared on the screen, taken from the security cameras inside the security offices themselves. She looked late twenties or early thirties, though it was hard to tell, average height and build, business dress, with brilliant scarlet hair. She was walking with Saldivar. "She came posing as an Interpol agent from Washington," he began, and detailed the entire encounter.

Mac considered his story for a brief time. "Who were the men the computer identified?"

Saldivar clicked the mouse, and three images appeared side by side.

Mac pointed to one and grunted. "That guy accosted Boone as we were heading to examine the plane."

"Accosted? I like him already," said Castillo.

"You check all of them out?"

"Naturally," she said. "The first two are ordinary. That one sells telecom systems for a large US corporation. The other was traveling with his wife on their first trip outside the US. The third, the one she was interested in and the one that confronted your Boone, was born British, married in the US, and was naturalized almost two decades ago. Wife deceased, himself an entrepreneur with his name on half a dozen businesses around the world. Interpol US located the other two quickly enough and exonerated them after brief interviews. We haven't been able to reach him."

"Interesting."

"But nothing that raises any flags, except perhaps that this man and Doctor Verone possess rather unfortunate tastes in their choice of neckties."

"Well, Boone told you about the mask we found, right?" Mac said. "This man could've been the one impersonating Doctor Verone."

She smiled. "It could be, but the ties would have to be identical." She flipped through her phone a moment, showing Doctor Verone's security photo. "They're not. And the CIA handler would've likely noticed."

It was true. Holcomb may have been duped, but he wouldn't have missed a red and yellow polka dot tie versus green and blue stripes.

She continued, "That said, he might have changed ties, and we're still tracking him down. So that returns us to my POI. As I say, she's been seen at several crime scenes, either before or just after, where the MO matches this one. Seeming magic tricks where the goods or devices simply vanished at some point without anyone seen coming or going. Sometimes despite lavish security."

"Okay. So what sort of—" Mac was saying when there was a rapid knock on the door.

A security officer with flushed cheeks blew in to all but shout, "Pardon, chief, but we think we've found them!"

A beleaguered baggage cart carried them all as fast as its battery could churn and deposited them outside a disused maintenance hangar at the airport's edge. Several security vehicles surrounded the place, lights flashing weakly against the noonday sun, as an urgent conference was in progress between a woman officer and two workmen in coveralls in the open hangar door.

She saluted as Saldivar, Castillo, and MacGyver approached. "Sir! We're pretty sure they're inside, stuck in an old shipping container. But the latch has been deliberately disabled, and the bolts are so corroded even Cuello can't get it open."

She led them into the dingy, dusty interior, infused with the faint scent of jet fuel and even stronger motor oil. More officers stood at hand, watching one of the largest men MacGyver had ever seen as he labored at an enormous wrench with both hands, using his own considerable weight and strength to no effect. He pulled and pulled, muscles bulging until his face was beet red, but finally eased off, sweating and panting. He turned to the group and shook his head. "Sorry, sir. It's stuck tight."

"I can still cut it open," said one workman. "But it'd be faster to go through the side, and that'd make things really hot in there."

Castillo shook her head. "They could be in bad shape, bound, piled against the wall you're cutting."

Saldivar turned to the officer. "Have you made contact?"

She shook her head. "Just banging and muffled shouts. We can't make out anything they're saying, and I bet it's the same in there."

"Let me take a look," Mac said, and went to the container.

Thick walls. Good steel, if old.

Yeah, go in through the roof if they have to cut.

He examined the latch.

Broken off?—no, cut off and pinned. Badly corroded, except here where they cut it.

The bolts attaching the latch to the container were in even worse shape. Someone had tried to scrub them, and some shiny residue caught his eye. He touched it and sniffed.

Oil. WD-40. Good idea, but maybe kick it up a notch.

Need a penetrating oil.

And something to eat the corrosion.

He turned around, scanning the hangar.

Maintenance hangar ...

"Uno momento," he said, and went looking through the dust-coated shelves. It didn't take long.

He returned with a plastic bucket, a dipstick, and two bottles: transmission fluid and acetone. He poured equal parts of each into the bucket, mixed it together with the stick, then poured the viscous fluid on each bolt. "We'll let that sit a minute," he told them.

"You might get medical services and an ambulance out here," Castillo told Saldivar.

He nodded and spoke into his radio.

"Who found them?" Castillo asked.

"I did, ma'am," said the female officer. "I couldn't think of anywhere else to look, but I remembered this old hangar. I didn't know this container was in here, and when I saw the fresh cut on the latch, I banged on the door. They started banging back."

"That's good work," Castillo said.

"Okay," Mac said. "Officer Cuello, give that another shot."

The huge man gave a skeptical nod, applied the wrench, took a deep breath, and pulled. Again, muscles bulged under his shirt with the strain, but after only a few seconds, the bolt gave a rusty squeak and the wrench moved. "Yes!" he shouted, laughing. He rubbed his hands together and got to work.

It took several minutes and another application on the second bolt, but the ambulance roared up outside just as the last bolt fell away and the latch came apart. They swung the container open and three men stumbled out blinking into the relative brightness of the hangar. "Thank God, thank God, thank God," one croaked over and over, voice nearly gone from shouting. He was an older man with grey hair, a huge beard, and a face like old leather. A bruise was fading high on his cheek. He nearly dropped to his knees, but Mac caught him, and they helped all three to the light and air outside.

The medics got them water and looked them over while the others examined the container.

Castillo played a light through the interior. It smelled faintly of human waste and greatly of rust. A lidded bucket sat in one corner (the source of the stench, despite being closed), and several sandwich wrappers and empty water bottles were piled in the other. "The kidnappers were humane at least," she murmured. She indicated several strips of duct tape, sliced in half, and a box cutter on the floor. Several expired glow sticks were strewn about.

"Yeah," said Mac, examining a wall. He rapped his knuckles on it and only got a hollow thump. "This is really thick. They didn't want them communicating with anyone, but not so thick that we'd never find them."

Another delaying tactic. Layers and layers of delays.

Saldivar approached as he closed a call on his phone. "An anonymous tip just got called in. It directed us to check this hangar 'in case we were missing anyone.'"

Castillo and MacGyver traded a look. "Very humane, indeed," she said. "What do the men say?"

"They were ambushed as they got to their truck to begin their rounds. Three men, speaking Spanish, the darker one with a strong Turkish accent. Took them by surprise. Pulled guns, then tased the younger ones into submission. The old guy dodged and fought back, earned that bruise on his face. They were hauled here, bound, tossed inside. One of their assailants broke some glow sticks for them, piled in water and sandwiches, and suggested they keep the lid on their 'toilet' there closed. He dropped a box cutter by the door, told them they'd be okay in a couple of days, and locked them in." Saldivar sighed. "Thank God for small mercies, I suppose. They could have simply shot them and dumped the bodies here. We'd not have found them until someone noticed a smell."

"I'll need to interview them as soon as possible," Castillo said.

He nodded. "I showed them your Person of Interest. They never saw any woman, let alone one with red hair."

"Damn."

"Doesn't mean she wasn't involved," Mac said.

"This is true," said Saldivar. "They'll be in the infirmary. They need food and a little more rest. Say half an hour or so."

"Tasers," Castillo said, then was silent, eyes distant.

Knowing that look, Mac asked, "What, Solana?"

"Food truck ... Saldivar, do you have a spare 787 we can use for a few minutes?"

An identical Dreamliner, where Castillo sat in the seat number Holcomb had occupied. She turned her head to view forward, having to crane her neck to see, then beamed back at MacGyver. "I knew it," she said. "Saldivar, the food trucks generally service the aircraft while they're boarding, yes?"

"Just before," he said. "They try to be done before general boarding is complete."

"So, they start towards the tail and move forward?"

He thought a moment, then sighed. "Yes. Exactly. I see what you mean."

"I don't," said Mac.

She led him to the nose and pointed at the restroom to port. "Doctor Verone went there." She pointed to starboard and the closed hatchway. "While the kidnappers were servicing the galley right there."

Mac looked back and forth, then down the aisle where Holcomb would've been sitting, his back turned directly towards them. "Abracadabra ... They waited for Verone right here; he walks out; they pull a gun, or maybe tase him, and walk him right off onto the food truck." He put the rest together, though it was clear Castillo had been way ahead. "And the man impersonating Verone just needed to board the flight normally, walk forward to this lavatory before boarding was complete, change clothes, put on the mask, swap ties, and join Holcomb. Took a sleeping pill to make sure they wouldn't talk and possibly clue Holcomb in. Two hundred twenty-five boarded. But only two hundred twenty-four ever took off or landed."

She was nodding. "He definitely never left Barcelona. At least, not with Holcomb."

"Well, now we know the how," Mac said. "We need to know the who, the why, and where Verone is now."

Saldivar said, "Once we interview the victims in more depth, we'll have some descriptions to review the footage by. Some camera somewhere *must* have seen the men that did this."

"How long?" Castillo asked.

"Medical revised to say another hour. They are much diminished, despite having had food and water."

She nodded. "Food and water sounds good, in truth."

"I'll have someone take you to the cafeteria while I finish up at the container."

"Very good," she said, turning to Mac. "Join a lady for a meal?"

He nodded. "And I should call Boone."

Her expression went flat. "You really know how to kill a mood, huh."

👓

MacGyver and Castillo sat across from each other in the spartan staff cafeteria deep within the bowels of the airport. Her expression was faintly amused as Boone's shouting could be heard by everyone nearby.

"So, you found them, and figured it all out. Great, MacGyver, just great. Oh, one minor thing, *where the hell is my asset?*"

Mac pinched the bridge of his nose, hoping to crush the headache beginning there. "We're working on it. When we interview the food truck guys—"

"You haven't even *talked* to them yet? What the hell?"

"They just spent over two days stuck in a metal box. I don't know if you checked the weather, but it's August out here, even if it was inside a hangar. Let them take a damn shower, at least?"

"And all the while, Verone gets farther and farther away. Great work, MacGyver, the DD was so right to trust you with this."

"I'll keep you posted." He ended the call without another word and dropped the phone on the table. He ran his hand through his hair and sighed.

"Such a charmer," said Castillo. "Do you think he's single?"

Mac grunted. "I wouldn't wish him on an actual harpy."

She did that Mona Lisa thing again as she stirred sugar into her steaming coffee and eyed him carefully. "And how about you? Anyone ... significant in your life these days?"

He felt his face warming under her gaze as he picked at his salad. "No. I guess not really ..."

"You're not sure?" she said, amused.

"Sorry. No, there's no one. And you?" He'd been expecting this conversation—wanting it, even. But still felt unprepared.

She regarded her coffee with distaste. "One, a year ago for about three months. Apparently, he did not appreciate his girlfriend whisking off in the middle of the night to points foreign, like every two weeks."

Mac cocked his head. "Didn't he know going in that was your job?"

She rolled her eyes. "This may shock you, but most men prefer to be the international person of mystery, even if they're only a deskbound investment banker."

Mac nodded. "I can't imagine getting upset about that."

"Because you do it too, no?" she said. "It would certainly make things easier."

"Things?"

She grinned. "Relationships. Those things that make you blush like a tomato."

He blushed furiously. "Who's blushing?"

She laughed, a delicate bite of pure amusement. "Don't lie to a cop. You never were good at maintaining a cover for long. Except for last time, of course."

He smiled back, sheepishly. "Well, there wasn't a lot of acting involved. And I know we said we wouldn't work together again, so I'm sorry it's me they sent out here."

She waved that away. "I'm not. This is hardly the same thing. It's an emergency, and we're not going undercover. I'm helping find your scientist, and hopefully it'll link back to my string of heists. It certainly fits the pattern." There was a long beat as they let the mutual attraction hang silently between them before Mac let it go.

"Yeah, what is that about?"

She sat back and picked up her phone to show him pictures and specifications. "Two years ago, a large number of military-grade atmospheric filters and scrubbers vanished in-transit from their manufacturing center in Madrid to Naval Station Rota. It was like what happened with your scientist. When the trucks departed under the tightest security, the cargo was aboard. When the convoy arrived, every crate was empty. Vanished without so much as a fingerprint, a lot like Verone."

"Yeah. Only now we know that Doctor Verone was never on the plane. Might've been the same with these?"

"Yes, that was one of our theories, but we could never conclude exactly how that happened. My team will reexamine the evidence now, of course." She took a long draw on her coffee. "The heist was significant, but no one got hurt, and while it did set back a joint naval venture between us and the States, they passed it to Interpol, as it was deemed non-terror related."

Mac wagged his head as he studied the specs and took another stab at his salad. "I don't know about that. These specs indicate they're good for everything from nuclear contaminants to biological. Outfit a sealed base with these, and the inhabitants could survive a nuclear winter."

She shrugged. "That's how the politics fell out, and international cooperation seemed likely, so it made sense for us to take the lead. And this was my first significant investigation as a Special Agent, so I went for it."

He grinned with her.

She continued, "Two months later, plans for a new tidal generator went missing from the developing firm in Nova Scotia. It's a—"

"Tidal barrage!" Mac exclaimed, his face lighting up as he scanned the details. "They're a real breakthrough. You build this long pier about three-quarters of the way across a bay that experiences heavy tides, or maybe even a causeway across a strait with navigation locks for passing ships. It works like a power-generating dam that goes both directions depending on whether the tide is making or ebbing—What?"

She was watching him, hand supporting her chin, grinning at his unchecked excitement. "You are too adorable sometimes, Mac. And blushing again now, *si*? But, yes, cutting edge tech to be sure. The firm developing this one had the plans stolen from a secured data vault. And, like the filters, it was there Monday night, and gone Tuesday morning. Nothing else disturbed or touched."

Mac was puzzled. "But the plans were digital, right? They didn't lose anything."

"The company does contract work for NATO, and some projects are more tightly controlled than others. Thus, they treat all of them the same. All digital work at the end of the shift is encoded onto a single drive, backed up once at a remote location, and stored in a vault along with a few hundred other drives."

Mac shook his head. "Seems like overkill."

"Perhaps, but the fact is the perpetrators snatched this in the same manner. It took a little while to reach my desk, but when it did, all the markers were there. And then, some months later, we've got others: a military-grade atmospheric regulator like they use on submarines, a revolutionary desalinization filter, and a significant stockpile of a material called graphene—"

"Graphene! So, you know about graphene, too?"

She was enjoying this—maybe even more than she expected. "Yes, and you can regale me with all its uses soon enough, including for solar cells and next-generation batteries, plans for which were also stolen. Again, in every case, no one saw anything. No evidence of the action in progress, cameras, motion detectors, audio, heat, nothing. No one hurt. No one missing."

"Until today."

She nodded. "Until today, it seemed like pure magic. But the one thing connecting most of these is this woman here."

The image showed the redhead from Saldivar's security footage.

"So, you think she's the one masterminding these things?"

Castillo shrugged. "All I know is that except for the first heist, witnesses and cameras have noted someone of this rough description in the vicinity." She flipped through several images, some grainy, some in color, though none as clear as Saldivar's.

"Different hair most times," he said.

"A small matter. More important is her manner of dress. Businesswoman, clubber, secretary, society girl, goth … This is a woman with serious training."

"An operative, then?"

Castillo shrugged. "It's possible, but no one is claiming her. Admittedly, it wouldn't be the first time the CIA or other agencies have refused to tell us. But Boone gave my query a definitive 'No,' where ordinarily the cue is 'No Comment.'"

MacGyver frowned. "And the other big agencies?"

"Similar." She sighed. "A little openness would be nice, but then, Interpol is police, not spooks like you," she said with a tight grin.

Mac scoffed. "Oh, yeah. Spooks like me. No gun and iffy even in a fistfight."

She reached to pat his hand but stroked it instead. "I like that part. You let me handle the guns and fighting while you really save us with one of your sorcerous concoctions."

"It's not sorcery."

"Acetone and transmission fluid to loosen a rusted bolt? You can call it chemistry, but I know better," she said with a firm nod. "I should denounce you to the Inquisition."

"There's still an Inquisition?"

"I think they call it the Congregation for the Doctrine of Faith now, but they can still dig up a rack and thumbscrews if they need it. I warned you about us Catholic girls long ago. We can be deadly serious in important matters."

"That you did." He nodded, still enjoying the feel of her hand on his.

They shared a long look, savoring that quiet pull for another moment, before she said, "Well, I think our food crew has had enough time to collect themselves. And I'm eager to learn more about our mystery woman."

The mystery woman lost count of how much coffee she'd had, except that this was the fourth pot she'd brewed. The calendar file had been intriguing, but ultimately useless. She'd been through the remaining few files, but none had been as useful. The last one's results appeared before her eyes.

Another calendar!

She leaned forward, reading each line, forcing herself not to skim.

The last entry made her pause. It was a series of numbers and times, the first of which was scheduled not thirty-six hours hence.

"Flight numbers, is it?"

The internet was her ally, though the final destination code puzzled her. LYR. Svalbard Airport? Longyear, Norway? "What in the bloody hell is in Svalbard, yae daft bastard?" she asked the numbers on her screen.

Again, the internet had the answers.

She muttered to herself as she read the entry. "Svalbard, Norway, archipelago ... largest islands halfway between Norway's mainland coast an' the North Pole, well within the Arctic Circle. Most notable attraction ... Oh! Yae fiend, yae. I've got yae now!"

Excited, the need for coffee vanished; she booked the next train to Paris and the next flight to Norway.

CHAPTER 7

THE WIRY OLD man's accent was so thick that Mac's Spanish, while fluent, could only catch every third word. Castillo had to translate, digging through the Turkish inflections. Of the three workmen, the old Turk had been hit hardest by their confinement and lay in a hospital bed in the pristine infirmary, receiving intravenous fluids. The doctor had asked that they be brief. He was in no danger, but utterly exhausted.

"He says they didn't tase him," she translated. "He fought, but they hit him. He's too old to fight now, but thirty years ago, he'd have had them."

"I don't doubt it," Mac said in English (his American-accented Spanish being equally baffling to the Turk). "So, they weren't speaking Spanish?"

"Kurdish," he said through Castillo. "They didn't think I understood, but I played dumb."

Castillo nodded. "Wise. Anything interesting?"

"They were in a hurry, and glad their man was first class. They'd tase him only if they needed to. They had a gun."

Mac said, "That confirms their involvement in the kidnapping, at least. What about your mystery woman? She may have had different hair."

The Turk examined her photo for only a moment. "No, I told

the other officer I'd certainly have remembered someone like her. They mentioned no women at all."

Castillo put her phone away. "Okay. Anything else?"

He shook his head, obviously weary. "They were chatting. In a good mood. Everything was moving according to plan, and they were eager for the next phase."

Solana and Mac traded a look. "'Next phase?' That's what they said?"

"It was their word. 'Next phase,' but it made no sense. One hoped the surfing would be good because he'd never surfed in arctic waters. His friend thought that was stupid, but the other insisted that surfing was always best on islands, even if they're freezing cold. Then his friend said they'd have no time if they were to get everything loaded on the polar bear."

His retelling was met with puzzled expressions from both of them. "Arctic surfing, an island, and a polar bear? You are certain of this?"

The old Turk looked at her wearily. "Young lady, all I've done is replay their conversations in my head for two days. Yes, I am certain. Their leader returned at that point, and they went silent, and soon locked us in." He closed his eyes and lay back.

"A polar bear," MacGyver said. "Like ..." He raised his arms like claws and made a growling noise.

The Turk chuckled, eyes crinkled in amusement. "Yes, young man, those were their words. Although they said it in Turkish while speaking Kurdish. It was a strange way to phrase it."

"What's the difference?" Castillo asked.

"In Turkish it's *kutup ayisi*." He spelled it for Castillo. "In Kurdish it is ... well, they spoke Sorani Kurdish, so it is difficult to spell in Latin script, but the spoken words are very different."

The spelling kicked something in Mac's brain. "I think I've read that somewhere before. Give me a minute." He got out his phone and did a brief search. It returned several news articles instantly. "It's a missing cargo ship!" he said, holding it up for them to see.

Enlightenment crossed the old Turk's face. "Ahh, yes, a vessel name. That would explain it."

Castillo scanned the article rapidly. "Reported missing six days now, last docked at Matosinhos, Portugal, for refueling, voyage planned for Sao Paulo, Brazil."

"The hell they are," said Mac. "They're headed to some arctic island up north to load a cargo. We need to spend some quality time with a map."

"Indeed," she said, and turned to the old Turk. "You saw their faces, though? You can describe them for Saldivar's people?"

"Perfectly," he said, eyes closing. "I am not a young man, but my mind is as quick as anyone's."

Castillo patted the old Turk's shoulder and motioned for Mac to follow.

MacGyver looked up from Saldivar's computer as Castillo entered while ending a call. "My team is looking into the *Kutup Ayisi*, its owners, holding company, captain, and so on. I wish we had more of a lead, but until Saldivar can get us perpetrator images ..." She shrugged.

Mac gestured at the screen. "I may have something here."

She rounded the desk, and her eyebrows shot up. "Svalbard, Norway? That's our island?"

"Spitzbergen is the island, technically," he said, zooming in to the largest island. "But yeah, it's the Svalbard Archipelago. It's the only place I can think of that might be a viable destination."

"What about Iceland?" she asked.

"It's a larger island, but not inside the Arctic Circle. Well, except for one tiny island a little bit north. But mainly, I was considering Svalbard in light of the other heists."

"Air filters, desalinization equipment, and such?"

Mac was nodding. "It all sounds like stuff you'd need to build a colony. Or a survivalist enclave."

"And you think Svalbard might be where it's located?"

"No, if our witness was accurate with what he heard, they said they were loading the cargo ship. I'm betting it's another heist. So, I looked up the kind of ship to see what they might be loading."

She nodded. "Sure, if it's a tanker, then liquids, if it's a bulk freighter, then dry goods."

He tabbed to a new window. "This is the *Kutup Ayisi*. It's a RoRo ship."

She chuckled, reading. "So, not 'row, row your boat'?"

"No, roll-on, roll-off. It's made for trucks and cars and farm equipment to drive themselves into the hold and back out again at the destination. Like a ferry but made for the open sea and long distances. Whatever they're hauling would fit on trucks. It's a medium to small ship, but even still, you could fit fifteen to twenty semis on there or other stuff about that big."

She considered for a moment, then asked, "So, is there anything at Svalbard worth stealing for a survival-minded mastermind?"

He opened another tab. "The Svalbard Global Seed Vault. Almost one million pristine samples of plant life from around the globe."

Saldivar opened the door and paused, seeing Castillo's surprised face. "Something come up?" he asked.

They brought him up to speed quickly on the current theory.

"Forgive me," Saldivar said, "but whomever this is does not lack resources. Could they not simply *buy* these seeds? Why do anything illegal?"

Mac answered, "Maybe, yes, but these are curated to be genetically authentic, and stored in quantities sufficient to repopulate a biome or grow new crops after a global disaster."

"Wouldn't GMOs be better though?" Castillo asked. "Higher yields, lower resources consumed, and so on."

Mac nodded. "Yes, but a lot of GMO seeds are specifically designed to be infertile. Some don't grow more than one to three generations. You have to buy next year's seeds from the company that designed them. A survivalist would want something with the potential for much longer viability, especially if they're preparing for global disasters like biological outbreaks or nuclear war."

"My God," said Saldivar. "And Doctor Verone is a nuclear scientist!"

Mac's brows knotted. "I suppose, but ..."

"Let's not speculate that far just yet," Castillo said to Saldivar.

"But he could be building them a bomb!" the man persisted.

"Easy now," said Castillo. "He's an expert in fusion reactors, not weapons. Right, Mac?"

"Yeah, the biggest challenges with fusion power are creating and sustaining the reaction without it melting your reactor. A runaway reaction that might explode is impossible. Also, they're usually non-radiological, so no fallout or contamination. Or very limited anyway, depending on your fuel. At worst, you destroy your prototype, not the city."

"But *could* Doctor Verone alter his prototype?" Saldivar pressed.

"Well—" Mac began, but Castillo cut him off.

"Saldivar, please don't ask MacGyver to theorize on how *he* might make use of a fusion reactor. We'll be here until Christmas. Now, did you have something for us?"

Saldivar took a calming breath and nodded. "Indeed, yes. Forgive me. Sleep is a faint memory. If I might use the computer?"

Mac hopped out of the seat, and Saldivar brought up three images from surveillance cameras, all decent shots of the suspects wearing food service uniforms and caps. "Here they are. We have no names or records, but I have sent this to Agent Castillo's team moments ago."

"Excellent." She leaned over to stare at the screen, a predatory gleam in her eye. "Now who might you be, *mis amigos?*"

●●

As much as he wished otherwise, Mac had to bring Boone up to speed.

"A seed bank," Boone said, voice lathered in sarcasm. "A survivalist conspiracy. A phantom cargo ship. Really ...?"

"This is the best we've got right now. Plus, you should already have the images they pulled off the cameras here. Those three guys are your perpetrators."

"Yeah, along with your mystery redhead and whoever pretended to be Verone on the flight. Anyone else you want to add? Carlos the Jackal? Bin Laden? Oh, wait, Bin Laden is dead. *Or is he?*"

Mac stifled a sigh. "Did you get a chance to check on that text I sent you about Kurdish terrorist groups?"

"Yeah, *I* was doing my job, at least. Every terrorist organization in the world wants a nuke, but no one really has the means, unless Verone can somehow make that happen."

Mac shook his head. "I was just explaining that to someone. Fusion reactors and nuclear weapons are very different animals—"

"Yeah, yeah, but *you* could probably do something with it, and Verone has ten times your experience in his field. We're not ruling out just how serious this could get."

"I really don't think I could—"

Boone ignored him and kept on, his volume increasing. "And speaking of doing our jobs, why the hell has it been five hours since I heard from you last? Taking a siesta? Walking the beach, maybe?"

Mac kept his irritation in check. "Jesus, Boone, what is your problem? We're making headway here."

"Not enough—and not fast enough. My problem is that I'm stuck here while you gallivant around Spain with your Interpol girlfriend."

Mac was too stunned to reply.

"Oh, yeah," Boone continued, "I read up on your 'working history' together. No wonder you were so eager to get out there. Meanwhile, my operation suffers."

Mac's tone suddenly hardened as he answered slowly, "Any 'history' between me and Agent Castillo is irrelevant to this investigation. And if you try flashing that card again, Boone, then you can explain to the Deputy Director why I walked away from this. Are we *clear*?"

Boone knew he'd touched a nerve but was smart enough not to press on it too hard. "I don't think taking a hike because I ruffled your feathers would be in your best interest right now."

"Or yours," Mac replied coolly.

"Then let's just stay focused on how much is at stake here, shall we?"

"For you, or for Doctor Verone? Because right now that's all I'm focused on. You copy?"

Boone was silent a moment. "I'll expect your next sitrep shortly." And then hung up.

●●

Solana Castillo sat at Saldivar's desk, finishing an email to her team updating them on the seed bank lead, and laying out their immediate objectives. Top of the list was Saldivar's perpetrators. The bottom was finding any trace of the *Kutup Ayisi*.

That was the rub. It was the weakest lead by far, but her instinct told her that even if they didn't find the vessel itself, where it went was where she and Mac needed to be. But how much time and effort to allocate towards that end? This was the burden of command. She did not have unlimited resources, not without a confirmed quarry in sight.

From her experience chasing smugglers, she knew that finding even a large ship in the limitless wastes of the North Atlantic could be almost impossible. But "almost" didn't mean "entirely."

She finished her email with directions to reach out to a colleague who had a man in Spanish Naval Intelligence. The Armada was a small, but integral, part of NATO, and he had gotten her answers before. The vast sonar listening network (SOSUS) across the North Atlantic was a relic of the Cold War, but still in use. Any ship picked up without a corresponding transponder track might merit at least a flyby from any of the airbases in Greenland, Iceland, or Scotland, to say nothing of any aircraft carriers that might be in the region.

Was it a long shot? Absolutely. Yet the conviction that this was worth chasing persisted. She sent the email and leaned back to collect her thoughts.

Is there anything else I'm not thinking of? she wondered, sifting through all the bits and pieces still churning around in her mind. But no answer appeared.

Just let it settle.

See what the team comes back with.

And wait here.

With Mac.

Yeah, Mac. Out of the blue.

And back in my life again, she mused, smiling privately. It had been good to see him. Better, even, than she had expected.

She could certainly have sent someone from the team to fetch him from the gate. And with any other intelligence spook, she probably would have. But she needed to see him for herself. To know if the sudden roil of emotions upon hearing his name ... meant something. And not just to her.

Appearing from the jetway here at the airport, she'd seen him first and saw the full range of his reactions when he'd finally spotted her. That lopsided goofy grin spilling across his face, his eyes wide with unexpected delight, his shoulders rising slightly as if ... renewed even after a transatlantic flight. But a bit nervous, not wanting to presume anything or get ahead of himself.

Oh, that grin.

The smile of a boy still.

In the strength and surety of a man.

Who wants to "talk about some things."

It was hard to suppress the rush of memories of their time in San Sebastián: the sheer ... joy of playing newlyweds. She hadn't felt anything like that for some time now.

Mieda, Solana! You're thirty-eight, not seventeen.

And you've got a job to do.

That's why he's here, remember?
Until that's done there's nothing to think about.
Still, of all the people they could've sent ...
It was Mac ...
Really just a coincidence?
Or a message of some kind?
God doesn't work like that.
Does he?

The door opened to admit MacGyver, looking worn and irritable.

Cheeky, God, too cheeky by half, she thought heavenward as she glanced at the time, then grinned at Mac.

"A long call. Eloquent, was your *Señor* Boone?"

Mac leaned back against the door, massaging the bridge of his nose. "Charming as always. But at least he could confirm there was no credible danger of any Kurdish groups constructing a bomb. They're just not that organized."

"That's something, I suppose. On my end, we're running down the men that Saldivar found for us, and I have a line out to NATO about the missing cargo ship. Interpol Norway will circulate my POI and Saldivar's perpetrators, and they'll have local police on the island check on the seed bank. One of my superiors expressed a concern about the island's international satellite relay, but I rather doubt that's in play."

"Yeah," Mac agreed. "Hard to haul that off on a cargo ship."

She gestured to the screen. "I found information on charter aircraft departing here in the immediate aftermath of the kidnapping. No less than three private charters left within half an hour of the time we've pinpointed as Doctor Verone's disappearance. Their destinations were Moscow, London, and Bamako in Mali. All three showed four private passengers, listing names only, no other details. The charters were made with three different companies, all in those countries of origin. However, the one to Moscow reported mechanical trouble and set down in Vienna. The passengers disembarked, and the plane returned to Moscow with just the pilots. We're finding them now."

Mac nodded, impressed. "Interpol moves fast."

"Modern policing, *mi amor*. Though I'm sure Boone already had this information in hand," she said, smirking.

"Oh, I'm sure," Mac groaned.

Her phone rang. "Castillo."

"Boss, it's me," said one of her people from headquarters. "We've got a problem ..."

She listened a moment, expression growing worried. She looked at Mac as she spoke. "What? Why not ...? *Fire!* When ...? Hold on." She covered the phone and asked, "Could that ship already be up there?"

"At Svalbard? *Hmm* ... 24 knot average speed for that class ... 3,456 nautical mile range for six days ...? Yeah, easy. Could've been there for a couple of days at the very least."

She went back to the phone urgently. "Get Oslo to send a team up there right now! We're on our way, too." She hung up and turned towards Mac's querying gaze. "There's been a big fire at a research village on the north coast. All the officers and their one coast guard boat are up there right now, and no one can reach the Seed Vault administrator at this time of night."

Mac's alarm was plain. "A big distraction. And another sleight of hand?"

"We need to get up there now." She paused. "But I'll need clearance—and with the cost of an emergency charter—*mierda!*"

Mac shrugged and pulled out his card. "How about we just put this one on the CIA? Boone wants results, no?"

"I love how you make the complicated so simple," she said as she all but beamed at him. "I'll find a plane. Maybe for this, I can get clearance by invoking emergency powers." She rang Saldivar.

Twenty minutes later, their co-opted Gulfstream G650 roared into the night sky.

Solana rubbed the seat's supple leather and admired the spacious luxury interior. "A cop like me could get used to this."

Mac grinned. "Yeah. Nice to have leg room, even if this is only to Oslo."

"We'll meet our team there, then travel with them to Svalbard. I'll call in a bit to brief them."

"Then tell them we'll need cold weather gear when you do. It's still the Arctic, even if it's not quite freezing in summer."

"*Hmm*," she said, looking pleased. "Maybe I'll finally have a chance to see the aurora. It's—how do you say it?—on my bucket list."

Mac shook his head. "Sorry, Solana. It's still daytime in August that far north."

"Pity."

The aircraft leveled off and the male attendant that came with the plane showed up to inquire about drinks. "A mixed drink? Wine, perhaps? We have a lovely Veuve Clicquot Brut in the yellow label that's perfect at altitude."

Castillo bit her lip and sighed a little. "Just some tea, *gracias*."

"Water for me," said Mac. The attendant bustled off, and Mac asked, "No wine? We're in the air for three hours. Plenty of time for it to wear off."

She shook her head. "Something could come in at any moment, and I want to be clear as crystal." She sighed wistfully. "But what did he mean about altitude?"

"Planes have almost no humidity. Dries out your olfactory senses, so you can't taste subtleties. I'd imagine that's important for wines costing a grand per bottle," he said, chuckling.

"Oh, Veuve Clic doesn't cost that much. More like sixty euros. I wonder why they'd have such a relatively inexpensive champagne here. Considering ..." She gestured to the lavish cabin.

"Seventy bucks a pop is *inexpensive*?"

She laughed. "For a good champagne, *si*. It's got plenty of flavor, though, which makes sense if your taste buds and nose are dulled. You know something about everything, don't you?"

"Hardly. I didn't know that was a champagne. Or what it cost, or what it tastes like, for that matter."

She considered him a moment, enjoying his humility almost as much as his encyclopedic mind. "Yes, as I recall, I ordered for both of us most of the time in San Sebastián, didn't I?"

"I'd only just started learning Spanish."

"It's improved considerably."

"Well, guess I was ... motivated."

She leaned towards him, close. "You don't say?"

This was usually where Mac's head emptied of words and he would blush. But a very different feeling was rising in him now as he met her eyes and whispered, "I do ..." And the moment hung, as something even deeper seemed to pass between them, when the attendant returned with their beverages and took their orders for the chef before retreating again.

Solana leaned back to sip her tea as if it were champagne as Mac raised his water to toast her. "All this *and* a chef."

"Welcome to how the other half lives," she said.

"It's more like the other point zero one percent," he replied. "But who's counting?"

"Either way, another world. Completely." She glanced at her phone for alerts. "Nothing new. I believe this is the first break we've had since lunch in the cafeteria. And you wanted to talk with me about something?" She sat back, cradling her cup, eyes innocent.

Mac nodded. "I've been thinking a lot lately about ... well, where I am in the world, if that makes sense."

"You're wondering if there's not something more to life than ... this thing we do?"

"In part, yes ... And if I'm really making any difference at all. I'm not a kid anymore, you know. Was a time I was pretty clear who I was serving and why. But that clarity—the black and white of it— has become, well, a lot more grey."

"You mean with people like Boone?"

"He's just a symptom," Mac said, nodding, "not the disease, but yeah. He postures like he's working for the greater good. But it's clearly about what's good for *him* first and foremost. Hell, he views me as more of a *threat* than an asset. And we're supposed to be on the same side. And I see that kind of thinking more all the way up the chain these days."

"Things have clearly become more ... political in all the intelligence services," she agreed. "And not just in America. The world is stressed now for reasons you know as well as I: climate change, technology, economic imbalance. It's all changing faster than we can adapt. And with uncertainty comes fear. And with fear comes—"

"Bad decisions. More often than not, *really* bad decisions." Mac could feel the simmering anger of that working its way to the surface as she countered.

"But you can't really believe you make no difference, Mac. Just as I know, when I sit in a courtroom packed with people victimized by the defendant that we've nailed, there's some sort of justice at work."

"Well, I never see that part," Mac replied. "Or almost never. But sure, if I bring aid workers out of a war zone in Africa or keep insurgents from overrunning a village in the Middle East, I see the results. So, maybe for them I made a difference."

"But now you're questioning if even that's enough for constantly putting your life on the line?"

Mac nodded. "Maybe. Or if I'm not just trying to empty the ocean with a teacup. And the tide keeps rising against me."

"And what tide would that be?" she asked, truly feeling his struggle and moved at how open he was willing to be with her.

"People look at what I do and think it's magic, but it's not. It's just science, logic, simple deductive reasoning. And even *that* seems to be under attack now. As if the same process that gave us jet engines, cell phones, and vaccines was now somehow a suspicious approach to be challenged or denied if it doesn't fit some agenda. What's that all about? Should we just dispense with educating the next generation in these things because the truth is ..."

"Inconvenient?" she interjected, nodding. "Another symptom, as you call it, of rising uncertainty and fear, no?"

"Well, then maybe I just don't want to think of myself as the cause of any more fear. I'm not looking for any parades or medals, but if even the people I'm trying to work for view me with suspicion, then what in God's name am I really doing?"

She put her cup down, leaned forward, and put her hand on his knee. "I can't argue with any of your concerns, Mac; they're valid. But we've always faced challenges—and not just in our work—in everything: society, culture, civilization. Those challenges may change and shift; how can they not? But, in the end, it always comes down to how we, each of us, choose to face those."

"Meaning ...?" Mac said, feeling more adrift than he usually allowed.

"Meaning the only important question in all this is what do *you really want now*, Mac?"

He took a moment, searching her face as he searched himself for a genuine answer. "Maybe just something ... solid. That I can hold onto for more than the length of the next mission?"

"Something? Or *someone?*"

Mac realized she was pressing him, like she might a witness or suspect, but he understood she was only doing it to help.

"Who says they can't be the same thing?"

"No one," she replied softly. "Certainly not me."

And suddenly, all the teasing banter, fetching smiles, and clever interplay between them got a whole lot more serious—the Inquisition indeed—and Mac knew it was either time to let go or fess up as he gently placed his hand on hers.

"So, what's to stop me from moving to Madrid? Maybe doing some work for Interpol. Or, if that's got too many complications, maybe just taking a teaching post at a university?"

"So that I—or we—could perhaps become that rock you're looking for?"

"We'd agreed to check back in with each other at some point

about whether that was a possibility. Granted, neither of us was expecting it to be like this, but ..."

"Here we are," she said, agreeing, as the weight of his proposal now sat on her as well.

"Yup," Mac smiled tentatively. "Here we are ..."

"And you want to know what I think about that," she continued, realizing that whatever her feelings for Mac, he deserved some answer that equaled his in openness and honesty.

"If you have any thoughts about it, sure."

"Fair enough," she said, looking at him, then at her hand on his knee still and his hand on hers before summoning whatever it took to face him again. "If I listen to my heart, the answer is clear: were I prepared to really build a life with someone, Mac, I can't imagine finding anyone better than you."

"But you're not there now?" Mac asked.

"I honestly don't know. I've put the idea of anything but casual relationships in a box somewhere ever since I was promoted. And now I have to find that box, open it, and give my head a chance to really think this through. I may be younger than you, but I'm not a kid anymore either. And the last thing I want to do is make promises I can't keep—especially to you. Can you understand that?"

"Of course," Mac replied, meaning it. "Like I said, this kinda came out of the blue for me, too. Not to mention we're in the middle of a situation that seems to have more twists than a strand of DNA."

"So, then maybe we both just sit with it for now and think it over —because I promise you, I will. And, when we find Verone or run this mysterious master thief to ground, we will come back to this. And I will know, for myself and for you, if I can give you what you want. Okay?"

"Fair enough." Mac nodded, knowing she was right, and somehow wanting her all the more for it, as he released her hand and she moved it from his knee to touch his face.

"Muchas gracias, mi amor," she whispered, grateful that he had the good sense to give her the space she needed to find her way to him if that was meant to happen.

And they shared a very different kind of smile, one of questions and possibilities as the attendant reappeared with their meals. He explained each plate in detail, checked if they needed refreshers on their drinks, and then slid away with a *"Bon appétit,"* leaving them to savor their meals in silence, at least as far as actual speech went. Because they could almost hear one another's minds buzzing with the images of being together: making coffee in the morning after a night of wine and tapas and unrestrained passion; her handing Mac a list of things that needed fixing around the apartment, knowing they would all be done right and she could toss her list of repairmen for good; Mac knowing she could be even more fearless at pursuing her career, because her people would know together they could decide to go private and companies, if not agencies, would pay a small fortune for their services as freelance agents. Their eyes kept checking one another as all these moments, opportunities, and images came swirling in so fast they could hardly hold them still before another replaced it. And it was somehow even more tempting than the five-star food they were eating. In silence.

But the heady, almost giddy, imagining was cut short as Solana's phone pinged and she suddenly snarled, *"Madre de Dios!"* As angry at what she saw on her phone as having been yanked from their mutual reverie, she quickly dialed.

"What?" Mac said, forgetting the food as she gestured for him to give her a moment while she listened to the rapid speech on the other end of her call. "Well, why the hell not ...? This is clearly a diversion! Look, can't the local police—Okay. Yes. Let me know of further developments. We're just over ninety minutes out. We still need gear, so have someone standing by ... Okay, good." She closed the call, eyes furious as she turned to Mac to report. "We just lost our tactical team. There've been bomb threats at the Regjeringskvartalet."

"Come again?" said Mac, not fully understanding. "Bomb threats where?"

"Norwegian government quarter in Oslo," she said. "And their Parliament building. Multiple threats, priority one, and deemed credible. Basically, they don't have five guys with guns to help us in Svalbard."

MacGyver considered: more feints, sleights of hand, delay tactics. Then, trying to put a better face on it, "I don't like guns anyway. We're still going to Oslo, though?"

She nodded. "They've got gear for us but no plane now, so we might need another charter."

"They haven't cancelled my agency card yet. We'll get there," he offered, shrugging as if to confirm that they were, even now, a tight team, as she caught his look—and meaning—allowing it to temper her anger.

"You're damn right, we will." And he passed her the card as she started dialing to find them another plane.

CHAPTER 8

A YOUNG, rail-thin Norwegian Interpol officer in plain clothes and perfect blond hair met them at their gate. "Special Agent Castillo?" he said in Norwegian-accented Spanish. "Agent Kristoffer Berg, Politi Interpol. I'm here to give you any assistance you may require, and please accept our regrets on the current situation. As you pointed out, the timing is suspicious, yet we can take no chances here."

She shook hands with a nod. "Agent Berg, a pleasure to meet you." She noted MacGyver's confused expression and said to Berg, "Do you know English? I fear Mister MacGyver's Spanish is not quite equal to your accent."

"*Ja*, of course," he said fluently. "Mister MacGyver. CIA, correct?" He offered his hand.

"Something like that," Mac said, taking it. "But we'll need gear, and I'd like to hear about this bomb threat."

Berg gestured as he led them from the plane. "The airport armory is open to you, and your flight to Longyearbyen will be ready in twenty minutes. The bomb threat reportedly came from a Jihadist group who have terrorized Oslo in the past. This time it has to do with editorials criticizing their recruitment methods in the harshest terms. We would have expected them to threaten the newspapers directly, as before, but this time it is the Regjeringskvartalet itself."

"But you haven't found any bombs?" Mac asked.

"No. Not as yet. This may well be a ruse."

Mac and Solana shared a look. "A ruse just as we're heading to the possible site of their next heist," he said.

She shared his concern. "These people have demonstrated an intimate knowledge of the intelligence community and our procedures more than once, using them for distraction and deception. I'm almost certain there are no bombs."

"This may be true," said Berg, apologetic. "If you can wait another four hours—"

She shook her head. "The fire on the other side of the island has me convinced that if something is happening, it's happening now. And Svalbard is *still* nearly three hours away. Have you had any update on the fire there?"

"Only that it is extensive. No casualties, but they're attempting to save as much of the research village as possible. The Kystvakten ... er, Coast Guard has sent a ship, but it won't be in those waters for some hours."

Berg got them past the security line and to the armory. Long racks of weapons stood opposite racks of parkas and heavy coats. The room smelled of gun oil, which Mac always associated with conflict—and casualties.

"Current temperature in Longyearbyen is three degrees," Berg said. "There is little fluctuation this time of year."

"That's about thirty-five, for you Imperial users, Mac," Solana teased as she tried on a long coat.

"Thirty-eight Fahrenheit to be precise," he added before turning to Berg. "Is there a utility closet or toolbox around here?"

Berg led him around a corner. Mac came back grinning and patting his pockets. "Duct tape, pliers, a hammer, paperclips, and even a lockpick set. Better not to be dropped in the middle of nowhere with nothing but my pocketknife."

Castillo was checking her handgun and spare magazines. "Lockpicks? You? I thought you could pick a lock with anything."

"Yeah, but why ruin perfectly good sunglasses when you can have the right tool?"

She holstered her weapon and noted his look at the sight of it. "I know you don't like them, Mac, but I won't shoot if they don't."

"Then let's do what we can to keep that from happening, shall we?"

"And you, Berg?" she asked. "Are you armed?"

The young man blinked, then blanched. "*Me?* Oh, I've never been in the field ... that is to say, I'm not that kind of officer—"

She and Mac traded another look. "Well, we need all the help we can get," she said. "Besides, you're at my disposal, yes? And we may need a translator. But you've been through the academy here. Weapons training is a requirement, no?"

"Well, yes, but ..." His objections faded upon seeing the piercing look in her eye before he drew a long breath, selected an automatic for himself and began checking it over. "Let's hope MacGyver is right and it won't come to that."

👓

The small twin-prop aircraft flew them north towards an encircling dawn, ringing the horizon as the aircraft penetrated the Arctic Circle. Mac caught a couple of hours to snooze, despite the constant drone and antiseptic smell in the cabin. Sunlight on his face brought him blinking back to consciousness, leaning against Solana as she worked with her phone. She felt him stir and smiled as he collected himself and sat up straight.

"Not exactly a G650, is it?" she all but shouted over the roar of the engines.

"Certainly cozier," he said, returning her smile.

She gestured with her phone. "No updates. We're twenty minutes out or so."

"Any headway on that fire? Just how big a place is this?"

She pulled up what she'd found in her research. Several dozen buildings—two large, the size of four-story office blocks. "All kinds of equipment, and about two hundred researchers and techs. Studying everything from marine life to the ionosphere."

Mac shook his head, ruefully. "Yet another blow against science, huh?"

"If it helps, Longyearbyen is a tiny town to search. Population is about twenty-six hundred. This is the height of tourist season, but there are only a few hotels and bed and breakfasts. We could cover it all in less than a day."

"Better to say, 'twenty-four hours.' Days up here last a while," he said, pointing at the sun well over the northeastern horizon at 4:00 AM.

"You know what I meant. And get some sleep so you won't be clanky with me."

"I think you mean 'cranky,'" he said, grinning to prove he wasn't.

"Either way our first stop is the Seed Vault's administrator's house. We still can't reach her."

"Another kidnapping?"

"Maybe, but Berg is doubtful."

"Yes," yelled the young man from the front seat. "Sleep can be difficult to obtain this time of year, and the administrator is new to Spitzbergen. Most residents take special care not to be disturbed. Blackout curtains and silenced phones are common."

The plane leveled off for landing. Berg craned his neck to look out the window. As they felt the landing gear deploy, he pointed. "There. You can see it."

The only snow on the mountain stood at the peak. Much farther down, the entrance to the Svalbard Global Seed Vault jutted up out of the rocky ground like the nose of some submarine breaching the surface. It overlooked the airport and the bay beyond, but little else. No other structures stood near it. No offices, no houses ... nothing.

"Tough place to rob," Mac said.

Castillo turned. "And there are a million seeds in there?"

"More. A million samples of up to dozens of seeds each," he said. "And it's still only about a third full, I think."

Once on the ground, they hurried to the terminal through the sharp wind that cut right through what little heat the arctic sun graced upon the tundra. A yawning, older customs official met them inside. He spoke to Berg in Norwegian. "Agent Berg? Identification? Thank you. Your vehicle is waiting, but you should know that I believe I spoke with one individual from your watch list, day before yesterday."

Berg translated, and the customs agent said in English, "Apologies, I did not know you preferred English. Although it was language that made me remember this woman so well. Her Norwegian was nearly flawless, with only the slightest British accent. I have an ear for these things in my job."

Castillo showed him a photo of the redhead. "This was her?"

"Dark hair, not red, but yes. She had a ... ah, regal bearing? Most striking. The airport opens at 6:00 AM, and she was on the first flight. Also a private charter, but without official clearance like you, of course."

"Did anyone come with her?" Mac asked.

"No. She did inquire about vehicle rental. I told her an agency opened here just this summer. Usually tourists walk or rely on shuttles."

"I don't suppose she mentioned where she was staying?"

"Sorry, no, but with the proper warrant, I believe you could obtain information on her vehicle. Or simply look for a brand-new Nissan. All their rentals are the same model, and all completely new." He shook his head. "Foolish. Winters are hard on vehicles here. They age fast."

"Good to know," said Castillo, nodding. "Tell me, which hotel might be closest to the Seed Vault?"

"That would be the Barracks," he said. "It's a common question, though she didn't ask it."

Castillo looked at MacGyver and Berg. "Berg, call the office about that warrant. In the meantime, let's take a drive by this place and see if there are any new Nissans in the lot."

"What about the administrator?" Mac asked.

"It's still four in the morning, and this is a tiny town. If we're to catch someone sleeping, let's make it our Person Of Interest."

Not five minutes later they pulled up to the Barracks in their aging pickup truck loaned from airport security. Mac had noted the salt stains and general disrepair of most vehicles in the short, gravelly streets. Roads were largely unpaved, made of packed earth, far easier to repair after months under layers of ice and snow but tough on transportation. As such, the shiny red Nissan backed into its spot alongside a couple dozen weather-beaten vehicles stood out like a gem among stones.

The Barracks itself was actually a collection of buildings, all refurbished from old mining barracks for some project abandoned long ago. Each building housed ten rooms, and there were ten buildings. A high chain link fence surrounded the place, built up a bit on wooden posts to avoid at least some of the winter's rusting snow. Beyond the fence towards town sat a diner attended by a couple of aged cars.

Berg finished his call as they got out. "Special Agent Castillo, your warrant is authorized, though it will be at least a couple of hours before anyone is at the rental office to honor it."

"That's fine," she said, eying the red car in the hotel lot.

"I'd want a couple ways out of here if it were me," Mac said, looking around.

"Yes, but I'm not sure I'd have picked such an eye-catching car."

"If there's no choice, there's no choice. And sounds like her cover is as a tourist. As is, that fence is pretty easy to get over, so if you find yourself blocked from the front, it's just a quick climb and sprint to your other way out."

"This is assuming that's her car, of course."

"If so, then she's probably here. I don't see anyone inside the diner."

Solana nodded. "Let's find out. Should be someone at the front desk, even at this hour." She led the way to the main building where they found a young woman who ran the place for her father, the owner. Her day had just begun. "Early starts around here," Berg translated. "Never know when someone will be on the first flight from the mainland."

"Do you recognize this woman?" Castillo showed her phone. "Though likely with different hair."

Her face brightened. "Mrs. Johnsen? Yes, she's here, but doesn't go out much I think, and likes her coffee strong. We do our best, but this is hardly the Mediterranean."

Mac felt his pulse rise with the news. "Could you point us to her room?"

Her face fell. "Oh, no, I'm sorry. I can ring her, if you like."

"No," said Castillo, showing her ID. "We just need a word with her, urgently."

The hostess wavered but shook her head. "No, I am sorry. The law is the law."

"That's okay," said Castillo with a smile. "Berg, we need another warrant. Mac, let's keep an eye on her car."

Outside in their pickup truck, Mac contemplated the car and its positioning. If she was an operative of some kind, she'd want quick access to it. Although where the hell she might flee to on this island and in this tiny town was beyond even his imagination.

Castillo alternately drummed her fingers and checked her phone as the minutes passed. "This warrant should be a minute's matter, except that it's four in the damn morning."

Mac smiled inwardly at how her accent dropped prepositions and mixed up adjectives when she grew agitated. "Wasn't Berg just on the phone with a judge?" he asked.

"Different department it seems between rental car and direct access to a hotel room," she said, drumming her fingers again.

"We could always do it Boone's way," Mac said lightly.

"So, you have a US warship and company of marines on standby ready to violate allied sovereign territory? And here I thought you forgot my birthday."

"July 29, 1981," he said quickly. "So, we just missed it, sorry."

She sighed with a grin, then turned serious as she eyed the car. "I just wish we could do *something*."

Mac thought a moment, staring at the metal fence, then glanced at the mechanic's shop across the street, its owner just arriving for the day. "Might be we could make some ... preparations?" he said as she perked up, realizing the wheels in his mind were busily turning.

●●

The red-haired woman was already awake and scanning footage when her alarm told her it was 4:30 AM. Tapping into the security feed at the Seed Vault had been child's play for her software. Similarly, the recorded footage proved remarkably easy for the computer to scan and halt at any activity.

The Seed Vault got virtually no traffic save for a few hours in the day when the Administrator and an operator or two entered to monitor the coolers and perform their daily routine. The most activity had been the day before with a new deposit from the mainland which she had watched live. Yet even that had taken less than an hour.

Further, the Vault had just two interior cameras. One covered the front door, and one the main tunnel leading to the three vaults themselves. There were only two interior doors besides the main, locked with keycodes (none tripped as of now), and each vault had an airlock with mechanical locks in place.

She'd been racking her brain for ways that her long-sought prey might smash-and-grab this place. She'd been over the schematics a dozen times, themselves bone-simple. She'd considered everything from a straightforward convoy to an elaborate system with cargo choppers and some crisis on the mainland to trick people into believing the evacuation was official.

The massive fire at the research village on the far side of the island had got her attention, and then the bomb threat at the Regjeringskvartalet had kept her glued to her cameras. But nothing had happened with the Vault at all, though she watched for hours. Finally, she'd let herself grab some sleep. The computer would've emitted an alert loud enough to wake the dead, had there been any movement.

Nothin', she thought.

Nothin', nothin', an' more nothin'.

If his calendar was correct, his plane should have arrived yesterday.

"So, wher' are yae, yae bloody bastard?" she muttered aloud. The computer did not reply.

She pushed herself up, stretched with a final yawn to dispel her lingering weariness, and threw back the blackout curtains. She blinked in the eternal sunlight outside, eyes scanning as they adjusted to the light. She saw a battered old truck from the airport as the only new vehicle in the lot, but otherwise nothing new. She didn't think much of it. At the tiny kitchenette she set water on to boil, then headed to the shower. She was brief by habit, not three minutes, but the computer's alert brought her flying from the bathroom wrapped in a towel, hair bundled up high and dry.

A man in a Seed Vault parka had walked past both cameras to the front door and stood there, holding it open. Another man followed, older, well-dressed, and looking like he was ready for an evening out with colleagues. He glanced around the room as the worker secured the door, spotted the camera, and grinned broadly with a mock salute.

"*I have yae!*" she exulted, already halfway into her clothes. Yet, caution and training dampened the moment into worried mutters. "But yae could'hae killed the feeds, spliced them to look clear, yae could'hae ..." Her voice trailed off with unsaid possibilities. The fact of the matter was that the man had made certain he was seen. Why?

It does'nae matter, she told herself.

Here we are, top a' the world, with nae witnesses.

Yae are mine!

She synced her computer's feed to her phone, donned a heavy coat, holstered her .45 in easy reach, and whisked the door open.

The shock from seeing her target on camera a moment ago could not compare to the jolt she shared with the couple standing just beyond the door. A tall, lanky man and a dark-skinned woman with expressions as startled as her own stood there, the man with his hand upraised, about to knock.

The Mediterranean-faced woman recovered quickly, ID in hand. "Hello," she said in accented English. "Interpol. I wondered if we might have a word?"

The mystery woman kicked the door closed and slammed the bolt home.

Not now, not NOW! she roared at the universe.

The room reverberated from a strong shoulder slamming the door.

Plan B.

She didn't need caution any longer. She just needed to get to that vault. If Interpol wanted to follow, then so much the better, but explanations would take hours she didn't have. The window went up easily enough, and the alley looked clear. It was just a short step around the corner to her car.

She hopped to the ground. A gun cocking behind her brought her up short. "Excuse me," said a man in Norwegian. "Interpol Politi. Please raise your hands."

She brought her hands up slowly, and heard his boots crunching the gravel as he approached. At the first touch of his hand on her wrist to bring it down into a hold, she spun the other direction, elbow angled into his ribs. The man's breath leaped from his body in a startled moan as her knee came up into his side. He thudded into the dirt beside his gun, which she kicked away.

She sprinted down the short alley, rounded the corner, only to see—

Her car was completely blocked in, hemmed on two sides by hotel vehicles, and at the front by the airport pickup truck. They had moved it while she was in the shower. She cursed bloody murder for half a moment, hearing running feet on the gravel in pursuit.

She dashed between the bunkhouses towards the fence. She saw her other car, a local beater, not nearly as shiny, waiting by the diner on the other side. She'd jimmied it last night and hotwired it in seconds as a backup she could steal if need be. Her hand closed on the fence, and she shrieked in pain and leaped away. She stared at the stinging burn on her hand, then at the fence, itself humming on and off with electricity. A rapid clicking sound drew her attention to a pair of car batteries sitting on the ground on the other side near a post ten yards away. The clicking was a turn signal assembly, rapidly flicking the power on and off to pulse the newly electrified fence. She stared at it, incredulous for a moment, then bolted away from the approaching footsteps.

They charged the fence?—Who in the hell?—

Does'nae matter.

But there was a wooden ladder by the pumping shed.

Just have tae ditch them long enough tae reach the Vault—

She broke off the thought as she rounded the corner and spotted the ladder, itself bound to the shed's hot water pipes by shiny new bands of duct tape!

She reached for her pocket knife, but instead drew her gun to the sound of running feet rounding the building, a man's thudding tread.

The lanky man in his parka skidded to a halt, duct tape coming up even as her gun did, and faced off for a tense beat, gun versus tape, before he broke the silence.

"I'd appreciate it if you'd drop that gun."

"Or what? Yae'll tape me up?" She cocked the hammer. "I dinnae think so, laddie. An' who the dev'l are yae?"

Another hammer clicked behind her. "My distraction," said the darker woman. "Gun down. Slowly."

The mystery woman's gaze went flat as she lowered the weapon to her side. Aiming with peripheral vision alone was difficult, but she took the shot, the gun banging once as the pressurized vapor billowed from the hot-water pipe, engulfing her and the man.

"Mac!" Solana shouted, but held her fire, all targets obscured.

The cornered woman leaped straight up, caught the shed's ledge, and pulled herself up in one smooth movement. Three quick steps and a leap, and she was atop the nearest bunkhouse. She took off at full speed, leaping gaps like a gazelle, back to the front parking lot.

Her car was still blocked in, but the airport security truck was unlocked. She leaped in and cracked open the column housing with a deft slam from her .45's grip. She got to work on the wires. It wasn't difficult, and she could do it almost by touch alone, but it would take a good fifteen seconds, and Lanky was already sprinting towards her. He was armed ...

Nae he's not. Is that a bloody nail gun?

She locked the doors and continued her work. He slid to a stop beside her door and lodged two nails into the side. She paused, with an incredulous look, as he blew out a breath. "You're kinda stuck," he said, breathing hard. "Come on. We just need to talk."

Still staring at the madman, she closed the connection and the engine roared to life. The tires spewed gravel. A loud thud brought her head whipping around to see he'd leaped into the bed. The rearview showed the little Interpol man and the other woman left in the dust, lowering her gun, unable to take a shot before the truck veered around the corner.

Just one a' yae left, she thought at Lanky clinging to the bed, as she floored the accelerator heading towards the Seed Vault.

She knew the way well enough now as there was really only one road heading to it. Lanky was on his feet, trying to keep his balance. She didn't make it easy on him. She swerved left and right with sharp jerks on the wheel, hoping at least to rattle him around. The more the truck worked him over, the less she'd have to do at the Vault. She even got him to his knees, curled up around himself for a brief time.

Finally, he got to his feet despite the erratic motion and grabbed on to the roof, his legs just beyond the rear glass. He was up there, doing ... something. She craned her neck but couldn't get a solid look. His hand slapped the opposite door, applying a long strip of ...

More damn duct tape?

He leaned well out to apply another strip. She took the opportunity to wrench the truck hard. She heard a curse, but he held on by a leg over the side and a death grip on the rim. He hauled himself back in through sheer strength and got to his feet. She hit the gas again, hard, which planted him on his ass and slid him to the back, but he didn't fly over.

"Persistent bloody gaberlunzie, ain't yae?" she swore as he crawled back to the front and levered himself up. She attempted to wrench him loose twice more, but to no avail as more duct tape slapped on. She heard the nail gun's muted thwaps four times, and concluded she'd need a battering ram to get that door open, to say nothing of what he'd done to the driver's door. She felt her fury rising, exacerbated by Lanky plopping himself down securely in the bed, and giving her a little wave and smile.

"Fine, then," she muttered, and roared into the Vault's tiny parking lot.

She readied her gun and tried her door. It was unlocked, but the handle had only the faintest give, stuck fast by whatever he'd done. Lanky watched as she slid to the passenger door and tried it for duty's sake. Sure enough, it was held fast by duct tape reinforced by nails.

She rounded on him with her full glare as he crouched there in the bed, peering in the window.

"Jammed the lever bar," he said, pointing to the driver door. "Just give it up. We don't need anyone getting hurt."

She brought her gun up to his face beyond the glass. He blinked, and slowly raised his hands. "Open it," she ordered. *"Now!"*

Mac rolled his eyes at her. "You shoot me now, you'll never get out in time."

Shite! she thought, *he's a nervy one—*

But his logic was equally inescapable as the sight and sound of a hotel vehicle squealing into the parking lot brought both their eyes. The dark woman and her little partner leapt out, her gun already up, and the little agent raising his as he clutched his side.

Her own glare and weapon stayed locked on Lanky for another long moment as they surrounded the vehicle and her mind raced through the possibilities ... which were exactly none. Not without starting a firefight, and not with her locked in a confined space with no cover. She lowered her gun.

She dropped her weapon behind the seat at their instruction, and Lanky peeled back the duct tape on the passenger side to let her out. This time the little Politi man stood well back while the swarthy woman barked at her in full-on cop command voice, "On your knees! Hands behind your head! Do it now or I will put a round in your leg and you won't be running anywhere for months!"

She complied as the skinny blond guy said, "Nice work, MacGyver," as Lanky climbed out of the truck bed.

Her mind froze. "Wait—Yae *know* me?" she said, truly surprised.

The dark woman narrowed her eyes, aiming the gun at her thigh. "All we know is that you're in the thick of this—and he wasn't talking to you."

"He was talking to me," Mac said, keeping a safe distance from her despite her submissive posture. "My name's MacGyver."

"*The hell yae say!*" she snapped. "And yae'r sayin' it wrong tae boot."

Her three captors shared a confused look as she finally broke the silence. "I'm *Ailsa MacIver with MI6*," she said emphatically.

"More tricks," Castillo said, dismissively.

"Check it out through Interpol," Ailsa said. "Go on. 'Cause we're no bloody good tae anyone standin' around like this, now are we?"

Castillo shot another look to Mac, who shrugged affirmingly before she said to Berg, "You keep her right where she is—and shoot her if she moves. Understood?" Berg managed an anxious nod as Castillo lowered her weapon and stepped away to make a call. Ailsa turned to Mac, still trying to wrap her head around the possibility. "Yaer name is really MacIver?"

"Yup," Mac said. "Though it's spelled with a *G* and a *Y*, not an *I*."

"Nae wonder it sounded bollocks. An' yae'r what, a Yank?"

"Right again," Mac replied.

"Then yae'r no bloody relation a' mine. Thank God for small blessings there." Mac rolled his eyes again as Ailsa seemed curiously relieved despite being on her knees with Berg's gun aimed at her, sort of, as she looked at the monolithic entrance to the Vault, her irritation plain.

A good fifteen minutes later, Castillo finished her call and returned, gesturing for Berg to lower his weapon. "Let her up."

"*Finally*," snarled Ailsa, dropping her arms and rising as Mac looked between her and Castillo.

"You mean she checks out?"

Nodding, Castillo sighed angrily. "Meet Ailsa MacIver, MI6 agent-at-large. Who could've spared us all a lot of trouble if she identified herself to begin with."

Ailsa glared right back at her. "*Bollocks*. The man in there has eyes in ev'ry known intelligence operation. Why d'yae think I'm classified as 'at-large'? He's seen yae comin' ev'ry time, has'nae he? With yaer reports an' status updates an' playin' matters by the book. I wondered why he gave the camera that cheeky little nod. I'll show yae the footage. It's yae that blew the grab, nae me."

"Well, the Administrator is on her way now, and there's only one way in or out," Castillo replied. "So if he's there, he's not going anywhere."

"Never met another MacIver before," said Mac, taking Ailsa in anew. "I knew the family had to come from Scotland way back. And the name could easily have been mangled in the shift to the States. Are you sure there's no chance we're—"

"Look, Yank—"

"He goes by Mac," Castillo said, cutting her off. "And you should be grateful he's averse to guns, because anyone else would've put you down in that truck cab, understood?"

Ailsa raised a hand to acknowledge the point, accepting her part in the misunderstanding as her tone softened. "Look, Mac, we can go chop down the family tree some other time, okay? I just hope, for all our sakes, we've finally cornered the bastard. Because yae would'nae believe the things this man is capable a'."

"I think Agent Castillo is more than aware," said Mac as the sight of an approaching car seemed to end the discussion. "This must be the Administrator."

Indeed it was, with her chief of operations in tow; the pair of them harried and alarmed. Introductions were barely made when the demands began. "Who could possibly be in there? Why would they want to jeopardize or do anything to a seed vault?"

As one they looked to Ailsa.

"His name is Victor Hart, former MI6 turned industrialist an' now master thief. He targets innovative technologies with diverse functions most often, an' he makes them vanish into thin air. Like a bloody—"

"Magician," Castillo finished. "We didn't even have a name until just now. And if you and your agency had been a little more helpful—"

"Well, we can debate all that soon enough," Ailsa replied, still trying to take things down a notch with Castillo, "after I've had a word with the man alone. But now, Administrator, if yae'd be so kind?"

Flustered, annoyed, and more than a little upset, she led the lot of them up to the entrance and opened the clanking, ponderous door. Castillo, Berg, and Ailsa had weapons in hand, the lights coming on as they entered. Mac noted Ailsa eyeing the camera on the far wall. She glared at it as though the thing had done her a personal injury.

The Administrator led them to an interior door, locked with a keypad, marked with a dull red light. As she entered the code, Mac said to Ailsa, "You said someone let him in?"

"Aye. A man with a parka like his." She nodded towards the operations manager. "They store them in here, though. Easy tae grab one."

"How did he get through this without setting the alarm off, then?"

"Cannae say," she said. "Fact is he managed it right enough."

The door swung wide to a gush of frigid air. This deep into the mountain, the permafrost struggled with the surface temperature for supremacy, and a faint icy rime touched every surface. The operations office was two-thirds of the way down towards the vault doors. Castillo, Berg, and Ailsa quickly cleared it, weapons leading the way. But there was no one.

"Not surprised," Ailsa said. "Someone was here, though"—indicating cold coffee and seats pulled out in front of the computer —"Likely wher' they got the codes." She hit a few buttons on the security feed to show the man in the parka enter the codes at the interior door, then at the exterior letting Hart in, and Hart's own nod to the camera.

"But how did they get *in?*" the Administrator demanded, still flustered. "That man in our parka, I've never seen him before, and he wasn't on the work crew that deposited seeds just the other day."

"Well, he's behind one of those three doors," said Castillo.

"Each has an airlock. We use only physical locks this deep down."

"Which vault has the most seeds?" Mac asked.

"Vault two." She indicated the door straight ahead.

"Okay. Give me the keys," he said.

The door itself was coated in a layer of ice a quarter-inch thick. Mac noted the clean lock and ice chips loose on the ground. Someone had gone through recently.

The first door opened on hinges whose complaints reverberated the length of the tunnel. Castillo, Berg, and Ailsa stood ready with their weapons. Nothing within but the inner air lock door, showing the same signs of recent use.

"Here we go," Mac muttered to himself, turning the last lock and throwing the latches.

He let the heavy door be his cover, and swung it wide as the trio rushed in.

Lights kicked on in the interior to display long, numbered racks, twice as tall as Mac and extending many yards to the rear wall. Each rack held standardized black plastic containers, labeled with contents, country of origin, and bar codes with serial numbers. Mac could barely see his breath, owing to the dry atmosphere, but he could feel a creeping tingling in his nose that said his sinuses were freezing up. Massive coolers helped the permafrost keep the contents in a state of suspended animation.

"It's clear," Castillo said from within.

Mac led the Administrator in. She looked around a moment, then breathed a sigh of relief. "Well. I suppose he could be in one of the other vaults. We'll do an inventory later, but this one seems intact, at least."

MacGyver wasn't so sure. There had been quite a few people in the room recently, judging by the footprints on the frosty floor. "Can I open one of these?"

The Administrator hesitated, then nodded. She led him to a shelf with containers marked for Norway. "These you may open."

Castillo sent Berg to watch the main tunnel while everyone else clustered around. Mac picked up the topmost container, and immediately his heart sank.

Too light. Too light by far.

He set it on the ground, cut the zip ties, and flipped open the lid.

"Empty!" wailed the Administrator.

MacGyver checked three more. All the same.

They spent the next two hours checking the remaining vaults and containers. All empty.

The Svalbard Global Seed Vault had been completely plundered.

CHAPTER 9

WHILE THE ADMINISTRATOR made panicked calls to her seniors on the mainland, Mac paced the Vault trying to figure out how such a total wipe of the place had been accomplished, while Castillo and Berg were on the Vault's phones to their respective commands. Ailsa, on the other hand, just stared in the empty space—and fumed.

Castillo ended a call and turned to Ailsa. "This Victor Hart, what more can you tell us about him?"

The Scotswoman's icy glare hadn't thawed since they'd found the final vault empty. "I told yae," she growled, aiming her anger at Castillo. "He worked for MI6 an' then built his industrial empire usin' department contacts an' resources in the '8os. He's yaer man, an' I'd've had him if yae all had'nae blown the gaff. What possessed yae tae fly all the way up here, an' put ev'rything out on interagency flash traffic?"

Castillo didn't even blink, scowling right back. "I've been tracking *you* for two years now. We had no idea this man was even involved! And if MI6 had seen fit to give us some clue of who you were, we'd've *both* had him."

"Dinnae be daft! He saw yae comin'! He has moles ev'rywher'. Why d'yae think MI6 dinnae tell yae who I am? Why d'yae think I dinnae tell Saldivar in Barcelona?"

"My point exactly," Castillo said, returning the shot. "If you knew Hart was there, why *didn't you* tell Saldivar? You could have grabbed him *right there!*"

"If he saw the likes a' *yae* comin', young Saldivar would'nae stood a chance in hell. The man is lethal when confronted, believe wher' I speak."

The two women matched exasperated glares for a long beat until the Administrator returned, visibly shaken, eyes rimmed with red. "The police will be here soon. The fire is finally under control. For all the good any of that'll do now."

Castillo noticed Mac had stopped pacing. He stood staring at the back wall. "What is it, Mac?"

He turned quickly. "How cold can those blowers make it in here?"

The Administrator had to think a moment. "Um ... minus thirty C. It's usually in the minus fifteen range. Why?"

"Kick them on at max and disable the fire alarm. And do you happen to have a first-aid kit and a lighter?" They had a kit, and Ailsa had a lighter.

The room got so cold that Mac couldn't help the childhood memories from welling up, smiling to himself.

Huddled as deeply into her parka as she could, Castillo caught his grin and wondered aloud, "You can't really enjoy this? My face actually hurts."

"Reminds me of Minnesota in winter," he said. "I'll take you there sometime."

"Maybe in the summer, otherwise ..." She let the thought drop to spare another word's worth of warmth.

The cold appeared to have little effect on Ailsa or Berg. *No big surprise for a Scot and Norwegian,* Mac thought.

The blowers shut off and the Administrator returned, hauling the heavy door closed behind her. "All right. What now?"

Mac opened the first-aid kit and began laying a long, uncut strip of gauze across the floor, not three inches from the back wall. "It's above freezing outside, right?"

The Administrator nodded. "Last I checked."

He needed a touch of tape in a couple of places to keep the gauze from rolling up. "And no one came in the front door, and no deliveries were big enough to hide a person inside, right?"

The Administrator shook her head. "We repackage all our deliveries in standard containers now, and they're too small for anyone but a toddler to hide in. There is no way."

Mac taped the far end and flicked the lighter. The gauze caught instantly at one end and the thin strip burned away an inch every few seconds, leaving behind a little residue and slight, wispy smoke that wafted upward slowly in the motionless sub-zero atmosphere. "Don't move or disturb the air," he told them.

The flame quickly consumed the strip. The burning smell reminded Mac of firing up the wood stove for the first time every fall on the farm, with its odor of burnt dust and charred paper before the kindling caught. Then, halfway along its length, the smoke eddied noticeably towards the wall, slipping through the tiniest crack in the natural rock face. "There," Mac said, pointing, motioning for Berg to join him as he moved to the spot. "Give me a hand."

Mac and the smaller man put their shoulders to the wall and shoved, Berg wincing in pain.

"Bah," Ailsa spat, as she plucked Berg aside and lent her shoulder. "I was a tad hard on the wee thing."

The wall budged, grated on the floor, and, with a united effort, toppled backward into a lightless space behind.

Smoke and dust swirled in the sudden mix of normal and refrigerated air. A moment later the lights from their phones played around a large, open space connecting all three vaults, and narrowing towards the back into a tunnel, itself so long no light could be seen at the end.

"*Madre de Dios*," Castillo whispered into the frozen air, turning to the Administrator, herself utterly flabbergasted. "Did you hear any of this happening? Strange noises? Rumbles?"

The Administrator couldn't speak, just shook her head, mouth wide, her reddened eyes like saucers.

"We need to follow this," Mac said. "I saw a little electric cart by the entrance, right?"

Shortly after, Mac, Castillo, and Ailsa were awkwardly silent on the cart in the tunnel, leaving Berg and the others behind to handle the scene. The vehicle wasn't intended for high speed, but it was certainly faster than walking, despite the bumpy ride over rails laid for minecarts to haul debris and the looted seeds.

It took a good ten minutes along the gradually curving tunnel before they saw light winking far ahead.

"How the hell did he manage this?" Castillo muttered as the light grew larger.

"Without being detected? You got me," Mac said. "The shaft itself had to be some kind of boring machine. Nine-foot diameter or so. Professionally done, too."

She grunted. "Glad you're impressed."

"Hey, if this was Hart's doing, it took experience, equipment, and planning. We've gone about, what, two miles? Maybe more? Either way, this is no small feat of engineering."

"I keep tellin' yae," Ailsa gruffed, "the man's capable a' bloody anythin'."

Solana checked an app on her phone. "Two and a half miles. This must have taken them years."

Mac rolled his head. "In prep, maybe. But at a hundred feet per day on average, it'd only be about four to five months of actual digging."

They could all hear the surf before they exited the tunnel. Not a quarter mile down a gentle slope and across a road of packed earth sat the boring machine in a long, shallow berth. Alongside it a makeshift jetty stretched out into the sea, likely built with debris from the tunnel's construction. And a half mile offshore, two seaplanes rode easy on the rolling waves—apparently watching for them. Because as Mac and the women emerged blinking in the daylight, the planes' engines turned over, and they both maneuvered for takeoffs.

Castillo put away her gun and got out her phone. She recorded them taxiing and lifting off into the crystal blue sky where they separated and flew in opposite directions.

"Did you get all that?" Mac asked without taking his eyes from the receding planes.

"I did. Complete with their registration on the wings. Let's get to the airport fast. We can see if they filed flight plans and alert the police wherever they're going."

"We should go after them," Mac said. "We can commandeer planes for this, right?"

"Yes. And we should split up," said Castillo. "I'll take one, you take the other."

"Yae'r nae leavin' me behind," said Ailsa. "Nae after chasin' that man tae the ends a' the Earth."

Solana shot him a look and Mac quickly offered, "Come along with me. You can tell me about Scotland."

Another twin-engine prop plane raced into the air, this one more cramped than the one which had brought them to Svalbard. Their destination was Reykjavik, where authorities already lay in wait for the approaching seaplane. Thus far, neither pilot had answered communications.

Mac finally turned to Ailsa, who stared out the window ahead as if her gaze could cross the hundred miles ahead and pluck their quarry from the sky. "So, what is an 'agent-at-large'?"

She glanced at him like he was a fly buzzing in her ear. "I operate with minimal oversight. My direct superior at MI6 is the only one who knows wher' I might be an' what I'm about."

Mac nodded. "Sounds dangerous."

"'Dangerous' is lettin' raw tyros get involved with a proper villain like this. Damn Yanks an' their CIA, always wher' they should'nae be."

Mac suppressed a sigh. "Look, I get the whole 'lone wolf' thing. And if being so pissed off at having to work with other agencies helps you across the finish line, so be it. But I'm not officially with the CIA—even if I am a Yank. And I find a head full of steam rarely lets me think clearly, that's all."

She tried to give him a hard, even offended, look but, once again, he was making more sense than not—damn him.

"Well, if yae'r nae CIA, then who *exactly* are yae with? Or d'yae just work directly for the President, eh?"

Mac smiled, refusing to take the bait. "Let's just say I'm more like an agent-at-large; when one of the intelligence services has a situation they think I can help with, I get a call. And if I agree with the brief, off I go."

"Just like that?" she said, eyeing him dubiously. "So, yae'r a bloody *freelancer*?"

"A freelancer, yeah, close enough. Though I do my best to avoid the bloody part if possible." Now Ailsa looked at him with a mixture of confusion and flat-out disbelief.

"Well, then how in the hell did yae get tangled up with Interpol?"

Mac related the story of Doctor Verone's kidnapping—with all its theatrical misdirection—and how that led to Madrid and Castillo before he turned it back to her. "But you've been dogging this Victor Hart for years, you said. What do you think he's really after?"

Keeping information to herself ran deep into Ailsa, so her response took a few moments to find its way to the surface before she finally ventured, "My guess? I think he's buildin' a haven a' some sort. Like a high-tech Noah's ark."

"Yeah," Mac agreed. "Makes sense with the list of stuff he's been stealing."

"But as tae wher' the place is? If I knew, I'd be there. Nae spinnin' me wheels out here after someone who's most likely just another decoy."

"You don't think the pilots will know anything?"

"Nae likely. Why sit out there an' wait until we appeared? Why show himself tae us durin' the heist? Yae cannae tell me they moved all that out tae their ship an' powered over the horizon in the short hours it took us tae find the tunnel. They'd handled the bulk a' it over the nights or days before. Nah, he was there for his showmanship. Just like his father."

"His father?" This was new.

"Aye." She paused again, uneasy with so much sharing, but she'd come this far so ... "Dinnae be tellin' me yae never heard a' the Amazin' Solomon Hart?"

It took an instant for Mac to register the connection. "Of course. A big stage magician in the fifties and sixties. Like a David Copperfield or something."

"Only far, far wealthier. An' when he died, management a' his foundation went tae his daughter, nae the prodigal son."

Mac considered that for a bit. "Well, it seems like Victor picked up a thing or two."

Ailsa didn't respond, but a deep anger stole across her face as she quickly turned away from him back out to the sky. Assuming it was more of her recent ire, Mac persisted.

"And you said he's a killer, right?"

She nodded slowly, keeping her gaze out the window. "I know he is."

"Because, from what I've seen, he's gone out of his way *not* to kill anyone. Assuming Verone's still alive. But he spared the food truck crew in Barcelona."

Her eyes finally swung back to find his. "Make no mistake, *MacGyver*," saying his name as if that too still offended her. "His low body count tae date is just a ploy tae keep from raisin' undue alarm. If his back's tae the wall, his clever tricks'll go by the board, an' his fangs will appear. He was a stone-cold operative for the Ministry in the days a' the Cold War."

"Sounds like you've got firsthand details on that, huh," Mac pressed. But it was clear she was done talking, as she ignored his comment, slunk back towards the window, and muttered, "Just hope this jaunt actually leads somewhere'."

Unfortunately, Ailsa's prediction proved all too accurate.

On the runway in Reykjavik beside the grounded seaplane,

surrounded by security, Mac spoke to Castillo by phone on the runway in Oslo. "Nothing?"

"Nothing," she confirmed. "The pilots work for the same company. Were paid to fly to that point and wait offshore. Mine has positively identified Hart as their contact."

"Ours, too."

"Hart and his man came out of the tunnel, met them at the jetty, and told them to wait, ready to takeoff should anyone else emerge from the tunnel. Then they left in a 'dolphin-shaped submarine.'"

Mac thought a moment, stung by yet another sleight of hand. "Yeah, I've seen those. They're two-man subs. Not built for much depth. You go reef diving in them in the Bahamas. He must have one modified for the cold."

"A submarine," Solana groaned, exasperated. "A damned *submarine*. He could have been right there, five meters under the waves."

Mac suddenly felt the weariness descend on him, even as he kept filling in the blanks. "Though I bet he took it out to a boat lying behind the horizon somewhere. It's what I'd do."

"Starting to think like a master villain now, Mac?" Solana asked.

"Apparently, I have no choice," Mac replied as he glanced over at Ailsa, interrogating the hapless pilot who looked just about ready to cry.

"But, for what it's worth," he continued, "this Ailsa didn't cool off much on our flight so a heads up that she's still pretty angry."

"Screw her!" snapped Solana. "I'm angry—and there's nothing *pretty* about it. We've lost him, Mac! And are back at square one!" At which point she ended their call without waiting for a response. Yet another sting caused by this Victor Hart. Mac closed his eyes and tried to collect himself while silently asking *Who the hell is this guy?* And trying *not* to think that, at some point, he was going to have to call Boone.

●●

It looked for all the world like a deepwater fishing vessel. It once had been, in fact, up until just a year before. Now the ship's dilapidated exterior belied the high-tech interior, where a suite of monitors and manned stations kept an eye and an ear on various locations across the globe.

A man and a woman stood watching a pair of monitors showing handheld camera footage of runways in Oslo and Reykjavik.

"You were correct, Father," said the slight, blonde woman with a studious face and the body of a dancer, in her British accent. "More than just Interpol was on to you."

"Indeed," said Victor Hart, every inch the British gentleman, and now sporting much more proper attire than the rumpled suit and cheap tie he had worn on the Barcelona flight and in the hangar at JFK. "Agent Castillo I know already. She moved rapidly on this one. Helped, no doubt, by Lady Ailsa there, a connection I was completely unaware of. She got close this time. Cleverly done. But, as to this man, beyond seeing him with Agent Boone in America, I've heard nothing. Is there a name yet?"

"Not yet. He's definitely an American, but beyond that, we're still waiting."

"He was at Barcelona working with Agent Castillo, too. Someone in the security office will know for certain."

"Already checking."

"Diligent as always, Minerva. Scuttle the submersible and let us get underway."

"We could simply store it in the hold," she said.

Victor regarded her, amused. "The pilots saw me depart in it, so no. I've made my appearance for the lights. Now, I return to the shadows to observe the audience. Lord knows, they should have enough to go on. I say we let them proceed and learn as much as we can in the meantime."

"And if they start getting close again?"

"Oh, they certainly shall, even though we won't make it easy. What's the new timetable for the good doctor's project?"

Minerva consulted her tablet. "Two more weeks, maybe a little less."

"Very good. I think he can serve more than one use. It's clear that his disappearance has involved this third player, and I should like to know more." He leaned towards the monitor showing the lanky man in a leather jacket. "Who the devil might you be?"

CHAPTER 10

AILSA HATED SEEING *herself like this. Young. Ten years old. Scarlet pigtails and a lavender sundress. Mother's choice of colors, perfectly complementary, of course. An idyllic scene. The annual family picnic in the commons. Expected. Proper. Her father threw the ball far past the hounds to watch them run. Ailsa ran, too, laughing, stumbling, and laughing louder. Then the scent. Faint, in the breeze at her back. Something burning? No. Something long-burnt. Her young self slowed, wondering at grey flecks of snow swirling in the air around her. No. Not snow. Ailsa yelled at her young self not to look, but she turned anyway, and the oncoming wall of ash enveloped them both.*

The plane jolted her awake. Heavy weather covered Madrid, and the pilot was wrestling with his controls to keep them on the proper descent. Already her dream—the same bloody dream again—faded as consciousness rose. The phantom scent of ash lingered too long. Unwelcome.

She glanced at the American MacGyver, who, impudently, had somehow ended up with *her* name. He noticed her and gave a quick smile, as if to say, "Everything's fine." Bloody Yanks. Bloody CIA. Hart had escaped again, thanks to them and Interpol. His smile persisted, despite her scowl, before he turned his attention to the window, beyond which lay nothing but dark clouds, sparking with frequent lightning.

She'd been in front of him. For once. Once in three years! All across the globe, living other lives, being other people, for three entire years, and finally she'd had a chance to get in front of a scheme!

Only you didn't manage anything, now did you?

Her inner critic's voice always sounded like Mother's. Proper British upper crust. The Queen's Own English. And it was right. She glowered for a long moment, then forced herself to take a completely impartial, professional view of the events as she saw them.

Hart had shown himself for the first time ever. Why?

He'd impersonated a high-level kidnap victim and had been under CIA scrutiny, even indirectly, for the duration of the holdover in New York. They'd figured out his heist, faster than he'd expected, and his face wouldn't remain secret for long.

The final point: he had certain knowledge of Interpol hot on his tail, but they'd not known him at all.

So why show yaerself, yae bastard?

The only reason tae forego a cover is when it becomes more trouble than it's worth, or yae'v got somethin' tae gain.

And was this more trouble than it's worth?

No, cannae see how.

So, what did he gain?

The plane touched down at last, bumping and jouncing, then smoothing out rapidly as gravity took hold once more.

A driver met them in the security office and whisked them across Madrid through curtains of rain that shrouded the street lights into feeble glowing spheres. Ailsa's thoughts stayed as dark as the weather. She forced herself to calm down and stop running in circles.

Yes, he tripped tae the pursuit, never mind how, so what can be usefully done at this point?

Interpol won't let this go.

I'll be hampered now, what with the Red Notice they'll issue, keepin' the bastard confined tae countries that pay little attention tae such things.

Damn Interpol. Damn MacGyver. Wher' in hell did he get that name? An' why does it bother me so much?

If it's an American offshoot a' the greater family, Mother would know. She shuddered involuntarily. *An' endure the usual lectures yet again? I dinnae want tae know that badly.*

They pulled into the parking garage of a midsized office building. State Security Forces HQ, where Interpol had its offices in Madrid. A woman in an immaculate suit brought them to Agent Castillo's office, herself behind her computer concentrating on the screen. Then the American walked in, and her eyes brightened.

"Back safe and sound, I see."

Ailsa glanced at MacGyver, himself wearing a warm grin. "Bumpy flight, but no trouble."

Ailsa suppressed an eye-roll. "Have yae anythin' new tae tell us?"

Castillo went straight to business. "No. Not on Hart, anyway. I did get news on you, though, Lady Ailsa MacIver."

Mac was confused. "'Lady'? Like, royalty?"

"Yes, I'm a Scottish peer. I know which knife and fork to use at high table, the proper forms of address for the aristocracy of most nations, and it's all quite irrelevant to this case." Ailsa dismissed it. "Have yae anythin' a' substance?"

Castillo grunted. "The pilots had nothing. They didn't even violate any laws and weren't inclined to ask too many questions for receiving such outrageous pay. Mine thought someone was filming a movie." She hit a button and indicated the screen. "Message from Berg. The mining operation on the other side of the island was sanctioned by the municipality three years ago. They got started late last year, shut down for winter, then this year an entirely new crew took over. They spent little time in the town, and none of them can be found now. One was positively identified from the vault security footage letting Hart in. His name leads to a fake identity."

"So, basically, it's everything we already know with dead ends at every lead," said Mac.

"Except that he's been planning this for at least three years."

"I could'hae told yae that," said Ailsa.

Castillo looked her in the eye. "Yes. You *could* have."

"An' if I had, what happened would'hae happened sooner. Findin' Hart now'll be nigh impossible."

"Then what is MI6's particular interest in him? You said he'd used your resources to build his industrial empire. What illegal thing got you involved? Misappropriation of funds? Embezzlement?"

Ailsa paused a moment and took a breath. "Nothin' that was ever proved."

Castillo's brows came together. "But you've been chasing him for three years, since before his first heist you said, no?"

"Never mind that," said Ailsa. "The question now is, can I rely on yae tae keep out a' my way?"

"Not a chance," Castillo said, firmly. "This man is wanted for dozens of crimes, plus Doctor Verone is still missing. He's dangerous, and I want him under lock and key."

Mac could feel the tension building between them and tried to cut through it—if possible. "You know we can't back off this now, whatever you decide to do, right?"

"Well, yae could at least rescind the Red Notice I imagine yae'v put out on him. I need the bastard free tae move about the world, so I can get back on his trail, nae snug in some third world criminal haven wher' even the dev'l would fear tae tread."

Castillo shook her head. "Afraid not."

"And what will yae do when at last yae run him tae ground, eh?" Ailsa shot back. "*Call the police?*"

"You may not approve of our methods. But we found *you*, didn't we?"

Ailsa's face flared. "Listen, lass!—"

"Okay, take a breath, *everybody*," Mac said, raising his voice uncharacteristically before dropping it again after a beat. "We're all exhausted. We've been running for three days straight, and maybe even longer in your case. But we're not going to find Doctor Verone *or* Hart by going after each other like this, okay ...?"

Ailsa and Castillo refused to drop their scowls, but their silence said they knew he had a point as Ailsa crossed her arms and Castillo sat back in her chair before speaking with whatever calm she could manage.

"He's right. We could all use a break. I've arranged rooms for both of you at the hotel next door. I'll get someone to take you over, Lady MacIver. But I'd like a word with you, Mac, first, all right?"

Ailsa glanced between the two of them and shrugged as she headed for the door, adding without rancor, "Ailsa'll do. Yae need nae use my formal title."

👓

Mac watched her shut the door, then turned to Solana. "She's a piece of work, all right. Not sure I've seen anyone with that much ... drive."

Solana sighed, relieved it was just the two of them now. "She and Boone would get along famously."

He chuckled. "Yeah, somehow I don't think so." He could see how tired she was, not that anyone else would see it with only a few hairs straying from her bun. But the weariness had settled in deep behind her eyes. "You need to get some rest, too."

"I will," she promised. "After I do a little more digging—on her."

Mac frowned. "MI6's confirmation still not enough?"

"She's not telling us everything."

He shrugged. "Almost no one ever does."

"No, I mean there's something more to what's going on, and I don't like being kept in the dark."

"Well, I'm not sure how much else you're apt to get. Seems like her own agency doesn't even want to know what she's up to. We had to get her on her knees at gunpoint before they came clean."

"I just don't like it," she replied. "She has authority without oversight. It's a dangerous combination."

Again, Mac shrugged. "That's how I do things mostly. I'm almost never in touch with my handler. This operation has been a little unusual."

"But *you* I trust. She's not there yet."

"Fair enough," Mac said, throwing up his hands slightly. "Just be sure to let it go and get some rest. You'd be amazed how many ideas come together first thing in the morning." And then, without even thinking about it, he leaned over and kissed the top of her head before letting himself out. Solana was as surprised by the gesture as he was. But, alone now, she savored it for a comforting moment before turning back to her screen.

The next morning at the hotel, Mac's elevator opened on Ailsa and the smell of coffee so strong Mac thought he might get a contact high. "Morning," he said brightly, hoping a night's sleep might've helped soften her edge.

Ailsa grunted and stepped in, taking a deep sip.

"Sleep well?" he asked.

"Yae'd be a mornin' person, then, eh?" she rasped.

"Guess so," he said, still cheerful.

She sighed right down to her core.

"So, a rough night, then, huh?"

"Sleep's a rare commodity for me, Mr. Mac."

"Sorry to hear it. I slept like a log."

She took another long draw on her coffee and said no more until Castillo's office.

Solana looked as though she hadn't left, although she'd changed clothes and now wore her hair long.

"*Buenos dias,*" Mac said with a smile.

She looked up from her computer. "That's a matter of opinion," she said, coolly. "Though I suppose the hour is technically ante meridian."

"I guess I'm the only one that got some good sack time, then."

"Is he like this ev'ry day, an' all?" Ailsa asked, taking a seat.

"Certainly one of his flaws," said Castillo, nodding at her computer.

Ailsa grunted. "Another reason I'm glad I work alone."

Mac could only shake his head and take his seat. "Well, we may not have a great line on Hart, but we know more now than we did twenty-four hours ago. I bet if we put our heads together we can come up with something."

Ailsa scoffed. "Yae have no idea what yae'r sayin'. The man is one a' the best ghosts MI6 ever produced. An' a bleedin' billionaire tae boot. We're lucky tae even know his name."

"I was contemplating that," said Castillo, turning away from the computer at last. "We should think on why he didn't simply purchase some of these technologies. If his resources are so vast, then why not do much of this legally?"

"None of them were for sale," said Mac.

"Not yet, but most of them were going to be," Solana continued. "I believe my air filters and scrubbers are the only military assets he's touched that would've been forbidden to him, and again, enough money can fix even that. Still, everything else was being developed for the greater market, even your fusion reactor. He could have simply waited and used his money."

"Nae anytime soon," said Ailsa. "I'm inclined tae reluctantly agree with the American pretender here."

Mac let the slight go as Castillo continued to Ailsa, "Do you have a compiled dossier on Hart that we could see?"

"I suppose it would'nae hurt tae pass that along now since yae neither seem inclined tae leave him tae me." Mac and Castillo just gave her a look confirming that was not an option.

"Aye," Ailsa conceded. "But still, yae'v little chance workin' within the confines a' official intelligence. Like I said, the man has moles in ev'ry major agency. An' nae one has been caught out, despite ongoin' efforts tae do so. He's got an eye for talent an' operates cautiously at all times."

Castillo sat thinking for a long moment. "You've got some knowledge of how he executes these operations, yes?"

Ailsa nodded. "His patience is his greatest asset. He makes no move until he's dead certain a' his result. Why do yae think I settled for a simple data dump from his phone at the airport? If I'd told security about his true identity, he would'hae aborted his takin' a' yaer Doctor Verone immediately."

"Kinda wish you had," said Mac.

"I dinnae know he'd planned a kidnappin'," she said. "I dinnae know anythin' about his plan at all. Gettin' in front a' the man is the only chance tae catch him."

"Well, maybe that's what we should have our teams work on. Wouldn't hurt to give Boone something to chew on other than me."

"No!" Ailsa's exasperation was plain. "He'll get wind a' what yae'r about. It would'nae surprise me tae find someone sittin' right out there passin' him information even now," she said gesturing at the door. "Dinnae mistake, Miss Castillo, he certainly knows who yae are if yae'v been after him for two years."

"Any more than he already knows you, Lady Ailsa MacIver, daughter of the late Lord MacIver who was one of Hart's colleagues at MI6?"

Ailsa paused, realizing Castillo had spent part of last night digging. "They were contemporaries, yes. But I'd suggest yae focus more on Hart than me. Certainly, he knows a' me, but what I've been about was a mystery tae him until yesterday."

"You think," Castillo amended.

"I may be mistaken, but I dinnae think so. The bastard flushed us out with his seaplanes an' antics. The pilots were hired only the day prior an' paid in cash. It was a last-minute alteration tae his plan, an' he'd nae had a word a' me from Barcelona. If yae can figure out what he's after next, that's the place tae go lookin'."

"Yeah," said Mac. "I've had something bugging me about that

maybe. Do you have all the specs on the stuff he's stolen so far? Could be I can find *something* there."

"You've got my files. Have at it," said Castillo.

"Okay," said Mac, standing. "I assume we should keep all of this between just the three of us?"

"Yae'r damned right, Yank," said Ailsa.

He grinned. "Good. Didn't want to call Boone anyway."

Mac burst triumphantly into Castillo's office an hour later. "Graphene!"

The women glanced up from their computers, at each other, then back at him. "Yes, Hart stole a stockpile of it last year," said Castillo. "So ...?"

"So," he replied, surprised it wasn't obvious, "he only has a small amount. He'll need a lot more."

Again, they shook their heads, uncomprehending.

"Okay, think about his goal. We don't know the whole story, but everything he's taken seems like part of some survivalist effort, right? Seeds from the Seed Vault, military-grade air filters, two kinds of energy generation with storage for the excess, and a desalinization filter for his water. He's using all the latest technology to build a safe, pure environment and keep it clean."

"Aye," said Ailsa. "Now try sayin' somethin' we dinnae already know."

"What he's lacking is enough graphene to keep it all sustainable. He's got enough for a good start, but those de-sal filters could wear out pretty quick. They can be changed and cleaned, but they lose efficiency each iteration. Eventually, you need new ones. Also, he only stole the specs and one prototype of the solar cells. They're on the simple side, but he'll need graphene to build more. Same with the high-capacity batteries. He could just go with lithium-ion, but he wants the latest and greatest, and that's these graphene batteries he took. In every case, he's got a requirement for more of the stuff. As I said, a *lot* more."

Eager for any new lead, Castillo urged Mac on. "Okay, and this takes us where now exactly?"

"Well, the problem with graphene has always been that it's difficult to make at an industrial scale. I mean, you can do it with number two pencils and scotch tape, but that's labor intensive and inefficient."

Ailsa's eyes were already rolling in Castillo's direction. "Pencils an' bloody tape, what—"

"MacGyver has a unique way of viewing the world," said Castillo, reassuringly, even as she smiled at him, her spirits lifting already at his excitement. "Go on, Mac."

"Right, so the big holdup on this stuff has been production. Have a look at this." He put a printout on the table. "This company announced a prototype fabricator made to make this stuff quickly and cheaply. This thing is just the prototype, but it scales up *real* easy. I bet I could design a much larger model just from seeing this one."

Castillo tapped the printout, thinking. "It certainly sounds like something that would interest him. Do you agree, Ailsa?"

"Aye, but I cannae see the point. If yae think tae trap the man, he'll find out long afore the job, an' never go through with it. He'll stall yae out, wait till yae'r weary a' lyin' in ambush. When yae leave, then he takes his prize."

"Only if he knows we're there," said Mac.

Castillo objected. "But we can't know this fabricator is something he's after. It's a good guess, but still just a guess. What makes this thing next on the list instead of something else?"

He turned to Ailsa for support. "He likes making a splash, right? He likes the looks on their faces when something seemingly impossible happens. He made a *point* of showing his face in Norway, didn't he?"

"Aye, like a dark shade a' his father."

Mac laid down another sheet. "They're doing a big demonstration of the device—in France, Grenoble to be exact—for the European Union Commissioner for Energy in a week. Large press event. Can you imagine the headline if the machine vanished before the unveiling? I mean, just look at the Seed Vault coverage." He gestured towards the three monitors on the wall, each tuned to a different news channel. Word of the heist had been released with the morning news, and now talking heads from around the world spoke about the blow to conservationism alongside archival images of the Seed Vault.

Ailsa sat for a long moment, considering, then turned to Castillo. "It's nae like we're drippin' in leads here, eh?"

Castillo let out a long breath. "All right. I'll let them know they need to keep a tight lid—"

"Have yae nae been hearin' me, Interpol?" Ailsa snapped. "If that's his target, he'll have a mole there, placed tae hear a' any official warnin' by police, yae, or anyone else. That's how he operates, nearly at ev'ry turn, save the Seed Vault which has so few onsite employees as nae tae matter."

"I can't simply *let* him make an attempt at this thing."

"Yae bloody well can, so *I* can make another swipe at him!"

"She's got a point, Sol," said Mac.

Castillo looked from him to her and back again, wrestling with herself. Finally, she said, "Okay. If you're right about how well-connected he is, then I won't file anything here either."

Ailsa stood. "Thank yae, for a change. Now, if yae'll both excuse me, I should be on my way. Yae'll hear about what happens in a week."

Mac stood. "I should go, too. My idea after all, no?"

Ailsa's back went stiff, realizing they were determined not to let her charge off after Hart solo no matter how angry or offended she behaved.

"I agree," said Castillo. "I can't go anywhere without authorization, but a couple of agents from the CIA and MI6 aren't quite so bound up by tape. And you could use the help."

Ailsa steeled a look at Mac. "Yae'd have tae go into this cut off like me. No access to Agency tools or resources, usin' only what yae can beg, borrow, or steal. No fancy toys or gadgets, an' certainly no tactical teams for backup. Can yae really handle all that, Yank?"

Mac and Solana shared a silent smile before he replied, "You know, somehow I think I'll manage."

CHAPTER 11

SOMETIMES, *things that seem like a great idea at the time don't exactly pan out. Take dynamite, for instance. It's basically nitroglycerin rigged with a blasting cap in a mixture of diatomaceous earth and sodium carbonate. Without the earth and carbonate to keep it stable, the stuff is vulnerable to heat or impact, and just waiting to explode. The stabilizing element is vital. Same thing goes for teams.*

And we'd left Castillo behind.

Ailsa worked alone in the harshly lit dining car aboard the sleeper train as it hurtled towards Lyon in the darkness. From there they'd rent a car for Grenoble, which was France's own Silicon Valley. The engineering firm based its research division there where they'd constructed the prototype graphene fabricator.

She removed a USB stick from her laptop and regarded it. She was ready.

Mac entered the car and sauntered her way. She resisted the urge to narrow her eyes and share her displeasure at his being there. She still had no clear idea why the name thing irked her so. Was she just being pompous?

Probably, she concluded. *Let it go, lass. Yae have tae work with the radge, after all. Maybe he'll be some use as decoy.*

He slid into the seat across from her. He indicated the laptop. "I thought you said no fancy toys."

"Does the CIA nae use laptops now?" she asked dryly.

He shrugged. "I usually don't. But I'm okay if someone else wants to handle all the clickity-clack."

"Yae do know how tae *use* one I hope."

"Oh, yeah. I've built a few from scratch. But if it comes to hacking or bypassing them, I generally find there's a better way."

Now she raised an eyebrow at him.

Was he just bein' cocky? Or simply daft?

"But yae usually work alone, yae said, aye? An' near all security is managed by computers these days, at least any place serious."

Mac rocked his head in agreement. "I just find that it's a lot easier to make the things not work at all than finesse them into working for me. Most people really don't understand them. So, if it goes down, they're apt to get so caught up in confusion and panic, they don't even see me coming."

She could see the point but wasn't sure she'd want to rely on something so ... random.

"But seeing as how we'll be working together," he continued, "I thought maybe we should talk about tactics?"

Ailsa's instincts utterly rebelled at discussing operational matters in a public setting, but they were completely alone, with only one sleepy waitstaff that wandered through infrequently. "There's little tae say until we see what we're dealin' with. I know the firm contracted for their security, an' their methods. Likely a hard-shell type a' place. Difficult tae breach, but relatively free rein within."

Mac was nodding. "Okay. So, we're after their employee records, a layout of the place, and the specs on the graphene fabricator. That sound right?"

"Aye."

So maybe he was'nae a complete radge.

"Then I think we should start with their computer network and then—"

She held up a hand. "What say I'll let yae know what I need when I need it, eh?"

He frowned. "Well, I tend to play things by ear. And I just don't want to run afoul of your plan."

"I've nae yet seen the place. So, there is no plan, yae ken?"

He shrugged with a nonchalance that made her teeth itch. "Fair enough. And if we've got to wing it, so be it. You never know what might be on hand."

"What have yae," she said, not really wanting to explore how they should work, *together*. "But once we've seen it, we can design our assault: fallback approaches, alternate avenues a' attack, an' so on."

He chuckled. "You make it sound like we're going to war."

"We very much are," she said, correcting him.

Mac's smile faded. "Look, I get it's a serious situation. But if we go in expecting a battle, we'll only find one. For all we know, it'll be a walk in the park."

"An' for all we know, it'll be armed guards, keycards at ev'ry door, an' a shoot first, never question policy regardin' intruders." The difference in their MOs was becoming more apparent—and irritating to her—by the minute.

He looked at her flatly, trying not to fan any flames. "This isn't a suspected terrorist front in the Middle East. It's an R&D facility in southern France. I doubt you'll even need your gun."

"I've no intention a' shootin' anyone, but we should still be armed an' prepared."

He sighed slightly, having heard that line all too often, knowing that talking an operative out of going in armed was utterly futile. "Whatever," he said, throwing her dismissive attitude toward him back at her.

Ailsa eyed him hard, skepticism rising in her voice. "Yae'r tellin' me that in all yaer time as an operative, yae'v never used a firearm?"

He shrugged. "'Never' might be an exaggeration. But for what it was designed to do, no. To me a handgun is a short tube, a few springs of varying tension, high quality metal and plastic, and if there's a magazine, then a handful of gunpowder with which I can do all kinds of things. By itself, though, it's only good for one thing. And if using a gun is the only answer, chances are you're asking the wrong question."

She crossed her arms and regarded him, bemused. "Well, yae'r still alive, so I can only infer that it works for yae. Tae me it's a tool tae intimidate, coerce, or otherwise prevent them from takin' hostile action."

"For fear of reciprocation," he said. "And what happens if they're not afraid to call your bluff?"

She smiled tightly. "It's no bluff, laddie."

He sighed again and shook his head. "I'm just more comfortable going in unarmed and taking it from there."

Ailsa was about to reply but didn't when the door behind her opened to admit the waiter to see if they needed anything.

She closed her computer and ordered a whisky, neat. He ordered water. The server quickly brought their beverages, then bustled out.

She eyed his water as he sipped, thinking. "So, do yae nae drink, either?"

He glanced at his water. "Sometimes. Not often, though."

"All I've seen yae eat are salads. Yae a veg head, then?"

"Not really. I eat meat on occasion."

She set her glass down and regarded him curiously. "Yae dinnae drink much an' yae hardly eat meat ... Are yae certain yae'r ancestry is Scottish?"

He laughed, sipping. "Pretty sure. Although Mom was the one that did all the genealogy stuff. Can't ask her about it anymore, I'm afraid."

"Ah," she said. "My own mother has been obsessed with it since Father passed. I suppose I could inquire with her about any connection tae 'MacGyvers.'" She winced to herself as she took a drink. "Though the only ancestor who went to America would be Angus the Betrayer from Bonnie Prince Charlie's day. Said tae have fled tae the New World. Yae won't be tellin' me that Angus is a family name, now will yae?"

Mac looked at her with an awkward smile. "Then best to drop it, I guess."

She set her drink down, hard. "Yae dinnae mean tae say—"

"Didn't say a thing," he replied with a shrug.

She now regarded him with suspicion. Her immediate superior at MI6 had confirmed MacGyver as an American operative but hadn't attached a full name. "Yae'r right. Better nae tae know. Tomorrow will be busy. I'm goin' tae bed." And downing the rest of her drink in one final shot, she stood to go.

This is goin' tae be a bloody disaster, she thought, heading to her cabin.

                      🕶

This is going to be a disaster, Mac thought as he scanned the perimeter through binoculars from the rental car.

They were parked a couple hundred yards from the facility perimeter, the gates controlled by a pair of armed guards checking IDs and waving people through.

Ailsa had deflected his renewed queries on a plan, citing that until she knew more about what they were dealing with, she couldn't form a complete path to the objective. So far as Mac knew, the objective itself was just access to their computer systems. He'd tried asking a few more questions on the drive down to Grenoble from Lyon, but she'd evaded them like a Jedi. She had a real gift for steering a conversation and putting up walls. He just wished there was some way to break though.

"Okay," he said finally. "What do you think?"

She lowered her own binoculars from the driver's seat. "It's what I thought. A hard-shell with cameras an' live patrols. If we even approach the fence, they'll be on us in less than a minute. Talkin' our way in would be ideal."

Mac considered. "Does a place like this receive visitors?"

"Hardly. I checked, an' certainly nae any walk-ups. I can likely forge identifications for us. From the security firm itself would be best. But that'll take time that we may nae have."

Mac nodded and scanned the nearby area. They were located in a light industrial district, though the research facility sat on its own plot of land with a good forty yards across a manicured lawn between the fence and the large building proper. His binoculars settled on the electric substation a few blocks away. He grinned inwardly. "Pop the hood and trunk. Are you done with your iced coffee?" he asked, shaking her cup, now mostly ice.

She regarded him a moment, then shrugged. "Help yaerself. What're yae about?"

In the trunk he grabbed the jumper cables and looped them over his shoulder and chest like a climbing rope. He fished out a clean rag and some heavy wire cutters he'd picked up on their way down. At the hood, he rubbed the rag all over the engine, collecting grease, then added oil via the dipstick. He folded the rag carefully to keep any residue off his hands and shoved it into his jacket pocket. At the car window, to Ailsa's bewildered expression, he said, "Be just a minute. Keep the engine running."

"What're yae playin' at?" she asked again.

"Going to have a look at the substation. It's got ... possibilities."

She was about to say something else, but Mac was already on his way.

No security at the substation except a high fence rising up into a cloudless sky. His wire cutters easily defeated it. He rolled back a section and ducked inside the perimeter. A hint of ozone tickled his nose, and the main transformer's hum raised tiny hairs all along his arms and neck. "Oh, yeah," he muttered as he uncoiled the jumper cables.

With all the caution of a surgeon approaching a patient wired with two hundred kilovolts of electricity, he attached the end of one cable to the transformer's incoming lead and laid the other end on the hard concrete. Even there, he could practically feel the bundled current, coiled like a viper ready to strike.

"Do not try this at home, folks," he whispered as he did the same with the second cable, this attached to the low-voltage outgoing leads.

He placed the cable ends two feet apart and laid the greasy rag vertically between them in a long strip without touching either lead.

From the coffee cup, he fished out three ice cubes of about the same size. He placed one near each jumper cable lead on the hot concrete, and one on the rag. When they melted, the water would spread and close the circuit with an electric arc of ridiculous power, instantly igniting the rag and blowing every circuit at the station.

He hustled back to the car and leaped in. "Okay, other side of the facility. Quick!"

Ailsa threw the car into gear. "What did yae do?"

"In about two minutes there'll be a big arc and a fire at the substation. It'll take the power down."

"*What?* We dinnae have tae do this *today!*" she shouted.

Mac gave her a look. "We're here, aren't we? And you didn't say this was just recon."

"I dinnae think I had tae! Another day a' observation would'hae given us more intel. At the very least, we watch them come an' go, figure out who the important people are, maybe do a little smash-and-grab tae one a' their cars for an ID template. Nae blow the damn place apart!"

Mac, miffed at her secretiveness, coolly replied, "Now you tell me. Well, I'm afraid that ship has sailed, Ailsa."

"Bloody Yanks! Cowboys one an' all! An' we need the computers inside workin', yae know?"

"They'll get the power back on soon enough. They might even have backup generators, so we need to be fast."

"An' do what? Hide inside a place we dinnae know with cover identities that we dinnae have?" She was furious. "Do yae even speak French?"

"You do. Isn't that enough?" he shot back, trying not to match her anger. She brought the car to a halt in a parking lot twenty yards from the fence without stomping the brakes, though she slammed the car into park with a jolt.

"Bloody brilliant," she cursed.

True to his word, within another minute, a bright flash from beyond the facility drew all eyes. Mac could hear the violent, sparking arc in the distance. As they hustled towards the fence, a thin column of black smoke rose into the crystal blue sky.

"Voila," he said dryly as he cut through the links.

Ailsa just glared as he rolled back the links for her.

With the power out, the magnetic locks on a side door had disengaged. Mac managed the mechanical lock with ease, and they slipped inside. This was the construction floor where prototypes were assembled and tested. The scent of machining oil, cut wood, and lathed metal spoke to him of home: a busy, safe place. But he didn't see anything that looked like the graphene production device, and there were no engineers or anyone else in the area.

The muffled voice of a megaphone from within the offices towards the front of the building caught his attention. It was in French, so he didn't understand, but Ailsa listened intently.

"They're instructin' ev'ryone tae move tae the front office durin' the power outage. Aye, look ..." she said, spying two people in white coats and hard hats leaving the main room. A sign for the locker rooms caught her eye. "This way. Walk calmly, an' dinnae stare at anyone."

Mac nodded, gesturing her to lead the way. "Not my first rodeo."

"Cowboys ..." she muttered derisively as she headed into the women's area and Mac went to the men's.

Empty lab coats lined the wall like a line of ghostly engineers. Mac did a quick look around and nabbed a pair of plain visitor's badges from an open locker. He handed one to Ailsa when they regrouped.

"Just keep yae'r eyes open an' let me do the talkin'," she said, clipping on her badge. "Yae can play the clueless American, I'm sure."

Mac let the dig go with a nod as they started off, making their way towards the offices as a tall, uniformed guard appeared from inside the door they were heading to.

Ailsa, suddenly smiling and sunny, quickly greeted him. *"Ah, oui, salut! Je suis navré, mais avec tout ce tohubohu, nous sommes éloignés de notre groupe. Nous cherchons les ressources humaines."*

Mac knew only a smattering of French, but the last bit was certainly "human resources."

The guard grunted. *"Vous auriez dû éviter de vous égarer."*

"En fait, c'est notre guide qui nous a perdu de vue. Est-ce que vous pouvez nous rediriger?" she asked, apologetic.

He held out his hand expectantly. *"Certes, mais d'abord, je dois voir vos papiers. Évidemment."*

She handed over her visitor's ID. *"Oui, évidemment. Euh, est-ce que l'on peut parler en anglais? Mon ami est Américain, malheureusement."*

He chuckled. *"Oui,* I speak a little English," he said in that language.

Ailsa turned to Mac and said in a thick French accent, "Ze officer needs your ID, *monsieur."*

"Oh!" said Mac, handing it over. "Right."

The guard scanned them with his phone, then scowled. "Ze computer is still down. *Le* power, eh?" He waved at the emergency lights on above the door.

"I understand," said Ailsa. "We are sorry to be such trouble. If you could just show us ze way, surely that would be sufficient, eh?"

The guard mulled a moment, then handed back the IDs with a shrug. *"Très bien.* So many strangers for ze visit next week. Confusion everywhere. This way. Just do not wander again, *s'il vous plaît?"*

He dropped them at the door marked for Human Resources with a nod to Mac and smile for Ailsa. As they passed through the door, her complaisant smile vanished like dropping a mask. Staff wandered here in the medium-sized cube farm, chatting mostly about the power, an unexpected break in the middle of a busy day.

Mac and Ailsa loitered near the printer/copier, observing.

She glanced at him. "Dinnae just stand there lurkin' like a specter, talk tae me about somethin'."

"Fine, just how many languages do you speak?"

She smirked. "I dinnae know. How many are there?"

Mac gave her a chatty-looking grin. "Really?"

"Nae. I can operate in Europe an' most a' continental Asia. Pass for a native in most places. More, if I have time for research."

"Impressive."

She shrugged. "Learnin' a language tae usability takes a week or so. Tae fluency is a couple a' months. It's just trainin' an' practice. How do yae do yae'r little tricks, an' all?"

"Training and practice," he echoed. "And I read a lot. Take classes when I can. Almost everything being online helps. MIT and other universities publish their courses."

The power came on at that moment. Everyone looked up involuntarily, and a few laughs and cheers rippled around the room.

Ailsa turned to him, with a smiling demeanor that belied the seriousness of her words. "We only have a few minutes before someone asks us what we're doing here. I just need access tae a computer long enough tae insert this thumb drive for fifteen seconds or so. Someone just noticed us, so grin an' give a half-laugh as though I'm sayin' somethin' funny."

Mac liked to think of himself as fast on the uptake, but Ailsa switched gears so rapidly that he was starting to feel a step behind. But he laughed as instructed and nodded effusively to maintain the ruse.

"Do yae see any stations unattended?" she asked, still sunny.

"Can't say I do," he said, glancing around casually. "And I think that guy is still looking our way."

"We're goin' tae need a distraction."

"That I can do." He thought a moment, glanced upward at the

air vent, then picked up a ream of paper from the copier. "Back in a minute."

She put a hand on his arm. "Yae'r nae goin' tae burn the place down, are yae?"

"Destroy a place of science and engineering? Please ..." he replied, shaking his head as he walked off.

She let him go warily, but maintained her plastic smile.

We do need a fire, though, Mac thought.

A small one.

Janitor's closet was back that way.

That'll do, but where to set it that it won't spread?

Gotta be some place for that.

The closet door was locked, but the hall was empty and free of cameras. Ailsa had been right about most security being primarily outside. He picked it open in six seconds and shut the door behind him.

Great. The one janitor in the world that doesn't have a metal pail or bucket. Keep looking.

Then, craning his eyes up and around the room.

Bingo.

He unscrewed the small vent near the ceiling and checked inside. The duct was aluminum, all metal, without much dust at all. He nodded to himself and piled several wadded-up balls of paper inside. He then took the tube out of a toilet paper roll, pulled some lint from inside the vacuum, stuffed it into the roll and soaked it all with an alcohol-based cleaning fluid. He placed it amid the paper balls and lit the alcohol with his lighter. It caught instantly, already giving off a faint wisp of black smoke.

He replaced the vent and returned to the office. Ailsa sat towards the front in what little reception area there was, ostensibly reading a magazine, but actually observing the place like a falcon on her perch. "Any minute now, there'll be a fire alarm," he said.

Her saccharine expression turned brittle. "Yae told me yae would'nae burn the place down, no?"

"It's a very small fire. But enough to trip the system. You don't want to pull the alarm in a place like this. They'll know someone did it and have guards there ASAP. Trust me, it'll burn out inside of three minutes, and nothing else will catch."

"*Excuse, s'il vous plaît,*" said a man standing over them. "You are *Anglais,* no? Can I assist with something?"

Ailsa rose with her sunny demeanor on, already speaking. Mac noticed a wisp, then a waft of smoke curling out from the vent beyond the man's head.

Uh-oh, his mind whispered.

The fire klaxon interrupted Ailsa with its wailing, accompanied by flashing red strobes overhead and in the halls. After a startled moment, the fire suppression system deployed, spewing smelly, stagnant water everywhere.

Shouts, screams, and confusion brought everyone running for the exit, shielding their heads with papers and jackets.

Mac moved fast, whipping off his lab coat and throwing it over the nearest computer. "Quick!" he hissed at her, as the water plastered his hair to his scalp. Ailsa, already resembling a dunked rat, ducked under the coat, found a port, inserted the drive, and counted to fifteen, until the I/O light flicked off. She yanked it out, then headed for the door, Mac in tow.

The sprinklers hadn't deployed in the hallway where Ailsa stalked dripping down the corridor. Mac was right behind and could hear her spew of expletives—in several languages.

"Look," he said apologetically, "not as elegant as I intended, all right? But it got us into the network, didn't it?"

She rounded on him, shoving wet strands of hair from her face. "This right here is why I work alone. Goin' off half-cocked like a bloody action hero. The real world does'nae work like this, Mac!" She didn't wait for a response, just turned and resumed her stalk to the exit.

Which was but a few, short strides away when the same security guard nearly ran into them from an intersecting corridor. "*Vous encore?*" he blurted, surprised to see them again, then noticed their dripping condition. His hand twitched towards his weapon. "*Pourquoi*—why are you wet?"

"Ask him," Ailsa growled, jabbing a thumb over her shoulder—just as her hand shot out to his wrist, twisted him around in a lock, and shoved him up against the wall. She kicked his leg from behind, sending him to a knee, and her other arm wrapped around his neck in a sleeper hold. He was out in seconds.

Mac looked at her like she'd just grown horns and a tail. "Is he okay?"

"Better than yae'd be if I dinnae now need yae tae get us out a' the country. It'll be police an' security services the whole way, an' they'll certainly know they were infiltrated. Happy are yae?"

Yeah, definitely not a team player, Mac heard himself think as they disappeared from the complex.

CHAPTER 12

AILSA MACIVER'S jaw was set and hard as she stared at the long wake trailing out behind the fishing boat, barely registering the glorious, warm morning that had risen on the Mediterranean Sea. Their harried escape from Grenoble to the coast had been a straightforward bit of routine fieldwork. She'd had to burn the ID she'd used to rent the car, of course. The Yank had been good for his CIA credit card, fortunately. It had taken a large wad of bills to bribe the fisherman to let them hide aboard for the night, then haul them to Spain at dawn, no questions asked. Even then, she'd had to handle the conversation, convincing the man to break maritime law.

Every time the "other" MacGyver crossed her mind, her jaw tightened further.

He's chaos. Raw, bloody chaos. No sense at all for the nuances a' the job. He's just ... technical. Why do they even let him out alone on a mission?

And yet, they *did* send him on operations of this sort. She'd gotten more word back from MI6. He'd assisted on several joint endeavors, always with stellar marks. The Libyan transgression, the Tehran defector, and even the averted debacle in Montreal. They all appeared in his file. Clearly, he *wasn't* incompetent. And some part of her had to acknowledge that her constant cauldron of anger had nothing really to do with him, even if his involvement or interference was an easy target for it.

But they'd been pursued after bungling an operation that should've been a simple day or two of data gathering, planning, and execution. The two of them were—to put it nicely—professionally incompatible, that much was certain.

He approached her now, sauntering along, phone in hand. "Morning," he said in his irritatingly cheerful manner. "Did you sleep?"

Not even having had coffee, Ailsa merely grunted. The fishing boat had but decaf, instant at that. Bollocks. But she couldn't simply ignore him and so offered, "The data worm has done its work. I've identified the mole. He's a deputy director a' security, an' thus, he's identified us. They'll step up their timetable now, assumin' he does'nae bolt."

"Not optimal then, huh?"

"Understatement a' the year, *Mac*," saying his nickname like she was spitting out a bug that had flown into her mouth.

"Did you find the schematics?" he asked.

"Aye. Or at least what looks like them. They're on yae'r phone."

He looked at his cell like it was venomous. "Yeah. Haven't turned it on in a couple of days. Not looking forward to what's waiting."

"Welcome tae my life. If things a' this nature occur too often, then I cannae expect them tae continue my at-large status, now can I?"

"Are you needing an apology?"

She sighed. "I dinnae blame yae, entirely. Though yae might'hae mentioned what yae were about with yaer jumper cables an' flash fire."

"Fair enough. But if you shut me out of your thinking, then I'm going to grab the ball and run with it. I'm used to working solo, too, remember?"

"Point taken," she conceded. "But I cannae imagine yaer girlfriend will be too pleased with us," she said as she gestured to his phone.

"It's not her I'm worried about." He paused. "And Castillo isn't my girlfriend."

She barked a small laugh. "Yae could'hae fooled me, with 'you must come visit Minnesota' an' all."

"Okay. There might be something there for us; we've worked together before. But we've tabled it until we're all through with this. And it might still not happen. Relationships in our business are ... complicated. But I imagine you already know that."

She did, finding herself nodding, and strangely feeling almost a pang of sympathy for them if not a void in herself that she had long since sealed. "So, then who are yae dreadin' at the end a' that line?" she asked, keeping the matter on him, off her and that gnawing abyss. "A nasty relative or an ex, maybe?"

"Flavors of both," he replied, glancing again at the silent but screaming cell in his hand. "In the worst possible ways."

👓

"Three days! Three goddamn days with no contact, in direct violation of my orders!" Boone bellowed, making Mac jerk his head away from the phone.

Mac closed the door to Castillo's office, where he sat alone. "Things were moving fast and any sitrep would've been piecemeal at best," Mac explained.

"I don't give a shit! This is priority one at the Agency right now. *Not* time for a pleasure cruise with your new MI6 girlfriend! Or did you think I wouldn't notice the card charges at Grenoble and the huge cash withdrawal in Marseille?—Not to mention the private charter to Oslo—"

Mac had heard enough. "If you're just gonna rant, I can hang up now," Mac said in that low, firm voice. "If you want a report then I suggest you shut up and listen. Copy that?" There was a beat of stony silence on the line before Boone finally replied with a terse,

"Talk." Mac detailed a brief summary of the events, including the information about moles. There had been one at the engineering firm, now confirmed, though the man was apparently nowhere to be found at this moment.

Boone was unimpressed. "So, at the moment you're nowhere. Literally *nowhere*. After spending a serious chunk of Agency cash and no less than *two MacGyvers*."

"It's not spelled the same," he replied, wearily.

"Ask me if I give a damn. You both still blew it!"

Don't respond to that, Mac warned himself, and checked his first reply in favor of "And we're not nowhere. We know it's Hart now, how he operates and some sense of his goal and targets. Which is a lot more than we had before I left. And it's unlikely he'll be making a move on the graphene fabricator now."

"It was a damned long shot in the first place. And I'd never have approved it," Boone rasped.

"Then it would've been stolen, wouldn't it? The mole was there. Hart is moving towards his endgame, and he knows we're on him, which could give us an edge."

"Or send him to ground for who knows how long. While we still *don't know* where or what he's doing with Doctor Verone, do we?"

Mac could feel his edge welling up despite resisting Boone's attempts to bait him. "Well, if you have something to contribute to finding him other than a list of complaints, I'm all ears."

"It's *your* job to have things for *me*, remember?" Boone replied, still trying to saw away on Mac's nerves. "That's why the Deputy Director insisted on you, against *my* advice, I might add. But I'm sure she'll be rethinking things now with you turning up on a wanted list in France."

"Interpol will handle that."

But Boone could sense he had Mac against the ropes and wasn't going to stop swinging. "You know, petty arson and vandalism doesn't show your usual style. Hell, any teenager could've done that."

Mac wasn't certain what missions Boone was thinking of, since he nearly always needed a fire or explosion of some kind, but he chose to ignore it, and move himself and the conversation out of a pointless corner. "Going forward, I say we try to get a line on this mole that bolted."

Boone's sarcasm dripped through the phone. "You know that whole informants story about Hart is a pretty serious accusation, and we're just taking this MacIver's word for it?"

"MI6 seems to buy it, so, yeah, I think that's solid. But if you want, I'll tell you everything about the next operation beforehand and if it goes belly up, then *you* can explain it to the Deputy Director, how's that?"

Boone paused, and Mac could practically see the sneer. "No thanks, Wonderboy. I think I'll just let you hang yourself with all this. Which reminds me, I have a message for you from the Deputy Director. She says, and I quote, 'Be more discreet.' This thing in France has the DGSE up in arms with us and the Brits, and the DD is catching fire from both the Director and SecState."

MacGyver groaned silently but said nothing. The last thing he'd ever wanted to do was cause this kind of trouble—and listen to Boone revel in it.

"I'll take your lack of a snappy reply as admission of guilt," he said. "And my money says your days here are numbered. Because there are consequences to blowing me off. So, go ahead, tool around the Med with both your hotties, invade a foreign nation or two, and commit all the vandalism and arson you feel like while Doctor Verone labors over fusion bombs for terrorists in some third world hellhole. You can bet I'll be here keeping score."

The phone clicked dead.

Mac just sat there for a long minute, relieved—and not—that the enemy was as much at his back as out there somewhere.

Jackass has a point.

Some days it really feels like it might be time to just hang it up, let it go, and leave the world to its own devices. Could this get much worse? he wondered, putting his phone away just as Solana snapped open the door with a harried and furious look.

"You need to come see this now, Mac!"

Apparently, it could.

●●

Mac and Castillo entered a conference room where Ailsa stared intently with arms crossed at news reports on the big screen. The volume was up, and Mac's Spanish was adequate enough to follow along.

"While no one was killed in the daring midday assault, one guard is in critical condition and three others suffered serious wounds. Stolen was what the company spokesman described as a graphene fabricator, in transit to a secure location after an accidental fire at the R&D facility in Grenoble."

Footage was that of a phone camera, shakily showing a large panel truck with the company logo under assault from at least six men in urban camo and black balaclavas, armed with submachine guns. They were firing to keep the guards contained in the truck, then threw in some form of tear gas grenade. In less than twenty seconds, they'd taken the truck and sped away.

"Police located the truck some miles away, with the fabricator missing. The search is ongoing, and citizens have been encouraged to come forth with any information—"

Castillo muted the screen. "Great," she said. "You thwarted one heist, so he took it anyway."

Mac felt suddenly even more deflated, if that was possible. "And we know this was Hart?" She handed over her phone. An email read:

AGENT CASTILLO AND COMPANY,

ONE MUST OCCASIONALLY ADOPT TACTICS ONE MIGHT OTHERWISE FIND DISTASTEFUL. REST ASSURED THAT I MEAN NO SOULS ANY HARM, AND THAT I REGRET THAT MY ASSOCIATES IN THIS ENDEAVOR WENT ABOUT THEIR TASK WITH NEAR-LETHAL EFFICIENCY.

YET, THE ENDS MUST JUSTIFY THE MEANS IN SOME CASES,

AND YOU HAVE CAUSED ME DISCOMFORT. THOSE UNFORTUNATE GUARDS WOULD BE AT HOME WITH THEIR FAMILIES NOW, BUT FOR YOUR DOGGED PURSUIT OF MY INTERESTS. I DO NOT CONDONE MY PEOPLE'S USE OF DEADLY FORCE, BUT SUCH IS THE HAZARD OF HIRING CONTRACTORS, IS THAT NOT SO?

SPEAKING OF WHICH, PLEASE GIVE MY KIND REGARDS TO LADY MACIVER AND MISTER MACGYVER, I PRESUME. RELATIONS, PERHAPS? THOUGH A CURIOUS COINCIDENCE, REGARDLESS, DON'T YOU THINK?

—VH

Mac looked at Castillo. "Seriously?"

"Received this five minutes ago on my private email address, before I'd even heard about the robbery. No way to trace it, of course."

"Of course," Mac said.

"He's baiting us," said Ailsa. "He wants us angry, demoralized."

"I got that part," Mac said, watching the silent screen play through the assault again. "And it's almost working. 'Cause he's got ID on me, now, too. But who are those guys in the heist? Does Hart have his own army?"

"We're looking into it," said Castillo.

"Mercs, almost certainly," said Ailsa. "Though the bastard will deal with the lowest a' the low, when it suits." Even she looked beat now. "So, yae can see why I've been workin' alone. Our excursion has done nothin' more than send him deeper into hidin'."

"Not entirely true," said Mac, searching for some ray of light in a very black cloud. "We're getting into his head, too, or he wouldn't be playing mind games like that with us. And it confirmed that he needs the fabricator. So, our picture of his plans is gaining focus. It's not just throwing darts in the dark if you hit actually hit something, yes?"

"Aye, but we've no other spots tae hit. Unless yae can conjure another long shot from all the spec sheets?"

Mac had been considering that since they'd left France, but just shook his head. "Sorry, right now ... I've got nothing."

Twenty-four hours later, and still nothing. Ailsa spent most of the time running checks, reading specs, and doing her best to avoid the people in this building full of international police. Any of them might be Hart's lackey.

Eventually, she found her way to the gym and changed into sweatpants and an Interpol halter. It had been days since she'd had a proper workout, and strength like hers needed honing to keep its edge.

Her mother had complained about her high-strength workouts more than once in her teen years. Had said that she'd end up with shoulders like a man's. Rot and nonsense. Women didn't bulk up, not without using steroids. As ever, her mother had fretted about her ever attracting a husband. If anything, Ailsa's strength training had been a boon in that department. And if the less than subtle gaze of the two men in the mirror across the room was any indication, she need only whistle for all the company she desired. Not that she'd desired any company of that sort in quite some time.

Yet it was with some irritation that she noticed MacGyver watching her with raised brows, also in an Interpol T-shirt and shorts. He wasn't ogling like the other two, yet the surprise on his face inexplicably grated.

She put down the weights with a heavy thunk, breathing hard, and looked at him in the mirror. "Have yae never seen a woman trainin' before?"

"My apologies," he replied, realizing he'd been staring a bit too hard. "I'm not much for gyms so don't see women working out quite like that too often."

"Yae mean really liftin' a weight rather than playin' with it tae catch a braw lad's eye?"

Mac picked up some light weights to warm up. "Something like that."

"Did yae find somethin'?"

"Sadly, no," he said. "Just that Castillo tripped over me behind her for the third time and 'suggested' I find somewhere else to think."

Ailsa snorted. "Aye." Now she watched him run through his quick set with a skeptical eye. "With arms like that, yae'd do well tae see a gym more often."

Mac paused in the routine and turned to give her a look. "Now we're gonna play body shaming? Really? I'm sure that would make Hart smile. But if it helps get you past whatever's really been eating at you, then have at it. Because I could probably stand to lose a few pounds, too, and haven't been able to run a mile in six minutes since I was forty."

Ailsa's eyes shifted off him, suddenly realizing it *was* a cheap shot. And that Mac wasn't just getting into Hart's head; he was getting into hers. Because there *was* something eating at her—had been for quite some time now. But she'd been expert at keeping it hidden. Only now, with having to work with him, Mac was beginning to see it, too.

"Just givin' yae a bit a' shite, an' all," she answered, trying to cover the misstep as she grabbed a pair of heavier weights and started another set of reps. "Dinnae mean tae hit a sore spot."

Mac let it go with a shrug as the two of them continued their routines in silence for a beat before he finally asked, "I don't suppose you've heard anything new yet?"

She grunted with her final repetition and dropped the weights, breathing hard. "Nay. Though I'll admit it's nice havin' Riverhouse analysts tae call upon for once."

"So, you've really been off the reservation for the last three years, just chasing Hart?"

She mopped sweat from her face and neck. "Aye, though there'hae been side ventures now an' again, tae be sure."

"I know how that goes," he answered, though she could tell he was still a bit on edge from her crack at him.

She picked up more weights, now feeling an unusual urge to somehow close the gap she'd just opened. "Yae know, I saw yaer file at last. Frankly, I'm ... amazed yae'r still alive after two decades a' doing this work."

"Is that meant to be a compliment?" Mac asked, finally turning to look at her directly again.

"Yae could take it that way if yae like." She finished her set and dropped the weights, still wanting him not to shut her out. "But truly now. Do yae always just walk into a scenario with as little info as the other day? Is that ... standard for yae?"

Mac switched weights. "The more I know, the better, sure, but I find that if I plan too much, it's a waste of time. As soon as you think you know the situation, it changes. Better to be fluid."

"Aye, no plan survives contact with the enemy, yet there's bein' fluid an' then there's tossin' caution out with the bathwater."

Mac mopped away his sweat. "What can I tell you? It works. They never see me coming, since they can never plan for everything."

"And all without havin' a gun?" she said, still trying to wrap her head around that one.

"I can't tell you how many times I've been caught snooping and they're just as baffled. How can I possibly be an American operative if I'm unarmed? Almost no one believes it. Being unarmed has saved my life more than once."

She merely nodded, almost approvingly, and resumed her workout.

After a few minutes, Mac asked, "So, what's your plan going forward from here?"

She finished the set and racked her weights, breathing hard. "Depends on if anythin' is found in the next day or so. If nothin', then I'm back tae the start. If somethin' crops up, I'll beg yae an' Castillo tae leave it tae me. For all the good that'll do."

Mac let a grin cross his face. "I know Grenoble was hardly a win. But I still think we need each other on this, especially if Hart is closing in on his final goal."

She faced him directly. "We just have vastly different ways a' workin', yae know? I cannae fathom how we'd function in the field if I dinnae know what yae'v got up yaer sleeve. Yae have tae agree it's a problem, aye?"

"Yeah, it's a problem," Mac conceded. "But it doesn't mean there's no solution." His phone pinged with an incoming text. He looked, then held it up for her. "It's Castillo. She needs us."

They arrived in her office in no time, still sweaty in gym clothes. Castillo looked at them curiously for a beat at the thought of them working out together before she pointed to her computer. "This just came through from your software," she said to Ailsa.

It was a location trace, but not in Grenoble. It was in Algiers, across the Mediterranean Sea due south from France.

"A malfunction?" Mac asked.

"Nay," Ailsa said, taking over and typing a few commands. "Nay, it's somethin' that was online at some point after I infected their network. A laptop, perhaps? It came up for half an hour, then shut back down."

Mac's eyes flashed with a spark. "It could be the fabricator!"

They looked at him as he started to explain. "It's computer-controlled. If they brought it up to test it in Grenoble before trying to transfer it, your trace would've jumped on it, right? So, we could be looking at it right now in Algiers if they were testing it themselves. Either way, it's worth a hard look."

"I agree," said Ailsa. "An' I'll let yae know what I find as soon as—"

Castillo stopped her with a gesture. "I know what you're going to say, and I'm going to tell you no. I have no authority to stop you, but I cannot and will not ignore this lead. Now, I'm the only one that knows about it. I won't tell anyone here, but I can't send you off on your own to track it down."

Ailsa rolled her head. "But, after Grenoble, Mac an' I at least agree we're nae the best a' pairings, yae know?"

"I agree," Castillo said. "So, this time, I'm coming with you both."

CHAPTER 13

*A*ILSA WATCHED *herself from afar sitting down for dinner, pigtails drawn back and pinned to keep them out of her soup. Father hadn't much cared, but Mother insisted, as she did with all formal events, and dinner was ever a formal event. Father in his suit, Mother her immaculate dress, and Ailsa, learning to be a "proper lady" in formal wear suited for an eight-year-old. White-gloved servants marched past with the soup tureen, candlelight reflected in shining silver. They placed it before Father, who stood to ladle out portions. He removed the cover and the scent filled the room, assaulting her nose and mouth. Metallic. Almost iron-ish. The servant placed a bowl before her, the soup crimson, dark, and thick. Blood.*

👓

Ailsa's alarm woke her in her hammock, swaying on the easy Mediterranean swells. The phantom taste of iron lingered in her mouth and nose for half a moment, then evaporated. She'd long since gotten past waking in a sweat, breathing hard from the panic these damned dreams sometimes brought. Still, she ran her hands through her hair and breathed deeply for a long minute.

They'd decided that arrival by boat would elicit less fuss than by plane. Time was a factor, but the trip from Cartagena to Algiers was under four hundred kilometers and would take less than ten hours. Arrival by ship meant less scrutiny, vital for a trio of agents with two of them bringing weapons.

She remembered Mac's disapproving glance as she and Castillo had discussed the matter.

Silly man, she thought.

It still boggled her that he absolutely refused to arm himself. She conceded that he must know what he's doing, but she'd stick with her gun for now, thank you very much.

They'd departed well before dawn, and she'd retired for some much-needed sleep. The early morning beyond the porthole matched her mood: grey and threatening. Late August's sizzling temperatures often brought rapid storms to the Med. Her sailor's instincts told her they'd make port long before it broke, though.

On deck she found Mac watching the weather to the west with some apprehension.

"Morning," he said, then did a double take at her jet-black hair. "Weren't you a redhead last night?"

She didn't feel like banter. "It's a wig, yae know. Nae lookin' forward tae wearin' it in this heat, itches like the dev'l, but hair like mine is uncommon, at best."

"Well, if it helps, the temperature will moderate when we get closer to shore. Warm day, but not quite as muggy. Did you sleep?"

She merely grunted. "Yae?"

"Like a log," he smiled.

"There would'nae be any coffee, eh?"

"I thought I smelled some in the galley," Mac replied, leading the way.

"For what we're payin' there'd better be." They'd chartered a yacht for the journey, three crew and a captain, all quite willing to make the journey quickly and discreetly without anything more than a cursory custom's check and fewer questions. Amazing what a pile of bills could accomplish.

They found the pot, though Mac kept himself to just one. She looked at it cupped in his hands as she poured her third. "Dinnae tell me yae dinnae fancy coffee, either?"

He glanced at it. "I usually don't need it to get moving. A light breakfast and some orange juice are stimulation enough."

She shook her head. "Yae'd never make it in the highlands, that's for certain."

"So, tell me about your title. You're royalty of some kind?"

She rolled her eyes. "Ugh. No, only Her Majesty's family are royalty. If yae want tae be technical, I'd be part a' the aristocracy, though there is'nae much a' that anymore. An' good riddance tae it."

"I know almost nothing about it," he admitted.

"Yae'r better off. Though if yae really want tae know, Mother would be the one tae ask, assumin' yae'v got a month tae spare."

"Might be fun," he mused.

She stared. "Is it *fun* yae'r wantin' now?"

"I don't mean the reasons why we're here. But, yeah, I like the travel, and the people. I'm glad we met, for instance. Never met another MacIver."

She poured a fourth cup. "It's a full clan, tartan an' all. The name is about as common as a Jones in yaer States," she said.

"Still wonder if we might be related. So, I'd welcome an intro to your Mom, if you wouldn't mind?"

She fixed him with her gaze. "That would mean callin' her. Yae'v no idea the sacrifice yae'r askin' for."

"That rough between you, huh?"

Ailsa drained the cup and stood. "Finish yaer coffee an' let's find Castillo. We should go over the plan."

◆◆

Castillo stood at the yacht's stern, facing the sky. While the day had dawned bright and rather warm, she eyed the storm trailing them on the western horizon and sensed the turmoil both within it and herself, her thoughts churning like the green wake rolling out behind the boat.

Should we run through the checklist again?

Why? Nothing has changed, nor will it until we gather more information.

Lightning flashed through the distant cloud bank, illuminating the darkness below, despite the bright sun rising behind her.

Why are you really here, Ailsa?

MacGyver. And MacIver.

What a pair. Have you ever seen a more mismatched team?

Once or twice. They get broken up and assigned elsewhere.

Can't do that now.

So then, how to make this work?

Consider them individually.

Ailsa. Razor sharp. Methodical. And monstrously focused.

On finding Hart.

A killer perhaps?

Possible. But not a murderer.

She could have used deadly force against us in Svalbard.

Or against Mac in Grenoble.

But didn't.

So, why does she still scare me?

Been at it alone too long to really see the rest of us, maybe.

And Mac?

A rock. Sure, steady, and used to flying by the seat of his pants.

With a big heart, bless him.

I'd follow him into hell.

But he wants to save everyone.

Which is rarely possible.

And could pull us all off mission.

And run headlong into Ailsa before I can stop it.

Not so bad in France.

But in Algeria? Madre de Dios.

Then best to keep them both so busy they can't collide.

Speak of the devil ...

Castillo turned to see them both approaching, Mac looking

bright as the morning, and Ailsa resembling the vast thunderhead behind.

"Good to go?" she asked. Mac nodded. Ailsa offered more of a shrug as Castillo went straight into command mode. "Okay. We have the general location for the fabricator but haven't nailed it down precisely. We'll have to search through an industrial district that looks more or less abandoned. The best way to determine if a site is in operation is to check their meters. If there's a significant draw on power or even water, that's probably the spot."

"Makes sense," Mac said.

"When we arrive, you'll find us some transportation, Mac. Something official, like a utility truck, or anything we can convert to look like one. Ailsa, I assume you read Arabic?"

"Aye, an' Berber."

"Excellent. I want you digging through public records on the area, particularly police reports, assuming those are available, if not then the newspapers. Look for anything in the last month. I'm betting these mercs kept a low profile, but I don't want to walk into a stakeout. For me, I'm on uniforms, like for gas or electric or phone, it doesn't matter. They only have to pass first glance."

"What happens when we find the place?" Mac asked.

"We'll figure that out when we have it. Anything else?" Both Mac and Ailsa shook their heads. "Good. We make port in about an hour."

"I'll get started from here," Ailsa said, turning to go retrieve her computer. "Assumin', a' course, the captain can get a stable internet connection."

When they were alone Solana turned to Mac. "You two going to be all right working together?"

"I think so. We just kind of collided last time."

"Kind of? You have a gift for understatement, *mi amor*."

"She said the same thing. But I'm glad you're here. For several reasons."

She looked at him without much of an answering grin.

Better be straight with him, she told herself. *He'll find out soon enough anyway.*

"No one knows where I am," she said. "Not even my boss. I'm on vacation."

"Really?"

"We can't afford another incident. Me especially. Agents like you two can get away with all sorts of games. But us mere police are as bound by the law as anyone."

"Copy that, though I doubt I'll be welcome in France anytime soon."

"Probably not," she said. "But they won't be putting cuffs on you, whereas I'd lose my badge and position at the very least."

Mac could only nod. "Understood. But why not get even tacit permission? Someone should know."

"I'm sure my boss has an idea, considering I put in for vacation with less than a day's notice and you two have disappeared along with me. He also said to be careful, so ..." Her voice trailed off as she watched him consider the situation.

"I suppose Hart's crew being American mercenaries helps. The Algerians aren't likely to get too angry," Mac said.

"Possibly. But Algeria isn't exactly a great place to get official help for Interpol. They have their branch of the agency, of course, but local police are hit-or-miss."

"On our own then?"

"Yes, unless you burn down another building."

"It was a tiny fire that consumed itself in three minutes—and the building's still there!"

She smiled, eyes alight. "Uh-huh."

Mac threw his hands up in mock surrender, but clearly enjoyed her teasing all the same.

👓

Once in port, Mac loitered across the street from an electric company dispatch office and watched the western sky. They'd outpaced the slow-moving storm, but it threatened to close in by nightfall at the latest.

The gate was automated, a chain linked rolling affair that slid back to allow access to trucks coming or going.

No guards.

No cameras even.

Probably radio control. Garage door openers.

Slip in?

Hmm. If the driver sees us, it's over. If the gate stood open though ...

Is the gate even latched? Force it?

Don't see one. It's the motor that keeps it shut.

So, just need to deal with the motor while the gate's open.

A monkey wrench in the works?

Done.

He scooped up a few bits of gravel from the street, then popped three sticks of minty gum into his mouth and started chewing. He wandered across the street, talking at random into his phone to no one on the other end. He loitered there, leaning against the wall, nodding affirmatives or negatives in his fake conversation until a truck arrived.

The driver merely glanced at him as the gate slid open and the truck drove through. Quickly, Mac hustled across the street, popped the gum wad from his mouth, stuck it to the gate chain, and affixed the gravel bits to the gum. As the gate closed, the gravel crunched into the main gear and threw the chain clanking to the ground beside the quivering gate, now loose on its track. Mac waited a moment, watching, but no one came out to check. He shoved the gate wide open, and walked in.

A half dozen trucks stood empty, all unlocked. Mac hoped the keys would be in the visors, but no such luck. The models were last decade, though, and hot-wiring was a quick bit of work with his pocketknife.

An overweight man had come out to check the gate and was puzzling over the gummy chain as Mac drove by, throwing his hand up to wave and hide his face as the man returned the wave and went back to the chain.

Mac exhaled, relieved. Ailsa's advice had been right. *"If yae'r somewher' yae ought nae tae be, smile an' wave, especially in passin'. Just be yaer annoyin', cheery self,"* she'd said. *"Most will avoid yae."*

At the hotel, Mac parked the truck away from casual view, and went to the room the three of them shared. Ailsa was within, scanning reports and listening to the police scanner on earbuds.

"Anything?" he asked.

"Nae a word. An' yae?"

"Electric company truck. We should probably scrape off the number or change the plates."

She waved to the bed where a set of corroded plates sat. "Already done. Yaer lady will return soon with our uniforms. Hopefully before evenin' an' this storm."

"I told you; she's not my lady. Not yet anyway."

Ailsa shrugged off the comment. "Whatever. But I doubt she'd risk both career an' credibility for just anyone, dinnae yae think?"

He looked grim. "Yeah. I know her risk here."

"Then it's on us tae do our best."

He was surprised. "Rethinking all that 'I work best alone,' are we?"

"Hardly. But this is my best chance tae get back on Hart's scent. So, I'll take my cues from yaer Spanish beauty. She's got a head for operations an' she's no doubt familiar with yaer flair for chaos, so I imagine she can keep things on track."

Castillo arrived bearing bags. "Mac, you're too tall for your own good," she said, shaking them out on the bed, three brown coveralls and baseball caps. She handed him name patches stenciled in Arabic. "Here. Needle and thread in that bag. Right breast pocket."

"On it."

Ailsa watched them, amused, as Mac set to work sewing. "Now ain't this downright domestic."

Castillo just shot her a no-nonsense look. "What do you have?"

"Not a whisper. The mercs are definitely Black Dawn, American private military contractors. Their reputation is a' the less savory kind, which is sayin' somethin'."

"Hard core then," Castillo answered, absorbing the danger.

"Aye, the worst," said Ailsa.

"Okay," she said. "Initially, our objective is intel. Where are they, how many are there, how are they armed, and so on. Beyond that, we're looking for information on Doctor Verone and on Hart himself, specifically their locations. Anything else is a bonus. Above all, let's avoid hostile contact until we know what we're dealing with."

"Works for me," said Mac, stitching busily.

Ailsa handed them each a USB drive. "On the off chance we get tae one a' their computers, slot this in. Like before, a good count a' fifteen will put my data gathering software on their network. However, they're likely tae have more complete security than a corporate concern. It might be detected at any time from the moment yae plug in."

"Good to know," said Castillo, pocketing hers. "So, we hold off on those unless it's a perfect opportunity."

Thunder rumbled in the distance beyond the open window across the sea. The rain hadn't begun, but the impending deluge dampened the salt air with its fresher scent.

"I just hope we find the place before that hits us," said Castillo.

Mac drove with Castillo beside him while Ailsa applied makeup to her eyes in the back seat. "Makeup?" Mac asked, looking between the women. "We're supposed to be a work crew, no?"

"If we're seen or questioned, I'll handle the talkin'," Ailsa said. "Battin' some eyelashes can give me an edge."

Mac saw Castillo nod, and let it go as she pointed.

"Turn here."

The area was a crumbling industrial district, fallen into disuse for reasons Mac could only imagine. Broken-out windows and open garages gaped at them like holes in a skull, reminding him of a post-apocalyptic zombie movie he'd seen. The area must once have been full of industry and work, given the number of corroding business signs they rolled past. Shipping, manufacturing, scrap, lumber ... Mac shook his head, thinking of the people who no longer worked here.

"This is the area," Castillo announced. "Let's start checking meters." She handed them clipboards and pencils.

Mac told them exactly what to look for, though one didn't need an MIT degree to see an electric meter spinning at full speed versus one immobile or barely crawling. The first couple of alleys showed nothing unusual. The third one caught Castillo's immediate attention. She whistled and waved them over. The meter spun like a music CD.

She was about to say something when a "Hey!" turned their heads towards the alley entrance. The man was dressed in urban fatigues with a submachine gun slung over his shoulder. He approached them cautiously, his weapon still slung, but his eyes suspicious. He looked them over and noted the truck. "What are you all doing here?"

Mac and Castillo looked flatly at each other while Ailsa smiled broadly at him. "Ah, um ... English, yes? I speak some. We, ah ... power company. We to check meters. More ... ah, draw, yes? More draw in grid than should be." She indicated the swiftly spinning meter.

The man eyed the meter, then looked at them. "Oh. Yeah, that's supposed to be taken care of. Nothing you need to worry about."

"Oh, you are opening new business, yes?"

"Uh, yeah," he chuckled. "Something like that."

She turned to Mac and Castillo and said something quickly in Arabic. Mac took up the cue from Castillo and nodded, hoping he looked like he understood.

"Okay," said Ailsa. "Well, we go then. Thank you, ah, Mister ...?"

"Not important," he said. "Just go on about your business, you hear me?"

As they turned away and headed to the truck, he began speaking into his shoulder mic.

"Be nice to know what they're saying," Castillo said.

"Yeah," Mac replied. "You drive. Take your time."

As Castillo pulled them slowly away in the truck, Mac tuned the CB radio to its highest possible frequency, then downward until he had an actual radio station piping in a lively talk show. He pulled out his pocketknife and removed the radio from its brackets, then flipped it over in his lap and began unscrewing the housing to reveal the dusty electronics within. He tapped the various coils until the station fuzzed out. "There we go," he murmured.

With the blade edge, he carefully spread the coils apart, forcing them to receive frequencies outside their usual range. Abruptly, they heard a clipped conversation in English that quickly fuzzed into static.

"That's got it," he said, and used the screwdriver to manually adjust the inner tuning mechanism.

"Bloody cheap radios," Ailsa remarked. "Not even scrambled. I retract what I said about their security bein' competent."

After a moment of tuning, the remaining conversation came through loud and clear.

"—to stop giving me crap. It was just some mooks from the electric company. Should've seen the one I talked to, though. She was hot."

"Great, did you get their truck number?"

"I can't read that scrawly crap they call writing."

The other voice sounded like it was suffering. "Not the company name. The numbers are just like we use, you idiot."

"Hey, you want to come walk the perimeter? It's gonna rain any time now, and I'll be real happy to come sit inside."

A third voice cut in. "Both of you, shut the hell up and stay off comms unless there's an emergency. We're expecting Noah soon. Out."

They all signed off.

"Noah?" Mac said, as the three of them silently shared the question.

●●

Victor Hart scanned the darkened western sky from the tarmac beside his private jet, counting the seconds between each lightning strike and smelling the impending rain in the breeze. He tutted to himself. A severe storm, and exceedingly rare for Algiers in August. "And people like to pretend that climate change is a hoax," he said to his daughter Minerva beside him.

"Here's the car," she said.

"Excellent. I'm curious to see this fabricator for myself. And to determine if our contractors were competent enough to follow my instructions."

"They did obtain the fabricator."

He scoffed. "By simple brute force."

"I wish we hadn't needed them," she said, opening the SUV door for him.

"Well, one cannot foresee every eventuality, particularly with this new MacGyver involved. And perhaps now allied with the dogged Lady MacIver? Quite formidable. I should very much like the chance to speak with them."

CHAPTER 14

EVERY NOW AND THEN, *you're going to lose your cool. Sometimes you're just overloaded and have to step away. Other times, the last straw busts the camel in half, and nothing short of a desk-flipping tirade will calm you down.*

But when agents on a covert operation let things get the better of them, well ... then all bets are decidedly off.

👓

They decided to stash the truck and hole up in a nearby warehouse where Ailsa's computer could still see the mercs' wireless network. Dusk was setting in, made all the darker by the storm whose long, dark clouds now covered the city.

Mac examined the power box outside their building while Castillo and Ailsa surveilled communications and worked on cracking the mercs' network from within.

Mac had thrown the main switch, but no power flowed. He tapped the meter, but it remained obstinately stationary. A corroded padlock secured the breaker box, but a couple of minutes and a little brute force pried it open. "Fuses!" he said, surprised, and most of them were missing. "Just how old is this place?" he muttered as he examined the two still in place. Both had burned through long ago.

Lightning played across the cloudy overhang, and thunder rumbled while he thought.

Simple to bypass.

Saw an abandoned scrapyard a couple of blocks back. Metal aplenty.

That's overkill.

Oh, wait. You stole an electric company truck, dummy.

He shook his head, bemused, and went to the truck.

A few minutes later he had rigged up bypasses with copper wire held in place by electrician's tape. He threw the main switch and the meter began turning. A voltmeter from the truck showed the power draw steady and low.

Low is good. Don't need another fire.

He went inside to find Castillo listening intently to the modified radio and Ailsa working on her laptop.

"Okay, power's on," he said, flipping the lights. They came on steady but flickered as lightning cracked and thunder rolled across the city from the west. "For now, anyway. This place has fuses instead of breakers, would you believe it? It's got to be almost a hundred years old. Find anything?"

Castillo said, "This 'Noah' is clearly a code name, and they hope he's bringing their money. They also talked about having made the delivery, but they have a man watching the machine at all times. It doesn't make sense. Did they deliver it? If so, where? Or is it the thing in the warehouse that they have a man keeping watch on?"

Mac thought a moment. "Maybe Noah is coming to pick it up?"

"Maybe," she said. "Anyway, there are two of them on the perimeter at any given time."

Ailsa grunted. "They need more. We bloody well walked straight up tae the place."

"I don't get the impression they're expecting any trouble. No more mention of us at all."

"Good," Ailsa said. "They've got cameras established inside, an' at least four computers. They're usin' a satellite relay for their network connection."

"How do you know they have cameras?" Mac asked.

Ailsa turned the laptop around and pointed. "Because the absolute geniuses have labeled them Cam1, Cam2, etcetera, on their wireless network. I'm no computer guru, but I know better than tae label each device accordin' tae function. Still no access tae their computers, however, so someone over there is providin' at least semi-competent technical support."

"Can you get past them?" he asked.

She could only shrug. "MI6 makes the best software, but if we want in undetected, it needs time tae work."

"So, what's the ideal here?" Mac asked. "Get into their systems, see what we can find, and then, if there's nothing, we grab one of them for interrogation?"

"Correct, though that will likely mean neutralizing the rest," said Castillo. "You might start thinking of a way to do that."

"Six to ten guys with machine guns, trained to fight. Sure. No problem."

Ailsa's brow knotted. "I cannae tell if yae'r jokin' or not."

"Mild sarcasm," he replied. "I've faced worse, though. But it's not too difficult with the right tools."

"Oh, this I've got tae hear," she said, leaning back.

"Well, you don't attack the men. They've got you outgunned and they're used to fights of that sort. You go around them and attack how they fight. Run them out of ammo, or never present a target, things like that. Or stay hidden ..." He trailed off.

She waited a moment. "... And?"

"Or make it such they can't see you at all. Yeah, that could work. It's only a distraction, though. A big one, but still."

"How long do you need to set that up?" Castillo asked.

"Depends on what's at that scrapyard up the street."

"Go see," she said. "Maybe you can beat the rain."

Thunder pealed outside. No such luck.

The rain began in thick, oily drops that filled the air with a rusty tang from disheveled piles of scrap. Rust didn't matter for what Mac needed. The metal just had to be sturdy.

Pipes. There we go.

No bolts or threading.

Yeah. Need a welder, too.

And a winching system to put it in place.

There's one on the truck.

Right. Handy.

Welder, though ...

This place hasn't been abandoned long.

Let's look in the office.

The place looked like it had been in a war zone, with scattered debris, junk, and signs of a fire, long since quenched. An old mattress and makeshift latrine made Mac think someone had been squatting here in the recent past. He picked up a heavy coat and shook it out. The dust and general mold made him sneeze, but it was thick-lined and sound. It would do.

He found what he needed in the closet-like break room.

Microwave.

Perfect.

Broken.

Well, if it wasn't already it was gonna be soon.

Need wire and rods.

Rods can be anything so long as they're the right gauge to melt, and we've got plenty of scrap to pick through.

We don't need much, either.

Let's haul all this back to the warehouse.

Mac drove the electric truck into the warehouse, wipers flinging water from the windshield, and lightning crashing high above. He began unloading his haul as Castillo closed the garage door. She and Ailsa watched him curiously as he set about dismantling the microwave and tapping the transformer's big coil with a screwdriver to clear any potential charge.

"What's he on about?" Ailsa asked Castillo.

"Could be anything," she said, amused.

"It's nothing too tricky," he said. "Going to blind them, temporarily, anyway."

The laptop pinged. "Got eyes inside!" Ailsa announced.

They gathered around her machine to see panels from six fixed-position cameras arrayed around the interior. Two covered the front and back entrances, one the loading docks, and the other three kept vigil over a large machine attached to a computer terminal. It had a tall upright tank like a water heater, some complicated-looking machinery on racks, and a wide, flat disk attached to piping.

"That's the fabricator all right," said Mac. "Storage tank, collection tank, and centrifuge there. Powered down, looks like."

"Aye, or I'd see it on the network." She tabbed through her readouts and shook her head. "Still no access tae their computer. The feeds we've got are just split from their router. Their security is solid, even if their network is rubbish."

"Sure you can crack it?" Mac asked.

She could only shrug. "I once worked with a man who could make a stock exchange do backflips, but I've nothin' like that level a' skill."

"But we got into the Grenoble system."

"Aye, but that was through a direct upload within the network. We'd need the same here. What I can do is overlay these camera feeds. I can record them, then pipe it back. But that trick only works for so long, and if they're payin' active attention, then nae at all."

"And I'm counting ten of them now," said Castillo, eyeing the camera feeds. "Seven on cameras in the facility, patrolling or off duty, two outside that we know of, and one not on cameras, but on the radio."

"Aye, that'd be their security room. It would be manned at all times."

"Ten guys," Mac said. "And we need access to a computer. Do you need to tune the software on our flash drives for this place?"

"I can prep one, aye."

"Go ahead then," he said, handing his over. "Start recording some fake footage, too. I'll ready my distraction, then make a run at this place."

Castillo's eyes widened. "You're going in there?"

"It's the only way, right? Keep watching and see if you can find me an opening."

She gave him an unreadable look, then went back to monitoring the screen and radio.

Mac went back to the microwave's transformer and wrapped thick wire from the electric truck's stock around the coils. He taped it in place, attached the free end to a rod, and picked it up with a clamp wrench.

"So, what *are* you doing, Mac?" Castillo finally ventured.

He was examining some protective goggles from the truck. "Arc welder. Kind of. It won't be pretty, but it'll get the job done. Just need a welding mask now ..." he said, looking around. He spied a cardboard box full of old junk and took the lid. It was easily big enough to cover his face. He used his pocketknife to whittle it down to size and cut holes for the goggle lenses and straps. He threaded the straps through, which set the goggles in place over the eye holes. He put it on.

"Welding helmet," he said, voice muffled by the box.

"It's quite an improvement," Castillo said with a fetching grin.

"I'm sticking my tongue out at you," he replied, still muffled.

Her smile widened—and became even more fetching.

He slipped off the mask and started laying out his pipes. "You two will want to turn your backs. Whatever you do, don't look at the welding. It can burn holes in your retinas faster than you'd believe."

"We could use that against the bastards," Ailsa said.

"I'm not looking to blind anyone for life."

She scoffed. "Such regard for men who'd gun yae down without so much as a wink."

"I don't have to be like them to beat them," he said, pulling on the heavy coat and zipping it up. He grabbed thick rubber gloves from the truck and the improvised mask. "Okay, here we go."

The women turned their backs as he lined up the first pipes and lowered his mask into place. The first few taps brought blinding arcs from the rod and left melted metal at the junction. He grinned as he welded the pipes together. It was slow, and the beads looked like metallic scabs, but it worked.

When he finished, he gratefully discarded the smelly old coat, now scorched in half a dozen places from sparks, and showed the women his handiwork.

"An' what good is fifteen meters a' pipe goin' tae do for us?" Ailsa asked.

"I'll park the truck in the next alley over from their building and rig it to winch the pipe straight up. With the frequency of lightning above, I bet it gets hit within five minutes. It should blow every fuse in a five-block radius."

Ailsa's mouth nearly fell open. "Are yae completely mental? We're to rely on lightnin' for the distraction? An' what about this place? Yae said we're runnin' a fire hazard with yaer jury rig."

"I'll show you the switch to kill the power here. Just hit it before winching the pipe up. Believe me, it'll be fine."

"If Mac says it'll work, then I'm in," Castillo said, looking at Ailsa. "When do we raise it?"

"If the fake footage is ready, and you can see me on the cameras, then we're good to go. I'll give you the signal once I've got a hiding spot." He examined the feeds. "Probably there behind those containers. That guy playing a game on his laptop in the break area is where I'll slot in. Then I'll hoof it for the exit."

"What about this Noah?" Ailsa asked. "An' how will yae see when the lights are out?"

"I'll be expecting the power to go out and can use my phone light. As for Noah, what about him? Unless he's got superpowers, he won't see in the dark any better than them. And since lightning killed their power they shouldn't think they're under attack. I'll be out before they get it back on, and we should get eyes on this guy."

Ailsa was looking pained, but Castillo was still nodding. "It's as good as anything else we've got. Let's get it ready."

Ailsa listened to Mac's instructions on the winch out in the rain, punctuated at quick intervals by lightning and thunder shredding the sky. Finally, she'd had enough. "Aye, I know how tae operate a winch, yae know."

"Okay, just raise it fast. The jack I rigged up as the anchor will hold, and the guy lines will keep it steady. You don't want to be anywhere near it when the lightning strikes."

"Yae think, do yae?"

"Okay. Good luck."

"Save it. Yae need it more than I do."

He flashed a quick grin and jogged off.

She watched him a moment, gave the winch one last glance, then stalked back around the corner into their own building.

"He's completely nutters," she told Castillo, brushing water off her coveralls and shaking out her cap.

"Yes, but it's a nutters that works more often than not," Castillo said. Her eyes hadn't moved from the cameras, nor her ears from the radio, though now she glanced at Ailsa, situating herself in front of her computer and checking her gun. "Could I ask you something personal?"

Ailsa cleared the chamber and ejected the magazine for inspection. "Cannae stop yae from askin'.'"

"What makes a Scottish aristocrat seek a career in intelligence?"

Ailsa thumbed rounds from the magazine. "It's hardly rare for the aristocracy tae have work in this day an' age. It's nae as though we sit about sippin' tea an' watchin' the peasants till soil. Although my mother wishes it were, for all love."

"I know, but I suppose it's more a question of why it interested you. You could have done anything. Why this?"

Ailsa tested the magazine's spring with a critical eye. "I could ask yae the same."

Castillo smiled. "Guess I just hate seeing criminals succeed and get away with it. Plain and simple."

"That sounds like a story," Ailsa said, inserting rounds back into the magazine.

Castillo's smile narrowed. "It might be, if we were talking about me and not you. But points for the deflection."

"Part trainin', an' part growin' up with a grand inquisitor."

"Your parents?"

"My mother, the Dowager Countess MacIver, as she prefers tae be known." Ailsa slid the magazine home and chambered a round. She looked at Castillo straight. "Yae know my father worked for MI6 as well, eh? It got him killed, an' they never caught the man. His work always interested me, an' it turns out I've a talent for it. Does that sate yaer persistent curiosity, Agent Castillo?"

"Sorry," Castillo said with a shrug. "I just like to know who I'm working with, as a person, I mean. It sometimes tells me how committed you are to the chase."

"As I've said, repeatedly, I work best alone. When I have more tae worry about than just meself, it's difficult tae seize the initiative as events unfold. If Hart weren't involved, or if I'd had any kind a' lead, I'd have departed some time ago. The man is a blight on the Earth, an' I'll see him ended one way or another."

Castillo's smile had faded as Ailsa spoke. "Ended? We're catching him, not executing him."

Ailsa said nothing, and a moment later Castillo's phone dinged.

"It's Mac. He says to start the false feed now. He's going in one minute."

Ailsa went to her computer and established the connection. "Starting feed." The camera panels on her right began displaying the last twenty minutes of footage. The ones on the left were the true feed where they saw Mac slip in through the back door and stash himself behind some crates, in full view of the camera, but hidden from the room.

"I wish we had voice comms," Castillo muttered.

"Phones are too risky, an' I dinnae have any earwigs. Dinnae need them, workin' alone." Ailsa watched the cameras like a tiger lying in ambush, eyes everywhere, drawn to any movement.

Mac spotted the camera and gave the signal.

"I'll be back," Ailsa said as she holstered her weapon and dashed out into the thundering rain.

Killing their building's power was as easy as throwing a heavy lever. The winch gave her no trouble, as the breeze was only slight. The rain came down straight and warm, as if from an overhead shower. The solid metal pole raised into the dark sky. The tiny hairs on her neck prickled as thunder rumbled like an angry beast above, just waiting for the pole to reach a critical height.

At nearly vertical, she gratefully killed the winch and fled from the area of imminent impact. Inside, she quickly shook off the rain. "Anythin'?" she called.

Castillo shook her head, illuminated by the screens. "He's still hiding. There's a merc in the room, but he hasn't wandered Mac's way."

For several minutes Mac stayed put as a soldier walked past the back door and lingered in the room. The soldier's radio spoke at the same time as Castillo's. "Noah arriving. Everyone to the front, repeat, to the front. Out."

Ailsa and Castillo traded a glance. They saw Mac lean his head out and watch the soldier stride away. He slipped from behind the crates to an interior door and inside to the break room where he slotted the flash drive into the laptop there.

"We've got it," Ailsa said, as her cracking software popped up an alert. She ran through the network from the inside and found several cell phones. "An' now ..." she said, entering commands, "we have ears from their own phones."

"Oh, damn." Castillo pointed. A guard had just positioned himself by the back door. Inside the break room, Mac removed the drive, went to the door, and peered out. He spied the guard and quickly shut himself back in. He grimaced at the camera and began poking around through the drawers and shelves.

"Where is that damned lightning?" Castillo muttered. Outside, the storm raged above the taunting rod but refused to take the bait.

"I think I have the commander's phone," Ailsa said, clicking the mouse.

"—hate this dog and pony show he wants every time he comes down from Ararat," they heard.

Ailsa pointed to the group's leader, an older man in a beret on the camera covering the open warehouse door. Most of the mercs had lined up at attention, and the commander took his place, still talking to the lieutenant. "We'd better get our bonus for this, after all that hassle. Dirty work on the Turkish border is one thing, France is another."

"Yes, sir."

"And then all these extra instructions ... We're soldiers, not engineers. He'd better like it."

"He did want to inspect our work. Or that's what his assistant said, sir."

"That the blonde he rides around with? Nice to be rich."

"I believe it's his daughter, sir."

"Well, she ain't *my* daughter."

They stifled their chuckles and drew to attention as a black SUV rolled into the warehouse. The driver leaped out and circled to get the door for his employer. Ailsa sucked in a breath as an electric jolt hit her spine. "Hart!"

"Hart is Noah?" Castillo said. "I was expecting a lieutenant or operative. And what is 'Ararat,' other than the biblical reference?"

Ailsa put it together. "Code name, certainly. The workin' theory is some sort a' sanctuary, no? Could be that."

"Could be," Castillo said. "And that's his daughter?" She pointed to a tall, slender blonde in an immaculate suit getting out behind him.

"Aye. Minerva Hart. She's his right hand, essentially. They've had close ties since her mother died." A brief memory flitted through her mind. She brushed the bitter thing away. "We can get him! Right here an' now," she said.

"What?" Castillo looked like she'd been slapped. "Are you

insane? It's the same problem as before, ten trained mercenaries, plus now two more bodyguards, plus whatever his daughter can do."

Ailsa scoffed. "She's no more a combatant than he is."

"Quiet. What are they saying?"

The trio had moved to inspect the fabricator. Hart was examining it, comparing it to images on a tablet. "Yes, that's fine work, Colonel."

"Thank you, sir."

"Well, I'd say you've earned your bonus, but we need to speak privately a moment."

The Colonel motioned for him to follow, and they walked off-camera.

On Mac's camera they could see he'd quietly flipped over a breakroom table and was unscrewing a leg with his pocketknife to arm himself with something.

Ailsa watched him half a moment, then dismissed him with a shake of her head. "Listen, lass," she said to Castillo, "it can be done. I'll lay an ambush for when the lightnin' strikes. We can do it!"

"*No! Absolutely, no!* We stick to the plan, wait for Mac, and then *maybe* we can do something about Hart."

Ailsa felt her temper rising. "I'll nae let him escape yet again!"

"You've let him slip before. In Barcelona you were within five meters of him."

"He was prepared then, an' he's nae now!"

"He has us outmanned and outgunned. That's pretty damned prepared!"

"He's vulnerable!"

"*I said no!*"

Just then an immense crack of lightning lit the windows and roared like a thunder god as it struck the makeshift tower, causing even the unplugged laptops to flicker and reset in the static burst that filled the air.

Ailsa broke for the door, ignoring Castillo's calls to stop. It was now or never.

Mac had the heavy table leg in hand, ready to wield it, when the lightning struck and darkness fell like a curtain. "Finally," he muttered, and flipped his phone light on. He opened the door and shined it in the guard's face, not six strides away.

"Hey, what the hell was that?" he called in a gruff voice.

"Lightning, dumbass. And get that outta my face. Hey, you're not—*ugh!*"

Mac swung the leg hard into his gut, then chopped it down on the back of his neck. The merc collapsed like a bag of bricks. Mac tossed aside the leg and opened the door to slip out into the rain when shots rang out from the front. He whipped his head around and stood there, uncertain. The gunfire was answered with angry shouts and return bursts from automatic weapons, quite a few of them.

It's got to be the ladies.

But why?

They must have seen something—and were trying to help.

But they started shooting after *the lightning.*

Now what?

He thought another half moment, then rushed into the storm. He jogged around the building. Intermittent gunfire echoed off the concrete walls, a few single shots, but mostly the barking staccato of three-round bursts.

He poked his head around the corner to see Ailsa in cover behind a derelict truck, firing into the open warehouse, then dropping back as the mercs returned fire. She didn't see the two hustling from the other side of the building to cross the street and flank her.

Oh, hell!

A loud *clack-clack* from a gun slide ratcheted behind him. "Don't move! Hands high! *Now!*"

Mac expelled a deep sigh and raised his hands. A moment later he saw Ailsa take careful aim for one final shot, then throw down her gun, hands up. The siege was over before it had begun.

CHAPTER 15

Mac and Ailsa were on their knees beside the black SUV, hands zip-tied behind them, still dripping rainwater, when the mercs hauled in a half-drowned Castillo to a peal of thunder outside. She must have led them on quite a chase.

They forced her down beside the two of them while four guards looked on. The power flickered back on and Mac squinted in the sudden light. Ailsa had shot out a tire on the SUV, which the bodyguards labored to change. She avoided both Mac's and Castillo's eyes. It was clear to Mac that she knew how badly this had gone sideways.

Okay, so what do we do?

Zip ties. Easy to break if they're in front of us.

Yeah, well, they're not.

I'd kill for a paperclip about now.

His thoughts broke off at approaching footsteps echoing on the concrete floor. Victor Hart, his daughter, and the stone-faced Colonel came to a stop before them.

"Ah, the MacGyvers, plural at last," Hart said, amused. "I expected you'd find this place, but once more you've impressed me with your celerity. That said, I do hope you had more in mind than simply shooting out my tires and laying a three-man siege."

No one responded, which made him chuckle. He gave a slight

bow to Ailsa. "Lady MacIver, a pleasure, as always. How is your dear mother?"

Ailsa's voice dripped venom. "Dinnae yae dare play courtly graces with me, bastard."

"As you wish, milady." He moved in front of Castillo. "You must be Agent Castillo. I regret we couldn't meet under better circumstances. I must salute your talents. Your investigation has been most perceptive, at times bordering on the precognitive. I predict a brilliant career ahead of you, if you can relinquish the particular obsession of bringing me to justice."

"Maybe if you'd tell me why you're doing all of this, I can contemplate shuffling you to the bottom of my case load."

He grinned. "I think you might, actually, but I'm afraid gloating isn't something I indulge in, nor is revealing my ultimate purpose."

"You could've fooled me."

He laughed. "You are a delight, madam. Ah, and now we come to our newest player, Mr. Angus MacGyver of the American intelligence services. Did you know you're something of a spectre in our little community? A ghost, albeit with a fearsome reputation."

"Good to know you're shaking even with me like this."

Hart spread his hands. "Ups and downs, sir, ups and downs. Treat every failure as a learning experience, and you'll never be defeated for long."

The Colonel had been fidgeting, growing noticeably more impatient. He stepped forward. "How many more of you are out there?"

No one answered.

The Colonel backhanded Mac hard across the face. "Talk!"

The blow rattled Mac's brain in his skull, but he'd had worse. "Okay, there's a CIA tactical team circling the place right now. If you surrender to us, no one needs to get hurt."

The Colonel looked at him a moment, then laughed. "Nice try. Maybe the ladies will be more cooperative," he said, moving in front of Ailsa.

"Colonel," Hart said, "I'd appreciate it if you'd refrain from damaging my guests. They've a long journey ahead of them."

The Colonel rounded on him. *"Your* guests? I don't think so, *Noah.* You canceled our contract just ten minutes ago, even after we built that mockup in there and loaded the real thing on your boat."

At that, Mac and Castillo traded a glance, trying not to feel as wet and tired as they were.

The Colonel wasn't done. "They assaulted our base, shot at my men. That makes them mine." He drew his pistol and racked the slide. He pointed it at Ailsa's face. "This is all of them, and I don't want any reports about this *anywhere.* No loose ends."

Hart looked from the gun to Ailsa and then the Colonel. "Very well, but you're throwing away a fortune. I'll pay you one million for each of them."

The Colonel lowered the weapon and said dryly, "Our contract was worth three times that."

"Very well, three times that for all three. Or we can make it an even ten million if you'd prefer?"

The Colonel stared at him a moment, then narrowed his eyes. "If they mean that much to you, then re-up our contract for the Turkey job."

Hart's pleasant demeanor hardened. "I think not. Your careless-ness in France drew too much attention. How else do you think these three mobilized so quickly?"

"That was *your* plan in Grenoble, remember?"

Hart shook his head. "Which would have gone smoothly had you not upset the timetable with your impatience, Colonel. No, I cannot take such chances. Our association is at an end."

The Colonel shrugged and put the gun back on Ailsa. "Then so are they."

"An interesting bargaining technique, Colonel, threatening to kill people who may be troublesome to me but are hardly a serious impediment. Very well, I concede the point. They're yours to do with as you please."

"As if you had a choice."

Hart flashed a tight-lipped smile. *"Hmm.* But before you do any irreparable harm, be aware that you have in your hands three people worth considerable value. No doubt you heard my greeting to young Ailsa here. She is indeed Lady MacIver, Countess of MacIver House, Scotland. She's worth a considerable fortune, far more than even my elevated offer. This is Agent Solana Castillo of Interpol, also heiress to the Castillo clothiers of Spain. You may not have heard of them, but I assure you, ten million is a fraction of what her father might pay for her safe return.

"And finally, there is Mister MacGyver, as I said of the American intelligence services, meaning everything from FBI to CIA and all points in between. While it's not their policy to negotiate for captured agents, consider the gains in catch-and-release. You become known as the man who bested MacGyver, and the Americans have no retributive axe to grind. Of course, if you'd rather execute them, then I imagine the allied forces of Interpol, MI6, and the CIA will make it a priority to hunt you all down and exact vengeance with, I believe the term is 'extreme prejudice,' is it not?"

While he spoke, the Colonel's gun had lowered. Now he looked at Ailsa speculatively. "Any of that true?"

"It's just ... rot an' nonsense," she said, so unconvincingly that Mac almost laughed.

The Colonel sneered at his three captives, weighing his options, as Hart continued.

"I can give you contact information for Lady MacIver's estate, if you'd like," Hart said. "Consider it severance pay."

"Dinnae yae dare!" Ailsa shouted.

Hart merely grinned and motioned for his assistant's phone. "There," he said, hitting SEND. "Check your phone, Colonel. And now, I believe we'll take our leave. Agent Castillo. Lady MacIver. And Angus. Best of luck to you."

They watched the SUV roll out into the flickering storm. "Stay here," the Colonel ordered a merc. "Watch them. I'm going to check this out. If it's crap, we finish it. Algiers won't care about three extra bodies."

The merc nodded, the same one they'd first run into in the alley before the storm.

The Colonel dismissed the other men and marched off for his office.

Mac's head started again.

What was Hart doing?

All that stuff about Solana is nonsense.

Saving us? Buying us time?

Think about it later. Get out now.

Legs are free, and the door isn't locked.

Just have to deal with the armed guard.

First things first: Zip tie.

Easy to break with the right angle.

Not from behind our backs, it isn't ...

While he debated the possibilities, the guard watched them, hands resting on the submachine gun slung loosely over his shoulder as his eyes couldn't help but linger on Ailsa. The ties held their arms pinned flat behind their backs, which had the effect of thrusting her chest out. She noticed his gaze and taunted him. "Enjoyin' the view, are yae, laddie?"

He smirked. "What if I am?"

"Then I'd say yae'v got good taste—for a cheap thug, at least."

He moved over to stand before her. "I'm not cheap, sweetheart. And I've got way too much combat under my belt to be a thug."

"Oh, so yae'r a professional, are yae? But we compromised yaer network with barely an effort, so yae can't be much a' one now, can yae, for all yaer *experience.*"

He crouched down right in front of her. "What happened to your cute Arab accent?"

"Dinnae like the real thing, then?"

"I dunno. It was kinda ... exotic."

She gave a smiling laugh. "An' Scottish is'nae? Yae must get around then for a simple Yank with a gun."

"I get around plenty. Enough to know hostages try to improve their odds by getting personal with their captors."

She made her exasperation plain. "I'm just pissed an' scared, soldier. Jabbing's just a way tae keep me from bawlin' like a babe at the thought a' what might happen next. But if this is goin' tae be the end a' it, would yae mind if I sit on my arse? This concrete is diggin' into my knees somethin' dreadful."

He looked her over again, enjoying his dominance. "Sure. Just slowly, and don't stand up."

She rolled to her side, slid her legs out, stretched like a cat, then rolled back onto her butt. "Aye, much better. Yae have my thanks."

"Don't mention it."

When she'd rolled, she'd moved off to her right. The guard, still crouched in front of her, had turned with her movement, and now had his back angled towards Mac and Castillo.

Mac caught Castillo giving him a look as she twisted to show her ties. She flexed her wrist, indicating her watchband. A small silver paperclip was attached.

Mac's expression changed to one of pure adoration.

As Ailsa kept talking and stretching her legs to keep the merc engaged, Castillo rotated quietly just enough to offer her pinioned wrists to Mac's back. By feel he found the paper clip and felt for the clasp on the zip tie that bound her. He carefully found the locking bar and used the paperclip as a shim to lever it away from the teeth. All the while he stared at the guard, thoroughly entranced by Ailsa as she nattered away in a mix of light condescension and flirty banter, even spreading her legs wide at times to ensure the man's full attention.

Finally, Castillo's bonds slid free. And, in a single instant, she leapt at the guard, grabbing his gun strap, yanking it around behind him and up tight on his neck. He flailed as the gun came up hard against his throat, choking off any chance of crying out—as Ailsa sprang to her feet, delivered a smashing kick to his diaphragm, and then a roundhouse foot to his temple. The merc sank to the ground in a camo'd pile.

"About bloody time," she said as Castillo used the guard's combat knife to cut her ties. "I thought the radge was goin' tae kiss me."

They freed Mac. "He sure bought what you were selling."

"Hormonal stupidity at its finest," she nodded, seizing the man's weapon. "We can still get Hart. He's alone now, an' we're armed."

"That Colonel said they put the real fabricator on a ship, so—"

"The harbor," Ailsa said, yanking the door open as the trio fled into the rain.

Mac's lightning rod had fried the electric company truck, so he hot-wired one of the mercs' jeeps while Castillo retrieved their gear and Ailsa put the knife to the tires of their remaining vehicle. They drove in silence through the slacking rain with Ailsa poring through the data dump from the mercs' computers.

But navigating Algiers proved significantly more difficult without their phones, even with Mac's natural sense of direction. By the time they found pier twelve, the rain had cleared and a brightly lit cargo ship was already pulling away from the dock. A man stood at the stern, watching.

Hart.

Seeing them jump from the jeep on the pier, he gave them a cheery wave and a thumbs up, as if expecting them, and then turned and went below.

"We can still get him—" Ailsa hissed.

"How?" Castillo demanded. "We have no contact to anyone. Hell, it will be difficult enough getting *us* out of the country."

"I'll find an open wireless connection or hijack the harbormaster's network. I'm nae lettin' the bastard just sail away!"

Castillo was unmoved. "The only people that could legally detain him would be the Algerians, and I'm here unofficially. I'd have to explain everything, convince them to get a judge's order, then muster their coast guard to detain the ship, all before it hits the three-mile limit, and they're underway already."

"Navy then, surely Spain—"

"No! Seizing a vessel of Turkish registry in international waters by an Armada vessel would be an act of war! You should know that. You were in the Royal Navy, right?"

"Then we'll steal a boat! Board them ourselves!"

"Piracy, then? I don't know if Turkish law allows deadly force in repelling pirates, but the Med is a great place to dump three bodies, no questions asked."

Mac just watched, knowing Castillo was right, as Ailsa twisted and snarled like a tiger in a snare: fierce and livid that its power and mastery of the kill were all useless to it now. But where he'd been the target of that fury in Grenoble, this time she directed it inward. She'd screwed up, and she knew it. Mac could sympathize.

"I say we look for a charter willing to take us back," he offered. "You've got a lot of data from their computers now. Let's go through it and find another thread. The mercs seemed to know a lot about his next operation, so there should be something there. And you can bet they'll be coming for us soon enough in this city either way."

Ailsa looked from Castillo to Mac and back. She cursed, shoved her knapsack into MacGyver's chest, and stalked back to the jeep.

Mac and Solana shared a resigned and knowing look before she said, "There's more to this than just her dogged pursuit. I don't know what her plan was, but her opening shots weren't to disable his vehicle. That was only the last shot when she knew the game was up. I saw it."

"So, she's got a target painted on Hart," Mac replied, nodding.

"Maybe MI6 and the CIA can get away with termination, but that's not in my package."

"Mine either, you know that. But I still feel we all stand a better chance of catching Hart and retrieving Verone if we work together."

"Don't tell me. Tell her!" Solana said. "Any time Hart gets within a half a mile, she goes *insano*. Which makes her unpredictable and unreliable, and that's not good."

Mac couldn't argue with that but did anyway. "I'm unpredictable, or so you've told me more than once, no?"

"Not the same. At all. Your kind of unpredictability doesn't get everyone captured at gunpoint ... Not usually, anyway."

"Okay. But we're still here. Thanks in part to Hart and all that stuff about you being an heiress?"

She shook her head. "He'd done his homework, and clearly knew about my father's job, but making millions? *Pfft.* The company he worked for stole most of his designs, all nice and legal. Surely, Hart would've known that."

"But the mercs didn't, and that's the point. He laid it on thick and bought us time."

Her lips soured. "I'll be sure to buy him a drink after I cuff him."

"But why do that at all?"

She thought a moment, pacing and keeping an eye out for the mercs before a thought struck. "All right, so what's the only thing the three of us have worked on together?"

"Hart."

"Right. We wind up dead or missing and suddenly he gets a lot more interesting. He wasn't lying about the American intel community and you; they've got a long reach and a longer memory."

"Maybe. But he wanted to take us for himself. He only spun all that after the Colonel turned down his offer to buy us."

"The mercs would brag. Hart is much more discreet. And I don't really see him as a blood-for-fun kind of killer, whatever Lady MacIver says."

"Agreed. He was firing those mercs after all their shooting in Grenoble."

"Exactly."

They grew silent for a beat, standing there in the mist, as Mac tried to ease all the tension and adrenaline. "Good thinking with the paperclip, by the way," he said.

She nodded with a half-smile. "I figured they'd have searched you. Did they get your pocketknife?"

"Yeah. No big deal. It's far from the first one I've replaced. But I've got to remember that paperclip on the watchband thing. When did that hit you?"

"When I heard they'd caught you on the radio. I stashed our stuff and got myself captured."

Mac eyed her, surprised. "You did that for us?"

"You'd do it for me."

"I suppose, but ... *mucho gracias* just the same. And I'm sure Ailsa will thank you, too, once she cools off."

Castillo shrugged as they turned and started back towards the jeep. "It shouldn't have been necessary."

"Hey, at least she helped get us out. She had that guy wrapped around her finger in no time."

"Yeah, she's a pro at that, all right. Much better than me."

"Aw, c'mon, you can totally do the pretty girl thing."

She shook her head. "Not like that. Believe me, cat and mouse with a gun to your head is far more involved when batting your eyelashes. That takes training. But we can't have any more stunts like tonight. Or I'll toss her ass in a cell myself."

"Fair enough. Lemme talk to her. I want to know why she's so gung ho. And what the deal was with that final shot."

They broke off the conversation as they reached the jeep with Ailsa, stewing in a stony silence in the rear seat, before they jumped in and disappeared off down the pier towards the smaller boats.

CHAPTER 16

PEOPLE SCREW UP. *I know because I screw up all the time. For every instance someone's said, "Mac sure came through for us," there've been ten where I was running like a rabbit, scrambling to escape, or just plain got caught.*

It's vital to know what went wrong—to avoid it the next time if you can help it. But it's even more important to give yourself a break. Beating yourself up over something that's already happened, well, that's just a waste of time and energy.

Ailsa hated her old school uniform, the white shirt and sweater and plaid skirt. At least she could wear her hair long while away from mother at boarding school, her first stirrings of independence coming early at age ten.

The headmistress walked her to the office to receive a phone call. Her face split in a gap-toothed grin when she heard her father's voice on the line congratulating her for earning the lead in the school play. She would be Tom Sawyer, and he hoped she'd practiced the accent. He promised he'd be there for at least one performance. Only his duty could keep him away, and he hoped she was old enough to under-

stand. Of course she was! If he missed all the plays, she'd give a solo performance at home.

A strange scent tickled her nose as she talked, then itching as the poignant smell grew. Gun smoke? She sneezed, excused herself, then stared at the smoking gun in her hand. She shrieked as it grew red-hot and seared her skin.

👓

Ailsa woke, bolt upright and sweating in her hammock, swaying with the Mediterranean swells. She grabbed her face, forcing herself to calm down. "Ev'ry time. Ev'ry Goddamned time," she whispered to no one. Then, to a soft knock on the cabin door, she said louder, "What?"

"It's Mac."

She took a long breath. "Come."

He peered in around the open door, the bright morning blinding in the small, dark space. "Making port in about forty minutes. You okay?"

She grumbled. "Fine. Just had trouble gettin' tae sleep. Unlike yae, I'm sure."

"Guilty as charged. So, was it the hammock or the boat? 'Cause Castillo said you were Royal Navy once, yeah?"

"Well, we dinnae use hammocks anymore."

"Right. Well, I should—" he said, starting to back out.

"No. Come in, for a moment, if yae would."

He stepped in and closed the door, then stood waiting.

She took another breath. "Listen. I want tae thank yae for nae goin' on about back there, even if I deserve it."

He shrugged. "We all made it out in one piece. And got the data dump."

"Aye, but we could'hae had him."

"Maybe. But that assumes your plan was to capture Hart."

She looked at him sharply. "Come again?"

"I saw you shoot the tire out, but that was your last shot. You used a full magazine before taking that one. Care to tell me why?"

Ailsa had incredible control over her physiological reactions, but still his question brought heat to her cheeks. "Suppression fire. I had tae take them by surprise."

"And then what?"

"I ... had hoped Castillo was behind me, an' that yae'd hear the shots an' assist."

Mac eyed her for a long beat, nodding as if to accept her story, but the pause spoke volumes.

"Right. Well, I've got coffee on, nice and strong." He opened the door and turned to go.

Her exasperation bled through. "Do yae *never* get angry? About anythin'?"

He closed it and turned back. "Everyone gets angry. But what's that going to get us here?"

"A little payback, for one. I gave yae what-for aplenty at Grenoble. If yae want tae hand it back, today's the day."

"Not really my style," he said. "But maybe now you know a little better why I'm not so keen on guns."

"Meaning what?"

"Meaning, if you hadn't had the gun, how would you have gone about catching Hart?"

She thought a moment before admitting, "I cannae say now."

"Exactly. The gun lets your emotions take over. Without it, you have to stop and think."

She sighed, exhausted, if not contrite. "Point taken. But I should'nae have flown off as I did."

"I won't argue with that, but mistakes happen. Things go wrong. How can they not? Like at Grenoble," he said with a tight grin. "But even there, we got the data and survived, which is always job one. And here ...? Well, you played that soldier guarding us like a violin."

She scoffed. "His bloody hormones betrayed him. I can see why they're a cut-rate company."

"Maybe. But Solana's not sure she could've made that happen, and you made it look easy, so don't sell yourself short."

She regarded him, head cocked. "Yae'r an odd one, Mac. Here I lay out my confession an' ask for penance, an' nae only do yae forgive without a second thought but offer me kudos tae boot."

Mac just smiled and opened his hands with a shrug. "What can I tell you? Must be the Angus in me. So, coffee?"

"Let me put meself together an' check the computer. It may be done siftin' all that rubbish."

It hadn't finished by the time they made port in Barcelona. Castillo got them hotel rooms, seeing little point in returning to Madrid, as she was still "on vacation," and had nothing official to report to her superiors.

MacGyver, however, wasn't so fortunate.

"*Sonovabitch, MacGyver!*" Boone's bellow was right on cue, which was why Mac was holding the handset on the hotel phone away from his ear.

"You lost your goddamn phone? The one with access to classified data?"

"I already sent it the brick command," Mac replied, just pulling the mic end of the phone to his face. "It's a paperweight now. I'll buy you a new one."

"Screw the phone! You blew yet another encounter and *still have no lead on Verone!*"

A familiar headache was beginning to stir across Mac's temples. "You're missing the obvious, Boone; Hart *wants* this game with us. He's sure he's got control. But he can't dodge us forever. We've got a lot more data to sift. We'll get something."

"So you keep telling me. But I'm not interested in your games. And I'm tempted to go on a little 'vacation' myself just to keep actual tabs on you."

Mac's patience wasn't infinite. "Be my guest," he said, hoping the offer would be enough to hold him off. "But if you don't have anything new for me, then I'm done with my sitrep."

Boone's tone changed to matter-of-fact. "I do have something new for you: the CIA is currently opting not to renew your contract and will recommend to the DIA to suspend your clearance across the board, making it impossible for you to work for law enforcement, and make you toxic for any government-sponsored think tanks or research divisions. You've got about two weeks left. How's that for new?"

Mac felt a sting in his gut now, too, which is exactly what Boone was after. But part of him almost welcomed the threat as he calmly offered, "Nothing lasts forever. You all do what you think is best."

Realizing he wasn't getting the rise out of Mac he was hoping for, Boone just shot back, "Find Verone. Soon. It's the only chance you've got." The call ended.

Mac sat there listening to silence until the busy tone began. He set it back in its cradle and lay back on the bed, trying to ease the headache with visions of he and Solana, on a beach ... *anywhere*.

👓

Mac found her in her room, in a hotel robe, having just showered, restraining himself from a wistful sigh. "How's it going?" he asked.

She shrugged. "Kind of nice not having the phone. Though I keep itching to check my email."

"You might be better off." He told her about the call with Boone. "Thing is, right now I'm not sure I even care."

"That's not true, Mac. 'Cause you know Boone's main concern is ... Boone. If anyone's more concerned with finding Verone and getting Hart, it's you."

"Fair enough," he said, dropping himself into a stuffed chair as he watched her work her hair dry with a towel. "But it put that talk we had heading up to Oslo in a sharper light for sure. Say we find Verone, and catch Hart, and return everything he's stolen. Then what? I fly off to another part of the planet while the Boones of the world grind their axes and wait for a chance to chop my head off? I'm having trouble seeing the point."

She sat on the ottoman beside the chair and took his hand. "You'll give Verone his life back. And keep Hart from victimizing anyone else. That's the only point now. Screw Boone. But you can't fix the world, Mac, no matter how clever you are."

He smiled, feeling drained, but squeezed her hand. "Copy that. But the clock's ticking louder now. And not just on this. I'll be fifty before you know it."

"You don't look it," she said in that flirty way that made him want her all the more.

"But I sure as hell feel it."

"And I'm sure, once we're through this, there are ways we could change that, no?" She had that Mona Lisa non-smile on her face again, saying everything he wanted to hear without a word, when a knock came on the door and they both released the moment, for now anyway, as she rose to answer it.

Ailsa blew in, oblivious to all the pheromones floating around the room. "Aye, good, yae'r both here," she said, handing bags to each of them. "Presents, an' penance: that we may never discuss my dreadful lapse in Algiers again."

Each bag had a new phone and an earwig. Castillo's had a .45, similar to the one that had been taken, and Mac's had two pocketknives, one Swiss Army knife like his old one, and another slimmer version. "Yae can sew that into yaer jacket linin' or elsewhere for emergencies. Should pass a pat-down easy enough."

Mac examined the offerings. "Thanks, Ailsa. Seriously."

"This is a beauty," Castillo said, checking the weapon with expert hands.

Ailsa gave a nod. "It's also untraceable, so dinnae mention it. Earwigs would'hae been right useful last run if we'd had time tae get them. They work through the phone, so keep it within fifty feet."

Castillo turned to look at the phone, impressed. "Decryption software, force pairing, security lockdown ... even better than the last one."

"MI6 does'nae spare expense, an' we may need all a' it."

"You've got something?" Mac said.

"Aye, though it means Castillo's vacation is over."

Later, in Ailsa's room, she turned her laptop around to show them the Middle Eastern man on the screen, late thirties in a spotless white suit as if to make him look more handsome and dashing than he really was. "This is Bilal Demir, known as 'Hayal' in the international smugglin' community. It means 'shadow' or 'illusion' in Turkish, which speaks volumes for his imagination. But there's nothin' cliché about his capabilities. Lately, his organization in Gaziantep has been supplyin' both sides a' the Syrian civil war just across the border. So, he's nae friend to NATO or Russia."

"Wait," said Mac. "You know who he is, where he is, and he's got no affiliation, but he's still free to operate?"

"It's the money," Castillo said, eyes dark. "As always. It's more than just being paid up with the right people, though. He's been on Interpol's radar for years, but our hands are tied."

"He's the soul a' discretion, that one," said Ailsa. "Knows whom tae pay, how much, an' stays afloat by dancin' on the blade's edge between East an' West."

Mac nodded, glumly. "Right, so how's he connected to Hart?"

"One a' Hart's earliest an' most profitable businesses was smugglin' arms. His shippin' concerns make it child's play tae buy in America an' move them anywhere people are fightin'. He does'nae care one whit about the morality on either side. If yae'v got the coin, he's got yaer weapons. This Turkish operation the mercs were on about is a large shipment intended for Demir."

"And where do the guns go from there?"

"The files dinnae say, but that's irrelevant. We're goin' tae follow the money."

"Another computer thing?" Mac asked. "Slip your software into his system and watch the transfers?"

"Nay, he uses actual cash. Part a' Hayal's security comes from absolute insistence on dealin' in cash. US currency, to be specific, whether payin' or receivin'. He'll pay Hart's representative in bulk, an' we'll follow that bag. This deal is for five million, which Demir will turn into twenty or more when he sells them across the border." She held up a tiny tracer, the size of a coat button. "The ultimate goal is tae find one a' Hart's many front businesses wher' he launders large payments a' this type. The places are often quite clean in themselves, but I've had success snappin' up threads on him in this manner before. An', on occasion, Hart himself makes an appearance, an' we may be so fortunate here."

"Only if our luck changes," Mac said. "But I'm guessing this Demir won't let us just bug the cash."

"Nay. As I say, he's cautious, paranoid tae the point a' immobility, in fact. He distrusts technology, carries no cell phone, an' has minimal staff made up a' people he knows personally. He'll pass on a deal if he smells a whiff a' trouble about it. We're goin' tae give him that whiff."

"But then he'll just walk on the exchange, no?"

She grinned. "Not if we also give him an urgent need for more cash at the same time. Or rather, Interpol does."

"Me?" Castillo said, dubious. "How? You have something I can take to Turkey?"

"By this evenin', I'll have an MI6 document detailin' a ledger a' his payouts tae Turkish police. It's nae real, but it needn't be authentic. It's just a tool tae make waves. The locals will use it as an opportunity tae squeeze him for hush money."

Castillo was shaking her head. "I can't use fabricated evidence to get a conviction."

"Aye, but yae'r nae goin' for a conviction, lass. Yae'r just makin' enough noise tae rattle his cage."

Castillo remained unconvinced. "This feels like entrapment."

Ailsa shook her head. "The goal is nae tae bring him in. Much as we might all like tae see him in prison, he's nae the target. We just need him jumpy an' desperate enough tae accept Mac an' I as the solution tae his problem, so we can get close enough tae bug the bag he'll be passin' tae Hart's people. So, much will depend on yaer bein' able tae put the fear a' God into the local police. I'd go so far as tae say 'righteous fury' would'nae be out a' line."

Castillo looked at the screen and the figures for arms Demir had moved in the last six years of the Syrian conflict. "Well, that shouldn't be too hard to summon."

"Good," said Ailsa, standing. "An' now, if yae'll excuse me, I have an authorization tae acquire, an' a call I cannae dodge any longer."

"Your handlers at MI6?" Mac asked, rising.

"That's the easy one," she said, her mouth souring. "This is a higher power altogether."

CHAPTER 17

"REALLY, Ailsa, if you must get yourself captured, you might find a more respectable adversary than American mercenaries. How trite." The Dowager Countess MacIver shared little of Ailsa's Scottish burr, but her clipped British tones carried all the derision that an aristocratic background could muster as she went on, "It's not that one minds being roused at all hours with impudent demands for ransom. But then, when I ask for a simple proof of life as is the custom in such things, I am left on hold for a frightful time only to be harangued by a slew of expletives and then hung up on. I simply can't abide such *thoughtlessness*."

Ailsa could only roll her eyes and suppress a sigh. "Aye, Mother. I apologize for disturbin' yaer rest."

"As you should. I haven't had a decent night's rest since. And it's 'yes, Mother,' not 'aye.' I thought you'd have grown out of your accent by now."

"Vestiges of a rebellious youth, I'm afraid."

The Dowager ignored that. "It's worrisome enough your gallivanting across the globe on this crusade of yours. But if I must be dragged into your adventures, you could at least do me the favor of making an appearance here even *once* during the Season. Now it's almost over."

Ailsa would rather spend the British social season being waterboarded in an ISIS prison than cavorting with all the socialites and aristocrats in their endless galas and balls. "Is it really? Pity."

"Don't be snide, young lady, it does you no credit. And how are your dreams?" she asked abruptly.

Ailsa took a beat, deciding what to say before settling on the truth. "The same, alas."

"Oh, dear. Is there no end in sight, then?"

"I've been in the bastard's presence no less than three times in the last few weeks. I just cannae seem tae knot the noose on him before it goes all pear-shaped. Whether by his doing, others, or even my own damned self."

"My poor Ailsa. I'm so sorry," she said, with what felt like genuine empathy, before the Dowager's tone returned to its former acerbity. "Then dare I ask if there's any chance you'll pause in your quest long enough to produce an heir some time before I die? You are thirty now, you know. And age rarely favors the female form."

"Yae'r soundin' like a character from a Dicken's book again, Mother. Must yae do that ev'ry time we speak?"

"Well, perhaps it would sound less so if my only child attended her duty to the House with some of the passion she seems to reserve entirely for her work."

A change of subject was urgent. "Speaking of the House of MacIver, are you aware of a variant on the family name? It's MacGyver, with a GY in place of the I."

"Really, Ailsa, what foolery is this now?"

"Faith, Mother, it's true. I met a Yank in my line of work with just that name. We have a file on him and everything."

"It's an alias," dismissed the Dowager. "It must be."

"Nay, I checked. It rang a bell from Angus the Betrayer's day, and I'm wondering if he might not be related."

There was a long, troubled pause before her Mother ventured, "Well, if so, he'd almost certainly be a fourth to sixth cousin at best, and only related in the sense that anyone sharing a common ancestry might be. Why? Is he attractive?"

Now Ailsa groaned audibly. "For the love a' God! I'm nae out in the wide world tae chase men!"

"As he's an American, I should hope not. But I'll look into the connection if you insist. It will give me something to do other than rattle around in this dusty old manor while my childless daughter does her all to get killed at an early age."

"Mother!—"

"Very well, I've nothing more to say. Except do try not to get yourself kidnapped again in the dead of night, darling. *Au revoir.*"

As ever, her mother got in the parting shot.

Ailsa tossed her phone aside and threw herself back on the bed, hand over her eyes—wondering if death might not in fact be preferable to this.

Southern Turkey hosted few airports, and no aircraft wanted to get anywhere near the Syrian border, so the trio flew into Kahramanmaras and rented an SUV for the half-hour drive south. The searing sun clawed at the arid shrublands like a hissing cat, making the air shimmer like water, and Mac grateful for the air conditioning roaring full blast. Though the terrain shrugged off the beating heat like a thick-skinned beast, Mac tended to sunburn easily, Minnesotan that he was.

And they were a long way from the land of English now, so he was somewhat surprised at how much English Ailsa was using. "But you're fluent in Turkish. Why drop cover?" he asked.

"No need tae play a role just yet," she answered. "But yae'v been tae Turkey before, surely."

"Yeah, but whatever agency had me here, there was always a translator."

"Wher' we're goin' yae won't need one. Antep is somethin' of a hotspot for the jet-set crowd who likes tae pretend they're visitin' a war zone when the fightin' is at least a hundred kilometers south. Most locals know a fair bit a' English."

"'Antep'?" he asked.

"Short for Gaziantep. Local parlance."

Mac glanced back at Castillo in the rear seat. "Right, who doesn't know that?"

She scoffed. "Google, Mac. Yae should give it a go sometime. But the city is perfect for a snake like Demir. Close enough tae the border tae conduct regular business, out a' the way enough tae keep the locals bribed, an' cosmopolitan enough for him tae show off his money. He should be easy enough tae find in the club scene."

"So, I take it your feminine wiles won't work with him?"

"Only as window dressing. Like I said, he's a pro *and* paranoid. If I approach him as a plaything, he will'nae take me seriously. An' if I did, an' he discovers I'm a threat, he'd snuff me like a candle an' dump me carcass in the badlands. We'll nae get close by direct approach. We need someone tae make the introduction, preferably a corrupt associate."

Castillo chimed in from the back seat. "If I do my job right, we'll figure out whom to target among the police."

"Okay. So, what do you need from me then?" Mac asked.

Ailsa replied, "We need yaer particular brand a' sorcery behind the scenes, especially once we engage Demir an' I keep him occupied with my antics."

Mac turned full in his seat to look at Castillo again, who wore her innocence like a mantle. "My brand of sorcery, huh?"

Solana shrugged. "I call it like I see it, Mac. Or did someone else summon a lightning bolt from the sky like Thor the other night?" He rolled his head back with a smirk as she pulled out her phone. "Let's do the equipment checks."

Everyone could hear each other on the earwigs, and Castillo's phone was serving as the mic they'd use to listen in on her at the police station.

The badlands gave way to outlying farms and ranches, then suburban housing, then abruptly to a buzzing, modern city. The difference between irrigated landscaping and barren, unwatered plots sitting side by side was startling.

Ailsa guided them to a block from the police station and threw the SUV into park.

She and Mac began dripping with sweat nearly the moment they got out. Castillo didn't even so much as *glisten*. "How do I look?" she asked Mac.

She wore a modest white blouse, grey slacks, and her jet-black hair was tied in a severe bun. She clipped her badge and gun to her waist and holstered her phone. "Formidable," Mac said.

She smiled. "You always know exactly what to say." Then, to Ailsa, "You have my files?"

Ailsa handed her a manila folder. "Remember, yae just need tae make enough noise so ev'ryone hears."

Castillo's nod was predatory. "One Spanish Inquisition, coming up." She walked off with a confident step.

☙❧

Castillo made her way through the lobby to the ELEVATOR OUT OF ORDER sign. The directory told her the Chief's office was on the sixth floor.

Naturally, she thought, heading for the stairs. And a long enough climb to find herself musing about Mac again.

Was a life with him after this possible?

How would that even work?

Or is it just a fantasy I'm playing with because he's here?

Stop it, Solana! Not now!

Head in the game, yes?

Wish Ailsa was doing this.

She's good at playing roles.

But a loose cannon.

She finally rounded the sixth-floor landing and took a moment to slow her breathing.

Mac and I, we've played a role. Together.

Is that what made it possible?

But we're ourselves here. And not.

Why can't I just let this go?

You know why.

Okay. But time to be Medusa.

And that you got, lady.

She breathed for another moment, steady and strong, then made for the stairwell door.

It opened onto two uniformed officers who saw her approaching. Almost by instinct, they stood straighter and saluted as she breezed through, nodding to them.

She clacked her heels hard on the tile floor leading to the Chief's office, building up a head of steam before striding straight at the Chief's assistant, a young officer, mid-twenties, in a crisp uniform, trying to grow a mustache that just wasn't happening. And she went for him with claws in her voice.

"This is your chief's office?"

"I—yes, madam," said the young man. "But I'm afraid he's—"

"Save it," she said, and brushed past him without a second look.

"Madam? Madam, wait! You can't—"

Castillo shoved the door with enough force to ruffle papers across the desk and send cigarette smoke swirling through the air. "Chief Soylu? Agent Solana Castillo, Interpol Madrid," she said as she slapped her credentials on his desk, assuring his attention. "Care to tell me why in the *hell* I found records of payments to officers in *your* department from one of the local smugglers in an MI6 file?"

The heavyset chief with a craggy nose froze in shock, as if hit by a brick. He was a big man, aging, but still broad across the shoulders and arms. He'd gone to seed, but his former impressive bulk had left its mark. Castillo noted scars across his knuckles. A man of action, once, perhaps. Yet now he resembled a deer in headlights, his jaw falling to form some response as Castillo pressed the attack, thrusting the offending document all but in his face. "This man is wanted in your own country, is he not? I checked. He's a significant threat to international interests in Syria. So, why in God's name is he not on the red-flag list for Interpol?"

Chief Soylu finally found his voice, afraid to take the document, and afraid not to as she dropped it before him. "Forgive me, Miss Casti—"

"*Agent* Castillo."

"Of course, Agent Castillo, I'm unaware of any connection between this office and this smuggler, ah ... what was his name?"

"I'm warning you, sir, do not trifle with me. You know good Goddamned well who I'm talking about. Bilal Demir is legendary in smuggling circles, apparently far-flung enough to reach us in Spain. So, when I finally bust a gunrunning ring out there and am poring through their files, I find *this?*" she said, jabbing her finger on the paper again. "I think some answers are due. Or is your *entire department* on the take?"

He flipped through pages, making blustering sounds. "I ... This is not possible," he said. "I don't even recognize many of these names—"

"They're aliases, Chief! Or code names. I need your immediate and enthusiastic cooperation on this, or rest assured this will travel upwards, *fast.*"

He sounded pained. "Are you certain this file is authentic? MI6, you say?"

"According to my source's own verification, it is. This file was compiled by one of their best agents."

Over the earwig she could hear Ailsa's smirk. "Yae go, lass!"

Castillo continued her harangue. "It does not paint your department in a flattering light, and *you,* as their chief, are lucky your name isn't in here. So, you should be grateful that I traveled all the way to Turkey—in person—to bring it to your attention rather than go through official channels. I should hate to think the damage it could do to the honest men and women on your force, and to you in particular, if this became common knowledge."

"Yes," he said. "Of course, I am most appreciative, Agent. I can only ask that you give me some time to examine the matter in depth."

"I'll email you the file," she said. "And I trust that you'll act decisively and swiftly. I can delay my final report to the prosecutors for a few more days. If this goes in without any positive steps taken by you, it'll make waves from Madrid to Ankara big enough to drown you all, even out here."

She brought up her phone, activated the force-pair application which began whirring to sync the Chief's phone with hers while she emailed him the file. The notification blinked green, and she heard Mac say, "Perfect! We're in."

"You must forgive me, Agent Castillo," the chief was saying. "I do have a great many pressing matters, but I shall give this my fullest attention—"

"The next word had best be 'immediately,' Chief."

They locked eyes for only a moment. Castillo won.

"Yes," he said. "Immediately. I thank you for your indulgence, madam. I shall be in touch."

"See that you do."

She half-slammed the door on her way out, startling the hell out of the assistant, himself on the phone. His expression told her exactly who and what he'd been talking about. The grapevine was already chattering about the Spanish agent and the arms dealer.

Castillo arrived back at the car, cheeks flushed. "Well, that seemed to go well. What's he up to?"

"Checking your credentials," said Ailsa. On the drive to their hotel, they listened to him place a call to Interpol in Ankara and could hear his consternation as the reply came back that, yes, Agent Castillo is a decorated Interpol officer based in Madrid.

The Chief hung up, swore loudly, then placed another call.

A smooth voice answered, deep and self-assured. "You are not to contact me directly. I thought that was understood."

"This is an emergency. We have a problem. And it is ... significant. Interpol has one of your files."

Mac's brows narrowed. "That's *Demir*? So, the chief is in on it."

Ailsa grunted. "Makes sense. I dinnae put his name in the file, just in case. Dinnae need him bolting. Maybe our luck is turning."

Their conversation continued. "One of *my* files? What are you talking about?" Demir's voice remained in control as the chief explained, but by the end he sounded much less self-assured. "God's blood, Soylu! I pay you to keep this kind of thing in check!"

"It is not gone too far. This Spanish agent is giving me time to fix the problem. I can intercede in Ankara with our man there, but it will be costly."

"I do not like being extorted."

"It is the cost of your business, my friend."

Demir was grumbling. "You sound too pleased with yourself, 'my friend.' I do not suppose removing her would be effective?"

"I fear not. Her disappearance would only raise an alarm and bring further scrutiny—and others. We could perhaps buy her off, but, if she is not open to that, it will only make the matter worse. And she seems most determined."

They ended the call with the chief's assurances that, with the right amount of cash, the problem would be dealt with. Demir was displeased but conceded.

"Now the fun part," Ailsa said as the chief dialed a number in Ankara. She checked to make certain the call was being recorded as they listened.

"We have a situation," the chief said again. He detailed the problem for the man in Ankara. "In short, we need this Agent Castillo recalled, discredited, or whatever you think best. Do this, and you're in for at least double the usual payment."

"Very well," came the response. "Stall for time."

"Yes, of course, very good," said the chief and hung up.

Ailsa grinned, counted to sixty out loud, then dialed the same number in Ankara. When the man answered, she toggled on the voice scrambler and said in American English, "You don't know us, but we know you. You just got a call from Chief Soylu in Gaziantep asking you to interfere with an Interpol investigation. Don't deny it, pal, because we've got you on tape. So, listen carefully." She played back the pertinent bit for him, then continued. "We don't want anything from you except to sit on your hands. Don't do jack. Who we are is not important. We ain't police, or you'd already be in cuffs. Do what we say, and you just may keep your little cash cow. Screw with us, and you'll regret it." She hung up. "That should keep Ankara out a' the way, at least for now."

Mac shook his head, impressed. "You are just full of surprises, Ailsa. Shouldn't we turn that conversation over to the authorities anyway?"

"Are yae daft? A' course nae, nae until we have Hart. Besides which, the whole thing was gathered illegally. Castillo can tip off her people after it's all over, but they could never use this."

Mac glanced at Castillo who also didn't look happy, but he let it pass. "So, what now?" he asked as she started the car.

"Now, we need tae buy yae a new suit."

👣

Ailsa and Castillo sat outside the changing room at the posh department store downtown, flipping through their phones. It was the kind of place that Ailsa frequented out of necessity rather than desire. She'd had more than enough shopping lessons in her youth to last a lifetime. Yet the training served well in that she'd picked the least pretentious and most expensive place in the city. If they could find something to turn that lanky American into a dangerous-looking, well-paid thug, it would be here.

However, they'd been through four suits for Mac, and none had worked. It was as if the man seemed utterly alien in anything but jeans and that battered leather jacket.

"Oh, *much* better," she heard Castillo say.

She looked up to see him in a dark grey jacket with matching slacks, white shirt, deep blue tie, and polished black shoes. Silver cuff links and tie clip rounded out the ensemble. She nodded. "Aye, so he *can* clean up well enough now, eh?" She twirled her finger. "Give us a show, laddie."

Looking like a long-suffering pack animal, Mac turned around slowly, letting them eye every inch. "Good. Broad shoulders, nice an' tall, firm wher' it counts ... Yes, that'll do. Yae look like a proper bodyguard," said Ailsa.

Castillo was savoring the image, quelling the thought of tearing it all off and jumping his bones something fierce. "I'll say," she said coolly.

"Now dinnae be droolin' on him, lassie. He's got some squirmin' yet, I'm thinkin'." Ailsa reached in to gauge the space beneath the breast pocket. "Because we'll be needin' yae tae wear a gun under there."

Mac's obliging half-smile vanished. "Not gonna happen."

"Yae dinnae have tae use it," said Ailsa. "Yae just need tae wear it. Yae'r playin' a role, remember?"

"We've been through this—"

"Yae can unload the magazine, if yae wish. But they'll nae buy yae as a bodyguard around here without it." Turning to Castillo for help, "Explain it tae him, will yae, love?"

Castillo threw up her hands. "I'm not getting into this one. But she's right, Mac."

He looked between the women, realizing he was outgunned, literally. "It's not enough you get to dress me up like a Goodfella, so I can lurk over your shoulder and scowl? I gotta be packing to make this work?"

The women shared a look, unmoved. "If they search us when we meet Demir, an' yae can bet they will, they'll think it odd that yae'r nae armed. We're there tae con the man, nae turn ourselves over for execution."

Mac sighed, knowing that further resistance was futile if not flat-out petulant. "Fine," he said, trying not to sound cranky. "But it'll be unloaded, and I won't carry a magazine with me"—he made a gesture of air quotes—"just in case."

"Deal," said Ailsa, glad they'd crossed that bridge. "Now, show me the kind a' look all those thumpers seem tae sport."

Mac rolled his head with another sigh, then drew himself up, squared his shoulders, puffed out his chest, and glared, eyebrows drawn together, lower jaw thrust out, looking for all the world like a cartoon tough guy.

Ailsa groaned. "We're all goin' tae die."

Castillo was giggling behind her hand. "We'll use sunglasses. It'll be fine."

"Darker the better," Ailsa agreed. "Now, I'll leave yae two tae settle with the bill while I find somethin' suitable for me own self. This evenin' we'll visit that chief at his home tae set things in motion."

It didn't take her long to find a light grey outfit, just a shade under business formal, that would set off her natural scarlet mane, worn long.

Castillo appraised her when they met outside. "Nice. And I like the earrings." Which also looked professional and expensive.

"Glad yae approve. An' I see our old Mac warmin' tae his part. Does'nae hurt he passes easy for ten years younger."

Standing there without any expression, Mac could've been Secret Service behind his sunglasses. When he grinned, however, the illusion crumbled.

Ailsa just shook her head and checked the time. The sun was lowering in the west amid dry, wispy clouds in the hot evening air. "Let's locate the chief's residence, an' I'll get me head into character."

Mac practiced scowling off and on into the visor mirror with mixed results. He caught Castillo's bemused eyes behind him, not turning back to look. "I always sucked at charades."

"You're trying too hard, Mac," she said. "Just don't smile—at anything—and never laugh. Just stare and hold still. Big predators do that before attacking, and it works on people at some primal level. Your height'll do most of the talking anyway. I've seen you unhappy. Believe me, you're more intimidating than you think."

He felt like a shoe that just didn't fit. "I don't know how you two do it. I can B-S someone in a jam, but this ..."

Ailsa said, "The man we're seein' takes money from a gunrunner who supplies arms tae fuel a brutal war for freedom against an oppressive regime that will gas its own people, children included—if that helps any."

"It does, sadly," said Mac.

She pulled the car over in a trendy, upscale shopping district. "We're close. Castillo, we'll drop yae here at the cafe. Mac, yae take the wheel now, eh?"

"And what's your cover for this?" he asked as he got out to take the driver's place and she climbed into the back seat behind him, Castillo flashing them a thumbs up as she left.

"The fight for independence still goes on, me boyo," she said with a full-on Irish accent. "Why else would I wear me natural hair, now?"

"I hope you don't expect me to do an accent," Mac said, adjusting the driver's seat back.

"Nay, laddie," she said, still accented. "You just keep thinkin' about the man we're against. And I'll be takin' it from there."

Mac drove a quarter mile into an upper-class neighborhood with large houses on small properties, most having white stone walls and only a small drive behind ornate iron gates. He supposed the true wealth of the residents within were reflected by whether the walls were actual marble or just whitewashed stone. Ailsa directed him to a stately manor, the largest they'd passed. This had a fifty-yard drive up to the main house and the walls were definitely marble. "Not bad for a police chief's salary," he said, punching the intercom button outside the gate.

When the response crackled over the speaker asking who it was, Ailsa leaned across him to reply at the box. "A friend regarding Chief Soylu's call to Ankara this afternoon."

"Who?" the man demanded in English. It sounded like it could be the chief.

"Someone who can fix your problem," she said firmly. "That's who."

There was a long pause, and then a loud buzz accompanied by the gate grinding open.

The chief met them out front, wearing a plush track suit that looked a size too small and carrying a gun still in its holster, with a wary expression as he moved to avoid their headlights. Still, he was nearly as tall as Mac and seemed tense without the trappings of his uniform and office.

Mac got out, casually raising his hands to show they were empty, before he opened the door for Ailsa, who stepped out, eyeing both the place and the chief for an unhurried beat before she moved toward him with a broad smile, offering her hand. "Well, it'd be Chief Soylu, would it? I'm Ellie Shaw. An' I believe we've got a bit o' business, we do."

The chief didn't move or take her hand. "You have something to say?"

She withdrew her hand. "Perhaps somewhere more private?"

The chief looked Mac up and down, hanging no more than a few steps behind her, then to Ailsa, "There is no one else here. Talk."

She pulled out her phone. "It would be a lie to say I came as purely an angel of mercy, for angels never expect payment for their miracles. But I could'nae help but overhear a little conversation, an' was sure you'd be interested. So, just listen."

She replayed her own conversation with the chief's man in Ankara, her recorded voice heavily altered with the scrambling, and the American English having no trace of the Irish she'd been using with the chief.

As it played, the chief's face darkened, and he eyed them both under heavy brows. When she clicked it off, the chief said, "What do you want?"

"Just to help, mate. You to be sure, but meself as well, you know. Because I can make that Agent Castillo go away."

"For a price?" he almost spat the word.

Her grin broadened. "We're all in business here, eh? But I imagine it'll be cheaper for you than the alternative. Or I would'nae've come."

"And how do you have this recording?"

"I'm familiar with the lads on t'other end of that call. Competition, you might say, though not quite friendly."

The chief considered a moment. "Tell me who they are, and I can give you something for your time. I will deal with them."

She allowed for a small laugh, just enough to imply her advantage but not enough to offend. "Oh, I'm afraid they're beyond your reach, matey. But not beyond mine. An' a bit o' coin will suffice for me to handle 'em, an' your problem is no more. So, you see, 'tis a simple proposal."

All his attention was focused on her now. "And how will you deal with Castillo?"

"Best not to share the details, you know. But, where you've got your man in Ankara, I've got me a man in Madrid."

Another long pause, but then he shook his head, and turned to go back inside. "I do not believe you. Good night."

She held her ground but raised her voice at his back, "Suit yourself then, Chief. But if you're needin' proof of my good word, that can be arranged."

He turned back towards her, eyes unblinking, trying to look bored but still on edge nonetheless.

She shrugged and held out a card. "There's me number. If she comes to call, send me a text."

He didn't move. "And then?"

"And then wait. And see what happens."

He stared at the pair of them for an anxious beat then stepped back and took the card, examining it and her face a moment, before gesturing to the driveway. "You can show yourselves out."

The morning sun felt good on Mac's back as he jogged through the sparsely populated streets, awash in golden light. He was tailing Ailsa, herself not half a block ahead and on the opposite side. Eventually, she stopped at an outdoor cafe, common in Antep, and sat out front breathing hard and sipping a large bottled water. He jogged on, then back, and joined her a minute later.

"No one, I take it?" she asked.

He shook his head, taking the bottle from her. "No tail. We're good," he answered, before taking a long, grateful gulp. "I'm glad the chief isn't as paranoid as Demir."

She checked her phone. "It's about that time."

Mac put in his earwig and monitored Castillo's mic along with Ailsa.

They heard her enter the police station a half mile away and make her way to the chief's desk.

"Ah, Agent Castillo," said the secretary. "If you'll wait but one minute, he'll see you shortly."

"Here it comes," Ailsa murmured. A text appeared on her phone in seconds to the effect that Castillo was at the police station. She sent back a simple к and continued to listen.

In the chief's office, Castillo began with an imperious, "Well?"

"Agent Castillo, good morning," the Chief rumbled. "I am afraid there is little progress at this time. I really must insist on at least the weekend to have something for you by Monday."

She slammed a fist on the desk and leaned in at him. "*That's not good enough!*"

Soylu remained impassive. "I am afraid that we perhaps do not move as quickly as you do in Madrid. Nevertheless, it pays to be thorough and professional, does it not?"

"If you think you can lecture me about professionalism, think again. *My* department isn't the one implicated in taking payments from a smuggler running guns into a war zone! You know what? Forget it. I'm just sending the entire file on."

"That would be a mistake!" the Chief said, rising and clearly ruffled. "Please, I must beg your indulgence. We need time. This is a great many names!"

"Time is something you do not have, Chief."

Ailsa was chuckling as she listened. "Time tae rescue the poor man from yaer Spanish armada, I think," she said to Mac's grin. She dialed Castillo.

Castillo answered. "Castillo. *Go.*"

"Agent Castillo," Ailsa said in Spanish. "We've got a situation here having to do with your expense reports."

"What?" she said, sounding offended. "What do you mean, my expense reports?"

"What can I say? I'm only a lowly official, carrying out my duties."

"This is ridiculous!" Castillo answered, voice raising in volume. "I'm in a meeting!"

"You know Madrid and its bureaucracy. We need you on your computer ASAP."

Ailsa could practically feel the heat boiling off Castillo's voice. "I will deal with you shortly. And never call me about something so trivial again!"

The call ended, and they heard the chief ask, "Trouble?" sounding somewhat relieved.

"Just ... bureaucrats. But nothing that's getting you off the hook. Though ... if it's just a little more time that you need, so be it."

"Ah," he said. "Thank you for understanding. Be assured, this has my full attention. As for bureaucracy, it is a plague set upon honest people, is it not?"

"You just worry about your problems, and I'll deal with mine, Chief," Castillo shot at him as she departed.

Not ten seconds later, the chief's phone dialed a number.

"You again," Demir said. "What now?"

"There may be an easier way out of our situation. Less costly as well, though we've not talked price."

"I'm listening."

CHAPTER 18

I LIKE WORKING *in the background, out of sight. The less my target knows what I'm doing, the easier it is for me to do it. That's ideal, anyway.*

Sometimes though, you have to be right out in the open. Completely exposed. With a friggin' gun hanging next to my chest, no less. The only advantage is that they don't expect you to try anything hinky—which is exactly what you're trying to do. So, it can all blow up in your face ... in a heartbeat.

That night Mac waited for Ailsa by the car in the parking garage that still radiated with the day's heat, even though the sun had set two hours before. The night air was cool, and carried city scents, a medley of food, exhaust, and concrete that made Mac strangely hungry, realizing he hadn't eaten since midafternoon.

But all that vanished when his phone rang. It was Langley. "Not now, Boone," he said, answering.

"It's not Boone," said Agent Holcomb in a low voice.

"Holcomb? Good to hear from you. I can't really talk now, but how'd the review go?"

"Well, I'm not fired, but it wasn't from the lack of Boone's trying.

He's got a real witch hunt going on here with the Verone case. Meaning, mostly me and you. I'm on restricted duty pending further review. Desk jockeying, basically. Just thought I'd give you the heads up."

Mac was nodding to himself. "As if the job wasn't hard enough."

"You got that right. But if it helps, I think the Deputy Director still has your back and is wondering why he's making so much noise. But if it comes to it, she'll cover herself politically, you know."

"Does Boone really have that much reach?"

Mac could hear the shrug. "He's a player, MacGyver. He's good in the field, but he's a killer in the office. Any word on Verone?"

Mac grunted. "Lots of running around after Hart but can't get him to ground yet."

"Dust in the wind, huh?"

"Something like that. But I gotta go."

"Okay. Be safe."

"You, too." Mac ended the call, turned, and nearly froze, completely unprepared for what he saw.

It was Ailsa, making her way towards him, wearing a long-sleeved black dress with pearls, cut low in front, slit up her thigh, hair worn loose, and carrying a designer clutch bag. Her stiletto heels added at least another four inches to her height. *Damn.*

"Yae can put yaer eyes back in yaer head, Mac," she said dryly.

"Sorry." He got the door for her. "I thought you weren't going as eye candy."

"I'm not," she said as they got in. "But the chief is takin' us tae meet Demir at some posh nightclub. I'd be out a' place in business attire. If it was yae doing the talkin', yae'd get away wearin' what yae have now. But a woman needs tae look spot on, an' a simple black dress will always do."

"That's your idea of simple?"

She sighed, tossing her hair behind her shoulder. "It's below me knees. What, were yae raised in a monastery, for all, Mac?"

"Minnesota, remember?" he said. "Same difference." They both laughed at that as he pulled the car out into traffic, then asked, "Gun in the bag?"

"Nay. Yae'r the one that's supposed tae be armed, even if it's useless. The boss would'nae carry in this situation."

"I feel better already."

"He should'nae cause any trouble. Worst case, he asks us tae leave an' puts a tail on us. As for yae, odds are his men will send yae away. That's fine as yae'll be listenin' in anyway."

"And if he tries to nab you?"

"I'll nae go down without a fight, as yae well know. But it's doubtful he'd try. We've nae shown anythin' more than knowin' who he is an' what he does. That's the rub with runnin' a criminal enterprise. Yae need clients, but yae cannae very well advertise on Craigslist. This is simply sizin' each other up."

"Got it," he replied, as impressed with her feel for the nuances of all this as he was with the way she looked.

It wasn't a long drive to the club district. The hour was still somewhat early at only 9:30 PM, but the streets were filling with people dressed to impress, from sober and upscale to outrageous and flashy. Heavy bass lines thumped through the walls and into the line stretching half a block down the street.

Mac parked and acted as chauffeur. "Castillo, you on?" he said to the air.

"Right here," she said over their earwigs. "Listening to you ogle our colleague."

"Working with you two, ogling is an occupational hazard," Mac replied, then to Ailsa, "You ready?"

"Aye," said Ailsa. "And time for me tae go full Irish," she said, her accent changing instantly.

Mac escorted Ailsa to the front of the line, already feeling uncomfortable with the gun pressing against his side beneath his jacket, as they both drew harsh stares from the partyers waiting impatiently for their turn to get inside. From behind his sunglasses, Mac handed the bouncer a card with the chief's name on it. The huge man looked both of them over, then removed the rope barrier and waved them in.

They found Chief Soylu easily enough, having a tall glass of something toxic at the bar. His eyes lingered on Ailsa a moment, then, "Good evening, Miss Shaw. If only your beauty wasn't equal to your danger."

"I'll take that as a compliment, Chief." She slid onto the stool beside him. "Be a good lad, an' buy a lady a drink, would you now? Is our man here?"

The chief signaled the bartender and said, "Yes. We may approach at any time."

They made brief small talk waiting for the drink while Mac got his eyes adjusted to the sunglasses inside the pulsing club. "Castillo, can you hear me okay?"

"Barely," she said loudly. "Trouble?"

"No, just a sound check. Scanning for Demir." His eyes passed over the crowd. The dance floor was the usual panoply of pulsing lights and gyrating dancers, surrounded by booths and tables where only the wealthiest or most influential patrons bought seats. Body sweat mingled with alcohol in the warm air. His eyes went past a wide booth with a dark-haired man and young blonde chatting, then locked back onto them.

It was Demir all right, wearing a perfectly tailored sky-blue linen suit, and the blonde was probably just some bimbo. When Mac slipped off his glasses to eye her more closely, his blood went cold. "Crap," Mac uttered out loud to Castillo. "Forget what I just said. We got trouble." Because the blonde was no bimbo. She was Hart's daughter, Minerva, who he recognized from their capture in Algiers. And who would certainly recognize he and Ailsa if they got close.

"What's wrong?" Castillo questioned.

"It's Minerva Hart; she's meeting with Demir now."

Ailsa couldn't respond, but he caught her eye. She gave a fractional nod, looking grim while the chief's attention strayed.

"Do we abort?" he asked.

Ailsa inclined her head towards the chief, then towards the restrooms.

Mac understood and put his sunglasses back on, heading her way. He got there in time for the chief to slide off his stool and say, "Shall we?"

Mac put a hand on Ailsa's arm and leaned in to whisper, "I think I can get rid of her for at least a few minutes. Bring your drink to the restroom."

Ailsa looked at him sharply as if he'd just passed her an annoying message. "Now? Of all the—two weeks they've had, two weeks tae get back in touch! And now of all moments—" She turned back to the chief, smiling again. "My apologies, Chief, perhaps you'd be so good as tae hold the bar for us? This won't take but a moment. Where's the ladies', if you please?"

The chief was eyeing them both warily again, but indicated the way to the restroom and resumed his seat to order another drink.

Ailsa preceded Mac, drink in hand. In the quieter foyer that still thumped to the beat, she handed him the drink. "If she's really here, I'm likely tae need that," she said wryly.

"Have the chief buy you another." Mac dumped the contents in the trash. "And wait in the restroom. I'll tell you when you can go back to the bar. No time to explain."

She made her apprehension known through a glance, then vanished behind the ladies' door as Mac headed for the men's, that damn gun now feeling hot against him for some strange reason. *Focus, stupid!* he commanded himself as he got into the bathroom and, seeing it clear, went straight for the soap dispenser.

Mac pumped the glass half full, then filled the rest with water. He stirred it vigorously with his finger, creating a slippery mess. He took off his tie, loosed his collar, and pulled out one of his shirttails, then messed up his hair, now looking like a businessman who'd had a few too many after a long day at work. "Ailsa, count to twenty, then go back to the bar with the chief. Stall until the commotion happens."

"Not settin' another fire, are yae?"

"Thought I'd try water this time."

He emerged back into the main room as the music shifted to an even more frenetic tempo. He went to a standing table a short distance from the booth where Demir and Minerva chatted pleasantly. He spotted the bodyguards easily. One stood beside their booth, and another across, between them and the door.

When Mac saw the cocktail waitress in high heels heading towards their table with a fresh bottle of wine and two glasses on her tray, he affected a slight stagger to his step and walked the edge of the dance floor towards their table, soapy glass at his side. He rubbed his temple with his hand, feigning head pain and shielding his face from them, and at the right moment dumped the soapy water on the floor in the server's path. With the low light and high noise, no one noticed.

He staggered past the bodyguard and disappeared in the crowd. Then watched.

The waitress, used to swerving easily among the dancers at a good clip, never stood a chance.

With a shriek that could be heard over even the music, her heels hit the soap slick and she pitched forward into the booth, soaking Minerva and herself with the red wine. Hart leaped up as the bodyguard stepped in and hauled the startled waitress to her feet amid a flurry of pleading apologies.

Mac hurried back into the restroom to straighten up and resume his role, returning in time to see Minerva's harried bodyguard trailing in her furious wake, her dress now thoroughly soaked and stained, before she stormed out the front door. "Even better," he murmured.

Most people had seen the incident, though none thought more of it than simply amusing, and the hazards one faces in a noisy, busy club. A busser was already mopping the floor while another cleaned the booth, and Mac saw Demir signal the chief as he and his men shifted to a new one. Mac slipped back to Ailsa's side.

She did little more than give him a glance and the slightest eye twitch that might've been amusement, putting all her attention on

Demir as the chief took them over to make the introduction. The remaining bodyguard moved to stand in front of Mac, who kept his face impassive behind his sunglasses as they glared at one another. *Big predator, big predator,* he repeated to himself, the gun in his jacket still making him far more uneasy than confident.

"This is the woman I told you about," the chief was saying. "Ms. Ellie Shaw, Mister Belal Demir."

He took her hand beneath a serpent's warm smile. "Ms. Shaw. A pleasure."

"Likewise, me good man. I believe we have much to offer one another. Though I hate to have interrupted anything important afore." She gestured towards the old booth.

Demir's urbane gaze went slightly pained. "Just one of those things. I would offer you a drink, but I am not certain I should risk another close call."

She laughed, then indicated his coat sleeve. "You seem to have taken some shrapnel yourself, boyo."

He glanced, then sighed. His sleeve had several drops of red soaking into the fabric. "Well, I'm all too familiar with shrapnel, I'm afraid," he said, removing the jacket. "Fortunately, it is only a surface wound."

She grinned. "Easier than white cambric, that's for certain. Will your lady friend be joining us again, at all?"

He glanced at the door. "Ah, I think not, and our business was concluded in any event. Please, let us sit."

Mac's face-off with the bodyguard had continued, and he wasn't sure how much longer he could simply stare at the man within arm's reach. The bodyguard might've been a monument.

Ailsa noticed, and said to Demir, "I don't suppose we should risk another reason to draw attention to our table, should we? I'll send mine off if you send yours."

Demir simply said, "Go." The bodyguard unclenched and wandered towards the bar, though his eyes stayed on MacGyver.

"On your way," Ailsa said.

Mac also relaxed somewhat, both in body and mind, and made

his way to the front door. He lingered outside, grateful to be out of the thundering noise. His whole frame felt like it had been put through a workout from the beat alone.

Getting old, he told himself, though he realized the gun was more of a burden than the music. *Forget it, will you? It's just for show.* But it was bringing up ... something he couldn't deal with now.

He listened to their conversation as well as the mic on her phone would allow. Demir was saying, "Thank you, Chief, for acquainting me with Ms. Shaw. Please, have another drink at the bar on me. I'll be in touch tomorrow." The chief bade his goodbyes, Demir pausing for his departure before continuing to Ailsa. "Now then, madam, what is it you think you can do for me?"

"Keep you in business, lad, an' perhaps add to it."

"And what business would that be?"

"Following all the proper forms this eve, is it?" she said, amused. "You're in the business of freedom. You provide the means for people tae rid themselves of oppression and rise out of the ashes wrought by tyranny."

"An interesting way to put it. Are you oppressed, Ms. Shaw?"

"Ellie, lad, please. And me country remains ever oppressed so long as it flies two flags, despite all the blabber of reunification. Some people need a bit of a prod. And so, your services could be of use, but only if I ride to the rescue from your current predicament."

"I see. But you would charge me for this privilege. Over what? A document purported to connect me with the police that has little meaning."

Demir was cool, but Ailsa was ready for it. "Were that the case, would your good chief have brought me here, now?"

"The chief is a nervous man at the best of times. Easily rattled. I, on the other hand, am not."

Mac thought that sounded like posturing, but Demir was impossible for him to read over the mic.

"You'd hardly survive in your business if you were," Ailsa replied. "Which is why I'm convinced you're the man I need. If only you weren't fixed under Interpol's unblinking eye. And let's not pretend you've no idea of that, shall we?"

"Very well. Yet, I must insist that this document contains any number of inaccuracies. I find it hard to believe its origins are authentic."

"Do you now?" she answered. "And from where did the chief say this document came?"

"The Riverhouse, you would call it."

Mac knew that was the nickname used for MI6. Much like the Agency or Langley for the CIA.

"I would indeed call it that. And I can vouchsafe its origin, even if not its contents. And yet, it's led the Spanish harridan straight to your doorstep, hasn't it now?"

"You have a relationship with this agent?"

Ailsa's reply chilled Mac to his core. "The kind that begs a bullet in her pretty dark face." She continued, "There's a reason I must go so far from home tae find good tools. Spain was reliable for those of us in the market for freedom. One could whistle for their wares an' get a good price. Until that bloody bitch rose in the ranks. An' so now, I find myself here."

It had clearly impressed Demir. "So why not then just handle her yourself here? Turkey can be a dangerous place, so close to the border."

Ailsa's tone eased back to its earlier pleasantness. "Because too many eyes follow her steps, and not just for her pleasing form. If a bullet could've solved the issue, we'd not be here now, would we? Besides, I'm sure the chief has told you of my competitors with interest in these matters in Ankara?"

"He has, which is why I find myself even more cautious than usual. So many moving parts. So much room for error."

"Well, set your mind at ease, boyo. Because them I can handle by the usual means and the proper tools, in course."

"And this curiously convenient problem—which only you can solve—" said Demir, "will cost me what exactly?"

"Two point five million US. Though I'll take it in Euros if you prefer," Ailsa said as if it were a bargain.

"That's quite a number," Demir replied, trying not to sound troubled by it.

"Supply and demand, lad," she said with a smile in her voice. "You've a demand, an' I've the only supply."

Demir scoffed. "Nothing I do here cannot be established elsewhere."

"Aye, I daresay. Yet, in my experience, a bit of cash is easier to move than an entire business, wouldn't you say?"

Mac could practically see Demir doing the math in his head, sensing Ailsa almost had him convinced.

But Demir was a tough customer. "No. This is a fine tale, Ellie, but it is not one I wish to buy. Certainly not at that price."

Ailsa sighed. "Well, what is it you want then, love? Because I'm afraid the price is nonnegotiable. And 'tis not for myself, you understand. But the puppet that pulls the Spaniard's strings will not take a penny less. So, are we done here then? And we let the chips fall where they may?" Mac could hear her finishing her drink as if getting ready to walk.

Demir paused for a long minute. "Perhaps not entirely. But then I will require two conditions. First, you pay this puppet yourself, and I compensate in product. Agreed?"

Ailsa also paused, considering. "It could be done with a shove I imagine, aye. And the second?"

"You must prove that file comes from MI6."

That was the most direct Demir had been yet. Ailsa's irritation came through in her response. "And just how is it I'm tae do that? Call the man and ask him for tea?"

"That would be acceptable," Demir said, cold as an ice cube.

Now she was exasperated. "You've no idea what you're asking, laddie."

Demir leaned in. "I'll tell you exactly what I'm asking. If what you say is true, then your Riverhouse—"

"Those bloody bastards are not *my* anything!"

"Fine, then this hostile agency has far more information on me than I prefer. I want to know how. Means and ways, and whom to deal with 'in the usual way' as you put it. That's *my* price."

Ailsa's pause grew uncomfortably long as Mac's mind went into overdrive.

She needs to give them something.

But it's all bull. There's nothing to give.

He just needs proof he's being watched. Proof of a spy. A hidden threat.

Like a bug.

Or a tracking device.

And it doesn't have to work, just look the part.

"Ailsa," he said into his mic. "Tell him you'll see what you can do for now and send me a text."

On his earwig he heard her share another sigh. "Fine. I'll see what I can do. But it might take a few minutes, eh? So, why don't you buy me another drink. And if the waitress can keep her wits about her, I'd like a glass o' Kayra Okuzgozu."

"You know your wines," Demir said, impressed and pleased that he was now in control.

"A girl cannae grow up as I did without learning a thing or three about the world," she said, texting. She made certain it would self-delete after a minute. The text read:

WHAT DO YOU NEED?

Mac was already on the move, and sent back:

TEN MINUTES. AND WHAT KIND OF CAR HE HAS HERE.

"And how did you grow up, exactly?" Demir asked, relaxing for the moment.

Ailsa kept him occupied with prattle about a life on the run and keeping in with wealthy patrons while Mac made his way to the club's kitchen door. Someone had propped it open against the heat inside. Mac slipped in and made his way through the kitchen, doing his best to keep a determined step, like he belonged there. He got a few glances from busy cooks, but no one said anything.

He swiped a strong kitchen magnet from the cooler door and

found his way to an office in the back. Deserted, thank God. A quick rummage through their supplies yielded a bottle of superglue and a clear plastic container of pushpins. He dumped the pins in the trash, pocketed the glue and plastic case, and picked up the cordless phone receiver. He powered it off and made his way back outside.

In the car, he cracked open the phone with his knife to get at the electronics within. He found the radio transmitter/receiver and compared it to the plastic pin case.

Chop the circuit board there, and it should fit.

He chiseled into the circuit board with his knife's saw-blade. Once he had a decent groove, a quick snap broke it off clean. It fit into the pin case perfectly.

He took off his watch and removed the button battery within. He affixed it to the circuit board with superglue, then attached the magnet to the underside, and set it aside to dry. It would only take a moment.

Meanwhile, Ailsa was doing her best to keep Demir engaged and look for a way to steer the conversation to cars, but he was growing impatient.

"It has been five minutes," he said. "How much longer will this take?"

"You've asked for something extraordinary, boyo, an' put me own self out in the process. I've no complaint with foiling their operation against you, but I cannae put my inside man in danger to suit your impatience."

"I am not certain you realize where the danger lies, Ellie."

She laughed lightly. "Come now, Belal—since we're on first names now. 'Tis only a sign of respect that has me willing to go this far if we weren't united in purpose."

"I am not aware of a mutual goal, Ellie."

"For finer things, and a world of freedom, lad," she said, amused. "Your watch, for instance. Breguet, isn't it?"

"You are most perceptive."

"You can tell a lot about a man from his watch—an' his car. Oh, I do miss mine. Aston Martin. Forest green. She's a beauty, she is.

There's a disadvantage to traveling the world so much; you hardly ever drive yourself."

Demir shrugged. "I suppose, though a certain level of status requires the chauffeur."

"An' so they get the pleasure of driving the machine *we* bought," she laughed. "An ironic state of affairs, to be sure. What has your status bought for your guard to drive?"

"For pleasure, a Rolls-Royce, white with silver. For business, nothing so stylish. A simple armored SUV."

"Black, I'm thinking? Just to complete the image, no?"

Good job, Ailsa, Mac thought as he tested the circuit board and magnet to confirm the glue was dry before slipping it into his pocket and starting the car. *Just a couple more minutes.*

Demir chuckled. "Yes, naturally. And now, to maintain that image, I must insist on a progress report or something to warrant my continued patience."

She played along without so much as a beat. "Very well, I'll text again, though office hours have been over in the UK for some time now, you know."

"Intelligence officers keep office hours?" he replied.

She grunted. "He's a bloody bureaucrat, not a spy. I'm lucky tae get anything from a query that was'nae submitted in triplicate."

Mac drove through the parking garage, scanning for an armored SUV. It'd be big, black, and heavy, riding low on its tires despite superior suspension. His experienced eye found it soon enough—along with the bodyguard he'd faced leaning on the hood, scanning through his phone.

Sonova—

"Ailsa, I have to deal with his bodyguard. Keep stalling," Mac almost shouted into his mic.

"Can I help?" Castillo asked. "I can be down there in five minutes."

"There's no time," Mac replied, thinking hard.

I just need to get over to Demir's vehicle for two seconds, tops. Sneak up between the parked cars?

He's too vigilant, despite the phone.

Indeed, the hulking lummox would scan a few lines, then glance around, back to the phone, then look around again. It was less than fifteen seconds between scans. No way Mac could approach, even on the blind side as the bodyguard began to pace.

The parking garage elevator opened about twenty yards away. The guard looked up immediately, and watched a laughing couple exit and make their way to their vehicle, then went back to his phone. A few seconds later, a couple of young men parked nearby and made their way to the stairs. The bodyguard watched them the whole way.

Mac looked at the guard and the stairwell door a few lanes over, behind a row of parked cars.

Everything is catching his eye.

So, what might hold it?

Something strange, possibly suspicious?

But ultimately no big deal.

That's the hard part.

So, no fires.

Mac eyed the elevator door again.

How about a malfunction?

Mac drove up one level and looked around. No one coming. He backed the car to the elevator door and popped the trunk. Tied together, the jumper cables he'd insisted on at the rental agency were a good fifteen feet long. Plenty. He forced open the elevator door with a tire iron and looked down at the elevator car's roof. It was still at the guard's floor just below.

On the earwig he heard Demir interrupt Ailsa's account of the horses her cover supposedly owned. "This is all fascinating, Ellie, but I am getting the impression of being stalled."

"Because that's exactly what I'm doing, laddie," she said. "My man will get what you're asking for, but you have to understand—"

"No. I do not. And I believe we're done."

"If you wish. But let me send one more text, and if me man does not reply at once, then we'll call it a night, eh?"

Demir made an exasperated sound as Mac whipped out his phone and returned her text with:

ARMORED SUV. WHEEL WELL. GPS TRACKER.
WE'RE DONE. NEVER CONTACT ME AGAIN.

Then he tore off his suit jacket—and that goddamn gun—and quickly secured the jumper cable jaws inside the trunk with an extra loop for support, using them as a rope to lower himself into the elevator shaft, tire iron clenched in his teeth.

"Well," Ailsa said, showing Demir the text. "I hope you're satisfied, Belal. This cost me more than your entire payment would'hae been."

"We shall see," said Demir. "You will come with me to look for this device. Now."

Mac dropped to the elevator car roof amid the reek of stale cigarettes, discarded beer cans, and urine. It looked like someone had been camping there. He used the tire iron as a lever on the door arm. The motor was designed to give way in case someone forced the doors from below. He jammed them open with the iron via the lever arm, then hauled himself back up and out.

He threw the cables in the trunk and ran for the stairs.

Outside the club, Mac could hear Ailsa say, "I'm hoping you're not parked too far. I'm not wearing hiking shoes, you know."

Demir was on edge now, even angry. "You'll go much farther if we do not find what you claim is there."

"Make all the threats you like, boyo," she replied casually. "I know how to deliver when it counts, as should you."

Mac eased open the stairwell door to see the guard examining the open elevator, puzzled. Mac dropped low behind the parked cars and shuffled to where the armored SUV blocked his view of the elevator and guard, then rushed forward, keeping his head down and as quietly as possible. At the SUV, he thunked the mocked-up tracker magnet in place under the passenger rear wheel well. Mac peered around the car. The guard was still fiddling with the elevator as he crawled away.

"And do yae also expect a girl to take the stairs in these heels now?" That was Ailsa signaling that they'd made it to the parking garage.

Mac heard the guard's cell phone ring as he continued away, still low. He got to cover in time to see the guard saying something on the phone. He could hear Demir's response in Turkish over the earwig. It wasn't hard to guess what he was saying, as the guard gestured towards the elevator, looking puzzled.

Demir hung up and said, "If the car is indeed traced, it's not moving a centimeter. My man will carry you up, if need be."

"Dinnae bother with it," Ailsa said irritably. "I'll add the inconvenience to your bill."

On his earwig, there was the sound of a heavy stairwell door opening, and echoes as they trudged up. Mac hid where he could watch through a parked car's windows.

A moment later the door opened, and Demir's man led their way to the SUV. The other guard hurried over from the elevator, began apologies, but stopped when Demir held up his hand. "Search the wheel wells for anything."

It only took them a moment before a guard handed him Mac's mock-up.

Demir glared at it, then Ailsa. "Well, what would that be now?" she said, sounding just triumphant enough.

"This does not look like something MI6 would use," he said.

"And you're a connoisseur of digital devices now, are you?" she huffed. "Looks a bit crude, tae be sure. Do you suppose they might've gone to Spies R Us for it?"

He dropped it and crushed it under his heel. "I do not appreciate your humor."

Ailsa's entire being and tone changed as she stepped into his face. "And I dinnae appreciate burning a contact over your paranoid antics! My price has just gone up another half million, and I dinnae think we'll be taking the payment in product either!"

Demir didn't back down, but the advantage had clearly shifted. Through gritted teeth he said, "I cannot pay you until early next week."

She laughed. "An' your chief can hold off the Spaniard that long? Good luck with you then, laddie." She turned to stalk off, but he caught her arm.

"Wait."

She looked pointedly at his grasping hand, then stared him down. Demir let his hand drop and said, "I am conducting a transaction tomorrow. The product goes for delivery and payment the following week. I can have your money then."

She scoffed, full of venom. "You'll not last that long, if I know the Spanish queen at all. Your own chief will drag you away to save his fat hide, mark me words. Payment. Tomorrow. Somewhere secure, because now I've no one tae warn me if the Riverhouse comes to town."

From his lowering expression and clenched jaw, Demir was not a man accustomed to taking directions. "I have told you that I do not have the funds on hand—"

"*Then go to the bloody bank!*" Ailsa snapped. "'Tis not my concern. I've passed your little test at great expense. So, we're past the pleasantries now, Demir. The money. Tomorrow. You have my number. I'm done here."

Her hair whipped behind her as she turned and strode in loud clicking steps to the stairwell.

Mac remained hidden until a furious Demir finished bawling out his bodyguard in Turkish and they drove off. Exhaling deeply, Mac tracked Demir's SUV out of the garage before taking the stairs to their car. Ailsa was waiting out behind the club.

At the hotel they entered Castillo's room to the smell of popcorn and butter.

Castillo looked up from the nearly empty bowl, licking her fingers. "Sorry I didn't save any," she said. "But that was as good as a movie."

CHAPTER 19

Dawn the next morning, they met in Castillo's room, which had more or less become the center of operations.

"I still can't believe you got in his face like that," Mac was saying.

Ailsa shrugged. "Criminals are predatory an' cowardly. If I dinnae push for some advantage after what he'd supposedly cost me, he'd have suspected I was a little too eager for his goodwill."

"Plus, as much as they like to pretend otherwise, arms dealers like Demir are not all-seeing nor all-knowing," Castillo said. "The tracker rattled him more than he let on. It was quick thinking."

Mac nodded his thanks. "So, what's the next step?"

"Keep him hooked on the line," Ailsa said.

"You fish?—Or just using the expression?"

"Both. Royal Navy, after all. Key here is tae keep reelin' without him noticin' the hook or gettin' any a' us killed. He'd have reason enough tae move operations now, but he cannae do so with Interpol hot on his heels. An' I'm sure he's curious about any new business young Ellie represents, bitch though she be. He's up against a wall, held by an invisible assailant, an' I doubt he slept much last night. We can expect haste an' paranoia, an' those are what we'll play on."

Mac was nodding. "Got it. And while you play, I find his stash and plant the tracker before he pays Minerva Hart for her delivery.

Do we have any idea where he makes those transactions? His house?"

"I was thinking about that," Castillo said. "While you two were podcasting your action-adventure last night, I went through our real file on him. As Ailsa said, he only ever deals in cash, and seems to do most of his business in a warehouse he owns in the center of an old industrial district north of town. It's likely he's got a way of holding cash there on its way in or out of a bank here."

"We'll know when he makes his arrangements," said Ailsa. "Now, on the off chance he's thinkin' more clearly today, a little nudge might be in order."

"What did you have in mind?" Castillo asked.

"How's yaer tailin' technique?"

"Not bad if I'm working solo."

"Good. Then do yae think yae can botch it, convincingly?"

👁👁

Demir's caginess returned with her midmorning call. "You will forgive me, Ms. Shaw, but after some consideration, I do not believe I shall require your assistance in this matter."

"Oh, indeed, laddie?" she said over the phone. "And now why is that?"

"This Interpol agent is far beyond her jurisdiction. If she had something actionable, she would have moved by now. It is my belief that she is simply, how would you say ...? Just fishing?"

"Ah, well, if that's the case, and you're certain you're in no danger, then we'll just drop the whole thing, and I'll take me business elsewhere. A very good morning to you, sir." She hung up.

Mac looked at her, confused, jaw dropped open. "You just blew him off? Am I missing something?"

"He's playin' games, gagin' my eagerness. I just told him that I'm done with his shilly-shally."

Mac remained apprehensive.

"An' he has'nae spotted Castillo yet. Has he, Interpol?" she said over the mic.

"No," Castillo said back. "I'm sitting out here near his house, making every rookie mistake without looking like it. But to be honest, I don't like my ass hanging out like this."

"I would'nae worry. He has his meetin' today. If his men are even slightly competent, they'll notice yae."

Ten minutes later, they intercepted a phone call from Demir to Chief Soylu. "That Spanish agent is watching my house!"

The chief sighed. "It is not surprising. She is most determined. Likely this is a tactic to put pressure on whomever you have in the department."

"It's working, then. I have *you* in the department, and well paid to handle these problems! Get rid of her."

"How? If I interfere directly, my involvement becomes plain."

"I don't care how! Just handle it!"

Ailsa smirked as the line disconnected. "One can see the poor chief turnin' red even now."

"Okay then," said Mac. "What now?"

She held up her phone. "A countdown. In three ... two ..." The phone rang. She smiled as she answered. "Why, Chief Soylu, tae what do I owe the honor on this fine day?"

"Ms. Shaw, good morning. I hope I do not find you indisposed."

"Nay, laddie, I'm up and about. What can I do for yae today?"

She listened, nodding, as the chief detailed the problem. "Can you assist me once more?"

"Aye, I believe I might. Only that our mutual friend has decided he does'nae require my assistance, all evidence tae the contrary. If he reinstates the deal with payment as agreed by noon today, and throws in another ten percent, I can remove the Spaniard from the field."

The chief paused. "I can make no promises, but this seems reasonable."

Demir had other words for it. "*Reasonable?* The witch is extorting me!"

"This may be," said the chief. "Yet, I see no other immediate solution. Can you postpone today's delivery?"

"Not even for an hour."

"I am afraid she has left you with few options, which makes her a dangerous woman."

"She's an opportunistic *bitch*!" he growled.

"Indeed, my friend. But such is the nature of your business, no? Now, what do I tell her?"

Demir fumed for a silent beat, and then caved.

"We give her the payment at my place of business. Noon," he said before hanging up with a string of Turkish expletives.

"And where might that be, Chief?" Ailsa asked when Soylu called her back. "I see," she said, scribbling it down. "Very well. I'll call me man in Madrid. And shall we be seeing you at this meeting, at all? Ah, such a shame. Well, my farewells to you for now, Chief. It's been a rare pleasure." She ended the call. "Done," she said to Mac. "On the hook an' in the net, he is."

Mac realized he'd been holding his breath through all this and finally exhaled. "Time for me to start the campfire, huh?" Then, off Ailsa's look, he quickly added, "Speaking metaphorically."

"There's a relief," Ailsa replied, before continuing into her mic, "Castillo, yae get all that?"

"Yes. I'll wait another ten minutes, then pretend to get an angry phone call, and roar off in a huff."

"Only so far," said Ailsa. "Once they've seen yae leave, tail them for real this time. I have a feelin' we'll want extra eyes on this meeting place."

"Copy that."

"An' wher' are yae off to?" she asked Mac as he grabbed the car keys.

"A little shopping. What's the equivalent of a Wal-Mart in Turkey?"

"They're leaving the bank now," Castillo said over the earwigs. "Three large duffle bags. I'm guessing one is ours and the others are for Hart's daughter. 'Cause his bodyguards are even more hyper than usual."

"Still just the two of them?" Mac asked.

"Yeah. He runs a very tight ship."

"They're both his cousins," said Ailsa. "He trusts no one." She checked the time. "Ready?"

"On your six, boss," said Mac, wearing his goon suit once more, sunglasses, empty gun, and all. "Let's do this."

The warehouse sat in the midst of a ragged industrial district outside the city that still saw partial use. Trucks came and went, and steam, smoke, and other atmospheric contaminants rose from random stacks across the skyline. Yet the place wasn't fully utilized, and a noticeable three block radius around Demir's warehouse showed no signs of habitation. "Likes his privacy," Mac said.

"So much the better," said Ailsa. "Castillo, let us know when he's there."

"Very nearly. You'll be right on time. I'm going to drop back now."

"He has'nae seen yae?"

"He'd hardly be behaving normally if he had."

"She's a pro," Mac said.

"Very good," said Ailsa. "Ready tae wear yaer grumpy face again?" she asked Mac.

He chuckled. "Getting my grim on now."

"Then lay on, Macduff."

Mac drove them slowly through the squared-off streets beginning to shimmer in the noonday sun. The heat had been merely blistering before; today would be a flat-out scorcher.

The guard at the gate was the one Mac had faced down in the club the night before. He let them through under his steady gaze without comment.

Demir himself met them at the warehouse office entrance, the other guard beside him. "Ms. Shaw," he said without any pretense of politeness or warmth.

She smiled sunnily despite his edge. "Demir, glad we could come tae terms. And might ye have anything cool to drink, at all?" She noticed Mac and the bodyguard doing their staring contest again and sighed. "Shall we leash them, do you suppose?"

Demir's silent fury only seemed to rise at the sight of her. "I cannot permit your man inside."

"Oh, indeed? And I'm tae walk into the lion's den all on me lonesome?"

"Presumably you have some precautions."

"Aye, that I do. And after your difficulty this morning, I think I can safely say you need my help now more than ever."

"I will make no comment, although I do require some proof of what my payment is buying."

Ailsa paused, thinking for a moment. She glanced at Mac, idly, then back to Demir. "Very well, you can listen to the phone call, if you like. Me man in Madrid won't mind taking a call."

Mac caught the significance. He'd just had another task added to his list for the day.

"But," she continued, "that will require complete privacy. No goons."

"Very well," said Demir. "Mine will remain at the gate with yours outside."

"Go get a shave, lad," she said over her shoulder. "I'll be texting you when tae return. Shan't be long."

Mac returned to the car, escorted out by the guard. He drove around the corner and out of sight, listening intently on the earwig to Ailsa and Demir's terse exchange in the warehouse office. It was clear Demir despised every moment of the situation but was willing to contain most of it as Ailsa's people skills came to the fore, keeping the talk light with speculation about future returns for his investment.

"And now I'll be wanting to see the cash, all 3.3 million of it, as I recall, 'cause I've no time or taste left for haggling, you know?"

222 / ERIC KELLEY & LEE ZLOTOFF

"Your money is right here in the safe," Demir said, pointing to the door of an old walk-in vault embedded in the wall. "But first you make the call."

"And this is not me first dance, Demir," Ailsa said with an irritated sigh. "I see the money and then I make the call. Or I'm out the door and you can take your chances with Interpol. So, do I text me man now or what?"

Demir paused, hoping to salvage some final bit of advantage to salve his ego, but it was clear Ailsa would have none of it, as he finally conceded. "Very well, then."

She watched him pull open the heavy vault door and retrieve a large duffle bag, placing it on the desk between them, before unzipping it to reveal the piles of bound stacks of hundred dollar bills.

"Count it, if you wish, but it does not leave this room until I am satisfied, understood?"

"It looks to be the right amount, and I take you as a man of your word or I would'nae be here at all," Ailsa replied, lifting her phone to dial. "But one does love the smell of fresh bank notes, eh?"

"Not to be rude, but I do have another appointment shortly."

"Yes, indeed. Do you speak Spanish, at all?"

"Enough to understand."

"Very good."

Mac's phone rang a moment later. Knowing she had put the phone on speaker, *"Hola?"* he said.

Ailsa's accented Spanish was barely recognizable. "Good morning, my friend. I believe it's time to rein in the Spanish Inquisition."

"Everything is in hand?" Mac asked, trying to keep his accent neutral, not that Demir had ever heard him utter a single word.

"Right before my eyes. There'll be no complications?"

"No. She'll be gone in two hours."

"Very good. Ta for now, lad," she said, and disconnected.

Mac exhaled hard, again, as she said to Demir, "Satisfied now, are you?"

"I shall verify this, of course."

"Have your chief put a man at the airport. She's easy enough tae spot. As you know from my getting her off your house this morning, no?"

"Guys," Castillo said over the earwig. "There's a convoy approaching. Two semitrailers led by a luxury sedan."

Mac went cold. "Uh-oh."

In the office, Demir's hand radio crackled to life informing him of the same. "Ah," he said. "My other appointment. We are done here, I believe."

"Indeed," said Ailsa, zipping up the duffle and throwing the strap up onto her shoulder. "One has no wish to overstay their welcome. Though I don't suppose you've a back door? Best I imagine if we're not seen together."

"Oh?"

"Well, you're receiving a shipment, yes? From a supplier? If you wish me tae make their acquaintance, I certainly would'nae object. Though, if I know them meself, why would I need a middle man such as you are, eh?"

Demir could not argue with that, nor would it help to explain why she was there at all, as he replied, "My man will show you out the side door. You can make your arrangements from there?"

"Naturally. I'm sure me man's not far. Mister Demir, I'll be in touch."

Mac picked her up at the side entrance fire door with the heavy duffle pulling down hard on her shoulder as she yanked open the rear door and threw it in before taking the passenger seat. He kept his demeanor calm as he pulled the car away, but his mind was anything but. Half a block down, it let loose. "She's here already! I thought we'd have more time."

"Confirmed," Castillo said over comms. "He's shaking Minerva Hart's hand right now."

"Take a breath, *amigos*," said Ailsa. "Procedure would be tae check the inventory before handin' over payment. Look at the hoops he made me jump through. He let me see the money but would'nae let me take it until I made the call. If it's two semitrailers, that'll take time, an' I know the warehouse layout."

"Did you see the money itself?" Mac asked.

"Aye, the other two bags are in there."

"Okay. What kind of safe?"

"A big walk-in vault set into the wall with a combination lock in the center a' the door, though it was'nae locked when I was there. An' it looked old; no writin' or brand on it that I could see."

"It would be strange if there was," Mac said. "Okay. Even if he's relocked it, should be manageable."

"An' we'll be in close support," Ailsa added. "If it goes sideways, the cavalry is'nae far."

"If it goes sideways, we lose the only thread on Hart," he said.

●●

"I don't like this, Mac," said Castillo. "We're cutting it too close." They were three blocks away in an alley. Ailsa was up on the roof keeping an eye on happenings at Demir's warehouse.

"Not a lot of choice," he said, stripping out of his goon suit. "Toss me my bag."

She retrieved it from the trunk. "This is far too rushed."

"So what else is new?" he said, slipping into his jeans. "Besides, we still got Verone and Hart on the line."

"For all that'll matter if you get yourself killed." A nice feeling shot through Mac as he realized she was worried for him.

"If I do it right, no one will see me. Heck, if I'm seen at all, the mission is blown." He buttoned up his shirt and shook out his old leather jacket. "Got my knife?"

She handed it to him, taking his hand. "Be careful, will you?"

Yeah, definitely a good feeling. He squeezed her hand with a reassuring smile, then called up to Ailsa, "How's it look?"

"The same," came the response. "Hart and Demir went inside. The truck drivers and Demir's people are outside in the shade."

"And the side door?"

"No one there, but it was a fire door, remember. One way only."

"No problem. Just let me know when they start moving those trucks around."

Ailsa looked down at him, then shook her head with a resigned sigh, and went back to her binoculars.

"I need some bullets," he said to Castillo, as he opened the car door and grabbed the floor mat.

"We're not going to shoot up the place," she said, ejecting her magazine and handing it over.

"That's not my worry," he said, opening the trunk and handing her a one-liter bottle of water. "Empty that." He began pulling the bullets apart with pliers, then paused. "And, uh, stand over there."

"That's not the least bit comforting," she said, draining the bottle into the dusty ground.

"Just being extra careful," he said, emptying powder from bullet after bullet into a thin lunch baggie. "Bottle. Thanks." He sliced open a bag of fertilizer in the trunk and began shoveling it into a funnel he fit into the bottle's mouth.

"Turning terrorist on us?" she asked, arms folded.

"Pretty bad one," he said, pouring a measure of kerosene into the fertilizer. "But this should do what I need." He capped the bottle and put all his components into his satchel. "Okay," he said, shouldering the bag. "Wish me luck."

She grabbed his arm and pulled him into a soft kiss that turned that warm feeling into heat radiating up and down his spine.

"Trust me," he said, grinning. "I got this."

He jogged around the corner, head still swimming. "Ailsa," he said into the air. "Let me know the minute they start unloading."

"Aye," she said over the earwig.

Fire door.

One-way latch.

Let's get a look at it.

He skirted the building and peeked into the alley. Nothing. Not even any cameras. Demir's distrust of technology worked both for and against him. The door itself was solid, built into the concrete with a steel frame.

226 / ERIC KELLEY & LEE ZLOTOFF

Old though.

Not a long latch, I bet.

Good.

He laid out all the car mats one on top of each other, duct-taped them together, and then taped the explosive bottle on top. He unscrewed the lid, then nestled his plastic baggie of powder into the opening. He took a spare rag, wet it with kerosene, then secured that into the powder with a bit more tape. He then taped the whole thing solidly to the door, with the mat covering the bomb like a heavy blanket and reinforced with double layers of tape.

"Mac," said Ailsa into his ear. "They're unloadin' the trucks."

Indeed, Mac could hear the big rigs starting up, beeping as they maneuvered in the yard. "Good timing. Let me know if anyone reacts."

"Tae what?"

He ignited his lighter. "About to make a noise." He lit the rag and ran. He crouched down around the corner, listening.

It took longer than he wanted for the flames to reach the powder. When it blew, the thumping bang seemed startlingly loud in the alley with only a scorching jet of flame from beneath the heavy mat. "Anything?" he asked.

A pause. "No runnin' or shoutin', if that's what yae mean. They've got a forklift ready for the first truck."

Mac nodded his relief, then hoofed it to the door through a cloud of dusty smoke and the smell of burned rubber.

The floor mat had held thanks to the extra tape, focusing the blast into the door as an improvised shaped charge. The door itself had bent inward, releasing the latch. He pulled it open easily. "I'm in," he said, then pulled the burned mat off the door and stashed it down the alley. Inside, he secured the bent door closed with a bit of tape to keep it from swinging open. It didn't look terribly deformed. Someone would have to walk up to it to notice anything amiss. A lucky break.

Ailsa's hand-drawn map led him quietly through the empty corridors towards the front. He peered around a corner into the warehouse proper, brightly lit from the open bay doors. He counted both Demir's guards and two men from each truck, all unloading the first one by forklift, hand cart, and manual labor. Demir and Minerva Hart stood off to one side, checking random crates while Demir ticked items off a clipboard.

Now or never, sport.

Mac slipped into the offices and quickly found Demir's. It was the only one with any signs of residence, the rest being bare rooms. The safe was even older than he expected, but still with noise suppressed tumblers. And it had been re-locked.

No such luck, damn it.

Screw luck.

Where's the restroom?

It took him only a moment to find the closet-like stall. He took the nearly empty toilet paper roll and stripped it of paper. From his satchel, he retrieved the funnel that still smelled faintly of fertilizer and cut off the narrow end. He placed it into the toilet paper tube and very carefully taped it together, making certain to minimize puckers in the tape.

"Ailsa, the safe is locked. I'm getting to work on it now. Tell me if Demir or Hart head inside towards his office."

"Will do."

With his makeshift stethoscope he set to work on the tumblers. Between the thin walls, idling trucks, forklift, and shouting workmen, the going was slow, but he made inevitable progress.

After ten agonizing minutes, the safe clicked open.

"Got it," he said. "Anything?"

"They're moving up the second truck."

"Great. I'm nearly out of here."

The two overstuffed duffels sat on the floor inside, containing the five million plus Demir was forking over for this shipment. Mac opened them both, took a bundle of hundreds from each, and slipped Ailsa's two tiny trackers into the band, making sure they were turned on. The batteries would last a good week. Hopefully that would be enough time.

228/ ERIC KELLEY & LEE ZLOTOFF

Zipping the bags, he shut the vault door and spun the combination dial when the papers on Demir's desk caught his eye. An inventory. He ran down it, scanning across lines of explosives, guns, and ammunition when he saw a line that made him pause.

Methylphosphonyl difluoride and methylphosphonic dichloride ... Oh, man!

"Ailsa! He's shipping the precursors for sarin gas!"

"Okay. An'?"

Her nonchalance caught him off guard. "*And?* That's all you can say? All he has to do is mix this, and he's got about five hundred liters of weaponized neurotoxin!"

"Aye, an' what're we tae do about it?"

"It's an indiscriminate killer that you know will be used against civilians. I can't let him do this."

"Yae can and yae will, MacGyver!" she said with heat. "If anythin' goes wrong here, we jeopardize our only line on Hart."

"We'll find something else!"

"Mac, there's no time to argue," Castillo said. "Don't forget what you said before. Your Doctor Verone is counting on us too."

Mac didn't curse often, but his mind ran through his entire vocabulary.

Okay, settle down. What can be done?

Nothing. They're right.

If you destroy it, everyone starts looking much closer at this entire day.

They'll find the back door a lot faster.

But this crap is a crime against humanity!

It's delicate stuff though.

Well, the components are stable. That's why it's shipped unmixed.

But after it's mixed, it doesn't have a long shelf life.

Especially not if the precursors are tainted.

Heck, even adding water messes it up.

"No," he said into his mic. "I'm not leaving yet. He can have the shipment, but I can make sure it never mixes properly."

"MacGyver!—"

"No argument," he said quietly. "I'm going to hide until after dark. It won't take me long then."

"Mac, listen—" Castillo began.

"I am listening. No one will know until they try to use it and it fails. I'm going dark. Take off. I'll find my way back tonight." He removed his earwig and shut down his phone.

👓

Castillo's finger dropped from the earwig, shaking her head as she braced for the imminent explosion from Ailsa beside her on the roof.

"Bleedin' numpty! Buggerin' bampot! Shite-peddlin' arsepiece!"

"Stop shouting! They'll hear you."

Ailsa's volume halved but remained loud. "Bah! They're a quarter mile away next tae roarin' engines! How in the nine hells is yaer man still alive if this is how he goes about his business?"

Castillo felt a coolness settle over her brow. She knew it was a warning to herself. "That's enough, Ailsa."

"Not by half, it is'nae. Yae'v let yaer feelings for the man cloud—"

"I said shut it. Now," Castillo hissed.

The coldness of her words still seared the air as she put up a hand to stop any reply and continued, "I will not pretend to hide the fact that I care for Mac, nor he for me. You're an expert at reading people, and you have eyes. I won't insult your intelligence, so don't insult mine. But you need to make room for a little trust."

Ailsa practically spat. "Impossible! The man goes off-mission at the slightest—"

"And Algiers?" Castillo leveled at her.

Ailsa turned a shade redder, and not from the afternoon heat, but pushed back in spite of it. "And Grenoble?"

"You both offered your penance, no? Sounds to me like the hatchets should be buried already."

"Nay, lass, trust is earned, nae forced. What do yae call this situation?" she asked, gesturing towards the busy warehouse in the distance. "He's given us no option here!"

"Wrong. You have two options. You could leave. But, with our help, you've made more progress on Hart in the last few weeks than you have in the last three years combined. You want to fly solo again, then do it."

"An' have yae lot buggerin' the works an' steppin' all over my feet? Nae bloody likely."

"Then just trust us. And trust Mac. Because he and I have both put a lot of trust in you."

Ailsa's eyes narrowed. "If yae'v nothin' sharper than Algiers tae point at me—"

"But I do. You were tracking Hart before his first heist. Before. Why?"

Ailsa's rage slammed into Castillo's wall of logic—and stumbled. "I'm nae at liberty tae tell yae ev'rything. Some things are classified—"

"Bullshit. You're a brilliant liar, but not on this one. There's more going on here—I can feel it. But you won't tell me or Mac. So here we are, again, with this trust issue, you read me?"

Ailsa blew out a breath, and turned uncomfortably in place for a beat, hands on hips before answering.

"You're no happier about this than I am."

"No," said Castillo. "I'm not. But if Mac says his sabotage won't be noticed for quite some time, I believe him. So, enough with the lectures and recriminations." She checked the time. "We stick with the plan. I'm due at the airport to put on the show of going through security for whoever Demir has watching. You take this extra food and water. And stay on the comms. Understood?"

Ailsa hesitated, then accepted the bag. "And if he calls?"

"Help if you can, but he should be fine. Mostly, observe. Note as much as possible. Take photos, memorize faces. There's still a lot of detective work that might be done on those trucks and people; enough that we could still get a lead if Mac should blow it. I'll be back after I'm certain no one is watching for me. Anything else?"

Ailsa thought a moment, then shook her head.

Castillo turned, heading towards the ladder down to the car behind their perch.

"Solana," Ailsa called.

She turned.

"Yae'r trustin' me with him just now, are yae nae?"

Castillo looked at the busy warehouse in the distance a moment, then back. "You have no idea."

👓

After the empty trucks departed and Minerva left with the duffels of cash, Mac spent the rest of the day hot, sweating, and beyond uncomfortable. He was glad he'd packed extra water and a couple of energy bars, but by the time darkness fell, his stomach was reminding him of the missing calories with regular grumbles.

Not long now, he thought.

The plan was straightforward. He'd gotten enough of a look around to remember the fire extinguishers were water-based, common in manufacturing zones where more complicated suppressants might mix badly with industrial chemicals. Rigging a couple up to the sarin mixing tank would be child's play. The guard was the problem.

Like a lanky specter, Mac rose from his hiding place atop the interior offices and surveyed the warehouse floor. Crates of guns and ammunition filled the room, categorized by type, and lined up for loading in the next day or two. The shiny steel mixing apparatus stood in the center, like some kind of sick altar in a modern temple of death. He glared at it as he listened for the guard.

He could hear what sounded like a sports program playing faintly in the offices. Light came from under the door.

Sitting in Demir's office.

We can't knock him out.

No one can know we were here.

The back door is bad enough.

Rigging the tank is going to make some noise.

Might even need some welding.

Nah, look. There's an intake valve.

Just rig up the extinguisher to discharge the contents into the central tank and it's done.

But that won't be quiet.

Well, it won't be super loud either.

Yeah, but not silent. You've got zero margin for error.

Right. Have to figure a way to neutralize the guard without him knowing about it.

Mac lowered himself to the floor, dropping the last couple of feet into a catlike crouch. No reaction from the interior. A search of the crates showed little that might be of use.

Not unless you want to kill him, of course, he groused.

A sudden light from the office door sent him ducking behind the crates. The guard emerged and began walking the room with a flashlight. Between the light and the noise from his sports program inside, Mac avoided him easily enough. The guard went back to the office and shut the door, leaving Mac in semidarkness again.

Just normal rounds.

He was yawning.

Guard duty is boring.

Do you smell that?

Coffee. Strong. Some chocolate to it, too.

It's called mocha, stupid.

If he took a nap, he'd be unlikely to report it.

Not hopped up on caffeine he won't.

Hmm. Let's search the place.

Except for half-hourly scans of the warehouse proper, the guard spent all his time in Demir's office or in the tiny kitchen renewing a constant supply of coffee. MacGyver essentially had free run of the place, sometimes using his phone on a low brightness as a flashlight. Unfortunately, he found very little. The medicine cabinet had nothing but aspirin, antacids, and laxatives. The bathroom had nothing but toilet paper and some paper towels. The kitchen had nothing but coffee and a few little bags of chips (one of which he swiped).

He waited for the guard to make his next round, then rummaged Demir's office quickly. Nothing in the desk but some pens and paper, tissues, and a gun with extra bullets. The sports recap show played on a tiny TV in the corner. The place was utterly spartan. He closed the desk and slipped back out before the guard returned.

Back in his hiding place, Mac munched his chips and drank the last of his water.

One guy. We've taken out entire military units.

Yeah, with preparation and equipment.

Or at least a better stock of chemicals on hand.

Cooking up some chloroform would be nice.

Got any chlorine handy? Or methane to mix it?

No.

And how would you apply it to his face without him noticing?

Bah.

Some sleeping pills in his coffee would work, even over the caffeine.

Again, got any?

No.

Ignore the guard for the moment. How long will the sabotage take?

An extinguisher will empty in about two minutes.

We need to pump in at least two extinguishers' worth to give the sarin a shelf life of hours instead of weeks.

So, it's only four minutes we need him out of our hair.

Say five or six to be safe.

How often has he gone to the restroom?

Pretty often now.

All that coffee.

... What if he had a mighty need to stay in there a bit?

Any port in a storm, bro.

Mac returned to the offices, ghosted to the restroom, and grabbed the laxatives. He hid in an adjoining office and removed double the recommended dose in little brown chunks from their packaging.

He's at least Ailsa's age and healthy. This'll be fine.

He crushed them into a brown, chalky powder that smelled faintly of chocolate, and waited. The guard took his tour right on time. Mac counted to five and went around the corner into Demir's office. He stirred the small handful into the guard's coffee with his finger.

Not very sanitary.

Yeah, well, guarding poison has its risks.

He returned to the warehouse, easily dodging the guard, and retrieved his fire extinguishers to wait near the sarin mixing tank.

It took twenty minutes, tops.

He heard Demir's office bang open, then running feet down the corridor to the bathroom as Mac turned to the tank, which sobered his thoughts immediately.

The connection between the extinguisher nozzle and the intake was easily accomplished with creative use of duct tape with minimal leakage. He discharged both extinguishers into the main tank, cleaned up his tape, then returned the empty extinguishers to their mounts.

When mixed, the two chemicals would still become sarin gas, but the excess water would rapidly destroy the fluorine/phosphorous bonds, rendering the sarin into a couple of nontoxic acids. Unless it was mixed and deployed inside two hours, it was ruined.

Mac exited the warehouse through the side door, taping it closed from the outside. He felt at peace with his decision.

So why am I still so apprehensive? he wondered as he began walking back towards the brightly lit city.

CHAPTER 20

SOMETIMES YOU CAN DO all the right things, and still get it wrong. That's another "devil's bargain" part of this job, and it's been bugging me for some time now.

If you get a chance to make a difference and don't, is that inaction just absolved by accomplishing the greater goal?

And who's to really say the "greater goal" is all that good anyway? Is Verone's life worth that of ten people? Or a hundred? How do you answer questions like that? Because I'm not sure I can anymore.

👓

Fire and fury awaited Mac in the form of the Countess MacIver. And even Castillo's presence was doing nothing to temper it.

"Bloody damned American cowboy!" Ailsa seethed. "Have yae no sense a' priorities at all?"

Mac hated that word. "Priorities. That's what we say when we'd rather not think about the consequences of letting assholes get away with murder."

"That's exactly what it is! An' it's nae just a bloody excuse! Say yae discover yaer mark is also engaged in drug smugglin', or human traffickin', or they've a fetish for kids, or any other of a *thousand* horrific things. Yae do *nae* set about jeopardizin' yaer mission for the sake of a quick win!"

"I can see that for some things, but not with weapons of mass destruction."

Ailsa was relentless. "Yae *compartmentalize*. Yae set it aside. I dinnae want the bloody villains gettin' away with these things either, but sometimes all yae can do is pass it off tae yaer agency. Did yae never think a' that? Yae accomplish yaer task an' get what yae need tae settle their hash once an' for all. If yae tip yaer hand, they get away with it an' yae'v done nothin' at all!"

Mac's calm was fraying, but he was tired and didn't want another fight. "Well, he's not getting away with this one. And no one will notice until they actually use the stuff and it does nothing."

"Assumin' they dinnae inspect their apparatus beforehand an' find yaer sabotage."

"They still won't be able to use it."

"It does'nae matter! If they find out what yae'v done, the first people they'll contact is Hart. An' do yae nae think he'll piece together who's after his hide? He knows we escaped his mercenaries, so he'll connect it tae us immediately."

She may have a point, part of his brain said, but the rest was too furious to listen. Instead, he stood there, jaw clenching, fists half-formed.

"Yae just best hope that money leads us tae him soon," Ailsa said. "I'm done lookin' at yae now. I'm goin' tae bed." She swept from the room behind a slamming door.

Solana let the silence hang for a long moment. "I hate it when you fight with the kids," she offered, trying to break the tension.

"You want a go at me, too, now?" Mac said as he let the red haze drain from his vision.

"I'm just glad you're back. And I love that you'd risk yourself for people you don't know and will never meet. But I hate that it might all be in vain."

He ran a hand through his hair and let out a long sigh. He sat down on the bed, slumped. "I know she's not wrong. That only makes it harder."

She sat next to him and took his hand. "She is, and she isn't. If I were one of the people targeted with that gas, I'd *pray* for you to ruin it, absolutely. If I were Verone—or his wife and family, I'd wish you didn't care. It's all relative, Mac. It just depends on where you stand."

"I stand with ... *all of them*. But it doesn't seem that's possible."

She put a hand on his neck to stroke it. "I know. And while she might be wrong about the urgency of the situation, she's not wrong about compartmentalizing things like this. If you found out about the gas but it was too far out of your reach, what would you do then?"

There was only one answer. "Call Boone, I guess. Hope he could get someone on it."

"That's her point."

He objected. "But I was right there. And *I could do something.*"

"And if you'd gotten caught? Or if they discover the sabotage?"

"I didn't, and they likely won't. At least not until after we've got our line on Hart."

She shook her head. "You threw variables into the situation that you didn't need to. You've read his file. Demir was protected from his government through a lot of murky layers, so long as he made the right payoffs. But, until now, he only sold conventional weapons, sometimes in big quantities, but he never crossed the line into this untouchable stuff. You caught him with sarin. That's significant. You pass that to your people, or through Ailsa to hers, or even just give it all to me, and suddenly the corrupt elements in the Turkish government would have a lot harder time protecting him."

He saw where she was going. "Yeah. But what if he'd still sold this batch? I stopped it."

"You stopped this one. What about the next? An active threat would give Boone or others that much more weight and urgency, wouldn't it?"

"Assuming he'd jump on it," Mac answered. "Which is questionable given that it came from me, and his 'priorities.'"

"You said yourself he's a climber. A missing nuclear physicist is important, but proof of weapons of mass destruction flowing into Syria is another. Look, Mac, you'll never hear me say that destroying sarin gas is a bad thing, but there is such a thing as bad timing. That's all she's saying."

His brain offered up a few more feeble arguments, but none of them were worth voicing.

Told you, that tiny part said.

Shut up.

"Yeah. I get it."

They sat there, silent for a beat, Mac feeling her hand in his and the other on his neck before he asked, "You don't think Ailsa's going to bail on us for this, do you?"

Solana shook her head. "I think we're too far along for that. But I did get an earful about 'bloody American cowboys' for hours on end."

"Yeah. Sorry."

"Next time, I'll go swim with the sharks and you can babysit the infuriated Scotswoman. Learned all sorts of new curse words, though. And was diplomatic enough not to point out that she did almost the exact same thing in Algiers. It seems headstrong stubbornness runs in the Mac blood."

He smiled for the first time since returning. "I'm not even sure we're related. Could just be a weird coincidence with our names. Anything else go down while I was gone?"

"Just did what we had to. I made my appearance at the airport for the chief's surveillance team. Waited an hour inside security, then came back here in disguise. Ran down the plates on those trucks. Fakes, of course. Tried to ID the drivers, but came up with nothing, that sort of thing."

"Guess we're cooling our heels until those trackers land somewhere."

"It'll be daylight in a few hours," she said. "Are you going to try and sleep?"

Mac shrugged. "Calling Boone, then I don't know. Some food maybe, before I collapse. You?"

Solana pressed her forehead to his temple, breathing her words more than saying them. "I know we agreed to put our personal thing on hold until we finished this. But being with you again, seeing you, hearing you, all of it. Life is short, Mac, and all the rules mean less to me now than you do. So, I'll leave my extra key here if you want to come by when you're done." And with that, she kissed him softly on the cheek, dropped her key on the nightstand, and let herself out.

Mac sat there, alone, looking at her key, his mind swimming in what can only be described as the best of befuddlements. Because, for all the mysteries of science he had learned to navigate so easily, he realized the mysteries of a woman would forever be beyond him. He was exhausted and still churning with the dilemma of his move with the gas, but felt none of it. He had backed off, given her space, put aside all his longing and desire and, just like that ... she had handed him the key.

Better think about this one, Mac. Though he didn't really want to. *Call Boone, then decide.*

Painful as it might be, talking to Boone was a reality check for sure. The days of black and white choices were over; *everything* was grey now. And there was no certain way to go, except the way he chose to go.

Turning his eyes from the key, he reached for his phone and hit the number.

"Boone's desk," said a familiar voice.

"Holcomb?" Mac said, startled. "You're at Boone's desk?"

"Yeah, weird as it sounds," he replied. "Boone's off on something classified. Didn't even tell the Deputy Director. She's got a sense for the ironic, so seeing as I'm deskbound she put me to service all of his cases."

"Something classified? And the Deputy Director doesn't know about it?"

"Yeah, man, I dunno. Something's up. But, upshot is, you've got a new handler for now. So, what can I do for you? Got a line on Verone?"

"Not quite, but our hook's in the water. We did find something on the scary side though."

"Whoa," Holcomb said after Mac filled him in. "Sarin gas. Damn. You got proof?"

"Images of the invoices, and of the equipment. Serial numbers from the crates, and like that. I'll send it to you as soon as we're done."

"Yeah, definitely. Looks like it'll be a late night for me, but good work, Mac. And on spiking that batch."

Mac huffed. "You're in the minority on that, I'm afraid."

"Hey, you're the man on the ground. Not my place to second-guess you."

Mac laughed. "Just don't let Boone hear you say that."

"Yeah, well, Boone ain't here."

"Amen to that." Mac ended the call and sent Holcomb the gas docs and pics, his mind still swarming. He'd been braced to take a beating. But the universe had given him Holcomb instead. Maybe it was a sign—if such things can be believed. But it's all grey now, right? He rose, slipped Solana's key into his hand like the jewel that it was, and made his way out.

👓

Not this one. Please, not now, Ailsa's dreaming mind pleaded.

It was no use.

Midnight in the House of MacIver. She was ten years old.

She should have been in bed, not wandering the darkened halls. Restlessness had kept her barely dozing on and off for hours. Sleep banished itself, and she walked the house, smooth wood cold under bare feet.

Light streamed from Father's study. The door ajar. He worked late sometimes, she knew. Or was he having trouble sleeping, too?

She hesitated at the end of the hall. Mother would be angry to know she was up. She'd already dodged a servant on his last errands in the kitchen.

A sharp sound startled her. A flash from the study. Thumping feet in the distance. She was scared.

Don't!

She started walking towards the door.

You know what's there, just don't!

A smell. Faint. Musky. Cologne?

Just stop!

At the door, the same scene. Father in his chair, head titled back, eyes open, surprised. And sad.

Blood on his chest. Dead center. A good shot.

"Lady Ailsa?" from behind her.

She turned, and it was daytime. A sunny afternoon. She was in black. Everyone was. The funeral.

A man stood over her, hidden by the sun. He stepped forward like an eclipse and leaned down, hand out.

"Lady Ailsa, I offer my most sincere condolences."

The cologne. Sharp. Strong. Her stomach heaved.

Victor Hart.

She screamed.

⬤⬤

Ailsa leaped up, sweating, shaking, fists clenched, her breath coming in gasps.

"God damn it!" she hissed.

She hated these bloody nightmares. She hated being reduced to ten years old, a young girl, helpless and innocent, then having it all ripped away. She was nothing like that child any longer, the one they'd ignored. Two decades of work and training had grown her into a formidable woman, an expert in languages, psychology, martial arts, and firearms. She wasn't a girl in scarlet pigtails any longer. Yet, just try telling that to her subconscious, the part of her that was still just a child who'd lost her father.

She stalked to the restroom and ran water to splash her face and stared at herself in the mirror. Hollow eyes, rimmed red, darkened beneath. "Yae'r nae helpless anymore. Hart will learn that before this is over." It was a frequent refrain to sustain her pursuit even if now it somehow rang hollow.

A knock on her door. "Ailsa? You up?" MacGyver's voice came through.

"Comin'," she called.

She drew on her robe and checked her phone. Nearly 8:00 AM and missed texts from Castillo. She pulled back the blackout curtains to blink in the blinding glare. It had been an especially bad dream. She'd had several nights of relative peace while they'd been tracking Demir, but now, left to twiddle thumbs, she was back in this place, hostage to her subconscious. She grunted, tossing the phone aside, and got the door.

He was dressed in his usual jeans and beat-up leather jacket, looking unusually bright and renewed—which for him, was saying something—though it came with a look of concern.

"Is there a problem?" she asked, with some edge.

"No, just checking on you. You didn't get your phone."

"Yeah, just realized. It was time I got up anyway. Yae comin' in?"

Mac nodded, shutting the door behind him as he followed her into the room and she threw herself into a chair. "Everything okay?" he asked.

"Just trouble sleepin'. That all yae wanted?"

He looked down. "Well, that and to apologize for yesterday. I made a judgement call and, for whatever good it might do, it wasn't a smart one. I still think it was a good thing to do, but you had a point."

She nodded. "Forget it. It happens."

His brows went up. "You sure?"

She shrugged. "Would be damned hypocritical tae condemn yae

for what I did meself, no? An' yae accepted my mea culpa without a blink, so ... no hard feelings. Let's just both work tae keep ourselves in check, eh?"

He smiled, relieved. "Fair enough. And I still think the three of us make a good team."

"Yae'r lucky tae have Castillo. She kept me from any drastic action."

"Really?"

"Aye. Nae that there's aught which could'hae been done. She sang sweet songs all day though. 'Mac knows what he's doing. You can trust Mac. He always comes through.' I think she's about tae start a bloody fan club."

Mac smiled more to himself than Ailsa, still savoring the way his night ended as he replied, "Yeah, she's a keeper, all right."

"Was there anythin' else?" Ailsa asked.

He was about to respond when his phone rang. "MacGyver," he said to it. His eyes widened. "You did? Okay, can you give me five minutes? The others should hear this, too. Call you right back. It's Holcomb, Boone's temporary replacement," he told her. "He's got something we need to hear. Can you meet me in Castillo's room ASAP?"

"Two minutes, an' I'm yaer man," she said, already moving.

Mac set the phone down on the table in Castillo's room minutes later and put it on speaker. "Okay, Holcomb, we're here."

"Roger that. So, you know how Boone just kinda vanished? I did some digging. He keeps a clean computer, but there was a reminder set to talk with the sound guys in analysis. I called and had them send me what they were working on. Apparently, Boone isn't just chasing vapor. He's gone after Doctor Verone. Listen to this."

A momentary static hiss and then a shaky voice, an older man: "This is Doctor Arnold Verone calling for Agent

244 / ERIC KELLEY & LEE ZLOTOFF

HOLCOMB. THIS IS YOUR PHONE, WHY AREN'T YOU PICKING UP?"

There was a pause, and a distant clanging noise, plus the sound of a very distant bell.

"I GOT MY HANDS ON A PHONE, BUT I CAN'T TALK. I HOPE YOU CAN TRACE THIS. I'M ON A SHIP, I THINK. THE MOTION IS UNSTEADY. I THINK WE'RE DOCKED SOMEWHERE. IT MUST BE THE MIDDLE EAST. I CAN HEAR THE ADHAN RIGHT NOW."

He paused, and they could also hear the Muslim call to prayer beginning in the distance.

"THEY'VE BEEN DRUGGING ME. ASKING ME QUESTIONS ABOUT MY WORK, THE REACTOR, EVERYTHING. I'VE NOT BEEN HARMED, BUT—SOMEONE'S COMING. FIND ME, PLEASE!"

Everyone was silent for a moment, then Mac said, "And Boone didn't tell anyone else about this?—Why not?"

"I have no idea," said Holcomb. "At the very least he should've told you. If I had to guess, he's run off to grab the doc and the glory for himself, trash you, and come out smelling like roses."

"Bloody cowboys, all a' yae," Ailsa grumbled.

Mac shook his head. "I really don't care who gets him first, but Boone usually goes in guns blazing, and that's never a good idea. How long has he had this?"

"About thirty-six hours."

"And Verone was on a ship, so he could be anywhere now. Did they trace the call back?"

Holcomb typed a moment. "No. Turkey is all we get. Details have to come from their telecom services, and their administration hasn't been the friendliest to our queries lately."

Mac groaned. "Great."

"The sound guys were asked to clean up the background and get any clues. They confirmed he's on a ship, the engine isn't running, and the bell is a buoy. The adhan is the Shia version."

"Come again?" Castillo asked.

Mac knew this one. "The call to prayer is slightly different between Sunni and Shia sects of Islam, mostly in how it begins. Thing is, Turkey is predominately Sunni."

"Aye," said Ailsa. "But some cities do both, especially in regions with a higher Shia population. That'd mostly be southern an' southeastern Turkey."

"So, we need a port to the southeast."

"Mersin," said Castillo, scrolling on her phone. "Largest Turkish port in the Mediterranean."

"Would Hart use such a large port? Seems like a good way to invite scrutiny," Mac asked Ailsa.

"It's also the best place tae find people willin' tae take a bribe," she said. "If he's shippin' weapons through there, yae can bet there's someone turnin' a blind eye. All that traffic makes it easy tae slip things through. An' stashin' a person aboard one a' his ships would be simple enough."

"Anything on the trackers yet?" said Mac.

"Still looks like they're in transit. But heading west."

"Which could be towards Mersin," Castillo confirmed. "It's still all pretty iffy, but it's the only thing we've got right now. I think we should chance it."

"Okay," said Holcomb. "Head to the airport, and I'll arrange a flight. You need anything else?"

"We're good, I think," Mac said.

"Okay then. Talk soon."

"I like that one," Castillo said when he hung up. "Can we keep him instead of Boone?"

"I shudder to think I could suddenly get *that* lucky," Mac replied as he and Solana shared a quiet smile, which Ailsa noticed but was now too focused to question as she pressed, "Are we movin' now or what?"

CHAPTER 21

"What should we do with all this money?" Castillo asked, hauling the duffel to the car.

"Ordinarily, I'd use it tae fund my operations," Ailsa said.

Mac was putting their other bags in the trunk, which were few, as they all traveled light. He paused at Ailsa's statement. "Three plus million? What kind of operations are you up to?"

"None a' it goes tae my pocket, if that's what yae mean. But an agent-at-large has broad discretionary powers. Riverhouse would'nae mind if I dinnae request any funds for some time, tae be sure. But we're likely tae be quite mobile for a time yet an' travelin' with that amount a' cash is cumbersome an' only makes yae a target. Though I'm thinkin' we should keep a few hundred thou just in case."

"Agreed," replied Mac, "but I've got an idea what we can do with the rest." He parceled out a hefty stack of the bills into each of their bags before re-zipping the duffel and tossing her the keys. "You drive."

Gaziantep had been awake for hours, though traffic remained light with the increasing heat and non-hurry of a Saturday morning. "Right up here," Mac said, indicating a mosque near the south end of town. Syrian refugees had erected a kind of makeshift shanty-town in the vacant lots next door and down the street. They made their way skirting the edge, where Mac saw the dispossessed and downtrodden up close. None seemed to be starving, but clean clothes were rare, and a disproportionate number of children sat reading in small circles or played with soccer balls made of string and trash in an empty field that would likely fill up with more tents and scrap sheds in the near future.

He scribbled a note on a piece of paper that said only FOR THE REFUGEES and taped it to the top of the bag. "Be right back." He entered the mosque with the duffel hoisted up on his shoulder to help cover his face as he slipped inside as surreptitiously as possible before hurrying back out moments later. "Okay, let's go."

"You shouldn't skulk, Mac. Anyone would think you were up to no good," Solana said.

"Just didn't want to answer any awkward questions," he said, head craned to watch the front. He was rewarded with sight of the imam rushing outside, the note in hand, eyes wild with joy and astonishment.

Mac grinned. "It's not enough," he told the women. "But everything helps."

"'Not enough,' he says," said Solana, looking pleased. "I could get used to playing Robin Hood. What say, if Boone ousts you, I'll quit my job, and we'll travel the world, stealing millions from criminals and giving it to the poor."

Ailsa shot them a look. "What's with the two a' yae now? Life nae dangerous enough lately yae want tae add the romance a' staying on the run for good?" she asked, pulling onto the highway.

"Says the MI6 agent who eats arms dealers for breakfast and hasn't been home in three years," replied Mac, deflecting.

"Point taken," she muttered, though she could sense *something* had shifted between her partners and neither seemed apt to share.

The flight was a twin-engine small-craft, much like what they'd taken from Svalbard to Iceland. A tight fit, but a quick flight. In Mersin, they were met on the tarmac by Holcomb's CIA contact. He got them to a car with directions to their hotel near the coast. "Nice not to scrape all this together by ourselves," Solana said.

"When the Agency is doing its job, the logistics handle themselves nicely," Mac agreed.

The sun was blushing on the western horizon when Ailsa summoned them with an urgent text. "The trackers have stopped," she said, staring intently at her screen.

"Where?" Mac asked.

"Local. It's narrowing it down." They watched as the circle narrowed, bouncing in and out, zeroing on the port.

"How accurate is it?" Mac asked.

"Ten meters or so. Depends on interference."

Another minute, then it hovered just off a long pier on the map. "Is that it?" Mac asked.

Ailsa said nothing but pulled up the satellite data. "This is from twenty minutes ago," she said as the image loaded.

The marker hovered right over a long cargo ship nestled against the dock.

"Bingo," Mac said.

Ailsa shook her head. "Hold on. All we know is that's wher' the trackers are. I'd have expected this at a business office, or even a bank. Nae aboard a ship. He cannae launder it there."

"Maybe he's transporting it," Castillo said.

"Perhaps. It's just unexpected, an' I hate it when Hart does the unexpected," said Ailsa.

"Well, we need to go look," said Mac. "Doctor Verone could be there."

"We should find out what ship it is, then how long it's been here, along with anythin' else from the harbormaster's office," Ailsa said. "We should'nae go chargin' off into the unknown."

"No argument," said Mac. "But we don't want them leaving either."

"Then we'd best do our work quickly."

Castillo already had her phone out, searching for information. "One other thing. If we board that ship, we're on poor legal footing. Probable cause only goes so far, and none of us are Turkish authorities."

"Can you arrange for local help?" Mac asked.

"Given this administration's view of Interpol and its ties to Hart, I doubt it. Not fast anyway."

Mac thought a moment. "Okay. I'll call Holcomb and warn him what's up. We might need to get out of town quickly."

But some hours later, Holcomb had even stranger news. "I went looking for backup in case you find the doc and need to exfil in a hurry. We've got plenty of assets in the area, what with Syria on fire these days."

"Copy that," Mac said.

Holcomb paused. "Thing is, I can't contact the team that we'd use."

"Can't?"

"As in even their liaison isn't picking up his phone."

"That can't be good. Are they in trouble?"

"Couldn't say," Holcomb answered. "These are black ops specialists. By design there's as little trail as possible, but we should get at least a callback from our agent, and we're not."

"You think this has something to do with Boone vanishing?"

"Don't know, but I don't like coincidences. Boone's no dummy, and he had the same intel you had with the phone call, and longer to work on it. I'll keep trying but ... for now at least, you're on your own. As for your ship, I've sent you everything we have on it, including its transponder tracks for the last six weeks. It's been in port in Turkey for five of those, so Verone could've been there the whole time."

"Where was it before that?"

"Spotty coverage. They can turn the transponders off, you know. Last port of call was in Indonesia."

"Okay, thanks, Holcomb."

"One more thing. If you get caught, there's not a lot we can do for you, Mac. And as bad as it'd be for you and your MI6 friend, Agent Castillo would probably be impossible to get released any time soon."

Mac looked over at Solana, a new twist of fear clenching across his torso as she checked her gear, getting ready to go. "Yeah, I hear you."

♪♫

They'd not been in the SUV more than five minutes, zipping through the nighttime streets, before the trackers went dead. No one said anything, but the engine roared louder as Ailsa pressed the gas.

The ship didn't take long to find. It was the only one on the wharf not lit up in the deepening night. Ailsa scanned it with binoculars. "No lights. No workers. No guards that I can see. Bloody ghost ship."

"*Hmm,*" Mac said. "Someone was here if the trackers were. And not likely both batteries would fail at the same time."

"It was'nae the batteries," Ailsa insisted. "Someone found an' destroyed the trackers."

"We have another issue," Castillo said, pointing. A small security office sat at the end of the wharf. "And there, and there," she pointed to cameras scanning the silent ships and deserted loading areas. "I don't think any are in position to have seen us."

"Think you can hack him?" Mac asked Ailsa.

"I can try. Drive us somewher' hidden within a couple hundred feet a' his shack," she said, swapping seats. But it was pointless. "It's nae wireless. Even the cameras are on cords. Must be ancient."

"Or just more secure," Castillo said.

"We need tae disable it. Yaer specialty, Mac. But without raisin' suspicion."

Mac thought a moment.

Anything that looks like sabotage will be fishy.

Yeah.

No cut power, no sliced cords. No fires.

Only way is at the computer itself.

"Can you keep his attention for a couple of minutes? Also, without raising suspicions?"

"A' course."

"You have to be vague. You can't give him any information he might check up on."

She smirked. "I'm Scottish, ain't I? Can yae fake me some car trouble? Somethin' simple?"

"Sure," he said. "I'll show you a wire to pull off the distributor."

"That'll do."

How does being Scottish figure in? Mac wondered as he showed her how to disable the distributor.

They separated, with Castillo heading up atop a stack of containers to watch the ship through binoculars as Mac hid himself among the stacks at ground level within a short twenty yards of the shack. "I'm in place," he said to the earwigs.

"Same," said Castillo.

"Goin' now," Ailsa replied. The SUV pulled in at the far end of the wharf, drove past the first camera, then stuttered and halted abruptly as Ailsa faked engine trouble. She got out, muttering something Mac couldn't make out and threw open the hood to lean in and disconnect the wire as she "checked" the engine.

The guard watched for a moment from a distance, then emerged from his shack to head her way after locking the door.

"Miss? Trouble?" he called in Turkish, not far away, hand near his sidearm.

She turned, exasperated and gesturing at the car. "Ken yoo bleeve dis bloodie wrek an'oll? Peyd top coyn fer a noyce moturr an' end uyp wid a bryck, soay did!"

"Ah, is that English, miss?" he asked, trying that language. "Do you speak English?"

"Whit d'ye meen, daft boggar? Am I nit makin sinse to ye? Itz me boggurd moturr heer, disnae wano sturt an'oll. Kin ye giv et a boggull?" she asked, pointing under the hood.

Even Mac could barely make it all out. He suppressed a chuckle as he made his way around the guard shack on its blind side. He easily jimmied the lock with his knife and paperclip. The computer was an older model, but not so ancient that it had no net connection.

He brought up the control panels, checked a couple of things, and found what he wanted. "That'll do."

It took him about another minute while Ailsa harangued the poor guard with her incomprehensible Scottish accent. Mac got the computer where he wanted it to be, clicked the mouse, and gave her the thumbs up through the window.

"Ah!" she said, pointing to the wire. "Giv tat basturt dere a qwik jimmie. Aye, ta wyre dere, huuk it in an' lemme giver uh crank." She hopped in while the guard reattached the wire. The motor started instantly.

Ailsa squeed with girlish glee that Mac didn't think she was capable of and hopped out, still babbling at the confused, but smiling guard. Mac snuck back around the building to his hiding spot while she pretended to need directions and snapped a smiling selfie with the guard.

She drove away while the bemused guard returned to his shack and Mac crept away to the rendezvous. She met him on foot inside of two minutes behind the containers opposite the darkened ship. She was all business once again, the babbling tourist replaced by her true self. "Did yae handle it?"

"Yeah," Mac said. "That's a helluva accent you can dish up there."

She snorted. "It's just the Queen's own English, yae know. An' again, I question yaer Scottish roots. How did yae handle his computer?"

"The cameras were all controlled through it locally, so I kicked on Windows Update. He hasn't done it in two years, so it'll be a while."

She stared at him a moment, then clapped a hand over her mouth, and let go a peal of honest laughter. "Oh, lord, yae'r a rare one, Mac! Could be yae'r Scottish at that. A bloody *update*. I love it."

"Oh, he can be wicked when he wants to," said Castillo over the earwigs, Mac and Ailsa each taking a slightly different meaning from her comment as she continued. "Guard is leaving in his cart, looking annoyed."

Ailsa still shook with silent mirth as they watched the guard's cart drone by.

"Okay," Mac said. "Time to go."

They quietly made their way across the hushed wharf. Two gangways extended to the ship, one at the superstructure and the other to the cargo deck. The superstructure entry was locked.

"Bolted," Mac said. "Not getting through this without a battering ram. Let's try the deck."

The other gangway led to the top deck where containers had been loaded and secured for the upcoming voyage. "These are all stacked on top of the main cargo hatches. Means the holds are probably already full," he said quietly. He looked over the shipping information on one, bound for Boston, USA. He motioned Ailsa aside to crack it open on groaning hinges. They played their lights over the crates. "Thyme, sage, cumin ... pepper," Mac said. "Pretty normal stuff."

"I doubt he's exportin' guns from here. A large proportion a' his business is legitimate."

"Right. There'll be access hatches for the holds and from inside we can make our way aft to the superstructure. Come on."

♦♦

Castillo watched from her perch as they made their way along the deck, looking for a way into the ship—then scanning ahead and behind them for any signs of movement—as the images, sounds, and sensations of last night with Mac kept spinning up through her. One of the hazards of laying back on recon: too much time to think. But it was more than just the passion and release of making love that held her now; she had found an answer in that moment, more than an answer, a certainty.

Pay attention, Solana, she scolded herself.

But such certainties were rare, and even harder to ignore.

254 / ERIC KELLEY & LEE ZLOTOFF

Mac and Ailsa scurried easily along the containers on the deck, as the sea was calm, until Mac stopped and pointed. "Here," he said, gesturing to a closed top-hatch, covered over with a metal cap and secured. "This is just battened. The metal rod clipped there holds the hatch—"

"Aye, yae'r talkin' tae a naval officer, remember," Ailsa replied as she unfastened the batten and slid it towards him. The top-hatch swung upward, exhaling the tang of pent-up rust and salt, and revealing dull metal rungs on the ladder down into darkness. Their lights showed a twenty-foot descent to a catwalk running fore and aft above the cargo containers in the hold.

"Castillo," Ailsa said. "We're entering the hold."

"Copy," came back. "Still quiet here."

Castillo watched them disappear into the hold, which only intensified her thoughts of the way Mac had held her, touched her last night. Offering more than he asked, giving more than he took. Wordlessly assuring her that it wasn't all about him. A man so sure of himself that he could see past his own needs to a higher purpose, even if, in that moment, the purpose was only her. That was the answer that filled her. That was the certainty. Yes, she heard herself thinking. If Mac wanted a life with her, then yes. She would make it work. *They* would make it work. When this chase after Hart is over, however it ends, I'll tell him yes. Though some part of her realized she already had. The way she'd looked at him afterwards, in the half-light spilling in through the curtains. He *knew* she wanted him, would be with him. But he claimed no victory, asked for no declaration. He just smiled that goofy Mac smile and touched her face as if the answer was obvious. I hear you. I see you. I know you, Solana. So, *yes.*

Mac and Ailsa hit the catwalk and paused, listening, but heard only the odd creak or thump the ship made as she bumped against the wharf, rocked by the swell, before they set off towards the stern.

They made their way through two more holds, also full of containers, each blocked with closed but unsecured hatches. At the superstructure itself, the primary hatch took no effort to wrench open, and they found themselves in something akin to an office building extending from belowdecks to six stories above.

"Castillo, you there?" Mac asked quietly. "Sol, do you read me, over?"

No reply. Most likely the hull was just too thick for the comms to penetrate. He'd try again when they got to a higher deck.

"If they've got Verone here," Mac said softly, "he'll be in an exterior room. Otherwise he couldn't have gotten a signal out."

"Aye. I'll check port, yae do starboard," Ailsa said.

They separated, Mac crossing the ship to the starboard side and reading door plaques as he went. It didn't take long to find the crew quarters, themselves just five bunkrooms for a crew of fifteen, each with triple bunks, a small eating area, and space for a couch, TV, and gaming console.

The last one was secured with an exterior padlock, bolted on.

"Ailsa!" MacGyver hissed around the corner. "Ailsa!" he said louder. She appeared at the end of the corridor and hurried his way at a quiet trot. Mac pointed at the lock. "Not exactly standard."

She nodded and readied her weapon, keeping watch as Mac went to work on the lock, again with his knife and the paperclip. It was somewhat more difficult than the guard shack had been, but it only took an extra minute or so.

Mac went through first to see a room identical to those he had searched. But the lowest bunk held a sleeping man of medium size and middle-aged paunch, his face drawn and breath shallow. Doctor Verone.

Mac approached and put a hand over Verone's mouth, whose

eyes shot open instantly. "I'm MacGyver with the CIA," he said quietly, subduing Verone's fear and writhing. "We got your call. I'm here to get you out. Do you understand?"

Verone sagged back into his cot with relief as Mac took his hand away. "Thank God, thank God it got through," the old man said. "I've been here for ... weeks."

"We need tae go," Ailsa said from the door.

"Are you hurt?" Mac asked.

"I've been alone for almost two days. Food ran out this morning. I'm feeling a little shaky. They used drugs on me for days at a time. Asked me questions—endless questions!—about my work." He sat up, haggard and haunted. "I'm sorry."

"Don't worry about it," Mac said. "Can you walk?"

"I ... yes, I think," he said, getting up with Mac there to steady him. Once on his feet, Verone looked a little better. "Yes, just light-headed."

"Castillo, do you read?" Ailsa asked by the porthole. It looked out over the harbor, the wharf being on the other side.

"Just barely," came the response through static. "Still quiet out here."

"Copy. We've got Verone," Ailsa said, wanting to double-check. "Nothin' on the wharf or the ship?"

"Still clear," Castillo confirmed, though the signal was weak.

"The superstructure gangway should be up two decks an' port-side. We should be able tae unlock it from within," Ailsa said to Mac, but she paused, shaking her head. "Somethin's off." She looked into the hall. "This is too easy, too easy by half. No cameras, no guards, only a ghost ship with yaer man in a room secured with naught but a padlock." Still, they needed to move. "Keep ten paces behind me an' let me check the corners."

Mac nodded. No other choice, really.

Doctor Verone kept up fairly well, strength growing with adrenaline and the promise of escape. Mac stayed close by his side while Ailsa swept corridors and poked her head and gun through hatches and up each ladder.

But the ease of their progress ended when Ailsa rounded the corner towards their escape and greasy smoke billowed into the corridor. Gunfire erupted down the hall, staccato sparks in the swirling haze. Ailsa fired three quick shots blindly, ducking back around the bend.

Mac had put himself in front of the doctor. "How many?" he asked.

"Cannae see," she said. "Sounds like one, perhaps two." Three more shots sent them crouching low.

"Are you there?" came Castillo in a reedy transmission. "Mac, do you read me?"

"Yes, Sol, but it's weak," Mac called.

"Mac, there's a team coming over the bow!" He could hear was she almost shouting on her end though it sounded barely more than a whisper. "Balaclavas and submachine guns. I count three. Repeat, three. Professionals. Heading aft."

"A bloody trap!" Ailsa said. More scattered gunfire from the hall.

"They're not in the hold yet," Mac said. "Maybe we can hide or sneak past. Let's go!"

They ran back the way they'd come, Ailsa leading and clearing each door and ladder.

At the main hatch from the superstructure to the hold, again they were met with smoke and gunfire, the bitter smoke filling Mac's nose and lungs, making him cough. "They're shooting at random," he said as they took cover again. "They're just keeping us contained."

Ailsa agreed. "Castillo, can yae read me? What do yae see?"

Castillo's reply was still weak but readable, "Your smoke bombs are keeping them pinned okay. But what position are you keeping them away from? I can't see you at all. They're firing back, but I don't see at what."

Mac and Ailsa traded a look of confusion. "I didn't rig anything," Mac said.

"No?" Castillo asked. "Then someone else is there. Because

the gangway is still clear." Then a pause before Castillo added, "Wait!—I can see movement on the bridge. There's a light up there now."

Mac thought a moment, tasting the smoke in his throat. It had a familiar tang to it, like rosin. Very familiar. He told Ailsa, "Stay here," and walked around the corner to the hold door. As soon as he moved, three more sharp bangs went off down the hall, but he didn't even duck. In a moment, he found the setup. The first-aid box beside the door had been rigged to blow open with a homemade smoke bomb made out of chemicals in plastic wrap. Spent blanks had been wired to go off via electric charge. No one had been shooting at all.

It had literally been just smoke and noise.

He gestured Ailsa and Verone to join him, showing them the device. "It's a trick," he said. "The bomb itself is just potassium chlorate and rosin. That's why it's bitter. I've done the same thing myself."

"But there are men with guns coming!" Verone said, looking panicked.

"Castillo, how far along are they?" Mac called.

"They're still fifty meters from the forward gangway but making progress. Hold on!—There's another team on the dock. They just unloaded from a van. Three more men, going up the ramp to the superstructure. They're taking positions to cover the door. Not going in, looks like, but you can't get out that way."

Ailsa swore loudly.

Mac's brain was in motion. "We can walk right past these smoke traps, but not those guys." He thought a moment, then looked up and above the door. He grumbled when he found the pen-sized camera taped to an overhead pipe. No microphone. "Someone is triggering all this manually," he said, yanking it down. He put it in his pocket.

"Probably whoever's on the bridge," Castillo barked. "Can you get to them?"

Mac looked to Ailsa who could only shrug. "Given time, maybe, assuming they've not locked themselves off completely or have anything more dangerous than smoke and blanks."

"Then I can probably make my way to it," Castillo said.

"With guys on deck shooting?" Mac answered. "No, we'll find a way."

"The team on deck have pulled back—Looks like they're regrouping. I can get to the forward gangway and from there to the superstructure—it has ladders on the outside—I can get to the bridge on its exterior—"

"Hang on a sec—"

"Mac, you've got six armed hostiles plus whoever's on the bridge. I'm useless to you here. Going now—"

"Castillo, wait! Solana!" Mac was shouting but she either couldn't hear him or had cut her comm.

"She knows what she's doing," Ailsa said, pulling his focus back to their situation. "But we should try tae get out a' here, or find a good hidey-hole. I vote we move rather than stay."

"Yeah," Mac said, nodding. "Doctor Verone, you okay?"

Verone's face was tight with tension, but his eyes were alert and all trace of shakiness had gone. "Yes. Yes, I think so. Just tell me what to do."

Mac looked over the remains of the first-aid box.

Simple bomb. Clever use of wiring on the blanks.

Yeah, can be triggered in trios or all at once.

Those guys outside aren't gonna be fooled much longer.

Already regrouping.

You know though ... can we find another of these?

He looked over the wires leading to the box, taking them in hand, feeling their smoothness and the crisp insulation. It had none of the wear and grime of the other exposed wiring leading to the overhead lights.

New. Rigged up special.

Could be all over the place.

"Do you remember passing any more first-aid kits?" he asked Ailsa.

"Aye, behind ev'ry bulkhead."

"Thought so." His pocketknife whisked out to cut the overhead wires. No one could trigger any more bombs or blanks on that circuit.

He opened the hold door and followed the wiring through the overhead channels that let pipes and other infrastructure pass through the interior bulkhead. Only a few moments brought him to the next door and its first-aid kit. He spotted the camera easily enough this time and took it down.

The intact kit had been emptied out and rigged with nine blanks and a smoke bomb which itself was little more than a chemical resin, cooked in a saucepan and molded into a ball with wires running out the top.

"Like I said, I've done something like this before," he said as he looked it over. "Easy stuff. Anyone with high school chemistry and Google can do the same thing." He was talking while his brain worked.

Got three guys to disable if we want to get out the superstructure gangway.

Smoke is a good start, but they've got real guns, and that's a narrow egress.

Yeah, hard for them to miss, even blind.

This smoke disperses pretty slow, which is fine in the corridor, but they're outside.

Yeah, it'll blow away a lot faster than in the ship.

Crushing the resin will speed up the reaction.

Need more accelerant, though.

And something to spice it up a bit.

They were in the hold. He glanced at the cargo containers and wondered if they had the same freight as on deck. "Check those containers and find me some pepper. Finely ground, if it's there," he told Verone. He removed the blanks from their tape and examined them.

It's just paper holding in the powder.

There's your accelerant.

He grabbed a nearby dustpan and handed it to Ailsa with his pocketknife. "Get the powder out of these blanks. You'll need a good twist, but—"

"Aye, I've done it before," she said, taking it all in hand.

"And I need to borrow your gun."

She looked at him quizzically a moment, then handed it over.

Castillo was back down on the wharf now, crouched behind a container as she took a final look through her binoculars. The first team of three men were grouped back on the bow, behind the stacks and out of sight of the forward gangway, no doubt deciding how to make their way down into the hold. The other three held their positions at the aft gangway that led to the superstructure, their van below them, where it would help provide cover for her crossing the pier.

She pressed her mic. "Mac, Ailsa, can you read me?" But there was no reply except static. Her perch up atop the stacks must've allowed just enough of a signal to get through, however poorly. But down here, with them in the hold and all the containers, there was just too much interference to make contact.

So be it.

She stashed the binoculars in her pack and strapped the gun to her thigh—no sense having it out until she reached the deck. The trick to moving across open space at night was not to run with your arms flailing at your sides; just move at a quick walk, even and steady, with as narrow a profile as possible. People are wired to catch sudden, frantic motion. Not so much something that conforms more to its surroundings.

Her heart was pulsing at a good clip as she rose and slipped out from behind the container, turning her head back and forth between the two hooded teams, should either react as she walked. She figured it would take thirty seconds, tops, to clear the pier. But there was no way she could hang back and just watch as Mac and Ailsa were pinned below in what could soon become a kill zone with no way out. She reached the gangplank and crouched low to stay beneath the chain railing as she made her way up, reaching for her gun as she stepped across to the deck. Swiveling her head again, she strode across the twenty feet to the stacks of containers, putting her back to them as she slowed her breathing and tried again to make contact.

"Mac, Ailsa, do you read me?" Still nothing.

Okay, gotta keep moving. Time to make her way along the containers to the superstructure. *Go ...*

In the passageways below, Mac went to work on the smoke bomb rigged into the first-aid kit. He detached its wiring and placed the device on the floor. Then he took the gun, ejected the magazine, and cleared the chamber before using its grip to crush the smoke bomb's resin in its plastic wrap, being careful not to tear the plastic.

Doctor Verone returned with a sack of pepper, finely ground. "I hope that's enough."

Mac looked at the loaf-sized bundle and nodded. "Plenty, thanks." He began unwrapping the crushed, grainy resin, again careful not to spill any.

"Yaer powder. Done with my weapon?" Ailsa asked.

Mac exchanged the pan of powder for the gun and poured it carefully over the smoke resin, adding a healthy dose of pepper on top. It was powdery and sharp to his nose, even when carefully dusted. "Oh, yeah, that'll do it," he muttered, eyes watering.

He bundled it all loosely in the plastic wrap, then shook it just enough to form a mixture of gunpowder, smoke resin, and pepper. "Poor man's tear gas," he told them, holding it up.

Adding the wires back in for the spark just took a bit of tape. "Okay, there was a machinist's shop we passed at one point, yeah?"

"Only the most basic tools an' supplies," Ailsa said, clicking a fresh magazine into her weapon.

"That's all I'll need. Lead the way."

In the shop, Mac immediately spotted a large flashlight. The light flickered on weak batteries, unfortunately, but the battery only needed a little charge for what he needed. Another minute of searching found what he'd really come there for. "Eye protection," he said, holding up three pair of plastic safety goggles. He sealed the vents with duct tape. "If this works, we'll be running through this stuff. It's not as bad as tear gas, but enough to mess you up. These aren't perfectly sealed, but they'll do if you don't linger, and hold your breath as you dash through. Got it? Okay, back to the hall before the main hatch. Let's hope they haven't tried to get in yet."

Ailsa led the way, gun in hand. They tried contacting Castillo more than once but met only silence.

Castillo made her way aft along the deck, hugging the sides of the containers until she found a break in the stacks about halfway to the superstructure, a corridor, in effect, that allowed for the crew to get to the port side if they needed. To avoid being seen by the team at the aft gangway, she rolled into the opening, gun up, and looked for any signs of movement. Seeing none, she hurried across the deck to the port side of the ship through the canyon of containers and then turned aft again and continued back towards the superstructure, feeling both determined and oddly fierce as if not only doing her job now, but somehow defending this new future with Mac. Her senses somehow even sharper as she could begin to make out the stairs and ladders leading up to the bridge.

Everything in the corridor below was as they'd left it, oily smoke and all, as Ailsa, Mac, and Verone retraced their steps. It had cleared considerably in the dim light, but the tang still left a bitter taste with every breath. Mac peered around the corner, then traced the wires overhead to the corner where they had cover. He cut the wires, then pulled them down to hang beside him around the corner. "Doctor, the ship's mess was two compartments back that way. Go see if you can find three dishcloths and soak them in water. Wring them out, but bring them back damp, okay?"

Verone left while Mac tested the flashlight battery. "Let's hope this does the trick," he muttered. He removed the battery and taped it to the wall between the two hanging wires. "Our trigger. Tap the leads to the battery and the circuit is complete. Just has to heat the connection in the bag enough to ignite the powder."

"Will it get hot enough?" Ailsa asked, looking dubious.

Mac sounded more certain than he felt. "Sure ... Well, it'll need a minute."

"Great," she said.

"I'll go wire this up. When I'm done, and you two are ready, I'll open the hatch and leave it ajar. That should get them curious. When they're inside, we trigger it, and dash out past them."

Ailsa nodded, looking grim.

Wiring up the bomb in the first-aid kit took only a moment. He closed the lid without latching it, then looked for Ailsa. She and the doctor were at the corner, goggles in place and damp cloths tied over their nose and mouth. He gave the thumbs up, and she nodded.

Mac grasped the latch mechanism, gave it a loud wrench that clanged through the hull, then pulled the door slightly ajar. He left it hanging there, barely open an inch, and quietly ran back down the corridor, smoke wisps spiraling in his wake. Doctor Verone handed him his cloth, which he tied on hurriedly as he peered around the corner. He poised the wires away from the battery, ready to complete the circuit, and waited.

The trio of men came cautiously and competently. The door opened slowly, followed by a laser sight, easily visible in the haze. MacGyver watched with one eye around the corner, himself hidden in the dim light.

Two men moved while the other covered them. When all three had crossed the threshold, he applied the wires.

And nothing.

He looked at the battery. The wires were touching positive and negative ends. He glanced at Ailsa, whose gaze was incredulous and withering.

Then the bomb ignited.

The first-aid kit blew open as the powder went off in a sharp retort, half burning, half fragmenting the smoke resin through the air. Still, it was plenty to send the men to the floor coughing and holding their eyes.

"*Run!*" Mac shouted, leading the way. Their feet pounded on the metal plating. He stopped at the door, motioning the doctor, then Ailsa, through.

"Gas!" one yelled into his shoulder mic. "They've got tear gas."

Mac froze. *English? American English!*

"Charlie team, report!" he heard over their own radios. "Report!" A familiar voice—*Boone?!*

⚓

Her gun back on her thigh, Castillo was scrambling up the ladder to the bridge when her eye caught movement just below—it was the aft team! They'd breached the door on the aft gangway and were coming up the stair beneath her—*Mierda!* She was completely exposed. No choice but to keep climbing—she was only meters from the walkway around the bridge—if she could reach it, it was just a few steps to the bridge door and cover—She flew up the ladder and threw herself flat onto the walkway, but she could hear from their shouts they'd spotted her—She lunged for the bridge door—

⚓

In the hold, the gassed men were all down, unable to see, more or less at Mac's mercy. He grabbed a radio from one's shoulder.

"*Boone?*" he shouted.

"MacGyver!" came the response. "What the hell?"

"Same question! Are these your guys shooting at us?" he said, stepping out of the smoke onto the gangway.

"You shot at them!"

"I don't shoot at anybody! You know that!"

Ailsa and Verone had screeched to a halt on the wharf. She ripped off her goggles and mask and stared back up at Mac. "They're bloody *CIA?*"

"Get Verone to the car," Mac yelled.

But gunfire erupted above. A quick three-round burst that brought all heads looking up. It had come from the bridge. Another voice came over the comm. "Suspect acquired. One target down."

A spike of freezing cold shot up Mac's spine, catching his breath in his throat. He fumbled for his earwig. "Castillo, are you there?" Nothing. "*Solana!*" he screamed, already running.

AFTER STASHING Verone at the SUV, Ailsa sprinted the entire two hundred yards back to the ship. She climbed the exterior stairs and ladders two and three at a time and burst onto the bridge to find her fears confirmed.

Two men in balaclavas with weapons stood covering Minerva Hart against the wall, while a third covered Mac on his knees—in blood.

Solana Castillo lay on her back, eyes open unseeing, her lifeblood oozing out across the floor. Mac didn't move, didn't seem to breathe, head bowed, her lifeless hand in his, his face a mask of anguish.

"Oh, my God," Ailsa said quietly. A hollow pain settled into her gut, though she knew it was a bare whisper of his.

One of the agents whipped his weapon up. "Hands in the air!"

Ailsa's pain writhed into fury. "Get that bloody thing out a' my face," she said, striding into the room. "Someone explain tae me why yae shot an' killed an Interpol agent!"

"Stand down! Stand down now, or we'll—urgh!"

The shooter had let Ailsa get too close.

Like lightning, her hands shot out to sweep the weapon away and yank the man into her upcoming knee. He doubled over, breath bursting from his lungs from the impact. She shoved him into the

268 / ERIC KELLEY & LEE ZLOTOFF

man on the right as the other two whirled her way. They went down in a tangle.

The third got off a quick burst where she'd been standing as she whirled into a roundhouse kick that broke his hand against the weapon. Continuing her momentum, her knuckles struck his throat with enough force to gag him without crushing his larynx. She kicked out his knee as he dropped the gun, caught it, and turned it on the two now getting to their feet. "Hands where I can see them! *Now!* Stay on the ground."

She kicked their weapons away and stole a glance at Mac, who'd hardly registered the lightning assault.

One of them started talking. "It just ... happened—We were coming up to the bridge—She had a gun—"

"Shut yaer gob. There'll be no more shootin' today."

Ailsa lowered the weapon and moved over to Mac. She had no clue what to say—but was spared in her silence by the sound of feet pounding on the metal grating outside.

"MacGyver!" a man demanded from the door. He was balding, of medium height and build, with sunglasses perched atop his head. He saw the scene from the door and groaned. "Oh, *for shit's sake!* Now I have to clean up a corpse, too?"

Ailsa's fury returned, but it was nothing to match Mac's eruption.

"YOU SON OF A BITCH!" Mac was on the man like a beast, face contorted, bloodshot eyes still streaming. He grabbed Boone by the collar, hurled him up against the wall, and delivered a one-two gut punch and right hook to the eye that sent Boone's sunglasses flying.

Ailsa tossed her gun on the counter and caught Mac around the waist from behind. "Okay. *Okay!* That's enough. Yae'v made yaer point!" She caught his arm as it swung back for another punch and locked it. "Enough! I'll handle this. Step outside! Now!"

Mac came away from Boone and flung himself out of her hold. He stalked to the open door and moved out onto the walkway, gripping the rail.

Ailsa stared at his back for a beat before turning on the man sagging against the wall and nursing a bloody lip. "Yae must be the notorious Mister Boone," she said.

"And you're that MI6 MacIver. You want to take a swing, too, or should we act like professionals?"

"Professionals dinnae go jumpin' into each other's operations, yae bloody burk. What in the hell are yae doing here?"

He pushed off from the wall and tested his blackening eye, wincing. "Making certain we got my asset back. Where is he?"

"Safe, an' as far as I'm concerned, he's *my* asset now."

Boone scoffed. "You've got balls, especially for a woman outgunned three to one." He only now seemed to notice all three on their knees, disarmed, one still clutching his throat.

It was her turn to smirk. "Unless yae plan tae add MI6 tae yaer list a' enemies today, I'd rethink that. Yaer here without any authorization. I wonder now, do yaer men know this, at all?"

The three of them traded glances before looking at Boone.

"Don't listen to her," he said off their expressions.

"I'd listen, lads," Ailsa replied. "Or does he have an explanation for vanishin' an' leavin' Agent Holcomb in charge a' his desk?"

Boone's eyes narrowed. "How do you know Holcomb?"

"Mac does. An' yae'r off the reservation, as yae Yanks say. Even yaer Deputy Director does'nae know what yae'r about, does she? I'm certain yae'd never have gotten these lads in the muck if they knew."

"They're paid to do as they're told!"

She glanced at them. "How about it, lads? Are yae just meat for his grinder? Ready tae take the fall for this woman's death there?"

"Lieutenant, your team is *mine*!" Boone said. "You take orders from *me*, understand?"

"May I interject?" Minerva Hart asked politely, the very picture of calm in the eye of a storm.

All heads turned her way, herself having been forgotten in the altercation.

"Thank you. Whatever you decide, I'd advise deciding it soon. The Turkish police are on their way, and I would not be at all surprised to find their Coast Guard sending a ship or two as well. You see, the moment I spotted the unfortunate agent here heading up to the bridge, I sent out the call along with all the video information I recorded during your assault. And, in fact, everything you've done and said since is now on record." She gestured, indicating two tiny cameras in the room. "Really, I would've expected more finesse from the CIA."

"Yeah, well, you're coming with us, Hart," said Boone.

"The hell yae say," said Ailsa.

Minerva smiled. "As a point of fact, I'm going with no one. Not unless you want the same sort of international incident as in Grenoble, but to another order of magnitude entirely. You're operating within Turkish jurisdiction, intent on carrying out a kidnapping. And while Lady MacIver and presumably Mister MacGyver are authorized to do so by their governments, you, Mister Boone, and your compatriots are not. I have this on even higher authority than Ailsa there does. I've never been in a Turkish prison myself, but I understand them to be somewhat unpleasant."

Boone was gritting his teeth. "This wasn't how it was supposed —" He cut himself off. "A double cross is it? Fine. You're implicated in a kidnapping. I bet your footage shows Doctor Verone, too, right?"

"I have no idea why he stowed away. In addition, this is Turkey, where my father's generous contributions to various political parties allows us a significant benefit of the doubt. Seize me, if you wish, but the odds of you escaping the country diminish by the second."

Cold, raw calculations of the facts told Ailsa there was no way out of it.

Also, we've got Verone tae look after.

An' Mac if his current state is any indication.

An' what're these Yanks goin' tae do?

One of Boone's men spoke. "I say we go." He retrieved his weapon, keeping it held low.

Boone's gaze was pure venom. "You certain you want to end your career right now in this room?"

The man was shaking his head. "We'll take that chance. But this has been funky from the get-go, and now some things are making sense."

"She is manipulating you."

"Wouldn't be the first time for that. We're getting our guys and bugging out of here now—*with you*. 'Cause you've got some questions to answer. You need us to take your gun to prove it?"

The two that could still hold weapons brought them up just enough to show Boone it wasn't a request.

Boone glared at them, knowing he was out of bluster and choices, but reserved his look of pure hatred for Ailsa. "This isn't over," he said, as he turned and left with the agents behind him, leaving Ailsa alone with Minerva.

"Why yae?" Ailsa asked. "Why are yae here? I thought yae Harts never got yaer hands dirty. Yae'v got minions for that."

Minerva was pitying. "Really, Ailsa, this single-minded persecution of my father has gone on for too long. He's not the man you seem to think he is."

"Yae have no idea what I think, an' dinnae deflect. *Why are yae here?*"

Minerva cocked her head, condescendingly. "In the first place, when we let Doctor Verone place his call, we knew a team would be coming eventually." She opened a metal box on the counter beside her and pulled out a brick of bills. She slipped the tracker out from under the band. "And this confirmed it. Very well done, by the way. Was this you, or Mister Boone?"

"Yae'll get nary a thing from me. It still does'nae explain why yae'r here."

"Well, we wanted to make certain Doctor Verone got away safely. We meant him no harm. We mean no one any harm, hard as that may be to believe."

Ailsa thought a few things about sarin gas and making arms deals but kept silent.

"And my father also wished to convey a message to Mister MacGyver. An offer, I believe."

Ailsa scoffed. "Yae want tae *recruit* MacGyver?"

Minerva shrugged. "To tell you the truth, I don't know exactly what he wants. Only that I'm to deliver the message and bring him with me if he wishes."

Ailsa regarded her with deep suspicion. "I could still take yae captive."

Minerva pursed her lips. "You do as you must."

A long moment passed between them as they stared at each other over Castillo's body. Ailsa looked down at her, wanting to scream, but kept herself in check then told Minerva, "Wait here."

She went in search of Mac, and found him, leaning on the bridge wall right outside the door. "Yae heard?" she asked quietly.

He nodded. His eyes were still red and glazed, his body slumped as if someone had snapped his spine.

"What do yae think?" she asked.

He took in a deep, shuddering breath and released it slowly. "I don't want Solana to have died for nothing."

"We got Verone back."

"But she was after Hart. And so are you."

"That does'nae mean yae should march into the lion's den, gilded invitation or no."

He looked at her, hard. "This entire time we've been strung along, jerked around by his strings. Every time we think we're ahead of him, we find out he was playing us. Every decision in this pursuit has gone from bad to worse. And you can bet Boone is already spinning this to be my mess. So, if Hart wants a sit down with me, you tell me exactly what I have left to lose."

"He could bloody well kill yae, that's what," she shot back.

Mac shook his head, almost as if he didn't care. "If Hart wanted us dead, he'd've done it in Algiers, and we wouldn't be having this conversation."

"An' the sarin gas?" Ailsa reminded him.

Mac paused. "Yeah, and guns. I know. I just—I can't let her death be for nothing. You understand?"

Ailsa did. "Aye. Yae'll be undercover then?"

"I guess. Kind of. Who knows anymore?"

She didn't like the sound of that. "Yae'r nae yaerself, Mac, sure as stone. After that shock, no one would be. He'll get in yaer head, twist yae around. I'm trained tae manipulate people, but I'm a pup next tae Hart at that."

"I'll be okay."

"Mac, please—"

"I'll be fine!" he said sharply.

There was no talking him out of it, she could see that now. "Then know this. Hart killed my father. Gun in hand, shot through the heart. It was him. I found the truth when I was still a child, an' no one believed me. Just yae remember that."

Mac stared at her, not as surprised as he should be. "I'm sorry, Ailsa. You never said, so I didn't know. But I figured he did something to make getting him ... an obsession for you."

Maybe in their newly shared grief, Ailsa's words, old and painful as they were, just poured from her. "He used tae wear this cologne. I smelled it in my father's study mingled with gun smoke, an' then again at the funeral when he gave his condolences. I screamed. Ev'ryone thought I was just hysterical. No one took me seriously, nae even Mother, nae until much later. An' what could she do by then? Nothin'. So, just remember that he smooth-talked his way past Scotland Yard an' MI6 *both* tae get away with murder."

Sirens could now be heard, approaching in the distance. Turkish police no doubt.

"I have tae go get Verone out."

Mac nodded. "I'm sure Hart's daughter will handle them for me. And I should see to Solana."

"Aye."

"I doubt I can contact you. Here." He handed over his phone and unlock code. "Call Holcomb and let him know what happened. Tell him I'm undercover or whatever. And try to figure out what Boone was up to here. Not everything he said clocks, including the case I was on before he steered me into this one."

"An' what was that?" she asked, taking the phone.

"Tracking down a stolen bioweapon for Homeland Security.

Some militia guys had gotten their hands on it somehow. Boone arrived to clean up that one, too. We never figured out how they got ahold of that stuff in the first place, and Boone seized the lot of them before we could do any serious questioning. There's something hinky about it, especially since Hart himself spoke to Boone directly in front of me before we knew who he was."

"Very well," she said, starting to offer her hand to shake before she dropped it and pulled him into a hug. "Good luck tae yae, Mac."

He returned the hug, harder than he meant to. "And to you, Ailsa."

Mac watched Ailsa sprint across the wharf and drive off with Verone, then steeled himself and stepped back to the bridge. Minerva had covered Solana with a blanket. She stood respectfully back while he looked down at the body for a long moment as the wailing sirens grew closer.

"Thank you for that," he said at last.

She inclined her head. "It was horrible to witness. I am very sorry, for what it's worth."

"You didn't shoot her. They did."

"Mistakes happen."

"With guns, often," Mac said, coldly. He cleared his head with a breath and forced his grief aside, though he knew it wouldn't be for long. "So, you're here, why?"

"On this ship? My purpose was twofold. First, we wished to return Doctor Verone unharmed."

"You could've dropped him at any airport or hotel."

She disagreed. "No, appearance is everything, as my father would say, and that sort of unforced capitulation would raise questions we didn't wish asked. And there were other factors which I can't elaborate."

Mac grunted. "And the second reason?"

"My father wishes to speak with you."

"I heard. Why?"

"I will leave that to him. This is an invitation, Mister MacGyver, not a threat nor an order. In exchange, I'll be keeping you out of Turkish custody and not raising any alarm over Lady MacIver or Mister Boone."

Mac felt a hot jet of anger at the mention. He gestured to the monitors and controls. "So why all the smoke and mirrors here?"

"We knew a team would be coming. We just weren't certain whose it would be. If you were here, so much the better. Were it the CIA alone, they'd have found Doctor Verone easily enough, and I'd have allowed them a rapid, if not simple escape. I did not anticipate you were part of two different teams."

"And Solana paid the price for that."

"If it's any comfort, her death was instantaneous."

His gaze hardened. "It's not."

The Turkish police arrived, full of huff and bluster, but ran straight into the wall that was Minerva Hart. She took over the scene like a sovereign ruler, gave them their orders to have poor Castillo's body cared for, and gave the investigators their official stories. Not all of them seemed happy about the arrangements, but a government liaison had arrived as well, and pulled rank to back up her smooth flow of instructions.

Mac remained on the bridge, now sitting in a chair, staring at the smeared bloodstains on the hard tile floor.

"Mister MacGyver?" Minerva called from the door. "Come. A car is waiting. We'll provide accommodations and give you a chance to rest. You can speak with my father in the morning."

"I'd rather do it now," he said.

She paused. "I'm afraid that would prove difficult. He'll be out of pocket for at least the next few hours." She held out her hand. "Please. You look … in a state. Let us at least get you some food."

"Not hungry."

"I'm sure, but nor can you stay here. The car, please?"

She's the bad guy, remember.

She didn't shoot Solana.

But she died because of all their games.

Your thoughts are circling.

Let 'em.

He got to his feet and followed her to the waiting limousine.

CHAPTER 23

Loss is inevitable in this kind of job. Hell, loss is inevitable in life. The months of grief and pain are the price paid for years of love and laughter, kindness and companionship. That's the deal. And, in the end, it's still worth it.

But I didn't get those years. Those were the years to come.

So why does it hurt just as much to lose a future as it does to lose a past?

But this isn't over yet.

Can't let that get into your head, Mac.

Can't not.

So be it.

Doctor Verone had slept all the way to the airport. Ailsa's brief call with Holcomb got a private flight arranged, and she agreed to escort him to Washington. Once settled into luxury seats with Doctor Verone dozing once again, she called Holcomb for the promised full debrief as the plane soared skyward.

"So, MacGyver went with her willingly?" he said, hardly believing. "He's not really an undercover kind of guy."

"I was surprised, too. Hart wished tae deal with him, an' we've been chasin' the man halfway across the globe with little effect, so it makes sense. We only truly have the doctor back because they'd gotten what they wanted," she said, annoyed with herself at having been played.

"Yeah, about that, has he said anything?"

She glanced at the man, sunk deep in his chair, head back, mouth open. "He's been asleep since takeoff. I'll ask him if he wakes. In brief, they were after his knowledge a' yaer new reactor, an' used drugs tae get what they needed."

Holcomb swore quietly. "Well, at least it wasn't for any bombs."

"Aye, I doubt yae need fear as much. Mac explained how a fusion reactor is very different."

"Yeah. Okay. Thanks, Agent MacIver. Langley owes you one."

"Before yae go, Mac wished me tae run somethin' by yae." She explained about their last conversation regarding Boone and his sudden appearance at Mac's last case.

Holcomb thought about it a moment. "He's not wrong about Boone being there. MacGyver's last assignment was the stolen bioweapon. Boone used a favor with Homeland Security to get those prisoners transferred to our control and held as enemy combatants."

Ailsa was struck dumb for a long moment. "I may nae know much about yaer legal procedures in the States, but they're yaer own citizens committin' crimes on yaer own soil! In the Middle East, I could see it, but—"

"I didn't say it was right, or that it would hold up. I don't do things this way. Very few of us have the authority. Boone has a lot more leeway."

Ailsa was incredulous. "Why?"

Holcomb's shrug was implied. "Office politics, favors owed, clout ... take your pick. Some deputy directors are more interested in results than rights. It's no different where you're from."

"Aye, but that does'nae make it right."

"No argument here, ma'am," he said. "But those are the facts. Boone gets it done. Even went rogue once, much like now. Only that time he was successful. This time ... well, we'll see how it all shakes out."

"Aye. Even though Castillo was technically on leave, this will raise hell in Interpol. Yae can expect somethin' formal, tae be sure."

"And from MI6?"

She paused. "My people are aware a' the incident, but as I'm the agent on the scene, they're followin' my judgment. The only issue a' official concern we have at the moment is yaer Mister Boone."

"Acknowledged. I expect we'll have something to say on that soon. Like I say, going rogue worked for him once before, but that went off flawlessly. This time it was a debacle, and he'd been using a lot of political capital here in his witch hunts."

"Witch hunts?"

Holcomb explained about Boone's persecution of both him and MacGyver over Doctor Verone's abduction. "He effectively had me all but out the door until he disappeared. Mac would've been the same in another few days when his contract expired."

Ailsa was no stranger to intra-agency rivalries. "Did he have some reason for this animus against the two a' yae, at all?"

"MacGyver stole his thunder more than once. Not intentionally. That's not his style, from what I hear."

"No, it's not." Ailsa had trouble imagining Mac either nursing a grudge or trying to outshine anyone.

"But, in the intel world here, MacGyver is a kinda rock star. His record is first-rate, and sometimes that makes enemies of people in the running for promotions."

Ailsa knew a fair bit about that as well. "An' what did Boone have against yae?"

Holcomb could only shrug again. "I'd shaken his hand at a company Christmas party once, and he ran an operation where I was perimeter defense. That went fine, and we didn't even speak directly. I have no idea why he had me in his sights after losing Verone. Hell, he was even suggesting that there was a sinister reason I'd volunteered for the assignment."

"He was suggestin' yae colluded with Hart tae kidnap Verone?"

"Not outright, but he's been dropping breadcrumbs about it."

A switch clicked open in Ailsa's brain. She leaned forward, intent on the thread. "Who else would have oversight into Verone's disappearance besides Boone?"

"Oversight?"

"Aye, yae were Verone's handler in Barcelona, so yae'd be involved. Other than yae, who would investigate?"

Holcomb considered. "If you mean who'd be in charge, it'd be Boone until the Deputy Director called Mac in."

"Right, an' the two a' yae were targets a' his official wrath. Nae yaer team members in Barcelona. Nae anyone in New York at the airport. Just the two a' yae—the only two with direct lines tae Boone's superiors that could tell them a different story than his."

Holcomb's long pause was borne of shock. "*Uhh*, okay, agent, hang on a minute. You know what you're implying?"

"I'm nae just implyin', lad, I'm bloody well sayin' it. Hart has long had someone with superior access inside a' Langley. Hell, he's still got moles within MI6, which is why an agent-at-large like me is on his case rather than someone with more support an' resources. Factor in Boone cleanin' up the bioweapon mess out from under yaer DHS's nose—that was meant as a distraction before the kidnappin' a' Verone, an' the pattern becomes clear."

Holcomb hedged. "That's a lot of supposition, ma'am."

"Enough coincidences tae give it a good look, if yae ask me."

Holcomb was wary, but not arguing. "It would explain a lot of things. But best to let it sit for now. We'll talk more when you get here."

◆◆

The hotel towered into the night sky, the tallest building in Mersin. Uniformed valets opened doors and pressed buttons to bring them to Mac's room, fully one half of the penthouse. In truth, he hardly noticed. His mind remained fixed on Solana's big brown eyes, looking at him the night before, seeing everything, and now, empty and vacant, seeing nothing at all.

"You really should eat something, and try to get some sleep," Minerva was saying from the door.

"What? Oh. Yeah." He glanced around at the gleaming wood furnishings, silver and gold appointments, and the pricey works of art adorning the walls. "Look, I'd just as soon get this over with, understand?"

Minerva glanced at her watch. "Very well. But it will be another hour or so. For now, please let us know if there's anything we can do to make you more comfortable." The doorman—a bodyguard, judging by his size and the shoulder holster under his jacket—closed the door behind her, leaving him alone.

Mac collapsed into a chair, cradling his head in his hands.

Make myself comfortable?

How? Right now, comfort just sounds ... obscene.

Sleep? Food? The pretense of normal?

Can't get there from here.

It's all just hurt.

And darkness.

And rage.

Mac forced his eyes to open, looking around at the perfectly appointed room. Wanting nothing more than to tear the place apart: rip the paintings, smash the furniture, break every goddamn thing he could lay his hands on. Make it match the chaos and havoc roaring inside of him.

And then what?

She's still gone.

And you're still here.

Waiting to face Hart.

How can I do that?

I can't even face myself now.

"*Then don't,*" he heard Solana whisper.

"*Take yourself out of it. Completely.*"

Mac closed his eyes again to shut out the offense of the pristine room and just focus on his breath for a moment.

I can't run from this. Run from myself.

There is no way out. Is there?

But

What if

You imagine Solana's here.

And you're the one that's dead.

How could you help her?

What would you say to her?

I'd say I love you.

She knows that.

Nice, but not much help. What else?

Help her! She needs your help now, jackass, not your gooey blubbering.

What do you say to her!?

Mac's mind went blank for a moment: no thoughts, no words, no images. Just the utter emptiness of being lost in the darkness. And then ... something. The tiniest flicker, barely perceptible, rising to the surface in all that black.

I'd tell her to use what she's got.

If all you have now, Solana, is grief and pain, then ...

Use that!

Make it into a tool.

No, make it into a weapon.

Take all that hurt and anger and hammer it into a frigging battle-axe!

And crush them with it. Hart. Boone. All of them.

Mac couldn't feel his body, not even his breathing. But he could feel *that*. Clear and sharp. Like a blade that could cut ... *anything*.

And if you could hear her now, if she was talking to you now, is that what she'd say to you?

Yes.

Yes. That's what she'd tell me to do. Want me to do.

Don't let me be your weakness now, Mac.

Let me be your strength.

Because I love you, Mac.

"I know," Mac whispered out loud as he opened his eyes, feeling the tears seeping from them. But, looking around, the room with all its privilege meant nothing now. The pain and loss and anger were all still there. But they were *his* now. He *owned* them. And would use them when the time came. Because that's what she would want. That's what she could give him now, as an almost surreal sense of gratitude washed over him, coursing through his veins, filling him, completely.

Rising from the chair, he went into the bathroom, turned on the faucet and stuck his head beneath it, letting the cold water soak his head. And rinse his tears. But, most surprising of all, it felt good. He pictured Solana, shampooing his hair, then sitting him down like a schoolboy to cut it, wrapping a towel around his shoulders, the way she had in their time together in San Sebastián. And he smiled. There would be no future together, he told himself. But she wasn't lost to him. And never would be.

He turned off the water and reached for a towel to dry himself, noticing the phone beside the sink. On a whim, he picked it up and tried an outside number.

"Apologies," said the automated message. "This line is reserved for concierge service only."

Of course.

Had to know I'd be cut off from everyone.

How will I get a line to Ailsa or Holcomb?

Not to worry about now. You'll think of something.

Eventually.

Now I have to sheath that weapon. Keep it hidden.

Act wounded. But "normal."

He hit the button for service. A smooth voice picked up instantly and took his order for fresh salad with salmon. It arrived inside of fifteen minutes, with a scent that made his dry mouth water, perfectly prepared and presented: crisp lettuce, juicy tomato, crumbled blue cheese, the salmon seared flawlessly.

But it was just a prop now. Part of the play he was acting out. He grabbed the fork and jabbed a bite of the salmon, recalling how he fed Solana grilled octopus, one little tentacle at a time, as they sat on the floor in their casita, wrapped in sheets, laughing their heads off. Nothing would ever taste that good. The salmon wasn't bad, but it might as well have been cardboard. He mashed the fish around in the greens to make it look like he'd tried, then found a bottle of water in the fridge, shut off all the lights, and returned to the chair to sip at it. And let himself wander through more moments of their time together. Not reaching for them, nor trying to hold them when they appeared. Just letting them come as they chose. For now, that was enough ...

He must have dozed lightly, as a knock on the door brought him blinking up from darkness, wondering for a moment where he was, feeling that hard pain of grief return, gripping at his chest and limbs, but not fighting it now. "Come in," he called.

It was Minerva, backlit from the light in the hallway. In another life, he might've even thought she was pretty. No Solana by a long shot, but who would be now?

"It's time, Mister MacGyver," she said from the door.

Mac rose from the chair, not bothering to turn on a light, and followed her across the hall to her penthouse, a perfect mirror of his own. She picked up a remote and the huge portrait above the fireplace slid upwards and back to reveal a massive curved-screen monitor. Another click, and Mac found himself face-to-face with a smiling Victor Hart, looking for all the world like they were merely convening for a pleasant business meeting. Mac let his mind run along the edge of that hidden blade but kept the mask of grief on his face.

"Ah, Mister MacGyver," Hart said. "I regret we can't meet in person, but, under the circumstances, I hope this will suffice."

"You got something to say, Hart. I'm here. So, say it."

"Straight to the point, yes, indeed. First, however, allow me to offer my sincerest condolences and apologies for the loss of Agent

Castillo. She was an admirable woman, extraordinary in so many ways. Such an unfortunate waste."

Mac held his gaze. "Yeah. And?"

Hart smiled sadly. "You doubt my sincerity. I understand. But she hunted me avidly and very nearly successfully across three continents. She had my utmost respect. Perhaps it is strange to you, and meaningless at the moment, but I recognize and appreciate talent, and I deplore its senseless loss."

Mac took in a quiet breath. "Still waiting for the point. For all it took to get me here, I'm guessing you have one?"

"You don't give yourself enough credit, good sir. You're a difficult man to track down. And a face-to-face discussion, such as it is, was necessary for my proposal."

Here it comes.

"Which is?"

"I've taken the last few weeks to study you, Mister MacGyver: your career, your missions, your successes, even your infrequent failures. And I'll confess, I've become something of a fan. You're obviously a brilliant man and, perhaps more importantly, one with a good heart, which in your line of work is rare. And though I may appear to you as the enemy, we are, in fact, not truly opposed in our goals."

Mac looked grim, and dubious. "And how do you figure that?"

"Simply this," Hart went on. "We both wish to help people, save them, in fact, from those that wish them harm and, at times, even from themselves. In short, we share a higher purpose."

"And what would that be, exactly?" Mac said, sounding irritated, making his resistance clear.

"A way to help humanity as a whole. As opposed to putting out spot fires for your intelligence services to little lasting effect."

Mac crossed his arms and cocked his head.

Hart nodded. "Skeptical, naturally. I know my proposition sounds wildly grandiose."

"More like absurd," Mac said. "I don't work for criminal organizations."

286 / ERIC KELLEY & LEE ZLOTOFF

"Oh, but I'm afraid you do."

Mac sighed. "Meaning the CIA?"

"As with all national intelligence agencies, they have the best of intentions and the worst of means. They also function at the behest of their governments, themselves run by the wealthy elite, who merely seek to enrich themselves at the world's expense."

Bait him. Make him work for it, Mac thought, as he said, "You got any tinfoil, Hart? I'm thinking I need to make a hat."

Hart's smile remained on his face but left his eyes. "That is unworthy of you, my good man. This is no cheap conspiracy theory. Your own country is no exception. The ultrarich dictate policy to the politicians to line their own pockets. When foreign interests interfere in corporate designs, the powers that be send in the intelligence agencies and their jackals. I have firsthand experience in these matters, or did Ailsa not mention my background?"

"You worked for MI6, I was told."

"A lifetime ago," Hart said, eyes briefly distant. "It was as bad during the Cold War as ever it is now. Very little has really changed, and even less has improved. I can't imagine you haven't noticed. Vanquish one rogue actor, one warlord, one deranged terrorist, and another just appears to take their place."

He's not wrong, Mac thought.

Ailsa warned me about this. He's a master.

And you have a blade now.

Yeah, but he's not wrong.

"Keeps me off the streets," Mac said, not letting himself agree.

"Glib and clever, sir. But a disingenuous response. Being used as a tool by such powers can hardly be satisfying for a man of your intellect, I should think."

"So, instead, I should work for kidnappers and thieves? Not my thing. Or did you miss that in your studies?"

Hart's smile widened slightly. "Ah, and now we get to the core of it, eh? Because you yourself are a kidnapper and thief, are you not?"

"Come again?"

Hart tapped a few keys on his computer and read. "April 2015, you extracted a nuclear scientist from Iran, correct?"

If Hart had reach into the Agency, he would know about that. He would know about all of it. Mac didn't even try to evade. "I didn't kidnap him. He was defecting. His government was preparing to imprison him on trumped-up charges."

"Did he mention that the CIA were the ones to trump them up?" Mac said nothing. Hart continued. "No, of course not. I doubt that he knew. Or that you did. Currently, his family remains in hiding in Iran, and his brother is imprisoned in his stead while your man walks free in America, or rather as free as a government asset and foreign national can. Or do you truly believe he'd have willingly left his family behind, and his brother to take the blame for his alleged crime?"

Mac knew Boone wasn't above pulling something like that. And he wasn't the only one. The Agency did what they wanted when they chose and wrapped it all in "national security." He'd said as much to Solana on the flight to Oslo. But it was too soon to bend.

"But that's just your version," said Mac, coldly. "And I have no way to verify it, do I?"

"Indeed," replied Hart. "Let's turn to the issue of your thievery. Which I'm afraid makes up most of your curriculum vitae. Going back for decades."

Mac shifted uncomfortably, as if to let Hart think he was scoring points.

"We have a chemical sample of a neurotoxin you appropriated in Libya. Plans for a ground-to-space laser you liberated in China. An orbital map for spy satellites you recovered in Tokyo, Japan. An ally of the US, no less."

"Someone had hacked them," Mac argued, "and they didn't believe us. We had to prove they weren't completely bulletproof."

"Then you robbed them for their own good, wouldn't you have to agree?"

"No comment," said Mac.

"And while you appear to avoid firearms entirely, which I find admirable, because—not unlike myself—you have no desire to inflict violence and suffering, the fact remains that there are consequences to even your most altruistic actions."

A video appeared from the Syrian badlands, the site of a convoy of armored SUVs, now wrecked in the burning heat. The cameraman jogged across the shattered ground to the twisted wreckage and looked in. A mangled man in what once was a designer suit stared back with ash-covered eyes. He'd been dead at least half a day, and the heat had accelerated the decomposition process. It was the arms dealer, Demir.

MacGyver stared a moment, the image of his body mingling horribly with that of Solana's on the floor of the bridge.

Hart was pressing now. *Let him.*

"You corrupted his product," he continued, "did you not? Surely you had to expect his customers would express their displeasure."

"He dealt in the business of death," Mac replied. "Sooner or later that catches up to you."

"Perhaps." Hart remained cool, calculating. Judging. "But you were the man who set that inevitable revenge in motion."

Mac's answer brought some heat. "Then maybe you shouldn't have sold him sarin in the first place! If there's blood on my hands, then it's on yours, too."

"My point exactly," said Hart, like he'd just snatched Mac's queen off the chessboard and was angling towards mate in a few more moves. "And who do you think paid me to deliver that gas to Demir? So that the Syrian regime would use it and permit the US to launch token air strikes to assure the world they were a country that stood for something and would punish such offenses?"

Mac took a beat, as if Hart's words were starting to hit home. "You're seriously trying to tell me the CIA paid you to deliver poison gas to the Syrians?"

"I'm telling you your CIA is one of my best customers," Hart replied with confidence. "And that gas was merely the latest in a long and sordid history of my work for them. But perhaps this will prove more convincing."

A transcript appeared on the screen along with a recording:

"THIS PRODUCT, YOU KNOW, VIOLATES YOUR OWN COUNTRY'S POLICIES AND LAWS, DOES IT NOT? ARE YOU SURE SUCH A PURCHASE IS WORTH THE RISK, MY FRIEND?" said Hart's voice.

"THIS COMES FROM UPSTAIRS," came the reply, garbled through a synthesizer.

"YOUR PRESIDENT, THEN?"

"YOU TAKE THAT AS YOU CHOOSE. BUT WE HAVE A LONG-STANDING ARRANGEMENT WITH YOU. AND, IF YOU VALUE THAT, I'M NOT INTERESTED IN ANY QUESTIONS OR OBJECTIONS FROM THE DELIVERY BOY. ARE WE CLEAR?"

A sigh. "VERY WELL. PUT HALF THE MONEY IN THE ACCOUNT, AND THE SHIP WILL BE AVAILABLE. DELIVERY TO YOUR TURKISH MERCHANT WILL REQUIRE THE OTHER HALF IN CASH."

"FINE. THEN WE'RE DONE."

The audio cut off.

Mac was shaking his head, keeping up the fight. But the recording sounded every bit like the agency often dealt with him. Still. "That could be faked. Easily," Mac said.

"As can almost any intel these days—even video." Hart shrugged. "But what reason would I have to falsify any of this?"

"You want to turn me. And get me to work for you. Isn't that why I'm here?"

Hart laughed. "Indeed, it is. But you both flatter and insult yourself, Mister MacGyver. First, that I would go to such lengths just to persuade you. And second, that you wouldn't discover it was just a ruse, given time. However, there is a simple enough way to resolve our debate, assuming, of course, you are prepared to accept the truth of what I say rather than cling to your current illusions."

"Yeah? And what would that be?" Mac asked, letting Hart back him further into a corner.

"A task," answered Hart, "well within your capabilities, I should think. You require evidence of my assertions, and I am willing to provide it. And, once you have that evidence, it will be your choice what do to with it. For my part, I only ask this evidence be erased from those who have it now. I have been cutting ties with my more complicated clients in the last year as my project moves into its final stage."

"Project Ararat, you mean? Your sanctuary?"

Hart nodded. "I'm not surprised you of all people would have deduced my purpose, based on my shopping list alone. Though, I didn't know you knew the name."

"And you'd be Noah."

Hart actually looked embarrassed. "My colleagues can be overly dramatic. But, yes, Ararat has been my ultimate goal these last three decades, and it is nearly ready to weather the coming storm."

"I'll bet. And what's this 'task'? You want me out there rounding up pairs of animals?" Mac said, trying to mock Hart just enough.

Hart smiled briefly. "The data concerning myself and my dealings at your government's behest is in CIA headquarters. I want it erased, along with the backups. You may view the data beforehand, then decide for yourself if my proposal carries weight."

Mac suddenly felt that edge waver in his mind. He wasn't sure where Hart was going with all this. But it never occurred to him it would go *there*. "You want me to bust into Langley—one of the most secure facilities on the planet—and erase their data?"

"And the backups," Hart said without blinking.

"Same difference!" Mac snapped. "You know how impossible that would be?"

"'Impossible' is not a word I associate with you, Mister MacGyver. I know what you can do."

"I helped design some of the security there!"

"Indeed." Hart shrugged. "Then what better man for the job?"

Mac rolled his head, his mind spinning. If Hart wanted him tangled up in the ropes, he was there—as he reached for a response, "And how would I even know what I'm looking for?"

"Minerva will assist you," Hart replied calmly, not wanting to rile Mac too hard. "She has all the necessary qualifications to defeat their internal computer security."

"Oh, that's just great. So, I'm not only breaking in myself, but a foreign national to boot." Mac groaned. "She could get caught, you know. Hurt, even."

"I think not. My money is more than enough protection for her in the event of an unfavorable outcome. And I possess damaging information on enough of your politicians to counter even the most damning charges. Of course, I cannot offer the same protection to you. It is a risk, yes, but, as I said, I have no shortage of faith in your abilities. More to the point, I have an equal faith in your curiosity and your conscience, sir. So, do you wish to know the beast you serve? Or go on telling yourself there are no monsters beneath the bed?"

Mac felt for that edge in his mind. It was still there, but he had no clue which way to cut with it now.

This is a bad idea, he thought.

But if this is true, what have I been doing with myself all this time?

Yeah, they could be monsters.

Still a bad idea.

But, either way, the info is there.

And if it proves it to be legit?

Then we've got a decision to make.

And if it's bogus? Then I hand Minerva to the agency.

And what happens to me then?

I'm finished. Or worse.

Right now. This moment. Do I care about that?

No, came the answer, that edge suddenly feeling even sharper than when he first found it.

I'm tired of all the grey. I need some answers.

If I can't hold Solana, then at least something solid.

Still a bad idea.

"Okay," MacGyver said finally. "But I'll need a few things."

"Minerva will get you anything money can buy. I regret, however, that you have somewhat less than seventy hours."

Mac sighed. "Naturally."

Hart smiled and turned. "Minerva, go carefully. Good luck to you both."

"Thank you, Father. And good luck with the reactor."

The screen went dark. And Mac felt like he had just jumped off a very high cliff.

The aircraft with Ailsa and Verone descended, jouncing its passengers as it passed through the storm front on descent to Dulles International Airport. Ailsa saw Verone stir and sit up, clearing his eyes and staring around, lost. "Oh. Hello," he said. "Where are we?"

"Landing in Washington shortly," she said. "Bit a' weather. Are yae feelin' all right? Yae'v slept the whole way."

"Yes, better now, I think, thank you. The drugs they used were ... potent."

"I'd imagine it was a combination a' drugs an' sleep deprivation."

He nodded, looking haggard and ancient.

"I'm sorry for all that. They wanted tae know about yaer fusion work, aye?"

He nodded. "Do you wish to hear the specifics?"

She shook her head. "I would'nae understand much a' it, I'm afraid. They were buildin' their own reactor, was it?"

He bobbed his head again, glancing out the window as lightning lit the cabin. "Believe it or not, it helped me work through a very tricky problem we'd been having keeping the containment field stabilized."

Ailsa thought for a moment, glad Mac had given her the rundown on how a fusion reactor worked. "Containment field for the deuterium that fuses tae provide the energy?"

"Correct." Thunder startled him. "Oh, I dislike flying—especially in stormy weather."

She smiled, reassuring. "We'll be through it soon enough."

"This whole thing has been too much excitement for a lifetime.

At least they won't have their reactor long. I can claim that much revenge for this torture."

Ailsa felt a jolt run up her spine. "What do yae mean—they won't have it long?"

He laughed hollowly. "I may have been strung out and drug-addled, but I know what I said. Not knowing who they were, or were working for, I left out how the field's interaction with the reactant would feed upon itself. That's part of the beauty in the ultimate solution, but it has to be properly configured and carefully controlled. With what I gave them, it will overload at a certain point, and the reaction will breach."

Ailsa stared at him. "Breach? As in explode?"

"Oh, not a large one, no," he said. "More than a meltdown, but it would self-sustain very briefly. Like a small fusion device."

Ailsa swallowed dry. "Doctor, please be very specific now. How large a detonation are we talkin'?"

He shrugged. "A kilometer radius, perhaps three-quarters. Certainly enough to eliminate whoever did this to me," he added grimly.

Ailsa's guts seized like a fist. "Then a nuclear explosion. Right wher' Mac is goin'." She couldn't tell if a bolt of lightning had just flashed outside the plane, or in it.

CHAPTER 24

"BUT HOW WAS I TO KNOW?" Doctor Verone repeated miserably for the twentieth time, seated on the couch in Boone's office, now co-opted by Holcomb. The storm lashed the window beyond, and the entire building smelled of stale coffee and a memory of cigarettes, not long ago banned, much to the CIA's particular collective regret.

"It's not your fault, Doc," Holcomb said. "You had no idea who they were or what they were after. Not sure I wouldn't have done the same."

"Aye," Ailsa said. "Yet, the problem remains. We have no way tae warn Mac that he's walkin' into a bomb until he makes contact." She turned from eyeing the storm outside the glass, arms crossed. "What news a' Boone?"

Holcomb sat back behind the desk with a dark look. "He's gone missing. Slipped away from our people in Turkey before he was due to come back here."

That perked her up. "The bastard's gone full rogue then?"

Holcomb could only shrug. "Looks like."

"I'd say that confirms our suspicions about him."

Holcomb waved to the computer. "Maybe, but there's nothing I can find that links him to Hart in any way. Not that I'd expect it to be easy. Plus, no one upstairs has issued a detainment order for him.

He has a standing order to return to Langley, but no one's released the hounds."

Ailsa shook her head dejectedly. "The man ran a black operation that resulted in the death of a decorated Interpol agent!"

"Yeah. Well, there's a reason they call them 'black ops.' No discussion, no acknowledgment."

"And no consequences, apparently," Ailsa said tersely.

"I wouldn't go that far. The standing order wouldn't be there if he was off the hook entirely."

With effort, Ailsa beat her temper into submission. "Aye. Sorry. She was a respected colleague an' one a' the good ones. It's Mac that should worry yae, though. I'd bet Hart has promised him some measure a' vengeance."

Holcomb's eyes widened. "What do you mean?"

"I know Hart. If he gets a hook in yae, all he needs is time tae reel yae in. Hell, he could convince the dirtiest a' lawyers tae take up charity work, or a priest tae burn his Bible. It was one a' his specialties in his MI6 days. He turned more agents than anyone else. The man's dangerous, especially in the emotional state Mac's in."

"I can vouch for that," Doctor Verone said, seeing ghosts.

Worry had crept into Holcomb's voice. "Yeah, I read your report." He paused, shaking his head. "But revenge? MacGyver? That's a stretch. I mean, I haven't worked closely with him, but his rep around here doesn't need any more shine to it; guy's a Boy Scout, if you know what I'm saying."

"It'll be somethin' insidious, then," Ailsa mused. "There's a reason Hart wanted him, an' it cannae be solely due tae Mac's noble works."

"Well, the word has been sent to keep an eye out for him, too. Especially with this reactor problem." His head tilted with a new thought. "So, then what about getting Hart a direct message? About the reactor."

Ailsa grunted. "Hart? I'm nae so very worried about the man blowin' himself up." But reason took only a moment to break through. "That said, I suppose we cannae let the bloody thing kill ev'ryone nearby," she conceded.

"I'm so sorry," Verone said again, looking wretched.

"Dinnae trouble yaerself, Doctor. There's no blame tae assign. But, if we could warn Hart, what could be done tae stop it?"

Doctor Verone hung his head, considering. "Nothing. Once powered up ..." He spread his hands helplessly. "Twenty minutes? Perhaps a bit more. It will build and build until the magnetic containment field collapses, releasing the reactant and allowing it to fuse uncontrolled. You see, the reactants are compartmentalized within the field, only sent into the primary chamber for fusion in precise bursts. There is literally no safe way to shut it down in this configuration without additional precautions built into the reaction chamber. I never told them of those precautions." He paused. "Am I making sense?"

"We get the gist, aye," she said. "So, tae contact Hart ... In truth, keepin' information from him has been our largest concern for some time. In theory, we just make it known that the reactor is rigged, an' he'd hear about it."

"Not if Boone was his source here," Holcomb said. "Unless you know who's feeding him intel from MI6?"

She shook her head. "It's why I'm at-large. An' would it reach him in time?"

"And would he even believe it?"

Ailsa had no clue. A thought occurred, and she suppressed a groan. "There may be one person who could get me in touch directly."

"Who's that?"

She sighed heavily. "Is yaer phone secured, an' might I have the room?"

"Calling your superiors?" Holcomb asked as they stood.

Ailsa picked up the receiver, eyes flinty. "*She* certainly thinks so."

Mac handed over a list of items to Minerva Hart.

She took a moment to peruse, her eyebrows slowly creeping upward in amusement. "You're quite serious?"

"Yeah. Any hardware store or electronics shop should handle most of that. Secondhand is fine, too. Oh, and I'll need a suit. Nothing expensive. More like something I could afford."

"How much would that be?"

"I dunno. Couple hundred bucks."

"Also found in the secondhand store, no doubt."

"Could be," he said without humor. "You'll need a suit, too."

"Skirt or pants?"

"Just normal business attire. Either is fine."

"I'm just curious what sort of acrobatics might be required," she said. "If we're to run at all, it should be pants and sensible shoes."

"No, we won't be climbing through any air ducts or suspended on wires or anything."

"So how shall we get in?"

Mac didn't bother to meet her gaze, looking past her as he answered. "Just like everyone else, through the front door."

👓

"Ah, the prodigal daughter remembers her mother is alive, should I be touched?" the Dowager Countess MacIver said, her acid all but dripping through the phone.

"Hello, Mother," Ailsa said. "If you've any caustic observations to make, perhaps we could save them for the end? There's a situation developing, and I could use your help."

Dead silence. "You've been kidnapped again."

"Please, stop. This is about Victor Hart."

Silence again. "Oh, him. Are you any closer to laying hands upon his neck?"

"Somewhat, but I need to get him a message, urgently."

"A message! What makes you think I can—"

"Mother, don't. Before I proved my accusations to you, he was still a family friend. He still thinks he is, all evidence to the contrary."

"Ailsa, you don't know what you're asking—"

"There's no time!" Ailsa snapped. "Either yae can or yae cannae. Which is it?"

The Dowager's tone dropped several degrees. "Where are you?"

"America."

"Specifically?"

Ailsa paused, then said, "Langley, Virginia."

"Oh, so you *have* been kidnapped."

"Mother!—"

"Never mind then. I may have the means to reach him, but I need to look for it. How urgent is this matter?"

"Extremely. Innocent lives are in danger right now."

Silence for a moment. "Very well. Contact me tomorrow."

"Tomorrow? Time is a significant factor here."

"Should I find something sooner, I'll call. Otherwise, dawn tomorrow on your side of the pond."

The Dowager MacIver hung up abruptly. Ailsa stared at the receiver a moment, then slammed it down—harder than she meant to.

♥♥

The Gulfstream G650 sliced through the night sky like a razor through silk. Mac was grateful for the smooth ride as he performed surgery on a gutted laptop computer.

Farther forward at the dining table, Minerva set her empty plate aside, and noted Mac's pristine salad, untouched across the table from her. "Not to your liking, Mister MacGyver?"

"You can just call me Mac," he said, glancing up from his work. "People who call me Mister MacGyver either want money or something else I can't give them ... And I'm not hungry."

She crossed her arms and regarded him as the stewards removed the setting. "As you wish. But, for what it's worth, excessive brooding does no good. Believe me, I speak from some experience."

He went back to his soldering. "You brood a lot, do you?"

"An occupational hazard, in this family business."

Mac just gave her a look, taking the moment to search for that sharp edge in his mind as she continued.

"Despite what you see, our endeavor has its burdens. Particularly as a great many employees and others depend on us for their daily bread."

"Like politicians?" he said, sourly.

She laughed. "They're more like parasites. Easily acquired and difficult to discard. No, I mean the various employees across our business ventures that fund this grand project. Everyone from sailors to software developers."

"To arms dealers and terrorists."

She sighed. "Really, Mac, the CIA must treat you like Rapunzel in her tower, shielding you from all the evils in this world, especially those they perpetrate."

"My hair's not that long," he said.

She smiled. "Well, perhaps it's just a trifle. Still, I'm glad to see your sense of humor remains in there somewhere."

With the mention, whatever lightness had lifted him for a moment evaporated. He went back to his work, mouth set in a line.

Minerva paused. "Ah. Forgive me. I know the grief is very near."

Mac didn't respond.

She watched him for a long moment, considering. "Not that I imagine it helps, but had I realized what was afoot, I would have kept your two groups separate on the ship. I am truly sorry that you've lost someone ... special to you."

"I got it," he said bluntly. "But you don't really know anything about us."

"No, I'm sure. But I am a woman, and it's not difficult to imagine how she must've regarded you. And you her."

Though he had no place for it, and wanted it even less, Minerva's empathy sounded genuine. And, after more empty silence, she finally stood. "Well, we do not land for some hours, and I believe I shall retire. You have the forecabin at your disposal, and both the steward and chef are on duty for the entire flight. Make use of them as you require."

He looked up from the computer again. "What I could really use is an internet connection to do a little research."

She made a pained face. "The aircraft's computer library is quite extensive. I'm afraid that's all I can offer."

"Oh? No satellite?" he said, skeptical.

"I'm afraid that perhaps my Rapunzel analogy was more apt than I realized. You are to remain sequestered until after our task is complete." She headed towards the aft door.

Mac nodded, resigned. "But then that makes you the wicked witch, doesn't it?"

She turned, trying to be amused and not offended. "Yes, I suppose it does. Good night, Mac."

Ten hours and forty-two minutes after Ailsa hung up the phone in Langley, Ailsa's phone woke her up in her hotel room, the light glaring in the dark. "Aye," she said into it.

"Ailsa. I have what you need. A phone number that may work."

"Good. Let me get a pen—"

"No. I need to see you. There are things you should know."

"Mother, I am not dragging myself all the way to Scotland."

"A video conference will do, but it must be completely secured. These words are for you alone, and certainly not for the likes of your allies. I want no one listening in."

Ailsa grumbled for a moment, then, "I suppose the embassy would have what we need, if your end is secure."

"I was married to your father long enough to develop the habit. Rest assured, we are well equipped at MacIver House."

"Fine." Ailsa checked the time. "I can be at the embassy by dawn."

"Very good. My regards to the Ambassador, should you see him." The phone clicked dead.

Securing Ailsa's credentials took longer than securing the line, with the sun well up over the horizon by the time she was shown to a "dark room," so-called due to its secure nature. Everything sent or received by the secure computer was immediately erased from its memory, and the line was "scrambled as twice-cooked eggs" the security tech said. Ailsa didn't see the immediate connection between eggs and digital security, but then perhaps the tech prepared his food in ways bordering on the arcane.

Ailsa sat before the monitor and initiated the call.

Her mother appeared a moment later. "Ailsa." Eleanor MacIver was the very image of her daughter, though with an extra quarter century of age and jet-black hair rather than scarlet red, now laced with silver.

"All right, I'm here. How do I contact Hart?"

"Straight to business is it? The first time we're speaking face-to-face in who knows when and not even the pretense of pleasantries?"

Ailsa sighed. "Greetings, Mother, how are the Highlands today? Grey as usual? You're looking well, you've redecorated the library, and was there any other nonsense we could chitchat about before a fusion reactor overloads, potentially killing untold thousands?"

"You are here to listen to what I would not say to another living soul, particularly not where it might be recorded. The embassy is secure?"

"Of course." Ailsa waited, then gestured into the pause. "Well?"

"I was engaged to marry Victor Hart before I met your father. This is why he was a close family friend for most of your early life, and why it took so long for you to convince me of his guilt in your father's death."

Ailsa was a difficult woman to stun. Between combat missions in the Royal Navy and MI6 training in psychology and covert operations, she'd learned to anticipate the unexpected, keep calm in dire situations, and accept tactical reversals with composure. It all failed her in that moment. *"What the bloody hell?"* rang from the office walls.

"So, my iron daughter is not quite so impervious after all."

"Why would yae hide this from me?"

"It wasn't precisely hidden, Ailsa. It was simply nothing worth mentioning."

"Dinnae split hairs with me, Mother! This was important, an' yae damn well know it!"

"Why do you think I wished to tell you face-to-face? You deserved to know. Albeit, perhaps sooner than now," Eleanor conceded.

"Next yae'll be tellin' me he's my actual father," Ailsa spat.

Her mother slapped the table, furious. "How dare you! Absolutely not!"

They glared at each other for a long minute before Ailsa unclenched. "Fine. It's unsettlin' tae discover that my mother was romantically involved at one point with the man who murdered my father."

"No less so for me," Eleanor said, regaining her composure. "Though I've had years to grow accustomed to it, and to realize I made precisely the right choice back in those days. The split was not mutual, but he came around. Alice was a far better match for him, God rest her soul."

"An' this is why yae dinnae believe me as a wee bairn."

"In part, though the general lack of evidence that convinced Scotland Yard and MI6 of his innocence contributed to that as well. However, had I been more insistent with the officials, well ... Who knows?"

Ailsa considered the new information for a long moment, doing her best to divorce herself from her immediate emotional reaction. It was not easy. "Do yae believe yaer former relationship had anythin' at all tae do with Hart's motivation tae kill Dad?"

Eleanor sat. "I've considered it off and on for the last decade. Truly, Ailsa, I do not know. Poor Alice had been gone for four years by that point. In that time, Hart never made a single improper suggestion to me, nor even a hint of interest. After your father had been gone eighteen months, and I was no longer wearing black to every formal function, I believe he may have suggested we consider the idea in a roundabout fashion. Just a general observation that it was unfortunate our daughters were growing up without two parents."

"I barely knew Minerva," Ailsa said.

"Well, they lived in London, after all, and Hart had quit the Ministry to get his business venture running," Eleanor said.

"But yae dinnae consider his suggestion."

"I wouldn't say I did not consider it," she said. "Raising a child alone is a difficult situation, even in a house such as this with servants and money, and you yourself were as truculent then as now. Yet, your crusade to convince anyone that would listen of his guilt had made inroads. And there was something ... unusual about him. He had changed, and not for the better. I trusted my instincts, and never followed up. And so, here we are today in this unusual position where you seek the means to safeguard the life of a man who took so much from both of us."

"Aye. But, again, it's for—"

"Yes, yes, for the innocents in proximity." She opened a small wooden curio box and removed a slip of paper. "I had forgotten I had this until you called with your unusual request. He gave me this note at your father's funeral. I show it to you now to use as you will."

Eleanor opened the message and held it where Ailsa could see it.

Eleanor,

    Words cannot express my deep regret and sorrow. If you or Ailsa ever need anything, now or in the future, you need only call this number.

    Affectionately yours,

    Victor

. . .

The number was local to London.

Ailsa took a deep breath. "Thank yae, Mother. For tellin' me the truth. I need tae contact him now, if yae please. We'll discuss this again in time."

❧

Ailsa spent several minutes composing herself in the dark room before dialing. The number rang four times before picking up.

"Eleanor, to what do I owe the pleasure?"

"Yae dinnae truly expect my mother," Ailsa said.

Hart's flickering smile was implied. "No, Lady MacIver, but it would have been a pleasant surprise. How is she, by the way?"

"The same. Let's keep this brief. Yae'v a fusion reactor, created with information yae tortured out a' Doctor Verone. Dinnae turn it on. It's rigged tae blow."

Silence a moment, then a sigh. "Oh, come now, rigged? For what? A meltdown? Surely not an explosion. Fusion reactors don't function that way."

"This one does. The man had enough sense still in him tae give yae false information. Can't say I blame him, an' were it up tae me, I'd have let yae destroy yaerself along with whatever project yae'v got goin'. But—"

"You deduced that I'm not quite the madman and villain you've built up in your mind, and you do place a certain value on human life, even in your self-declared enemies. Is that it?"

"Half. I do value human life, namely those yae may have gathered into whatever lair yae'v built for yaerself. As for yae, feel free tae flip the switch an' stand next tae the bloody thing."

He laughed to himself. "So *dramatic*. We should contact the Academy of Film about an award."

Angry heat blossomed in her brain.

DON'T! she commanded herself.

Dinnae give in tae his barbs.

Aye, that's what he wants.

"Were it just drama, I'd appreciate the compliment," she said. "I've delivered my warnin', so do as yae like. Their deaths would be on yaer hands, nae mine."

"Very well, Ailsa, I consider myself so warned. I absolve you of my imminent demise. Truth be told, when I heard your voice, a warning was the last thing I expected."

Careful now, lass.

"Oh?"

"Quite. I supposed you'd demand to know where your American colleague is."

She shrugged. "He's a grown man and can do what he likes."

"Yes, but no concern at all? He was hardly in a fit state to make important life choices."

"Aye, thanks tae yaer daughter's manipulation a' events."

"Come now, it is hardly Minerva's fault that Agent Boone's minions can't control their violent outbursts. I fear it has left poor Mister MacGyver in quite a state. It's good that he's in friendly hands."

"What're yae about, old man?"

He sighed. "As I've tried to explain multiple times, my intentions are far from nefarious. Though I wonder indeed at yours. I cannot help but recall shots fired in Algiers. No warning given, no attempt to corral and capture, and the first bullets striking the vehicle rather near my head. One might think there was blood on your mind."

The red haze in Ailsa's vision had cleared into a cold, furious calm. "After ev'rything yae'v taken from us, yae wonder at it? Pray that Mac gets tae yae before I."

"I am guilty of a great many crimes, but—"

"Stop yaer gob. Enough lies. Yae'v been warned. The next time I see yae, we settle this for good an' all." She slammed the phone so hard that this time it shook the desk.

Ailsa stood resting on her fists, breathing hard for a long minute.

Oh, very calm, very collected, lassie, well done.

Shut it.

He won again.

SHUT IT! He got his warnin'.

Aye, an' confirmation that yae intend tae kill him.

He'll take more precautions now.

Yaer temper just made the job harder.

An ugly truth, but she couldn't evade it; wouldn't help if she could.

An' what a' Mac now? Hart could very well use him as an unwittin' hostage.

We need tae make contact, both about this an' the reactor.

How, exactly?

There lay the problem. She tried to think, but the dark room's utter silence weighed in upon her. The embassy itself was old, built along traditional lines with wood furnishings and leather appointments. It reminded her much of MacIver House, and having just spoken with her mother, she had the uncomfortable sensation of being home.

Let's get out a' here.

Aye. Wher' tae?

"Langley," she muttered, rising, with the hope Mac would get word to her from wherever he was in the whole damn world.

CHAPTER 25

Mac drove himself and Minerva Hart to CIA Headquarters along the DC Beltway. The day was bright, sunny, and turning into a real scorcher, highly unusual for late October.

"Can I ask you a question?"

"Certainly," she said.

"What's with the magic tricks?"

She half-smiled. "Ah, yes, my father's showmanship. Well, you know who my grandfather was, of course?"

"The Amazing Solomon Hart, wasn't it?"

"Quite. Grandfather taught my father everything he knew about stagecraft. As it happens, these skills can translate well into an espionage career. Consider: by the time an opponent realizes something is amiss, you could be halfway around the world. Doctor Verone was in Indonesia before anyone realized he was missing."

Indonesia, eh?

Did she just slip?

She may have just slipped.

How do we keep her going?

"Oh?" he asked innocently. "So, then you needed a jet fast enough to get to Indonesia in one flight in under ten hours or so. Probably be a big runway."

Minerva rolled her eyes. "Keep digging, Mac."

Hell.

Ailsa makes this look so easy.

"Worth a shot."

"Of course."

"The disappearing act was a good one," he continued. "Though once you know the trick, it's not so mysterious."

"I'd imagine it's much the same with your own techniques," she replied. "Speaking of which, did you bribe the waitress to slip and spill her drink on me? Or was it something even more mundane?"

Mac felt a touch of heat in his cheeks. "You figured that was me, eh? Just soapy water on the floor."

"Yes, but to land on *me* specifically and not all over the entire booth?"

He shrugged. "Mostly just luck. But the angle the server was approaching from, her carrying the tray balanced on her right hand instead of left, her high heels, and then the soapy water on the floor. I honestly didn't think about it enough to gauge the variables. But you get a feel for these things."

She nodded, amused. "It's much the same with Father's techniques, though luck and improvisation are to be avoided. Preplanned contingencies are far more effective."

"Yeah, I suppose. But sometimes you just have to make do."

"Which I imagine is what Father sees in you. Had you been present for the second attempt at the graphene fabricator, perhaps those fool mercenaries wouldn't have caused such casualties."

Mac grunted. "And did Grandad use his stagecraft for something more than entertainment, too?"

Her mouth quirked. "No, and Grandfather did not agree with Father's choice of career."

"And so, Daddy turned to a life of crime."

She looked at him oddly behind her sunglasses. "Again, with the accusations. What would you have made of Robin Hood, I wonder?"

"Robin Hood wasn't a billionaire."

"He was a wealthy man, a landed noble. He sacrificed much for

the common people against the worst depredations of the aristocracy of his time."

"I'm missing your father's sacrifice amid all the private jets and
penthouses."

"You mock, but if you saw what dealing with people like your
government really cost him—but that's the whole point of today,
isn't it? You'll see."

Mac glanced at her, unconvinced, as he pulled into the line to
the security gate. "All set?" he asked as they waited.

"I believe so. My cover identity is in place and can withstand a
fair amount of scrutiny. Is your ... 'toy' ready?"

He glanced at his bag. "Yep."

They got through the parking lot checkpoint with no trouble.
The walk to the building was through a humid ninety degrees, as
summer's stranglehold remained at the height of its powers. Mac
found himself sweating as he held the door for Minerva, who looked
as unruffled and calm as ever.

A smiling security officer greeted him at the checkpoint. "Mac-
Gyver! Hey, man, how are you?"

"Arjun," Mac said, bumping the offered fist. "How you been?"

He passed them baskets for their keys, phones, and other items.
"Pretty good. Car's still working, too, thanks again for that."

Mac was jarred. "Arjun, that distributor is just jury-rigged! It's
been, what ... four months now? You gotta get that fixed."

Arjun grinned and shrugged. "You do good work. But yeah, I'll
get it fixed soon. Promise." He removed their phones, checked that
they were turned on, then slipped them into security pouches
designed to block all signals. "Name, ma'am?" he asked, holding a
sharpie to mark the pouch.

She held out her ID. "Alice Hare. Like the rabbit."

He glanced. "Gotcha. Keep your ID for the next checkpoint.
Visiting?"

"Yes, a guest of Mister MacGyver's."

"Can't really talk about it," Mac said.

"I didn't hear anything." Arjun shrugged, returning their items except the phones, and grinning at Mac's pocketknife. "Have a good day now."

The greeting was similar at the next checkpoint as a suited agent grinned when she saw them. "Hey, Mac. No flight jacket today?" She took their IDs.

Mac patted his suit. "Meetings, Marcy. Important people, or something. You know how it is."

"That I do," she said. "And you, ma'am?"

"Alice Hare. A guest of MacGyver's."

Marcy took their IDs, scanned Mac's, then typed information into her computer for Minerva's. "Stand over there, please, toes on the line, and look directly at the camera."

The photo done, the printer took only a moment to spit out a laminated ID card labeled Alice Hare. "Wear this at all times. MacGyver is responsible for your presence. At no time is your entry past one of the red security doors permitted without official authorization. If you are found anywhere alone, you will be detained and may face criminal prosecution. Do you understand?"

"Yes, thank you," Minerva said, accepting the ID.

Marcy smiled. "Welcome to Langley, Ms. Hare."

The sweltering heat brought Ailsa hurrying to CIA HQ's front doors sweating and grumpy. She'd forgotten how much she missed Scotland's cool mists as the view beyond the window in Mother's call showed a grey, wet day. Still, she was glad she'd stayed away. Seeing the place even on video had jolted loose a fistful of memories that she'd shelved for good reason.

She handed her items and temporary ID to the security guard who proceeded to sequester her phone in its bag. He looked at her, curious. "MacIver, huh? Say, you wouldn't know our MacGyver, would you?"

She grunted. "Who does'nae?"

"So, you related or something?"

"I dinnae think so, lad," she said, passing through the scanner and taking back her things.

"Yeah, he doesn't have your accent," the guard said smiling. "You just missed him and his guest by like three minutes."

She paused. "Missed him? Guest?"

The guard nodded. "Yeah. Just went in for some meeting. Sorry though, I ask too many questions sometimes."

Her instincts kicked in, and she merely nodded. "Oh, aye, the meetin'. Which guest was it then? Older man? Slim? Silver hair?"

"No, it was a woman, white, about your age. Blonde."

Electricity jolted her spine, but long training kept it from her face and out of her voice. "Ah, very good. Well, I dinnae wish tae be late. Thankee, lad."

Ailsa rushed through security in record time and burst into Holcomb's office. "Mac is here!"

Holcomb recovered without spilling his coffee and set it down. "Here? In Washington?"

"Here inside the bloody buildin'! He went through security nae five minutes ago with a guest!"

Holcomb scrambled for his terminal and pulled up the security logs. Sure enough, there on the camera, going through the detector was Mac and—"Minerva Hart!" Holcomb turned to Ailsa. "What the hell is he doing *here* with *her*?"

Ailsa had been thinking of little else for the last few minutes. "This has tae be some form a' test. Victor Hart would'nae let him into his confidence without a display a' some kind."

Holcomb reached for the phone. "I need to alert security."

"Stay." Ailsa put her hand on the receiver. "Can we track them internally? Without alertin' security or anyone else?"

"*Umm.*" Holcomb typed a few things on his computer and brought up some internal feeds. "Yeah, I can track where he uses his card to get through doors, and we can get an idea of what they're doing from the cameras. We don't have cameras everywhere, though. I mean, once you get past a certain security layer, the last thing we want is cameras recording what's going on."

Ailsa knew it well from MI6. Cameras missed nothing, and lips could be read even without sound. A security breach in the heart of a nation's intelligence apparatus could compromise operatives around the world. Which made her even more wary of Minerva Hart's presence in the building, a pressure taking root in the back of her mind.

Holcomb was feeling it as well. "I have a bad feeling about this. Are you sure we shouldn't have them picked up?"

"We could be ruinin' whatever his plan is."

"Whose? Mac's or Hart's? And who's to say he doesn't *want* us to catch him?"

Ailsa didn't have an answer. "One of us should tail them. Any earwigs on hand?"

"Yeah, but we can't just jump straight into it. Frequencies are being monitored, and security will hear us quick. I need a few minutes to get all this set up and alert the proper people."

"Without tellin' them Mac is here with a hostile?"

"I'm not fully comfortable with it, but trust me," he said, handing her an earwig. He glanced at the monitors. "Besides, it looks like they've been held up a moment. He could get himself busted without us lifting a finger."

❦

The security station to the computer labs was new, and the guard was uncompromising. "I'm sorry, Mister MacGyver, no laptops or other unapproved electronic devices past this door. And the lady will need to turn over her purse."

Mac looked at his bag which held the laptop they intended to use for scanning a security ID card with high level access. There was no way to get into the backup vaults without one. "I need it for a meeting with the Deputy Director," he said.

The guard was implacable. "I'm sorry, sir. She can authorize exceptions, but we'll need her direct word and have to hold it here until we get it."

Mac traded a glance with Minerva and sighed. "Well, okay. Sorry to hassle you. I know you're just doing your job."

The guard smiled and accepted their bags. "Don't worry about it. You're cleared to proceed."

Once past the checkpoint, they paced rapidly between cubicles with various people working quietly in intense concentration and stepped into an empty conference room. Mac closed the door. "Well. That's a little problem."

Minerva narrowed her eyes. "A *little* problem? You built that laptop to conceal the card scanner and let us duplicate a clearance card at two meters away. How else will we get into the backup vault?"

"I don't know yet. Lemme think on it," Mac said, at a complete loss for the moment.

"Indeed? Didn't your hand in consulting on this place's security involve placing the vault three stories down into the bedrock at the end of a long hallway covered by guards and cameras?"

"Yeah."

She paused for a beat, then said, "Time for airducts and hanging from the ceiling then?"

"Ah. No. Well, probably not."

"I shouldn't have gone with the skirt," she said.

"We can at least get to the first part of the plan, which involves getting you in front of a terminal. Are you sure you'll only need ten minutes to find what you need?"

She inclined her head. "More or less."

"Okay. While you do that, I'll work on part two."

"Remember, I'm also here to keep an eye on you. The thinking you need to do will have to be from whatever cube you stash me in. You're not leaving my sight."

"Really," he hissed. "I'll probably have to build a new scanner. That means getting materials, and a place to work with a solder iron for a few minutes—assuming I can even find one. I need time to scavenge."

"Make your list and contemplate the plan. We'll go together

when I'm done. Besides, don't you wish to see the evidence my father promised you?"

"Every minute we're here the risk of getting caught goes up."

"You walked in the front door, using your actual credentials. Anyone looking for you could already know you're here. 'Hide in plain sight,' as you said?"

"Look—"

"No," she snapped at him. "Until you've seen what I'm going to show you, you are under contract to me. These are the terms. If you decide to reject the evidence and return to their fold, then so be it. Until then, you will follow our instructions. Besides, you'll never find it without me, hidden as it's likely to be in the CIA's labyrinthine archives, and I imagine you wish to see this with your own eyes."

She's right. Damnit.

But you know, after seeing that, this building may become a very dangerous place.

For both of us.

Pandora's Box, Hart called it.

That maw of darkness was already opening as Mac finally spoke. "Have it your way then. Come on."

☕

Ailsa returned to Holcomb's office wearing thick secretarial glasses and a black wig clenched in a tight bun at the base of her skull.

Holcomb did a double take. "If I didn't know it was you, I might not have noticed. You just had all that handy?"

"Aye. Never know when a quick disguise is needed. An' a touch a' makeup can change yaer face more than yae might think. It's the shadows, really."

"Right. Okay, test the earwig. Security thinks we're training on protocols."

It worked fine.

"You should still avoid notice, I think," Holcomb said. "At least until we figure out what's what."

"That's the plan. Wher' are they now?"

"In the Icebox ... Sorry, that's the massive cube farm where they do a lot of digital analysis. It's always dark and a little chilly in there, so—"

"Aye, I get the notion. Yae'r certain they've nae left?"

He nodded towards his three monitors, now covered with camera feeds. "Not that I've seen, and Mac's card hasn't been used on any other doorways."

"Very well. Wish me luck."

"Luck," he said. "'Cause you're gonna need it," he muttered to the closed door.

◉◉

Mac watched Minerva typing away, the monitor reflected in her glasses, in an abandoned cubicle at the edge of the Icebox where they hoped to avoid notice. That said, Mac himself tended to draw greetings at intermittent intervals as people noticed him.

"Mac."

"Heya, MacGyver."

"Howdy, Mac!"

"Do you know absolutely everyone here?" Minerva asked, annoyed.

Mac rolled his head. "I'm a people person. Sue me."

She continued typing. "Doesn't that make covert operations somewhat difficult?"

"Only when I'm infiltrating my own workplace," he said wryly. "But that's why we went in the front door. Hiding would've been impossible. How's it coming there?"

"Getting it. The security is considerably less formidable internally, but no less perilous. And have you devised a solution to our card problem?"

"Getting it," he echoed.

Not very well.

I'm supposed to be good at improv.

But I can't mix up a potion to read and write data to a card.

A reader is easy.

Any door reader can do that.

So start there.

Okay then, some batteries, a memory stick, and a door reader will scan one.

Tape it together—

Carefully!

Shouldn't even need solder if I do it right.

What about writing the new card, though?

And that rig is going to require almost direct contact to scan the security card in the first place.

Door scanners have almost no range.

And whose card can we possibly find?

One thing at a time.

Minerva typed, paused, hit Enter, then sat back, thoughtful.

"Trouble?" Mac asked.

"A slight obstacle," she said, squaring herself to the keyboard. "Nothing a quick script can't fix, but a brief delay."

"It would really save us time if you'd let me go gather some things while you work."

"We've been through that."

"Still don't trust me."

"Trust is earned, Mac," she said, typing away. "It is not a gift."

Mac sat back, letting out a slow breath, and waited.

◆◆

Holcomb's clearance got Ailsa into the Icebox easily enough. Finding Mac and his 'ally' proved more difficult. She didn't dare ask around for fear of raising suspicions, and the grey, uniform cubes stood at shoulder height, impeding a quick survey from any safe distance.

"Whole lotta nothing so far," she muttered to Holcomb using her American accent.

He replied through the earwig, "The only reason to be in there is to get on a computer."

"I doubt they'd use someone's assigned cube though."

"Right. Probably one of the hot-swap stations for traveling agents."

She clucked her tongue. "Spotty security."

"They're not exactly for public use, you know," he said defensively.

A quick query with a passing analyst pointed her to the two banks of hot-swap cubes, bracketing the vast room. Ailsa picked the rightmost, and walked past the long line of twenty stations, some in use, most empty. No Mac, no Minerva. Same with the second. "Okay, nothing—" she was saying, but stopped when she saw a frumpy man wave to someone unseen inside a cube.

"Yo, MacGyver!" she barely heard.

"One minute," she told Holcomb, and made her way that direction.

A surreptitious approach brought her close enough to see over without peering in. Side-on, she saw Mac sitting beside the desk, lost in thought. Minerva was concentrating intensely on the screen, typing like the devil himself was on her tail.

Ailsa walked quickly away. "Okay, got them. Cube seventy, row twelve. She's on the computer. He's just sitting there. Can you snoop on what she's doing?"

"On it," Holcomb said.

●●

Mac saw Minerva pause, smirk to herself, then push back from the workstation. "Here you are."

Mac came around and saw an open folder marked simply VH. Inside were files upon files of spreadsheets and photographs, video and audio recordings. "That's a lot to take in. Where do you suggest I start?"

She pointed to an encoded transcript. "Perhaps here. Initial contact for an operation similar to the one you disrupted in Turkey. My father does nothing without a good reason. This should be your Agency man laying it out for him in full here."

Mac moved the mouse to click, but an alert covered the screen with ACTIVE TRACE DETECTED!

"Damn!" she whispered, shoving Mac out of the way. A few quick presses, and she glared. "Someone found us. I need to delete this now!"

"I need to see it first," Mac said.

"There is no time."

Mac glanced around in the cube but saw nothing. He poked his head over the wall to the neighboring cube and spied a flash drive. He slipped out, grabbed it, and held it up. "Copy it off. We'll look at it somewhere else."

"No," Minerva said, hitting a button. Her deletion program began running, the files scrambling into digital garbage. "You'll just have to look at the files on the backup. There was no time left."

Mac's hand dropped helplessly as he watched the proof vanish. "So, what's to stop me from calling all this off right now?"

"Nothing, except that you still wish to see it, and only I can find the backup files," she said, watching the last file vanish and the trace complete. "Someone clearly knows where we are. That was a targeted attack. Let me clean this up quickly and we'll move." She began deleting temporary files from the workstation.

The hairs on Mac's neck tingled as he glanced around. No security inbound, no alarms, no flashing lights. It was the Icebox, operating normally, quiet and dark, taking no notice of him. He spied a woman with dark hair in a tight bun turn away from them and walk out of her cube, taking her time, reading a printout. She turned the far corner and seemed familiar, but MacGyver couldn't be sure at this distance. She vanished into a hallway.

"What?" Minerva asked, eyeing him.

"Just keeping a lookout," Mac said. He slipped the flash drive into his pocket. "All done? Come on. I've got a plan."

●●

Ailsa breathed out her relief when she broke line of sight with Mac. He was just right over there! She practically wanted to scream that the fusion reactor was rigged, but she had no way to know if it would compromise him or not. "Get anything?" she asked Holcomb.

"No. She protected herself really well. I got in, but whatever she was doing was gone. It was in Boone's server space though. If she's in there deleting things, you can bet it's a link between them."

"Right. Makes sense," she said, sticking with her American accent. "But don't you have backups?"

"Yeah. We'll go looking after they've left the building."

"What if they destroy those, too?"

Holcomb chuckled. "That's down in the Crypt. Air-gapped protection with the finest in sneakernet technology," he said, meaning one had to physically carry the drive they wanted and plug it into a terminal to read it. There were no connections to the outside world, wired or wireless. "And it's all behind a clearance higher than Mac's. Hell, even I barely qualify for Crypt access. There's no way they'd get in there."

"This is Mac you're talking about. Care to put a few bucks on that?"

His smugness melted away.

CHAPTER 26

THE MAIN PROBLEM with swiping a card reader from a door was finding one far enough out of the way to escape immediate notice. The second issue was that any door important enough for a card reader was also important enough for a camera. The camera might not be actively monitored, but it was not impossible someone would be watching live, and it would certainly be recorded.

He and Minerva sat in the Icebox breakroom, a surprisingly luxurious space with comfortable chairs and secluded sitting areas encircling a large central table in need of a wipe down. Coffee rings, tea drips, and crumbs from lunch littered the place. Analysts were busy creatures, but on the slovenly side.

Minerva read from the daily newspaper. In a place where any smartphone might be a bug, newsprint and hardcopy remained popular. Mac watched some of the Icebox's denizens laying out supplies and decorations for the upcoming Halloween party, complete with blow-up pumpkins, orange and white tinsel, and little plastic spider rings. His mind wandered freely.

We've been hunting Hart nearly two months, and now here we are in the middle of Langley with his own daughter, and what are we doing?

Chilling.

Hardly.

The problem is solvable, but the subconscious needs to handle it.

What would Solana say about this?

She'd laugh.

I loved her laugh.

Stop. Not now.

Card reader.

Right.

It can be from literally anywhere.

But someplace no one's going to notice for a while? Where is that exactly?

This place is manned twenty-four seven and three sixty-five.

Not everywhere though. There's a reason the parking lot is so huge.

Right, most work is done during normal office hours.

So, it's gotta be from somewhere that won't be looked at until after five.

Or later, if possible.

His eyes wandered over the table again.

What a mess.

Janitorial!

God, why didn't I think of that sooner?

There's at least one closet on every level.

With a keycard, thanks to you.

Well, they asked what stuff I'd need to cause trouble here. The janitor's closet is a first stop.

But how do we deal with the camera?

Arrggghh.

"Any brilliant notions?" Minerva asked politely, as if inquiring about the weather.

"Maybe," Mac said quietly, watching the analysts joke around with their decorations. "I can get a reader off a door simple enough, and the battery assembly from the hand mixer in the kitchen over there can power it. I can rig it to write to this flash drive, and with some decent tape, it'll all hold together well enough to sit in my coat pocket. Just need to brush up against someone's key card. That'll be a trick, but one thing at a time."

"Yes. You have no tape, for one. That was also in your bag."

"The janitor's room I swipe the reader from will have everything I need. It's the camera I'm worried about."

"I'd've thought finding a way to write the new card would prove more problematic."

"Overwriting my own card is easy enough. We just go back through security and claim my bag, plug in the flash drive, and write the new clearance."

She eyed him skeptically. "You make it all sound so simple."

"There's a gap between sounding and doing. Sometimes a big one."

"Yet here we sit." She flipped a page. "I have never failed my father in any of his significant operations, and I do not intend to start now. I must admit that I am unaccustomed to basing the outcome on random chance and improvisation. If we do not succeed, it complicates matters significantly. Are you listening?"

Mac's vision had focused on the decorations. He snapped out of it with a grin. "What? Oh. Yeah, improvisation. Let's get moving then."

👓

"I have no eyes on them anywhere, and they haven't used his card since you tracked them down in the Icebox," Holcomb said, pacing in front of his monitors. "Ailsa, I am not comfortable with this."

"You sounded so sure of yourself not half an hour ago," Ailsa reminded him.

"Yeah well, half an hour is plenty of time for my imagination to run wild. At the very least, I should get in touch with the Deputy Director and get authorization on this."

"Not until we know what Mac is planning."

"How do we do that without *asking* him? And how do we ask

without blowing his cover? This is a chicken and egg kind of nightmare."

Ailsa had no immediate answer. "For my part, I'd settle for lettin' him know the reactor is rigged. They could wipe the entire archive for all I care."

"Well, we see things a little differently here."

Holcomb's computer beeped with an alert on the screen. He leaped into his chair and pulled it up. "He just used his security card on level three," he said, already accessing the camera. "Oh, come on!" he exclaimed when the feed came up.

A spider had crawled over the lens, and sat there hugging the video, obscuring all but the very edges from view.

"So, he commands animals now?" Ailsa asked, amused.

"This is serious, okay? He's in a janitor's closet! He could be building a death ray, for all we know. Do you want to go back down and trail them?"

"Nay," she said, still thoughtful. "Minerva Hart does'nae know yae at all, does she?" she said, dropping her American patois.

"Depends on if she was in on the Verone kidnapping. I've certainly never seen her before."

"Nay, she was'nae on the plane. Yae could speak with him, face-tae-face. Office acquaintances an' colleagues catchin' up briefly, that sort a' thing."

Holcomb was nodding. "Yeah. Okay, it could work. But how do I warn him with her right there?"

"I cannae hold yaer bloody hand. What kind a' field agent are yae, for all?"

"The kind that's more on the enforcement side than the grifting one," he said, rising and grabbing his suit jacket. "I'll think of something. Keep your earwig on."

☙☙

"Okay, that should do it," Mac said in the tight confines of the janitor's closet.

Minerva Hart looked over the proffered device. It was a mash of wires and duct tape, holding the reader, battery, and flash drive in place. A dull red light glowed on the reader. "Lovely."

"I'm not aiming for elegance," he said, slipping it into his suit coat pocket. Only a slight bulge indicated there was anything in there. "Good enough. I just need to get within a few inches of someone's card."

"How will you know if it succeeded?"

"The light will turn green, just like when you scan a card to open a door."

"Very well. Now, where do we find an access card with elevated access?"

"One step at a time," he said, getting the door.

"As far as I can tell this *is* the next step," she said, following.

"MacGyver?" a voice called down the hall. Holcomb walked towards them. "Hey, man, how are you doing? I didn't even know you were in Washington."

"Oh! Ah ..." Mac fumbled for words. "Yeah, just a quick meeting."

Holcomb eyed the janitor's closet and Minerva Hart. "A quick meeting? In the janitor's closet?"

Mac's mind scrambled. "Uh, yeah, you know—just a quick demonstration of—well, you know how I use chemicals and things in the field. I was just showing that to my guest here."

Holcomb nodded slowly. "Okay, sure. Anyway, we haven't been introduced, ma'am. Lorenzo Holcomb."

She took his hand. "Alice Hare. A pleasure, Mister Holcomb."

"Say, do you mind if I borrow Mac for a minute? Company business."

She regarded MacGyver, eyebrows up.

Mac's mad scramble continued. "Oh, say, Holcomb, I can't really leave her alone. You know how super strict they are with visitors past the line. I tell you what though, call me, and I can get in touch early next week."

"I, uh ... yeah, okay. I mean, this is kinda urgent."

"Okay, just email me and I can get to it in another day or two. Promise."

Holcomb looked like he wanted to say more but kept glancing between them. "Um. Yeah, okay. Sorry, Mac. I won't keep you."

Mac tried not to let his relief show visibly. "Thanks, Holcomb, good to see you. We'll catch up soon."

They shook hands again but bumped into each other as Holcomb moved past. The usual apologies, then they went their separate ways.

Only when they turned opposite corners did Mac let out the breath he'd been holding.

"Did it work?" Minerva asked.

He opened the flap on his coat and saw the green light staring back at him. "Yep. Okay, let's go overwrite my card."

Holcomb returned to his office and ran straight into Ailsa's withering glare. "Did yae have tae make it a bloody nightmare for the man?" she demanded.

"What do you mean?" he asked, surprised.

"Yae dinnae bloody well question yaer contact's story right in front a' their mark! Or is there another way tae interpret 'What were yae doin' in the closet'? An' then, yae might as well bring in a skywriter tae say, 'Hey, MacGyver, I've got an urgent message for yae, but I want it hidden from the person yae'r with.'"

Holcomb grumbled, "Look, could you have done any better?"

"*Yes!*" she said unequivocally. "Bloody CIA."

Holcomb sat heavily. "Okay, yeah. I'm usually the guy behind the scenes coordinating or out in the field with a gun and a target."

"Yae could'hae at least gotten rid a' the bloody spider," she said, gesturing at the cameras.

"It was a kid's toy taped up there. Little plastic Halloween ring, you know? Anyway, that didn't work, so what now?"

"Yae cannae run into them again without arousin' yet more

suspicion. Do we know for certain that they're aimin' for this Crypt a' yaers?"

He pointed to an active camera feed aimed at a security checkpoint around a solid steel door with two armed guards and an agent in a suit. "He'll have to get through there. I don't see it happening."

Ailsa looked, then glanced at the access log. She did a double take. "Did yae take a side trip tae the Crypt, at all?"

"No. Why?"

She pointed. "Because accordin' tae this, yaer badge went through that access point not three minutes ago."

Holcomb stared, jaw open.

"Do yae have yaer card or did he swipe it?"

He unclipped it from his belt and held it up. "Right here. My name on it and everything. He bumped into me in the hall, almost literally, though."

She was shaking her head slowly, disbelieving. "Somehow he copied yaer ID."

"Son of a ... Okay, look, we have *got* to tell security about this, right now!"

"An' risk compromisin' whatever he's got runnin'?"

"He's running it too Goddamned well!" Holcomb said, heat rising to his voice.

"It comes down tae this, Holcomb," she told him. "Do yae trust Mac or nae?"

He ran the security footage back to see Mac scan in and sign for Minerva Hart. Ailsa could practically hear his teeth grinding. "I don't know," he said. "Do you? Didn't you tell me he might be getting played? That he's not himself, and Hart is a master of reprogramming people to do his bidding?"

That's exactly what yae said, lassie.

Aye, but ...

No answer was forthcoming. "Either way. We have until they leave tae figure it out."

The massive vault three stories beneath CIA headquarters called the Crypt housed every scrap of data collected and analyzed by the agency. Three stages of backups brought the data to its final rest in the massive vault, stored on rows and rows of removable drives, themselves encoded and stored without physical connections to any data transmission method. To find a desired archive, one looked up the original server address on the archive library computer then physically walked to the drive on its shelf. Minerva Hart typed away as Mac looked around the gloomy, chilly artificial cavern, filled with looming rows of storage racks, stretching away into darkness. "Always feels like a dungeon down here. Guess the name fits."

Minerva entered a final command and turned towards him. "This way."

She brought them two hundred yards to a rack of drives, counted the numbers, then pulled one loose. "Here you are. The evidence you require. There were terminals towards the front where you could examine it, yes?"

Mac took the drive in hand, quite light to hold such weighty data. "Come on."

At the front, Mac sat before a laptop designed to slot in the backup drives. "What am I looking for?"

She drove the mouse to the correct folder in Boone's archives labeled VH. "There. That is all the data your Agent Boone collected on my father, presumably as an insurance policy both against my father and against your own Justice Department."

Mac looked up sharply. "Justice Department?"

Her words dripped with sarcasm. "This may shock you, but not everything the current administration gets up to is necessarily in your country's best interests. Scapegoats will eventually be required, and Mister Boone has the foresight to picture himself in the crosshairs. Mind you, he still eagerly performs his nefarious tasks, so judge that how you will."

Mac watched her for a long moment, uncertain how to take all that. With an unwilling hand, he clicked on a video transcript.

A split screen of Victor Hart and Agent Boone appeared. A conversation followed.

VH: You're receiving me?

DB: Yeah, I see you. Okay, here's the deal. We have to make a show for the press to get them off the President's back. Our vodka-swilling pals will play their part, but we need a real attack to retaliate against.

VH: <sigh> I don't suppose your president would simply stop going on about Russia?

DB: I'm not here to judge, I'm just here to set the stage. Can you get the material into the right hands?

VH: <pauses> Yes. I'm increasing my fee, of course.

DB: <sarcasm> Oh, of course.

VH: I also wish to see the official authorization from your superiors.

DB: <scoffs> Yeah. And we'll put it in a gilded envelope with White House letterhead, signed by the President himself.

VH: I am quite serious.

DB: Why? Are you recording this?

VH: How can I be? This is the computer your agency provided. It is completely tamper-proof.

DB: That doesn't answer my question.

VH: Because up until now these ... morally ambiguous operations have been done in the dark—

DB: Not completely.

VH: Certainly, but always as the lesser of two evils. This is why we've built such a solid working relationship. I shed no tears for weaponeers who fall victim to their own trade. This new situation is quite different. Deliberate civilian casualties are ... distasteful and go against what I stand for. Indeed, why do you suppose I'm no longer an intelligence agent? So, I must insist on seeing proof that your country is fully prepared to walk this path. Think of me as the genie in the lamp. I'll grant your wishes, if it's truly what you want, but I require proof of that.

DB: <suspicious> Hmm ... Okay, hang on ... Here. This is the digital authorization with code.

A document appeared on the screen with an encryption key that decoded into the CIA Director's name with an image of the digital signature. It ordered Agent Demerest Boone to facilitate operations in concert with the Russian SVR for "all matters as requested and required by either government."

VH: <impressed> That is quite the document.

DB: Happy now?

VH: Not in the least. You're about to commit an act of terrorism on foreign soil with full authorization from your government, and you seem almost eager to go about it.

DB: I NOTICE YOU HAVEN'T SAID NO TO THE JOB YET, "GENIE."

VH: I HAVE BILLS TO PAY, AND A SIGNIFICANT PROJECT TO COMPLETE. THESE FUNDS WILL AID IN THAT ENDEAVOR ENORMOUSLY. ALSO, I'M JUST THE DELIVERY BOY, AS YOU'VE PUT IT BEFORE. THIS BLOOD WILL NOT BE ON MY HANDS.

DB: THIS DOCUMENT MEANS IT'S NOT ON MINE EITHER.

VH: YET I NOTICE YOU'VE NOT CONSIDERED RESIGNING IN PROTEST.

DB: DO POTS CALL KETTLES BLACK WHERE YOU'RE FROM, LORD BRITISH? ARE YOU IN OR NOT?

VH: VERY WELL. ARRANGE YOUR SHIPMENT, DEPOSIT THE PAYMENT, AND CONTACT ME WITH THE DETAILS. GOOD DAY, MISTER BOONE.

The video ended, and Mac was seeing red, practically steaming in the chilly room.

"I was off-camera in the room when that went through," Minerva said. "It's perfectly authentic, if my statement means anything to you."

"I knew the Agency sometimes made ... expedient decisions. I just didn't think they'd ever willingly create this kind of havoc."

She suppressed a smile. "Forgive me, Mac, but your cover should be 'Alice,' not mine. This entire file is a vast rabbit hole for you. Look at the date."

He did. "This is from February of last year! Almost immediately after the inauguration!"

"Indeed. Did you think the recent sarin shipment you spoiled was the only one in question? The initial attack occurred in March last year, and the 'retaliation' in April. Your press ate it up, and all at the low cost of several million dollars and a few hundred innocent Syrian lives."

"Everyone needs to know about this."

"Absolutely not. As my father said, he was merely the genie granting wishes. It's not his doing if the asker wishes for self-inflicted wounds."

Mac turned towards her, finger stabbing at the screen. "This is bigger than your father! This is a betrayal of everything we're supposed to stand for!"

She regarded him like an alien being. "Well, Father did give you the option of refusing his offer and keeping this data for your own use. If that's the case, I'd ask that you escort me to the front door, then do as you will. We'll not contact you again."

And they'll go underground, Mac told himself.

Making them even more impossible to find.

We got Verone back. My work here is done.

Not Ailsa's.

Not Solana's.

Goddamn it!

So, we either get this information into responsible hands, or stay on-mission.

Hell!

... What would she want us to do?

Find a way to do both.

"Look," he said. "There's a lot here. I need to spend a little time with it. Let me copy it off and get us out of here. I can make the decision later."

"No. It's all more of the same," she said. "You'll find nothing in there to exculpate Agent Boone or your government. You must face it. The CIA creates as many villains as it takes down. It's a circular process in service to the American Empire. My father is not wrong, and he left the business for that very reason."

"And became a facilitator himself."

"In pursuit of a much greater goal," she said, clenching a fist, eyes alight. "I wish we could've shown you Ararat first to understand that."

"This place in Indonesia? There's a file here labeled Indonesia, in fact."

She paused. "Yes. No point in hiding it now, but you'll get no more from me until you decide. It's the moment to choose, Mac."

You can't let this data disappear.

And I can't lose this opportunity to get Hart either.

He ships sarin gas to help kill civilians!

Genie of the lamp. It wasn't his idea.

Yeah, but he still granted the wish.

Damn it. Damn it all straight to hell!

If I could just get Minerva to look away for a minute, maybe we could do both.

How's my sleight of hand?

Good enough?

"I need a minute to think about all this. Alone, okay?" Mac made himself sound both wounded and insistent, as if ready to cave if only given a moment to process what he'd seen. And hoping her empathy might once again kick in.

Minerva lifted her chin to regard him, sensing his dilemma, and his struggle before conceding. "I shall retreat a few paces down the row here and give you space. I will not leave you to your own devices, however, nor do you have more than a minute at most. So, choose wisely."

●●

Ailsa paced while Holcomb brooded in front of the monitors.

"They're leaving the Crypt," Holcomb said at last.

She rounded the desk and indeed, there they were checking back through security. At one point, Mac looked at the camera and held their unseen gaze for a count of three.

Ailsa straightened, head cocked, thinking.

Now what was that about?

He knows we're watchin'.

Cameras followed them at strategic intersections down to the ground floor. They were clearly heading for the exits.

"It's now or never," Holcomb said, hand on the phone.

"It's yaer agency. But I say leave them be." She took a deep breath. "I trust Mac."

"Enough to let him get away with whatever they were here for? And maybe walk into an overloading fusion reactor wherever they're going? Even with him possibly being compromised by Hart?"

That was the most damnable part. She could save his life by catching him now. But also lose Hart *again.*

"Curse me for a bleedin' numpty, but I trust him," she repeated.

Holcomb watched them walk to the front doors. Mac held it open for Minerva Hart, and they were gone. He unclenched his hand from the phone. "Well. What now?"

"Let's go see where they were. He looked at the camera for a reason."

Holcomb's clearance got them to the Crypt. It was larger than Ailsa expected; she wasn't terribly surprised, but it presented a problem. "This place is huge. Where do we look?"

"The only reason to come here is to review the backups. They deleted something from Boone's main files, so I'm betting they deleted the backup, too."

Ailsa examined the area. There were a few terminals by the wall where the removable drives could be slotted in. One of the chairs was ajar. At a glance nothing appeared out of the ordinary. She checked the computer, but it wasn't even on. On a hunch, she knelt to look under the desk. "Holcomb!"

He got to her as she stood, a flash drive in hand. "Taped tae the underside. Bloody duct tape," she said, laughing. "Let's see what our man left us."

CHAPTER 27

People will surprise you.
Always.
That's why it's a bad habit to apply labels.
"Villain," for one. Just when you think you're sure what someone's all about, things get grey on you.
Like everything else these days.
Still, for all his talk of ideals, Hart sure had a nasty way of going about attaining his noble ambitions.

👓

ANOTHER LONG FLIGHT chasing the sun beyond the western horizon, and Mac stepped out of the luxury jet onto a beachside tarmac at dawn. The air smelled of green things growing and briny sea air. Indeed, the pink eastern sky showed a limitless expanse of gently rolling sea beyond the swaying palms.

Across the tarmac stood his ultimate quarry: Victor Hart, himself, looking fresh and bright, all smiles, and backed by his security detail, serious men in dark suits, almost certainly armed.

Hart met them halfway, embraced Minerva. "My dear, you're looking well. All went as planned it seems?"

"Yes, Mac knew his business thoroughly."

He shook Mac's hand. "My thanks, Mister MacGyver, and I must say I am pleased you decided to join our little enterprise."

Mac remained noncommittal. "I don't know if 'joined' is the right word yet. Not sure I'm a fan of loyalty tests."

Hart waved them towards the cars. "Nor am I," he said, once they were settled and driving through narrow streets towards the dim city light, succumbing to the rising dawn. "Loyalty is an unreliable concept. It implies an unconditional devotion, which is unrealistic from any standpoint. A certain amount of leeway can be expected in trying times when trust has been earned, but even over the long-term, one cannot show loyalty to any employer, friend, or even loved one that provides no reciprocity. At its worst form, loyalty is a form of control and abuse. Indeed, look at loyalty as employed by nation-states to justify their wrongs under a flag of patriotism. I believe you discovered that in the very files I wished destroyed."

"Those could have helped bring the real perpetrators to justice," Mac said.

"And also put the hounds directly on my scent? Thank you, no," Hart said. "Your administration will face its reckoning soon enough, and it's that very event which has hastened my timetable."

"You're saying that you began all this because of the last election?"

"No, this project began nearly three decades ago. I would have been perfectly satisfied with purchasing the necessary technologies in the next five to ten years, but events in the United States have not gone as any rational individual could wish. The CIA has always been your hidden blade, but this administration wields it like a bludgeon."

"It's a difficult time," Mac agreed. "But we'll handle it. We always have. Presidents don't last forever."

"Nor do nations. The slide towards autocracy is accelerating. How long until agents like your Demerest Boone are turned inward?"

Mac had no answer.

"As I thought," Hart said.

Mac had been watching for the rare street sign, reading them as best he could. A large banner with a smiling man stretched above the road ahead. Mac didn't speak much Indonesian, but he knew world geography well enough that a name jumped out. "Larantuka. So, this is Ararat?"

Hart's smile reached his eyes. "No, not exactly. We'll be crossing the strait shortly. That's part of it."

"The Larantuka Strait," Mac said, feeling like he'd just opened his eyes. "The massive tidal barrage Indonesia is building. You stole the plans for it as one of your first crimes."

"Indeed. Whom do you think holds the majority backing for this project?"

"But this is a *perfectly legal project.*"

"It is *now,*" Hart laughed. "The engineering design firm was less than forthcoming with their technical specifications. I had to be certain it would suit my needs, particularly in this location."

"This is supposed to generate power for Larantuka and most of Flores Island, though, almost two million people. Not your Ararat."

Hart shrugged. "Why can't it be both? And after civilization collapses, the barrage will continue to generate power."

"So why kidnap Doctor Verone, then, for his fusion expertise?"

"Would you let the fate of mankind's survival on Earth rest on just one power supply? I think not. I had no desire to repeat the steps of fission or fossil power with all their poor trade-offs. As I say, Doctor Verone presented us with too fine an opportunity in attending his conference."

They were in the city now. A collection of storefronts, new and old, faced across from a Muslim mosque and Christian church, both looking ancient and implacable, as if carved from the island itself.

They passed a security fence and construction yard, where men in orange vests got their equipment in order to continue work on the causeway that would cross the strait and house the massive tidal generators beneath. All the water moving through the strait with the daily tide would pass under the causeway, and thus, through huge turbines to generate electricity. It was a marvel of engineering under the guise of an ordinary bridge.

"I had no idea the project had gotten so far," Mac said.

"Again, we had to alter the timetable, thus incurring additional expense. The causeway itself is complete, leading to Ararat on the far side."

The causeway was a little less than half a mile, bisecting the Larantuka Strait and dividing the Banda and Sava seas. They passed a cargo ship, waiting patiently in its lock for the water levels to equalize and the roadway to close and sweep aside, allowing passage. Mac turned his head to look as they went by. "They really have built a marvel here."

"It's nice to be appreciated," Hart said. "Look now. We're nearing the end."

The far end anchored on the mountain island of Adanora, itself sparsely inhabited except by wildlife. They traveled past the gates and security fence, a mirror of the causeway's anchor on the city side, then north along the coastal highway to a dock built to service nothing that Mac could see. No buildings save a small dockmaster's shack. He recognized the ship in port, however. "The *Kutup Ayisi*," he said. "You brought the Svalbard seeds here."

"Of course. I greatly enjoyed watching you puzzle out my little trick. A temperature-induced air differential to find our hidden tunnel," he said, nodding. "Very clever."

"Watching? There were no security cameras in the Vault."

Hart smiled. "None of *their* cameras. I had to know when to time my escape and the diversionary planes. Showmanship, Mister MacGyver! It's kept you misdirected for the better part of two months."

"And destroyed a science village on Svalbard."

"Nothing a grant of forty-two million plus insurance money won't fix by next year."

Mac grunted. "The blow to the Seed Vault was heavy. I assume the seeds are here?"

Hart pointed to their right, where they were turning into a road leading towards the mountain. They topped a small rise, and descended towards a massive cavern maw, large enough to swallow the entire cargo ship Mac had just seen.

"This ... can't be," Mac said, awed by the sight.

Hart was grinning wider. "You correctly guessed that this was a sanctuary. Perhaps you did not appreciate the scale."

The caravan entered the cave, headlights blinking on in succession, and made their way through a modern-built tunnel to vast vault doors of impenetrable steel, themselves flung wide, allowing the master of this place to enter freely. "We'll stop at the overlook," Hart told the driver.

Another minute, and "Good God," Mac said, getting out. They stood at the crest of a sweeping road that curved along the vast cavern wall then down to the encampment below.

It's a whole damn ... city!

I don't know what else to call it.

A titanic steel pillar supported the Ararat cavern, looking like something out of a science fiction movie. It was a cross between a skyscraper and a supporting structure, obviously inhabited, judging by the lit windows dotting its surface and elevators traversing the exterior. Surrounding its base was nothing less than a small metropolis, full of office blocks, apartments, entertainment and eatery districts, all the way to outlying farms, fed by artificial sunlamps and elaborate irrigation.

"This is ... beyond words," Mac said.

"You are too kind, sir," replied Hart. "The cavern is nearly fourteen kilometers in diameter, with a height of three hundred thirty meters. Or about the same as that of a hundred-story building, more or less."

"But this can't be a natural cavern?"

"More than you might expect. I believe it may have been the largest naturally occurring cavern in the world before we improved upon it. You can see some of the supports added strategically along the walls just there. But, of course, the majority rests upon the central arcology itself. The citizens have taken to calling it the Ark for short."

Mac looked in genuine wonder for a long moment, then turned to Hart. "Well, you didn't do all this just to impress me. You said before this was to safeguard humanity against the coming storm? What's that about?"

"Let's talk in my office."

⸙

Ailsa and Holcomb had barely slept and eaten less. Boone's files were engrossing and horrifying, the portrait of a man who didn't consider the morality of any situation, but rather where it would advance his career. The veneer of "national security" had long lost its shine for Ailsa, but reviewing these documents had given it a dingy patina covered with grime. "This data is a bloody bomb," she said, setting aside her loaner tablet.

"Nuclear," Holcomb said behind his computer, sounding miserable. "With the Director himself authorizing most of this, there's practically nothing I can do."

She sneered. "Then give it tae me, an' we'll see what Number Ten has tae say about it."

"Wish I could. I'm sure you're not even supposed to be seeing this. And I'm seriously jeopardizing my ass here. Maybe my freedom, too. As damning as it all is, though, I'm kinda seeing Hart as the one in the white hat."

"Except for the bloody sarin gas," snarled Ailsa, disbelieving.

"No, what I mean is how he sticks it to Boone in every exchange. He gets no points for his role in everything, but I get where he's coming from being the genie in the lamp."

Ailsa had no comment on that. "Well, we're nae much closer tae findin' Mac. What did yaer half a' the files have?"

"Not a lot. And that Indonesia file was all about some big power generator they're building there."

"Power generator? Fusion?"

"Tidal. A, uh ..." He paused to look. "A tidal barrage. They build a barrier across an area that has strong tides and—"

Ailsa's spine had tingled at the word. "Aye, I know what it is. One moment." She accessed her own case files and found the data that Agent Castillo had shared long ago, then handed over the tablet. "Right there. Plans for a tidal barrage were stolen by Hart as one a' his first high-profile crimes. Does that file contain the location?"

"Yeah. Larantuka on Flores Island. But this is about a project under government contract. It all looks legit."

Her mind was racing a mile a minute. "I'll bet all the apple pie in America that if we dig down far enough, we'll find Hart behind that contract."

Holcomb could only shrug. "Where do we start?"

She began gathering her things. "On the scene."

Holcomb was skeptical. "Just based on this?"

"I've made bigger leaps before," she said. "Can yae get me a flight?"

Holcomb wrestled with it for a long moment. "Yeah, okay. Head to the airport, and I'll charter something."

"Thank yae."

"Do you even speak Indonesian?"

"I'll learn it on the plane," she said, seriously, as she was already heading for the door.

●●

"The end of days," Hart said, as they settled into his office, a huge room that dominated most of the Ark's uppermost floor with windows viewing the span of his underground domain. The windows were dark for the moment, solid black, allowing total privacy. "For the majority of mankind, I fear they are not so very far off."

Mac had heard this on internet discussions and tabloids for most of his life. His expression said so.

Hart held up a hand. "I know, you think I should be fitted for one of your aluminum foil caps, perhaps, but hear me out. Even if the current wave of nationalism, populism, and demagoguery passes without a decisive eruption, climate change will ultimately create an untenable situation. Indeed, as a man of science, you understand that the damage is already in motion, and it's far too late to reverse."

"Not fully, but we can curb it substantially, and new technologies are in the works that could reverse it before the problems become too severe."

"Indeed, *if* the world's capitalists were so inclined to take action. Sadly, they have the ear of every politician in all the countries that matter, and resolve has been slow to coalesce. Even those politicos that desire swift, sweeping changes drag their feet when they achieve office. Again, your country is no exception."

"So, all this is in defense of what might happen in another forty years?" Mac said, gesturing.

"Correct, though America's dalliance with fascism and authoritarianism has emboldened these movements around the world. Indeed, hindsight allows that it was always heading this way. I do not regret my decision to leave government service some decades ago. I doubt you'll regret the decision now, for much the same reasons."

Careful here.

Don't commit.

Didn't we do that when we helped wipe the data?

It's not wiped.

Then what are we doing here, really?

"Look, Hart, I can't honestly say what's brought me here—curiosity, maybe? Or why I'm even considering going along with this. Maybe the sudden loss of a future I can no longer have? It's been a rough few days, you know."

Hart's smile was slight. "I'm no psychic, but your words say more than you intend. 'Going along with,' for instance. Perhaps you began this venture as a way to get close to me and continue the work your unfortunate Agent Castillo began. But I've read the interest in your questions, and I saw your reaction to this place when you laid eyes on it for the first time. A true, scientific community dedicated to pure research and the pursuit of knowledge above its promise of survival should that become necessary. Tell me that doesn't stir you."

It does. Dammit.

"Okay, sure, but you can't just expect me to forget or ignore Solana's work. You've committed a number of crimes."

"Yes, and to further this, I *would commit more*. But we've been over that. We, you and I, both *do what we must* for the causes we think just and beneficial, despite their lack of legality, however momentary or relative they may be, do we not?" His tone turned mournful. "And I am so sorry, again, for your loss. I can see the wound is still fresh. I should say it gets better with time, but all time does is dull the edge, losing someone so vitally important to you. A senseless waste of talent and potential, to say nothing of intelligence or beauty. For you this is similar to a moment I experienced decades ago, and I do not mean my beloved wife."

The insight struck Mac like a fist. "You're talking about Ailsa's father, aren't you?"

Hart's face was a tight mask except for his eyes. "Yes. Only there, I was not only a friend, mourning his loss, I was the very *cause* of his death. I pulled the trigger."

"So, you admit it. You killed him."

Again, the mask. "Under orders. *From my government.* Or so I've been rationalizing it to myself for the past twenty years. Which is why, no matter what court I should be brought before, it remains a crime I will never be charged with. Too many secrets would be revealed. Too much history would be undone. This is why I left my service to MI6. And why Lady Ailsa's pursuit has been—and will be —quite in vain. I've made my peace with it as I could and worked on my penance for the last two decades."

"Penance?"

Hart turned his chair towards the solid black window. The touch of a button cleared it to transparency. *"This place is my penance.* For my failure to protect the world from those that would do it the ultimate harm. That has brought us to this precipice.

"You see, Mister MacGyver, the world is being destroyed by those that think themselves above the fray, who think that somehow their money will feed them when no crops will grow; when the water is more poison than potable and the air is no longer fit to breathe. Having now stood there as a billionaire with unlimited resources at my command, I can understand the illusion. But I once lived apart from that blinded fantasy. I have lived hand to mouth and day to day."

He turned back. "In short: I see no hope. Nothing will save this civilization from the reckoning a very shortsighted few have wrought for the great majority. I will survive it, along with a few others. We shall endeavor to create a better society on the ashes of the old. A true phoenix, if you will. That begins here at Ararat. And you, sir, would make a fine addition to those efforts."

Not sure I'm buying all this doomsday prophecy stuff.

Doesn't mean it can't happen.

But as a think tank and research community?

Yeah, I'm tempted.

Can't forget how this place has been funded—guns and sarin gas.

But it's all grey now.

Including who you've been working for.

Is Hart any more grey than they are?

Is there even an answer for that?

Keep asking.

"Okay, then," Mac said after a beat. "What is it you expect of me here? A researcher?"

Hart smiled as though a weight had lifted from him. "Eventually, certainly. I've reviewed your work for the CIA, Homeland Security, and FBI quite thoroughly. I believe in the short-term, we could use you as a recruiter, of sorts."

Mac rolled his eyes. "Like door to door with pamphlets or something?"

"Not exactly. This is a rather exclusive community. Handpicked for individuals of great value and their families. We're two thousand strong right now, with room for another eighteen thousand. Recruiting individuals from first-world countries isn't terribly difficult where access is relatively free. However, there are persons we desire in more problematic nations where even my money and influence do not necessarily guarantee an interview, to say nothing of bringing them here."

"Hang on, didn't you say my extraction of the Iranian nuclear physicist was essentially *kidnapping?*"

"In that incident, it was. The situation was fabricated entirely by the CIA, and his family was left behind. I would have had you meet the man, persuade him to our cause, then extract him and his family, the expense be damned. This is somewhat different compared to your agency's normal modus operandi, in that no one is forced to join us. You yourself can be very persuasive when speaking of causes you believe in, and as for operating behind hostile borders, well, you'd be a remarkable asset."

"That's a matter of luck more often than I'd like."

"You give yourself too little credit, Mister MacGyver. You have the training to evade security services the world over, the acumen to improvise in any situation, and the humanity to bring everyone out safely. In short, you were *made* for this mission."

He ain't wrong.

I was. And would be.

But there's something here.

Something off.

Beyond all the words and logic.

Hart's smile widened. "Still weighing it, are we? Well, if material gain is any factor on the scales, Minerva dug up your contractor's salary. I'll offer you ten times that annual sum and call it a bargain."

Mac scoffed. "We'll need money after the world ends?"

Hart shrugged. "No, but while the world lasts, why not enjoy it? Besides, as you pointed out, I could be wrong about the short-term. Perhaps they'll struggle on a bit further, beyond my own lifetime, even. But I very much doubt it. My predictions have proved all too accurate thus far."

Mac sat in silence for a long beat, trying to quiet his internal debate before he finally responded. "It's a lot to think about. I don't suppose there's somewhere I could catch a little food and a nap?"

Hart nodded. "Of course. You've hardly slept nor eaten for the last few days. I understand completely." He touched a button and the door slid open to allow Minerva's entrance. "Minerva will show you to temporary quarters and see that you're fed. Tomorrow we'll tour the facilities, and as a special event, we'll be firing up the fusion reactor for the first time." He rose with Mac and extended a hand. "You'll forgive the presumption, perhaps, but, welcome aboard, Mister MacGyver."

Right or wrong, Mac shook it.

CHAPTER 28

MAC AWOKE SUDDENLY, uncertain of his surroundings. As he sat, blinking in darkness, it started trickling back to him. He wondered what Solana would think of the last day or so when he told her, meeting Hart, and seeing Ararat.

But she's gone.

She's dead. Remember?

That reality hit his heart like a stab, bringing an ache that welled in his throat and stung his eyes.

I miss you. Her. Us.

He recalled the same thing happening when he was a kid. His father had been alive one day, then gone the next. But for the following weeks, each morning he awoke thinking it had all been a dream, and everything was fine.

He swiped at his wet eyes and got out of bed.

It was still one in the morning, local time. He'd slept for almost fifteen hours. The quarters were spacious and comfortable, with every amenity, except for a working computer. He was still cut off from contacting anyone on the outside. "For a little while longer," Hart had said. But there was still no clarity about which way to move.

Do I just chuck the life that brought me here?

And take him up on his offer?

Or take him down?

Damned if I know.

But they're certainly making a full-court press to have me, he thought, opening the closet to find not only his clothes but a pair of designer suits cut to fit him, plus jeans, shirts, and two new leather jackets identical to his own battered G2 flight jacket.

He selected a blue plaid shirt and jeans, all his size of course, but donned his own jacket. Something about changing that just felt wrong.

In search of food, he found the dining room easily enough, and was not alone. Minerva Hart sat over a bowl of steaming French onion soup, reading her tablet.

"Mac. Up and about I see, and rested at last?"

"Yeah, I slept. Could use some of that, though."

"Of course," she said, tapping her tablet. A steward appeared with water and took Mac's order. He vanished through the far doors.

"So, am I getting out of quarantine anytime soon?" he asked, indicating the tablet. "At what point do you trust me to follow the rules and not try to put cuffs on your dad?"

"Today, most likely, assuming you're accepting our offer. Personally, I thought it a foregone conclusion from the moment you erased that data in Langley. Committing treason, even as part of a deep cover, is not to be done lightly."

"Or maybe my cover is just that complete," Mac said.

"Perhaps," she said laughing. "If you were Ailsa MacIver, I wouldn't believe a single word you'd spoken, no matter how sincere. But then infiltration and psychological manipulation are her specialties, not yours. I've seen how you reacted to this place, and when you get the tour today, I'm certain you'll be clear about your opinion of us and the work being done here."

Soup arrived, and Mac consumed it like it was a new experience. A salad with grilled chicken followed, vanishing down his throat as if by magic.

"Your appetite has returned as well, I see," Minerva said, amused.

"The food is good here. How sustainable is it without outside help?"

"Foods not native to Indonesia would either be farmed or substituted for something local. Thus, when imports are no longer possible, some variety may diminish. But as for overall capacity, once we're operating at peak, we'll easily feed all twenty thousand inhabitants with room to grow and plenty left over for emergencies."

"What about manufacturing and raw resource acquisition? A technological society, even one this small, needs a pretty constant influx of spare parts, replacement equipment, and such."

"Stockpiles for the short-term and the ability to machine and build our own parts in the long-term. Would you like part of your tour now? Infrastructure is one of my responsibilities. Father won't be up for a few more hours, but we both appear to be on western hemisphere time."

Mac found some relief from his dilemma by sorting through the technicalities and logistics of this improbable wonderland. And he could use the break. "Why not?" he said with as much enthusiasm as he could muster, however real it was, or not. "Let's have a look around."

Mac had seen some fairly impressive facilities in his time, but, for all his doubts, he had to acknowledge, even to himself, that nothing came close to Ararat. No expense had been spared on massive 3D printers capable of creating complex parts such as advanced fabrication equipment and even vehicle engines and cars themselves. They could print anything from buildings to tools to complex appliances and machines. They spent a couple of hours touring the darkened industrial district, lights popping on as they went, and passing a few random patrols that nodded and smiled at Minerva.

"Of course," Minerva was saying, "building something like a helicopter would require some specialized manufacturing apparatus, but that, too, can be designed and fabricated, given time."

"Impressive, to say the least," Mac said sincerely.

"Thank you," she said. "I think you'll find our defense labs even more to your taste. They're just up ahead."

"Guns? Not really."

She simply smiled as the lights came on and a door unlocked at her approach.

A large workspace illuminated before them with research and design stations lining the near wall. Proving grounds with sensor-laden humanoid and wildlife targets covered the far wall.

Mac's eyes narrowed until he got a look at what was being built. "Gas, sprays, electroshock ... all nonlethal?"

"Of course," she said, with as much a sense of pride as amusement at his surprise. "Father believes mankind has had too much experience with deadly weapons, and I agree. Naturally, after the current civilization implodes there will be enclaves of survivors around the globe that will require our assistance. Some are certain to be hostile. We'll not be party to exterminations, no matter how convenient that might be, but we will defend ourselves in a humane manner."

"Good to know," he said.

"And in the short-term, profitable. This device, for instance," she said, picking it up, "may resemble an ordinary stun gun, but unlike modern models, this will render the target unconscious for a good half hour rather than dazing them for just a few minutes." She clicked the trigger and a brilliant bolt tore the air between the contacts.

Mac blinked at the sudden streak that lingered across his eyesight. "So, you develop things here to market and sell to whoever now? But then wouldn't these other survivor enclaves have them, too?"

"Well, we're thinking they're more likely to have firearms, but if they wished to arm themselves exclusively with nonlethal weapons, that would be fine." She smiled and put the stunner back on the workbench.

"So, no guns at all?"

"We have an armory, certainly, well stocked and capable of outfitting a third of the city as troops in the event of something catastrophic. There is also hunting to consider in the short-term until proper ranching can be established topside. We can retool to manufacture even more arms and ammunition, if necessary. As I'm sure you know, modern gunpowder is a relatively simple substance. The capacity for lethal force is not to be lightly thrown aside. Where possible, though, we prefer nonlethal means. Should you like to see the armory as well? They're working on body armor at the moment, utilizing graphene layers. Early tests have been promising, capable of stopping a .45 at close range."

"Show me everything," Mac said, feeling strangely exhilarated.

You're really loving this.

Maybe too much.

Can't hurt to look, right?

The more you know, the better to deal with ...

Whatever.

And, as she turned to move on and he followed her past the workstation, some old instinct made him slip the small stunner in his pocket just for ... whatever.

<hr />

Ailsa stepped onto the same tarmac on Flores Island twenty-six hours after Mac had arrived. The sun was up over the horizon, and the day would be tropically warm, but not unpleasant if the sea breeze held. It reminded her of her time in the Royal Navy, aboard ship and up with the dawn as a daily exercise. It put a welcome spring in her step, which she surmised she'd need to run Mac to ground.

A broken conversation with a transportation clerk demonstrated that her rapid study of Indonesian during the flight wasn't nearly as comprehensive as she'd have liked.

Goin' tae be tough tae question anyone subtly.

Aye, but perhaps simple recon will be all we need.

This Ararat is connected tae the causeway. Has tae be.

A place tae start.

But as the rickety cab deposited her and pulled away spluttering in its own exhaust, she eyed the construction yard anchoring this end of the causeway.

Fence. Simple enough.

Guards. Nae as simple.

They're nae armed.

No, but the police would be.

Tonight, we could slip through easily.

We cannae wait that long.

Aye, the bloody reactor could be powerin' up even now.

A small group of protesters caught her eye. They stood off to one side, holding signs and chanting something that she thought was "Keep Water Free!" though she couldn't be certain. There were only five of them, so clearly it was a concern not shared by the local majority.

"Me excuse," she said to one of them. "Am curious signs. Upset about you something?"

The young man blinked at her butchering his language, deciphered a moment, then said slowly, "They're building a bridge and putting my uncle's ferry service out of work. People won't need it anymore! And they're blocking the strait!"

He spoke so rapidly that Ailsa wasn't certain she followed. "Ah, project important is not? Power free everyone or cheap?"

This time the young man just shook his head slowly. "I'm sorry, I don't understand."

She tried a few more iterations, to no avail. Ultimately, she sighed and muttered, "*C'est la vie.*"

His surprise was palpable. "*Français?*"

"*Oui!*" she said, continuing in that language. "You speak French, too?"

He grinned wide. "Yes, my grandmother insisted we keep the language in the family. Yours is perfect."

"Thank you. My Indonesian is horrible, I'm afraid."

"No, no, it was fine," he said, lying.

"Well, I'm glad we have a common tongue. The protest is about the ferries?"

"Yes!" he said and explained again.

"Surely there would still be work for your service, no? There are locks built into the causeway that can take hours to pass a ship."

He grunted and shook his head. "It's still a disruption, and he bought a new boat just before we found out about this. How will he make the payments on that now?"

Ailsa had no answer.

"And people are still asking questions about how all this got funded so quickly. And what's the rush? And what are they building on the other side behind that big gate of theirs with armed guards? *Armed guards*, madam, I assure you!"

Aha, she thought, but pressed for confirmation. "Armed? Surely not."

"It's true! It's off the main road a little north from this damned causeway. Helicopters come and go, and there's a dock with cargo ships that arrive in the night and leave before dawn ... It is all very suspicious."

"And no one has asked any questions?"

"Bah!" he spat. "The company employs many locally and pays a high wage. No one asks questions, not even the reporters."

She smiled. "Is your uncle's ferry for hire at this moment?"

•••

Mac had received the complete tour, beginning with the helipad atop the arcology tower topside, which proved to be the only other means of access to the cavern besides the main vault door. The place had every convenience of a modern city from state-of-the-art medical facilities to education campuses. Restaurants and stores had a sampling of cuisines from around the world. Entertainment ranged from stage plays to blockbuster films to libraries and archives, all in a dozen languages.

For protection against whatever Armageddon humanity ultimately decided on, modern desalinization plants would provide water, advanced air filtration systems would provide air, and the cavern was deep enough to withstand both any nuclear fallout and the worst depravity climate change could conjure. Even volcanic eruption, a pure act of God, would only inconvenience the arcology, as it was built to withstand earthquakes up to eight point nine on the Richter Scale.

Power generation was a mixture of solar and wind with the tidal barrage powering what would become massive graphene-based batteries. Ultimately, they came to Doctor Verone's own T-X reactor, replicated on a large scale in the arcology's base, when Victor Hart finally appeared to join them around dawn. They'd power up the reactor later in the day under Hart's personal supervision.

The entire operation hearkened to what a modern colony might look like on a distant planet, all right here on Earth.

Minerva went off to oversee the checklist for the reactor start, leaving Mac and Hart alone to share a leisurely meal in an open-air cafe on a huge balcony overlooking the cavern, until Hart finally posed the question. "Well, Mister MacGyver, you've seen everything our hand holds. The offer is genuine and sincere, and, perhaps, we now seem somewhat less like the mustachioed villains to your eye. So, what is your answer?"

The simplest move?

Tell him you're in.

And then decide.

More grey? More lies?

Sick of that crap.

Then play it straight.

"Still somewhat conflicted, I'm afraid," Mac said. "Look, I think you're building something amazing here, without question. And if you'd gone about it by more legitimate means, I'd have jumped in with both feet years ago."

Hart waited a moment. "But?"

"But this isn't a simple decision. This is a *life choice* you're asking me to make. To completely abandon my past ... allegiances and start again from scratch. And I'm gonna need a little more time to get there, you know?"

"Then why do I have the impression you're stalling?"

"For what? I could tell you I'm all in even if I wasn't really, couldn't I? But that's just not me. Not about something like this. And say, for whatever reason, I don't take your offer; you've said I'm free to go, yes?"

"Correct. Under the proviso that you'll say nothing about this place nor continue harassing my endeavors in the greater world."

"And, as insurance against that, you'd inform the CIA of my deleting that data, right?"

Hart's grin had no warmth. "We understand each other perfectly."

But you didn't delete the data.

Yeah, though we did commit a number of felonies getting to it.

Then which of us really holds the ace here?

"So then I've got nothing to stall for, do I?" Mac said, before adding, "You asked me for an honest answer. And I'm giving you one."

Hart considered, then nodded. "Very well, but I cannot hold your place at the table forever."

"Fair enough. Then how 'bout I take the rest of the day until you power up the reactor. And I'll let you know my decision by then."

Hart exhaled a sigh. "Well, in your shoes, I'd have jumped by now, but I cannot fault a man for caution. Meet us there for the grand moment, and, hopefully, for the celebration that follows. Today shall be one for the history books."

"I wouldn't miss it," Mac said.

👓

Having reached the island by boat, Ailsa made her way through the jungle to the outer edge of Hart's Xanadu. Though she'd seen prisons with easier access than the Ararat compound. She was crouched in the tropical foliage overlooking the road into the facility, and the guard house and electrified gate surrounding it. It wasn't so much overwhelming security as concentrated. Too many cameras, too many eyeballs, and not really enough gaps in between to exploit. Only the jungle provided any real cover, and it had been cut away from the fence line surrounding the area.

She used her phone's zoom function as binoculars to study the guards. The protester had been right. Submachine guns dangled from straps on every shoulder, with body armor and tactical vests protecting each man. That said, they were not in alerted state. They'd break off to patrol the fence line in pairs as others returned, sweating and gratefully accepting a fresh canteen. Ailsa considered the fence as she drank from her own bottled water, wiping sweat from her brow.

They've clear-cut out tae thirty meters.

With cameras at ev'ry ten meters.

Aye, an' I can almost feel the electric hum from here.

No chance a' climbin' over.

Wait, listen.

A cloth-covered truck was trundling up the path, stopped at the gate, then was waved through.

They dinnae check the back.

Aye, they dinnae check anythin'! Nae even the guard's ID.

They knew him personally, clearly.

They're nae expectin' any trouble. Completely stood down.

Aye, an' they were nae watchin' the road.

Think I can catch one a' those?

It took some time to work her way through the dense jungle, but eventually she hunkered down where the foliage grew right up to the road, out of sight from the gate, and settled in patiently.

Her predatory instincts proved accurate, as another truck nearly identical to the first rumbled towards her inside of an hour.

She'd chosen a sharp bend, and as the truck slowed to a crawl to navigate the turn, she dashed from her hiding space, leapt up to grab the tailgate, and vaulted into the back—straight into a shocked worker standing among the wooden shipping crates.

"Hello, lad!" she said brightly.

The man drew in a breath to shout, but only exhaled in a deflating groan as her fist connected with his solar plexus. A sleeper hold put him down for the count.

A rapid search found no weapons, and the crates were full of various foodstuffs, all packaged for long shelf life. His ID card had his own picture, useless to her.

"Oh, well. This was a temporary ride anyway," she muttered, hid the unconscious worker behind the crates, and hunkered down herself.

Again, the truck was stopped, but not searched. She watched the gate receding behind them, then darkness as they entered a tunnel.

I'm on the clock now. As soon as he wakes up, the place will be on alert.

A disguise would be useful.

An' an ID card.

One thing at a time. Let's get out a' this truck first.

She kept watch, peeking through the back flaps. The tunnel was long, and well lit. They passed another pair of trucks leaving the tunnel. She was wondering how long they'd travel when abruptly the tunnel fell away, and the wall stretched upwards into darkness.

Am I outside?

The air smells earthen. Like a cave.

Nice an' cool, too.

She risked poking her head out the flap and was stunned by the same view Mac had had on his arrival.

It's a bloody city! she thought, eyeing the central pillar.

With a fusion bomb in here somewher'.

Time tae get off this motor.

The opportunity arrived shortly in the form of a receiving center at the town outskirts. The truck pulled in, parked, and Ailsa snuck away unnoticed as the driver chatted with the tablet-bearing manager.

Without anywhere particular to go, Ailsa started towards the monolithic central pillar. If she knew Hart, he'd have his residence and offices there, likely on the top floor. It was as good a place as any to get started.

The place was indeed a fully functioning town, not unlike any planned community in a major metropolitan area. The industrial zone gave way to housing, condominiums built tall for extra floor space, then eating and entertainment centers. It was approaching evening, and people gathered in outdoor cafes and eateries. No need for roofs in a place that would never see rain.

She overheard languages of all sorts, though largely Euro and Indonesian dialects, with English as the most common.

"Excuse me," a woman said, stopping her. "Are you new here?" She was about Ailsa's height with lighter red hair and smiling, friendly eyes. She wore casual business attire, loose collar and business jacket, somewhat rumpled as if after a long day of work.

Ailsa donned her smiling American mask. "Yes, hello! Ellie Shaw," she said holding out a hand. "Just arrived recently, and still finding my way around."

"Hannah Norman, Human Resources," said the woman, smiling and taking her hand. "I could tell you're new, because you've forgotten your badge."

Ailsa noted Hannah's badge on her belt, looked at her own, and groaned. "Not again. Ugh. Sorry. I'm not quite used to wearing one all the time."

Hannah grinned. "It's okay. There's no lockdown in effect, and you only really need it if you're leaving the city or going to the Ark," she said lifting her chin towards the pillar.

"I'm still not quite used to this place. It's amazing."

"Isn't it? Mister Hart is an absolute wonder."

"He's certainly something."

"Were you looking for a place to eat? You could join me, if you like. I'm meeting some friends in a bit to watch the broadcast. New arrivals are always welcome."

"The broadcast?"

"The fusion reactor, of course. You must be *really* new."

"Oh, that! Yes, of course, that's very nice. But I should really hurry back and get my badge for later, huh?"

"Well, good thing I spotted you, then," said Hannah. "We hang out at this place often, so feel free to drop by. Ararat can be a little lonely at first, but I'm sure you'll fit in famously."

Ailsa said her goodbyes, shaking hands again. As Hannah turned, Ailsa deftly unclipped the badge from Hannah's belt. She examined it walking away. Hannah wasn't a perfect match for her, but the hair would do for a casual glance.

She headed for the pillar.

CHAPTER 29

Mac found a place to sit outside the Ark. He settled on a park bench across from a modern-art fountain made of spiraling angles with water forming curves as it spilled forth. Trees grew in graceful arrangements in the little park area, fed by artificial lamps spreading diffuse light across the whole area, simulating a somewhat dimmer than normal early evening.

Solana would've liked it here.

Though she liked the sun on her face.

But the goal of it? For sure.

Or would she look past it all to put Hart behind bars?

Impossible to know now.

He took in a long, deep breath, smelling the cool cavern air. Not quite fresh, but still refreshing. He turned the question over in his mind again and again.

I don't know.

There's a flaw in his logic somewhere.

I can't see it.

But I can feel it.

"Well, hello there, stranger," said a woman walking up behind him.

He turned and nearly did a double take to see ... *Ailsa* standing there before him—as he realized saying her name might not be the best move.

"Yeah. I'm new here. And you are?"

"Hannah Norman, Human Resources," she said indicating her badge. It took him a second glance to realize that wasn't her photo, and she was using her American accent.

She continued, "Is there somewhere we could talk privately a moment? Inside, perhaps?"

"Definitely. This way." He led her into the Ark, his badge getting them through the front door without trouble. The place wasn't fully occupied as yet, and the lowest levels held empty offices and conference rooms aplenty. He took her to a vacated office, shut the door, and darkened the interior window.

Finally, he let his relief and surprise show. "Ailsa, how the hell did you find me?"

"The files. It was touch an' go in Holcomb's office for a while there, I'll tell yae that. What in the hell were yae thinkin' leadin' Minerva Hart into the belly a' the bloody CIA?"

"They were convincing me to work for them, and sort of vice versa, I guess, to see if I could be trusted."

"Well, yae'r nae in chains, so the ruse worked."

"I guess."

"But it dinnae matter now, the fusion reactor is rigged tae blow."

His spine jolted with electricity. "*What? How?*"

She briefly explained what Verone had done.

Mac mulled it. "Damn. And clever."

"Not tae mention *deadly*. Look at all the people this will kill."

"Right," he said, picturing the buzzing city past the blackened windows. "Even if it's a small radius, it'll be enough to bring this all down on their heads. Well, lucky for everyone you got to me here. They were planning to start the reactor today. I can go to Hart and stop it. I'm sure even without Verone, there's a way to fix it."

"Aye, we'll go tae Hart," she said darkly. "An' sort him out, once an' for all. But what do yae mean, 'find a way tae fix it' ...? Dinnae tell me yae've *drunk* his bloody Kool-Aid an' thrown in with this lot?"

"No. But thinking about it. After Solana, Boone, and that data I hid for you ... Not sure what's left out there for me. Or if I even *want* it anymore. And look at this place; it's an engineer's wet dream."

The full force of her withering glare hit him. "*An' its lord is a Goddamned murderer an' thief!* It does'nae matter what shiny objects he's dangled before yaer eyes. *He has no right tae walk free on this Earth!*"

"I get it. You want him dead. You have from the start of all this. For killing your father. Which he admitted to me."

Ailsa jerked back involuntarily—suddenly unable to speak before she found her voice. "*He told yae that? Tae yaer face?*"

Mac nodded. "Said MI6 ordered him to do it. And that's why he left the agency. Lost all faith in the 'system' you and I work for and support. And turned his life to building this. Called it his 'penance.'"

"*An' yae believed him?*" Ailsa said, groping for a truth that was melting faster than she could grasp it.

"I don't know *what* to believe now. Or *who*. Guys like Boone? The CIA? MI6? *You?*—Who sees nothing but blood when you get within a *mile* of Hart?—You tell me who I'm supposed to believe now, Ailsa. Because Solana's gone. And there's a hole in me the size of this cavern. And I haven't got a *clue* what to fill it with! All right?"

She could feel how shaken he was—because she was equally at sea—as she raised a hand, like to calm a raging beast, and spoke slow and soft. "Look, Mac, I hear yae. But right or wrong, we swore an oath tae serve our governments—that were chosen *by the people*. An' maybe it's all shite. Maybe the people choose badly at times. Maybe they need tae rise up an' choose again. But *nobody chose Hart*. He's set himself up as a bloody *God*. An', for all his fine words an' reason, if we go down that path, there's only chaos an' madness—*for ev'ryone*."

She paused to let her words take hold, watching as Mac's head sagged slightly and his shoulders sank. But she knew he was right—

about her. Revenge had driven her for so long, it was the only truth she had left. And nothing could stop that now—not even Mac. And, almost despite herself, as he looked up to answer ...

Her hand lashed out, striking him in the throat.

The sheer force made him cough and splutter as she flew into motion around him, fists hitting his diaphragm and kidney, expelling all air from his lungs and sending a shock through his side. Before he knew it, she was behind him, kicked out his knee, and his neck was locked in her arm with a viselike grip.

Spots appeared in Mac's vision as he gasped helplessly for air. Blood flow to his brain had ceased, and he had only seconds remaining. He yanked on her arm with all his might, but she might've been made of steel. He fumbled for his jacket pocket, vision fading, numb fingers finding the stunner. He brought it out, flicked it on, and jabbed down into her leg.

She yelped, released him, and stumbled backwards, falling to the ground convulsing. Mac took a long moment on his hands and knees, choking and gasping for air as his vision cleared.

God. She's like fighting a tornado!

But she's down.

He crawled over and checked her. Unconscious, and breathing steadily.

Now what? Hand her over?

Hart would love that.

No. Just secure her for the moment. I've got to stop that reactor.

He found a roll of packing tape in a box two rooms over—not exactly duct tape, but it'd do—and returned to kneel beside her to start binding.

Mac found Victor and Minerva in the control room overlooking the fusion reactor core. The place looked like something out of mission control at NASA, and the reactor itself—beyond the meter-thick safety glass—appeared to be straight out of *Star Trek*. Mac eyed the chamber, imagining the preignition reactor as a predator waiting to pounce. Hart and Minerva stood by the main console, watching the people working on the floor below. A readout showed the reactor in a ready state, awaiting only the final sequence and the control lever to be pulled.

"Ah, Mister MacGyver, good," Hart said upon seeing him, sounding concerned. "You should be aware that Ailsa MacIver may be in the cavern and—have you been in a fight, sir?"

Mac touched his tender throat, purpling with a bruise. "Yeah. I kind of ran into her. It didn't go well. She's secured on the premises and poses no immediate threat—to anyone."

Hart's face went from surprise to suspicion in seconds. "I see. Well, now your hesitation appears to make more sense."

"You think *I* let her in here? Believe me, I was as surprised as anyone when she turned up in the park outside."

Hart's eyes remained narrowed. "You do indeed seem pummeled. But she's a deadly hand-to-hand combatant and your resume shows only modest skill in that arena. Not to mention her being more than a decade your junior. And yet you prevailed?"

"Stun gun," he said, pulling it out. "A memento from your tour this morning. Old habits die hard, I guess," he said to Minerva.

Minerva looked at him with more amusement than alarm. "Shall we add petty larceny to your resume as well, then?" she asked with a smile. "Though it seems we owe you some thanks for ... containing her."

"Perhaps," said Hart, "but telling me she's secured 'on the premises' is disturbingly vague. Could you please be more specific?"

"If your stunner works as advertised, she'll be out for a while regardless. You can have your men search the Ark if you'd like. But Ailsa's the least of your problems now. Because she found out from Doctor Verone that the reactor is rigged. If you turn it on, the reaction will overload the containment field inside of twenty minutes. It's not a full bomb, but it's powerful enough to destroy the Ark and a good chunk of Ararat, if not bring the cavern roof crashing down."

Hart's skeptical expression said as much as his words. "I see you had a conversation with her along with your bout. Yes, she tried to convince me of the same thing not thirty-six hours ago."

"What? *You knew?*" Mac asked, confused and startled. "Then at least let me see the specs and crawl in there for a look. If there's an issue, then there's a shot I can fix it."

"There's nothing to fix," Hart said. "This deception is transparent. And I'm surprised that a man of your knowledge would fall for such nonsense. Fusion reactors do not melt down or go critical, as it were. Such a thing is materially impossible."

"I'd agree under most circumstances, but this thing is still experimental. And the way this one is built, why even take a chance—"

"Enough," Hart cut him off. He pondered Mac and the reactor in turn, then sighed heavily. "And, if I permitted this, exactly how long would finding this supposed 'sabotage' take?"

Mac shrugged. "A few days? A week maybe? I'm not sure. I'd need to call Verone to consult—"

"And all the while your allies continue narrowing down their search for this place, which has already been compromised by the appearance of your female namesake, if not yourself." Hart turned to one of the guards at the door. "Have the premises searched for Lady MacIver." Then, to Mac, "And I fear my offer for you to join us now appears moot. As you say, old habits die hard, and it's clear now your allegiances, however misguided, lie elsewhere."

"Look," said Mac. "If it helps convince you, Ailsa's in one of the offices on the second floor, okay? And my only allegiance right now is preventing a disaster to your creation and the thousands of people living in it."

Mac turned to Minerva with a desperate look as she quickly interjected—"Father, perhaps just as a matter of caution, we should delay the initiation, and consider the situation further—"

But Hart cut her off with a curt wave of his hand. "No. I have played these games too long to be outmaneuvered by a fix-it man, however gifted he may be." Then to the guards, "Please secure Mister MacGyver, and his accomplice if she is indeed in those offices." The two guards stepped forward, each taking Mac by the arm before Hart continued. "And, as for your claim that the reactor is defective, here is my response."

And with that, Hart turned to hit two buttons on the console, turned a key, and threw the switch to start it.

"For God's sake, Hart, don't—" Mac almost yelled. But Hart ignored him as Minerva looked anxiously between them and—

A thrum suddenly echoed through the room as readouts flickered to life, and a bright, brilliant light shone through the observation ports, themselves rapidly darkening as the light grew near to blinding. Cheers came from the control room below with clapping and whistles.

"Attention citizens," Hart said into a microphone, his voice echoing through the room and across the cavern. "It is a time for celebration. Ararat's energy will now be fully self-sufficient. My congratulations to you all on a job well done." He released the mic and put the key back in his pocket before turning to Mac with a triumphant look. "You may have the honor of witnessing this moment before my forbearance towards you and Ailsa must, alas, come to an end."

But his gloating was short-lived as Minerva, her eyes fixed on the wall of readouts, raised her voice again, pointing to a digital display, "Father, look—" The meter clearly showed *something* spiking well above the nominal line. "It's the containment field. *It's not holding.*"

Hart looked at it, then Mac. "*What have you done?*"

"Unfortunately, *nothing!*" Mac snapped as the meter's level continued to rise. "*You* threw the damn switch!"

The celebratory mood on the floor below faltered, halted, and then totally evaporated. People got to their consoles, typing, checking, and rechecking their instruments. A murmur of fear rippled through the room.

"It's rising well above the safe limit," Minerva said.

"Shut it down," Hart ordered.

"No!" Mac shouted. "You can't shut it down normally! That'll trigger the explosion!"

Hart looked from Mac to the readings to the reactor and back again. His face grew redder, his fists clenched, jaw locked. "All of it gone in mere minutes. *Damn it to hell!*" he shouted, punching the console. "Minerva, we're leaving. To the helipad. Come." He turned to go.

"Father, we should sound the evacuation!" she argued.

"To what end? Few would escape, and most will live their last moments in terror. No, we must go. Now."

"No," Minerva said firmly. "We can't leave." Then, turning to Mac, "Is there any chance you can shut it down?"

"I don't know," said Mac. "We've only got about twenty minutes, but I could try. And it's not like I've got anything to lose now, do I?"

"But I do," said Hart. "And one must know when to cut one's losses." Then, to his daughter, "This can be rebuilt, the people replaced. *Please*, Minerva."

Minerva looked frantically between Hart and Mac, a lifetime of obedience suddenly called into question, as even the guards holding him shifted uncertainly. Seeing this, Hart barked, "Bind the man securely and then you can escape with us. *Those are my orders! This is over, Minerva.*"

Grateful for direction if not the chance to survive, the guards pushed Mac to his knees as the one on his right reached to pull out a zip-tie to strap his hands. But Mac's hand dove into his pocket for the stun gun and whipped it into the guard on his left. The man collapsed in a writhing pile, as Mac whirled up towards the other. But the guard was quicker and knocked the stunner from his hand with a slap, his gun already coming out of its holster. Mac seized the gun hand and wrestled with the man, keeping it held high. He had time to see Hart fleeing the room before he brought his elbow down hard into the guard's gut. Mac then spun, putting momentum into an uppercut that knocked the guard out cold.

Mac grunted, shaking his aching hand and bruised knuckles as he turned to see Minerva still there. "Not running?" Mac asked.

She glanced in the direction her father had fled and then turned to face him. "No," she said coolly. "And I will help you however I can. *Please.*" Mac just nodded as she turned to hit a few buttons on the console. A blaring klaxon echoed throughout the Ark and broadcast into the vast cavern before she picked up the mic and announced, "All citizens: you must evacuate immediately. Keep calm and proceed to the main exit. This is not a drill. Repeat: *all citizens are to immediately evacuate.* This message will repeat." She switched off the mic and turned to Mac. "What do you need me to do?"

"I need to make a call," he said.

She tossed him her phone.

"This'll work in the cavern?" he asked, catching it.

"There's a relay to the surface," she said.

"Great," said Mac, dialing. "Keep an eye on those readings while I do a quick consult."

❦

Ailsa MacIver blinked awake, imagining the klaxons to be from her navy days. Another instant and her eyes flew fully open, remembering exactly where she was. Minerva Hart's repeating voice warned everyone to evacuate the facility immediately as Ailsa saw even the guards at the door abandoning her down the hallway.

Ailsa swore loudly, glad MacGyver hadn't taped her mouth. Instead her ankles were bound and her wrists behind her back. She wrestled at the tape a moment but didn't exert much energy. There was enough wound around her to be nigh unbreakable.

She rolled into a sitting position and hunched up her elbows, bringing her hands to her waistband at the small of her back. The blade she'd secured there had been in case of just such a predicament, and she was relieved Mac hadn't thought to search her, nor had he taken her firearm, feeling its comfortable mass in her jacket pocket.

It took some maneuvering, and she suffered a small cut, but she finally managed to slice through the tape on her wrists, then ankles. She leaped to her feet, sucking the cut on her wrist, and still a little unsteady from the massive jolt she'd taken. Adrenaline banished that soon enough.

How long has that been goin' on? she thought to herself at the relentless klaxon.

From the office windows she could see people streaming towards the two great ramps curving along the cavern walls to the entrance. Most moved calmly, some ran, though even they weren't near fast enough as she realized:

Hart dinnae listen.

Tae me or Mac.

The reactor's goin' tae blow.

In minutes.

How many?

Less than twenty for certain.

Bloody hell!

She felt her phone vibrating in its hidden pocket. She looked, surprised she could get cell service in the cavern. "Holcomb," she said, answering and putting in her earwig. "Mac got the jump on me."

"I have him on the line," Holcomb said, anxiously. "Let me connect you."

"Ailsa? You there?" Mac said. "And you're free. Good."

"No thanks tae yae, bastard," she spat.

"You can kick my butt again later," he said. "Holcomb can't reach Doctor Verone, and I need to know exactly what he said about the containment field. Everything you can remember."

"Let me think ... Aye, he said the field will draw power from the reaction in progress. It makes the field stronger, lettin' more an' more reactant flow freely into the field until the emitters cannae contain it any longer."

"So, it's a self-feeding, recursive chain reaction?"

"Aye, recursive, he said that exactly. What're yae about?"

"Trying to stop the reactor without blowing us all back to atoms."

"To help Hart?"

"It's just me and Minerva. Hart's running for the helipad on the roof."

She pulled her gun, checking it. "Nae if I get there first," she said.

"Ailsa, don't. He's not worth it."

"He is tae me. An' the only way tae stop me is tae let that damn thing blow. He's dead either way. Yaer choice, Mac." She ended the call.

CHAPTER 30

MAC STARED at the phone a moment.

Forget Ailsa.

Stop the bomb.

"Okay. Science time," Mac said to Minerva. "Fusion reactions come from creating the same conditions inside the sun. That means heat and pressure. We can't do pressure of that scale, but we can substitute a stupid amount of heat, so it's hotter in there than the sun's core."

"Yes, that's true," Minerva said, nodding. "About one hundred million kelvin."

There's no material on Earth that'll let us get close to that.

Crap.

That's why they use magnetic containment suspended in a vacuum.

"And this reaction is feeding on itself," Mac said, "and cannot be safely deactivated. What about shutting off the reactant flow?"

Minerva hit some buttons, read her console, and shook her head. "By design it draws what it needs as it needs it. Ordinarily we throttle it via the containment field, reducing the energy requirements. But it's already peaking into the red. If we just shut it off or reduce the field, it'll collapse—"

"And the residual reaction will explode," Mac finished.

Gotta find a way to slow the reaction itself.

But it's a self-feeding, recursive chain reaction.

Too big an interruption, and boom.

We can't kill it cold turkey, so a bomb in there wouldn't work either.

Nor disabling any of the apparatus.

"What are your reactants? Deuterium and tritium?"

Another head shake. "No, we were able to improve on Doctor Verone's design by increasing the scale. This is straight deuterium-deuterium. No stray neutrons."

"No radioactivity," Mac said, with a hint of relief.

Handy.

We were due for a break.

'Cause it's been nothing but obstacles since he turned the switch.

Wait.

Obstacles.

Barriers to fusion!

"What if we can slow the reaction down?" Mac said, his mind spinning. "If we can get heavier atoms into the reaction chamber, the rate of fusion is hindered, reducing the energy output—"

"And the containment field reduces on its own!" Minerva's eyes flashed with the possibility. "Yes! Anything heavier than helium would do."

"Even ordinary air," Mac said, nodding.

Her face fell. "The field is in a vacuum, but the reaction is so energetic, air would hit the plasma state and ionize. Just as the magnetic containment keeps the deuterium inside—"

"—the nitrogen and oxygen in the atmosphere are kept out," Mac completed her thought. "Not to mention we'd be creating plasmatic air that would need venting somewhere."

Damn.

Fix one problem, make two more.

Then you need a solid mass to toss in there.

Yeah, but it has to be magnetically neutral.

Practically everything is magnetically neutral.

But not most metals when the temperature gets that hot.

And a metal is about all that has a chance of making it past the containment field before it vaporizes into ionized plasma and gets repelled.

Because it's still got to get through *the field to mix with the deuterium.*

Plus, how the hell do I stand anywhere near that?

But it's a vacuum, right?

And all the heat is thermal radiation, mostly infrared.

"I'm going to need something that'll let me get into the chamber," he said aloud to himself and her.

"Are you insane?" she demanded. "Nothing can do that!"

"Just from the airlock here," he said, pointing to a diagram of the core. "It's a vacuum in there, so there's no air to vent back and cook us all. You've got oxygen masks in your medical ward that I can tape to my face for the thirty seconds I'll need. I'm thinking I could stand from there, and hurl something into the containment field."

"Even with a heat suit, you'll die almost instantly, not to mention going blind from the raw light."

"What about the advanced body armors you had under development? There was heat shielding that could take it for maybe thirty seconds. And it's crazy reflective."

"That'll still cook you in less than—"

"It doesn't matter! It's me or them," he said gesturing to the cameras showing the evacuating people.

She stared at him a moment, then called down to one of the control room techs, still trying to monitor the situation below. "You, there. Get down to the advanced materials lab and bring the fire suit. Go! *Run!*"

"And don't forget the hood and faceplate!" Mac called after him.

"Okay, so we know how we might shut this down," she said. "Now, what can you throw in there that can get through the containment field without melting first and bouncing off?"

"Still working on that," Mac said.

"And how will you even *see?*"

Mac blew out a breath. "Working on that, too."

●●

The power fluctuations began as Ailsa was finding a map of the Ark. A touch-screen directory had just pointed her to the correct elevator for the helipad, when the entire hall and screen went dark, flickered back on, then dark again. The disruption settled down to random pulses of bright light and utter darkness, like an enormous heartbeat, rising in pace.

Yae cannae chance the elevator in this.

It'll slow Hart down too, though.

Do we even know wher' he is, at all?

Dinnae need tae know. We know wher' he'll be.

Helipad. Top floor.

Stairs it is.

That's a shiteload a' stairs, lassie, an' he has a head start.

Two at a time, then. Yae'r young. He's old.

Go.

She hit the nearest emergency stairwell doors at a run, gun in hand.

●●

Mac was studying his sunglasses, mind running at light speed, when the tech returned carrying the hyper-reflective fire suit. It looked like he was holding a mirror made of cloth.

"That'll do," Mac said, feeling the material, slick, almost silky.

"But how will you see?" Minerva asked. "The suit was never designed for temperatures anything like what's in there," she said, gesturing to the core. "And I'm still at a loss for what we can throw in there to slow it down."

"What's this suit made from again?"

"A composite of aluminum and graphene."

"Really?" Mac said, intrigued. "I wouldn't have thought it good for that."

"Oh, its specific heat is incredibly high—" She stopped, eyes wide as they both stared at each other a moment.

"*Graphene!*" they said in unison.

"Yes," Mac said. "It's carbon, so the atomic weight is plenty to interfere with the reaction."

"And its specific heat is so high, it might just breach the containment field before vaporizing to ions," she finished before turning again to the tech. "Get down to advanced fabrication. Look for the graphene bins holding the rods, about two meters long each. Grab as many as you can carry. Run!" she yelled after him.

Mac was studying his own reflection in the fire suit faceplate. It was as much a mirror as the rest, but he knew from experience with simple welding just how energetic light could be. Without darkening, he'd sear his retinas in half a second.

The lights flickered out and remained out for a count of five. He glanced up. "The batteries are handling this worse by the minute."

"They're overloading and switching to backups to cool down. Soon we won't have any left, and it'll all go out. Ironically, too much power was not something we anticipated."

Mac grunted as they were bathed in darkness for a moment, the room lit only by overflow from the core itself.

Pitch black.

The lights returned. "Got any black spray paint nearby?" he asked.

♥♥

Eight minutes of running up flight after flight of stairs had Ailsa's legs and butt burning as hot as the core, sweat pouring off her as she rounded another landing.

Then she heard a voice and jerked to a halt in the echoing chamber. "—watch here, in case of pursuit." It was *Hart's voice* from far above. "Did you hear something?—" he began, but her legs were already in motion, all aches banished.

In a glance she caught sight of a guard four stories up leaning over the rail. He shouted, and his gun came up. She jumped aside as gunfire exploded in the well, ringing in her ears. Bullets ricocheted off the rail and steps.

They'll be ready for yae.

Not for this, she thought, grabbing a fire extinguisher.

At the right floor, she waited for the lights to flicker off again, then hurled the extinguisher up the next flight with her left hand, as she dove sideways with the momentum. Useless, startled gunfire was their answer, as she popped off two reflexive shots. One bullet struck the extinguisher, causing a veritable geyser of suppressant and sending the depressurizing extinguisher careening among the two men. She was on them in seconds; a precision punch to one's temple and a pistol-whip to the other put them down.

This was the top floor, a long hallway leading to the helipad door. In the clearing mist and flickering light, she saw her prey hurrying away, nearly at the far door.

She broke through the smoke at a dead run.

"Hart!"

He looked back once, saw his death approaching, and ducked through the heavy metal door.

She could hear the chopper already spinning up outside as she barreled through the door into the dusk, the western sky outlining the helo in deep red fading to purple.

Her gun came up and fired once at it. The helicopter engine erupted in black smoke, the rotors still turning but now with a grinding noise.

At the shot, Hart slowed to a limping jog, then halted, his hands rising slowly in surrender. The pilot bailed and ran for the far fence. Ailsa ignored him completely, walking slowly towards her man.

"Here we are, at long last," she said, stopping just outside arm's reach.

"Indeed," Hart said. "I don't suppose the imminent fusion

explosion matters, at all? You may indeed get your misplaced vengeance, but you'll not have long to savor it."

"So long as yae'r in hell two steps before me, yae bastard," she said, raising the gun.

●●

The tech staggered through the control room doors with an unwieldy armload of two-meter black rods, each a thumb's width in diameter and weighing a good two kilos. Mostly he was having trouble keeping the stack from sliding out of his grip.

Mac paused from spraying the faceplate interior with a thick, oozing layer of black paint to toss him a roll of duct tape. "Here. Bind them up together good and tight."

"That has to weigh almost thirty kilos," said Minerva. "How will you throw that?"

"With the will to survive," Mac said, examining his paint work. "Guess that'll have to do." He pulled out his sunglasses and gave them a thick coat, too, front and back. "I'll be blind as a bat until we open the airlock. Then it'll be almost too much. You'll have to guide me into the airlock and then operate it from here."

"Got it," Minerva said.

"Okay. How long do we have?"

She checked. "Four minutes, maybe less."

"Piece of cake," he said, not sure if he was trying to calm her terror or his own.

"Mac," she said. "Whatever happens, thank you for trying."

Mac nodded and set to work.

Looking like a disheveled spaceman wearing a suit of shiny mercury, Mac let the tech hoist the rod bundle onto his shoulder before guiding him into the airlock. The rods were as heavy as an old big-screen TV. And he could see nothing, but gave the thumbs up when he heard the tech shout they were leaving the airlock.

"Depressurizing," Minerva said over the loudspeaker. "The instant you throw, I'll shut the airlock."

Another thumbs up, and he steadied himself with a deep breath. The mask was already hot against his face, and uncomfortable, taped as it was with an imperfect seal.

Just another minute, and it'll all be over.

One way or the other.

Searing, horrid light bit straight through the mirrored faceplate, its blackened interior, his sunglasses, and his own eyelids. Even opening them a crack was a lesson in stabbing agony.

Just enough to aim!

He allowed one eye to open just a slit to make out the containment field as a blinding, donut-shaped ring containing the plasmatic deuterium. Sweat was pouring off him in rivers, and he could smell something burning that was too much like burning meat.

He gripped the graphene bundle, heaved it off his shoulder, reared back, and hurled it with an animal yell that contained every ounce of strength his body could muster.

The stack of rods came undone as the duct tape incinerated midflight, but he could see enough blackness against the brilliant blur to know some of the rods had intersected the containment field. It may have been his imagination, but he could've sworn the searing light dimmed before the airlock doors slammed shut.

His hearing returned a moment later, with the burning smell now spreading along his wrists and forearms. The suit had caught fire!

Minerva and the tech were there with fire extinguishers the instant the airlock opened. They put him out as he clawed his way out of the suit. He could feel the burns along his arms, painful to the touch, but they didn't matter right now. "Did it work?" he was yelling, half-blind, his vision little more than peripheral with a white-blue blur dead center.

"It's dropping!" Minerva shouted, excited. "One hundred eighty percent, one sixty-five, one fifty! Oh, hell, it's stabilizing, and it's still too energetic to shut down safely!"

Mac staggered towards her voice, using what little vision he had.

"It's still dropping," he shouted. "Just slower. If it levels off at all, you've got to shut it down."

"That'll destroy the chamber for certain, and possibly us with it!"

"It's that or the whole damn place."

"Yes," Minerva conceded. They continued to watch for a count of fifteen, Mac's vision slowly clearing. Minerva's eyes suddenly widened as she examined the console. "The key! We need the key to shut it off!"

"Where is it?"

"My father's pocket!"

"There's no duplicate?"

"In my office," she said miserably. "One hundredth floor."

Mac swore, but remembered his watch. He slipped the paperclip from the band.

Thank you, Solana, he thought.

"Where's the keyhole?" he asked as he groped for his knife with his free hand.

She put his fingers on the lock. *"But you can barely see."*

"It's all by touch anyway," he said, maneuvering the clip and the thin, short blade of the knife into place. "Say when."

"One-ten, One-zero-eight, zero-seven ... Zero-five ... Holding at five and—it ticked up to six! *Do it NOW!*"

Mac twisted the clip and the knife as Minerva hit the kill switch.

Darkness fell instantly, the room rocked with a muffled detonation, and another high-pitched klaxon.

They all stood in darkness, breathing hard for a long minute. Then the lights started coming back up, and the consoles along with them. Minerva examined them and reported. "Reaction chamber destroyed. Fire suppression is working. The field is off. *You did it.*"

"We did it," Mac said. "Now, how do we find Ailsa?"

"Surveillance. Next office over," she said, leading him by the elbow.

Ailsa's finger was tightening on the trigger when they felt the detonation far below. It rumbled through the entire Ark to the platform they stood upon at the surface. The floodlights outside had shut off, then came back up. A moment later, Minerva's voice was speaking over the intercom, canceling the evacuation.

Ailsa took careful aim between Hart's eyes. "Perhaps I'll be savorin' my vengeance a bit longer, after all."

"*Ailsa!*" Mac's voice boomed from rooftop loudspeakers. "*Don't!*"

She looked around, spotted the camera, and shouted, "*Nae yaer business, Mac.*"

"*Listen to me,*" he echoed back, pleading. "There's nothing I can do to stop you, but he's beaten, a fraud. When it came down to his life or theirs, *he ran.* Abandoned even his own daughter. Shouldn't he live with that shame behind bars?"

Hart's jaw clenched, but his eyes held no fire. He simply looked away, awaiting the shot.

"It does'nae wash away what he did tae me an' mine," she bellowed, staring down the sights.

"No. But it doesn't bring your father back either. And that gun offers only one solution. 'Cause *it's only good for one thing.* And we both know it won't end your nightmares. Just prolong them. Is that *really* what you want?"

Her finger tightened on the trigger, just a hair, as Mac's words seemed to echo around her. The nightmares had been her demon: restless, relentless, consuming. Would killing Hart finally end them? She had convinced herself it would. Knew it for certain. But Mac had been right about her blood lust whenever she neared Hart. And here he was. Awaiting his death. Ready for the kill. With Mac as her witness.

Bloody Yank! she thought, as that wire within her snapped.

And with a deep, shuddering breath and an exhalation that left her deflated, she lowered the weapon.

She and Hart stood that way a long moment, facing each other barely two meters apart, before Hart sensed his deliverance. He straightened up slightly, standing taller, as if to regain his familiar, regal mien, adjusting his jacket, aligning his cuffs, before he deigned to speak. "Perhaps I have misjudged the name Mac—" But he never got the rest out.

Like lightning, Ailsa flipped the gun in her palm, caught it by the barrel, *and bashed it across his face with the grip.* He went down like an antelope, felled by the smack of a lion, and lay there, old, helpless, and bleeding from his temple, even if still breathing.

Ailsa turned towards the camera, holding up her gun by its barrel as she shouted to it, "*Two things.* A gun is good for *two things.*"

She looked at the gun, then Hart.

And tossed the weapon aside.

In the security room, his vision still marred, but clearing, Mac exhaled his relief and sat back before turning to Minerva. "Ailsa and I will be leaving," he said, definitively. "And we're taking him with us." As if it was clear that was his price for saving Ararat, and her.

"I understand," she said, nodding. "We all make our choices. And must accept the consequences. He would expect no less. Nor do I."

And with that, she reached out with a hand towards his sunburnt face and suffered eyes and simply touched his cheek, imagining for a moment she had met Mac in another life.

"Let's dress those burns, shall we?" was all she said, and nothing more.

CHAPTER 31

Closure doesn't come easy.
In the end, it's just about forgiveness.
For the person that wronged you, whatever they did.
Even if that's dying too soon.
And for yourself.
For whatever you did wrong.
Because nobody's perfect.
Sometimes that closure comes quickly.
Sometimes it takes years.
But, either way ...
It always leaves a mark.

👓

THE HOUSE OF MACIVER, Inverness, Scotland, sat at the head of a long loch, swathed in cooling grey mists on a chilly day early in November. Ailsa helped Mac unwrap the bandages on his forearms.

"There we are now," she said. The skin beneath was pink and relatively hairless, and only lightly scarred in places. "I'd say yae came out lucky, for all. An' yaer face does'nae hardly look like a raccoon mask anymore."

He ran his hands over the new skin grafts done by a Swiss clinic

Minerva had arranged and paid for. "I guess I owe you both one now, huh?"

"Like hell," said Ailsa. "This was the *least* she could do."

"And Hart?" Mac asked.

"In questionin' still. By my colleagues, Interpol, an' ev'ry other agency that wishes tae pile on, I'm sure. They've seized all his assets like hounds on a fox an' will see tae it he rots in his own private cell. But what about Boone? Any further word on him?"

"Last I heard, he's completely off the reservation and in the wind. But like he used to warn me, the agency has a long memory. So, I doubt he'll be coming up for air anytime soon."

"But a bad penny can turn up anytime, eh?"

MacGyver just nodded, looking at the mist outside making tiny beads on the window in the growing light.

Ailsa had brought him to her estate after they laid Solana to rest in Spain. That had been fitting, and brutal. A lump formed in his throat, familiar and raw.

Ailsa watched him for a moment. "Still aches, I see. An' I dinnae mean the burns. Well, a proper fret is the right weather for it."

"Fret?"

"A Scottish word. It's a heavy mist driftin' in from seaward," she said, indicating the weather.

"Ah, right." He forced a smile. "Thanks for everything over the last couple of weeks. I'll have to show you Minnesota some time."

She snorted. "The ancestral home a' Angus the Betrayer, then?"

"Something like that. And maybe in midwinter. I'll introduce you to hockey. It's high-speed, high-impact, and full of potential for violence. You'd like it."

She nodded appreciatively. "Perhaps I would." Then her tone shifted slightly, a tad more serious. "But what will yae do now?"

He shrugged. "I haven't decided yet. I'm still technically unemployed. Sky's the limit." The silence resumed.

She stood and patted his shoulder. "Yae'r welcome tae stay for as long as yae like. Mother insists, in fact, so I suppose I should say as long as yae can stand her."

"She seems ... lovely."

"That'll wear off soon enough," Ailsa said, souring. "But savor the illusion as yae wish."

Mac turned to look out the window again. "Think I'll go for a walk in the fret."

She half-smiled. "Then yae best wear somethin' warmer than that beaten leather a' yaers."

⁊⁊

A short time later, Ailsa looked out her windows across the estate towards the loch, its usual expanse of fluid leaden grey under a morning overcast. She felt ... quiet. And for once, she didn't mind.

Mother had taken the news of Ailsa's leniency of Hart with a deep sense of relief, if not gratitude. And then proceeded to make a fuss over Mac, sensing he had more to do with that than either he or Ailsa would say. She showed him the house, extolling the history of every room, sculpture, and painting, and taking special delight in talking about Ailsa's past: the more embarrassing, the better. Mac slurped it up with a spoon, but Ailsa let it go. Because it was time for that: to let things go. But her reverie ended with a knock on the door, announcing her mother's appearance as she entered the room.

"Ailsa," she said. "Up and dressed early, I see."

"Mother," she said, not turning. "I've been around the globe so many times, I'm not certain what day it is."

"Friday. Your friend MacGyver has been awake for hours as well."

"Aye. We got his bandages off at last. But he's still in mournin' for Castillo, I think."

"So you've said." Eleanor walked to stand beside her daughter before the streaking windows. They saw Mac emerge below them and walk to stand in the ivy-twined gazebo, its bare vines seeming to match the desolate man among them. He watched the loch, hands in pockets, himself almost a statue. "Your friend has hardly slept. And was her passing a trial for you as well?"

Ailsa looked down. "Takin' my gun off Hart was harder. I wanted him dead. Dead as dead can be."

"For what it's worth, your father would approve of your final decision."

Ailsa could only grunt. "Well, if Hart was'nae lyin' about his orders, then he's nae my true target, is he?"

Her mother sighed. "Ailsa, have you considered perhaps that some secrets are better left buried?"

Ailsa looked at her mother, her expression saying more than mere words.

Eleanor rolled her eyes. "Very well. Speaking of secrets, you might be fascinated to learn what I've uncovered in our family tree."

"Oh, for the love a' ... what now?"

"Mister MacGyver there is indeed related to us in the form of a sixth cousin."

"So, essentially no real relation."

"No more than two Smith's from the same town might be, no, but there is a direct lineage from Angus the Betrayer and the House of MacIver to your American friend. From a technical standpoint, if anything were to happen to you, God forbid, then he's the only one left that has a claim to MacIver House."

Ailsa could only blink a moment, looking from her mother to the distant Mac and back. "You dinnae tell me so!—"

Eleanor shrugged. "Until you bear an heir of your own, of course."

Ailsa groaned. "Oh, for Christ's sake!"

"A mother worries about these matters, Ailsa."

"An' little else it seems!"

※※

Mac looked out across the water from the gazebo, the chilly breeze filling his lungs like a tonic.

Ailsa was right, he thought. *About this being a good place to brood.*

Yeah, but you've said your goodbyes.

Time to get on with your life?

That's what she'd want, you know.

He found himself staring at nothing in particular for a long, drizzly while.

So, what is my life now?

The Agency? Research? Teaching?

Give Minerva a hand at Ararat? Now that the World Bank and the Nobel Foundation had stepped in?

Damned if I know.

Then just let it go.

When it's time, you'll know.

No real answer materialized in the misting rain.

And then the phone in his pocket buzzed.

He pulled it out and contemplated the number a moment before answering. "Holcomb, how are you?"

"Mac, thanks for picking up. Would understand if you didn't."

"And ...?" Mac said.

"Look, this is under the radar and not sanctioned by the agency. But I've got some people in trouble out there and, well, nobody else I can trust to call. That is, if you're feeling up to it."

Mac took a long moment to just breathe.

He could practically hear Solana's voice.

What you do might not have a global impact.

But for the people you help ...

It means everything.

He wiped the mist from his face and smiled.

"What do you need?"

ABOUT THE AUTHORS

Eric Kelley is a veteran writer of fiction for board games and war games for the last twenty years. He's done work for CMON Inc, Reaper Miniatures, and Games Workshop. His credits include multiple award-winning games including the Zombicide series of board games, A Song of Ice and Fire miniatures war game, Trudvang Legends, Massive Darkness 2, Cthulhu: Death May Die, Wrath of Kings, and Arcadia Quest. *MacGyver: Meltdown* is his third novel.

Lee David Zlotoff is an award-winning writer, producer, and director of film and television. Among his more than 100 hours of television credits, he was the creator of the original hit series *MacGyver* as well as the writer and director of the independent feature film *Spitfire Grill,* which won the coveted Audience Award at the Sundance Film Festival. In addition, he is the director of the MacGyver Foundation and author of the best-selling book *The MacGyver Secret: Connect to Your Inner MacGyver & Solve Anything. MacGyver: Meltdown* is his first foray into fiction.

For more info and updates about all things *MacGyver* visit MacGyverGlobal.com

Printed in Great Britain
by Amazon